"YOU'VE GOT A LOCK-ON. CLEAR TO FIRE."

Bud Pritchard rested his thumb on the launch button and watched the MiG-21 bounce in the turbulent air. He said, "He doesn't have a clue we're here."

"You're clear to fire," Dale repeated.

The pretty jet danced in the sunbeams and Bud couldn't bring himself to shoot. There was something wrong about shooting someone in the air who didn't see you. . . .

"Hey, Bud! He's not going to stay there all day, Captain Marvel."

Bud's thumb mashed down and he watched the Sidewinder streak away from the Phantom.

The explosion was spectacular. A fireball erupted in the aft fuselage, the tail fell off, and black smoke poured out in a great streaming cloud. At first Bud thought the pilot would eject, but he was either dead or badly wounded. Then the front half of the MiG followed the tail section down, the sunrays glistening off the spinning wings, fuel spewing from the ruptured tanks in a spiral of white vapor.

A DISTANT THUNDER

A POWERFUL NOVEL OF VIETNAM

Richard Parque

ZEBRA BOOKS
KENSINGTON PUBLISHING CORP.

ZEBRA BOOKS

are published by

Kensington Publishing Corp.
475 Park Avenue South
New York, NY 10016

First printing: February, 1989

Printed in the United States of America

For Donald, whose memory inspired this book, and for all the Marines on The Wall, and the others too.

Chapter 1

The girl child lay asleep on the reed mat. The air was very still. Every few seconds her flower-petal lips would lazily flap, the escaping air making a quiet purring sound in the thinning darkness of the hooch. A rag doll with the stuffing coming out sat in the corner staring at a rat poking its head out of a hole in the dirt floor. The child rolled over on her side. A pink toe caught in the torn mosquito netting wiggled around in slow motion, then abruptly stopped, hanging suspended from a tiny foot, trapped in the threads while her family slumbered on mats and in hammocks.

A broken chair sat next to a plank table. A cracked rice bowl and a pair of wooden chopsticks, burned on the tips, lay on the grease-stained table. A bottle of fish sauce, some loose peppers, a jar of peanut oil, and a pot of cold rice were huddled together at one end of the plank; and on the other end of the table was a chipped teapot and a single teacup without a handle. The painted dragons were missing a leg and their tails.

The little girl's lips fluttered tenderly, her breathing even, the small chest moving rhythmically. The hooch was quiet except for the rat scurrying across the floor to the rice bag. The girl's perfectly sculptured miniature hand reached up and aimlessly pawed at her flat nose, then fell back to rest on the mat, and she began snoring again.

A soft predawn rain began falling on the hooch. The yellow water collected in the hollows of the roof thatch and dripped off the edge of the overhang, making peening sounds on the red soil and drilling shallow grooves around the hooch. A duck waddled under the overhang and stood in the drip.

The rain soon stopped. The darkness thinned some more and a faint gray showed through the wall of bamboo. A moist, swelling redolence of ripe rice wafted across the dark paddies and spread through the hooch. The child stirred; she rolled onto her back and woke. She sat up and rubbed sleepy, long eyes, brushing away silky strands of raven black hair from her chubby round face. She undid her toe from the net, the jade bracelets jingling on her wrist. The woman next to her slept quietly.

The child yawned and blinked a few times. Parting the mosquito net, she crawled off the mat and went to the doll and stuck a thumb into the ragged hole where the arm used to be. She tried to pull her own arm off, then put the doll on her lap and talked to it; she kissed it.

She picked up the doll and carried it back to the mat and for a long time she caressed the doll; then she fell asleep again, the tiny lips waving in the wind of her baby-sweet breath.

The Phantom crawled along the taxi strip, hot gases seething from its entrails, and hissed low, cutting its way past the sandbagged dens. Then the amplitude changed to a high-pitched whine, its single front foot pivoted on the steel leg, and the specter swung onto the runway, accelerating in a burst of venomous energy.

Slowly at first, then gaining speed, the body began to pitch up and down, undulating rhythmically, straining to fly. With a roar from its open fiery throat, the Phantom leaped from earth and clawed at the air, control surfaces fighting for purchase. The elevators swung up on their actuators, and the F-4 arched with authority, climbing higher and higher into the fluid ether.

The Phantom breathed deeply, sucking the life-giving air down into its innards, squeezing it with great spinning metallic muscles, then pushing it out its great rectum in a blast of red fecal rage—up, up, up into the elastic vapor—climbing ever higher.

The brainless aluminum picked up a heading on its master computer and turned west. It flew away from the pallid glow that was creeping across the horizon and spreading into the ancient land thousands of feet below. It flew faster and faster, as if afraid of the light, seeking the sanctuary of darkness, its rudder nervously flicking from side to side like the tail fin of a giant fish being chased across the sea of air. On it sped, sniffing here, sniffing there, turning in big circles, then back again in wide arcs, but always away from the light, into the darkness.

The tiger dragged its kill through the elephant grass, momentarily looked up at the phantom-bird, and snarled. Crossing the clearing, it waded through the stream, teeth embedded in the fawn's neck, and lay down in the shadows. The animal's dull senses heard the quiet murmur of the stream. It blinked at the infantryman's boot washed up on the bank, then began feeding on the muntjac.

The F-4 flew west. When it came to the Cambodian border, it didn't cross but changed direction and flew north. It climbed into the dark clouds and stayed hidden there for a long while, still flying north. Then it changed course again, dropped out of the clouds, and flew back along the border. Once it came down to the treetops and cruised above a road for a while, but that wasn't for long because it climbed back up into the clouds and began circling once more.

The circles began widening until they were many miles across. Then they became smaller and smaller until there was very little distance across the circle. As if bored with this the Phantom broke out of the flat circle and dove down to the trees again. Leveling off, it found a river and began following it. There was a sampan on the river, and the Phantom came back around several times to fly over it. Once it flew very low and the people on board jumped into the water. The steady staccato hammering of the F-4's 20mm cannon vibrated through the jungle, but nothing stirred. It flew a wide arc, climbed a bit, then rolled out and came down along the treetops again, flattening out over the river. The gun pounded and splashes of water could be seen among the bobbing heads. A red smear began spreading over the surface.

The Phantom came around a last time but there were no more bobbing heads. Chunks of yellow bamboo and wood splinters flew into the air, floated down and settled on the river. The sampan split in half and sank level to the surface. Then the F-4 was gone, tail pipes winking back at the floating wood. The engine roar faded, and a long line of spent shells, the first rays of sunlight glinting off their brass casings, drifted down and splashed into the river, each shell making a little hollow *ploop* as it hit the water and sank to the bottom.

The Phantom circled high and began another series of patrolling turns in a southerly direction. The stark camouflage battle colors were faintly discernible in the sallow flame of daybreak. The jet twisted higher and higher, then rolled inverted, suspended motionless for a fraction of a second, and screamed down the backside of the loop in a long sweeping fall. The altimeter unwound in a frenzied rush.

The birds dance where I fly,
The butterflies smile.
I wander among the fish of the air,
Breathing the firmament;

The solid, earthy smell of dreams awakened.
My wings are steel.

Free now to be what I am.
The tears now sing and bathe me clean.
The gray turns to white and the butterflies sing.
My wings are steel. I'm war. I'm innocence.

Where am I?
I'm here—where I am.
Not there any longer—but where I was.
I'm found—I'm free.
My wings are steel.

The rice grows tall,
The river bends.
The wind sings—the birds dream.
Where am I?
I'm here, I'm there.
My wings are steel. I'm war. I'm innocence.

All is well now, time is only a memory.
I wait, it comes.
I am what I was.
How will it be—no matter—it will be.
My wings are steel.

I fly, I fly, I fly away;
Away, away, away home;
Home, home where I came from,
Where I will return.
No matter—take it all—there is no more.
Yet I'm infinity.
My wings are steel. I'm war. I'm innocence.

To this day no one in the village knows what the truck was

doing there or where it came from. No one really cared. Why the Phantom picked it out is understood even less. No one cared about that either. The first rocket hit the truck. The second one missed; it hit the house. A rag doll with an arm missing flew through the air.

The skintight black glove on Bud Pritchard's right hand was torn along the seam of the index finger, his trigger finger; the other glove lay on the wooden floor of the Quonset hut, abandoned and soaked through with sweat, discarded next to a scuffed boot that hadn't seen polish since he began his second in-country tour ten months ago.

"How'd it go?" the debriefer asked as he lit up a cornel pipe polished smooth by years of use. He rubbed the burl against his cheek and looked thoughtfully at the aging captain, who had been passed over for promotion several times, and knew that Pritchard would receive his oak leaves in the same envelope in which he received his discharge papers. "You have a rough one?"

"Yeah," Pritchard said, his attention focused not on the debriefer, but on a freckle on the back of his ungloved left hand: a bead of sweat had popped out of it and was crawling down to the base of his thumb.

There was no air conditioning and the room was hotter inside than it was outside. Like most things in the Nam, the Quonset hut smelled like warm urine and exploded gunpowder, and a whiff of rotting garbage from Cung Mai Dong floated through the windows. The metal tables and chairs, along with the file cabinets and chart holders, and even the five-gallon coffeepot, were all painted the standard Marine Corps olive drab (OD) and gave the room the unmistakable cold starkness associated with anything military, from the insides of mess halls to Phantom jets.

The debriefer's pipe smoke drifted past Pritchard's nose, and he heard the man say something, maybe asking questions, but he wasn't listening, the words lost in the explosion, the fire, the smoke—the hooch coming apart in the Phantom's gunsight. A tremor had begun in his hand, which he knew nothing about, but the debriefer had noticed, and he made a note at the bottom of the form.

"You were fragged to Quang Hoa, weren't you?"

Pritchard looked up at him as though he had just noticed the man sitting at the table. He picked up his helmet bag and got up to walk away, the air bladders on his g-suit loose around his thighs and the pencils and pens in the sleeve pocket falling out on the floor.

"Where are you going?" the debriefer said.

"I've got to have a beer."

"Let's finish the debriefing, Bud."

Pritchard fell back into the chair and saw the glove alone and pitiful lying under the table, begging to be picked up.

"I think you ought to see the doc after we're finished here," the debriefer said. His look went from the tremor to the haggard face and red eyes.

Bud Pritchard scooped up the flight glove and pens and pencils. "Stick to your job, Thorbus, makes for better relations."

The muscles around the debriefer's mouth tightened. "You're talking to a major . . ."

Bud looked long and hard at the silver wings on the chest of Ralph Thorbus and tried to remember when it was that the major last flew. It seemed that on the rare occasions when he was fragged on a mission he somehow got out of it by reporting that he had a rough-running engine or was unable to get tones on his Sidewinders or was needed to plan a *special* strike that conveniently popped up.

Pritchard studied the back of his hand. "Stuff the 'major' crap. You want to say something to me, say it. Don't hide behind your oak leaves."

Someone brought in a floor fan and turned it on, but the hot, stale, still air was merely changed to hot, stale, moving air and provided no refreshment. Ralph Thorbus tapped his pencil.

It was a no-win situation for Thorbus, goading Pritchard, who had an intense dislike for him; it only succeeded in creating an even wider rift between the two men, and Bud would become sullen and uncooperative as usual. He tried a different tack.

"We got an OV-Ten report on that sampan you creamed: nothing left of it. The body count was a confirmed *six.* They were all floating on the surface among the debris. . . ."

Pritchard came over the table after Ralph Thorbus and had him by the throat with his hands. The chair went over backward with the debriefer in it holding onto the pilot's wrists and crashed to the floor, the table also tipping over and spilling papers, half-filled coffee cups, file folders, and a stack of flight manuals.

Immediately the other pilots in the room came out of their chairs and pulled Pritchard off Thorbus.

Straining against the strong arms, the cords in his neck standing out, Bud shouted: "You're a freaky sadist, Thorbus, a blood-eating ghoul. I want no part of your lust for body counts, and don't ever again remind me of the dirty little jobs you're sending me out on." He pulled harder against the arms hooked under his shoulders and wrapped around his neck and chest. "If I ever catch you up in the sky with me I'm going to flame your butt, but there's fat chance of that, isn't there? The planes you fly are always in the shop or you conveniently leave yourself off the scheduling board so you can BF the CO."

As the squadron's executive officer, or XO, Ralph Thorbus had authority over Pritchard, but he knew there was little he could do to punish the maverick pilot. Bud Pritchard had less respect for authority than any Marine in the Corps and had already been busted in rank three times and as far down as Headquarters Marine Corps would allow without a general court-martial.

"I'm going to see you hung from the mast for this, Pritchard, and I don't care what the old man says; I'll get you before the commandant if necessary to see you busted all the way down to a lance corporal cleaning hydraulic pumps in the maintenance shops."

"Ha!—you *poagy bait.*"

Bud knew that the worst he could expect was for Thorbus to schedule him for the most dangerous missions and the maximum number possible. The colonel couldn't spare any pilots and he would make Thorbus keep Bud in the air.

The room became quiet and the major and the old captain glared at each other. The men released Pritchard from their hold and pushed him to the door. Someone handed him his helmet bag and oxygen mask and the .38 Smith and Wesson pistol that had fallen from its shoulder holster during the scuffle.

Outside the door of the Quonset hut he unzipped a pocket on his survival vest and withdrew a pack of Kent cigarettes. He looked at them for a moment, then tossed the pack to the ground. *I don't need these crummy things anymore.* He decided to quit again. He walked a dozen feet down the gravel path, then went back and picked up the cigarettes.

In the locker room he stripped off his equipment, threw it into the locker, let his flight suit and skivvies lie where he had dropped them on the floor, and walked the few feet to the showers. The strong GI soap quickly foamed up; he spread it over his tired body and with head back let the hot water pour over him and run into all his grooves and folds until his skin turned pink like a newborn baby's. With eyes closed he stayed under the shower for ten minutes, until he heard boots stop near him. He opened his eyes.

"I saw you have it out with Ralph. I finished the debrief for us." Dale Keilman, Pritchard's backseater, his radar intercept officer (RIO), leaned against the wall, one boot resting on the shower floor riser, his helmet and oxygen mask in one hand, a half-smoked cigar in the other. "You're going to get your sweet cheeks grounded this time."

Pritchard soaped his crotch and looked at Keilman with one eye, the shower water pasting his sandy hair to the sides of his head. "If the old man clips my wings it will be for no more than a week. Any longer than that and Ralph will have to fly my spot, and no way is he going to let that happen."

The water ran over his body and carried the suds down the drain hole. He reached out his hand and Dale gave him the smoking stogie. He took a couple of drags and handed it back.

"You still upset about the hooch?" Keilman said. "It was a mistake that couldn't be helped."

Pritchard straightened to his full six-foot height and slicked the hair back from his eyes. "Mistake or not, I killed an innocent family."

"Maybe the hooch was empty."

"Come off it, Dale—at that time of the morning? The people were sound asleep. No one was stirring in the village." He turned off the water.

Keilman threw him a towel.

"If Thorbus and his pinheaded planners would give us decent targets—targets that are definitely identifiable and of military value—then these so-called *mistakes* wouldn't happen. A sampan and a truck—what kind of mission is that? What idiot called that one in? And why didn't Thorbus confirm it before fragging us? Dumb . . . just plain dumb . . . and a whole family wiped out. God, how I hate it." He tore at his wet body with the towel. "And Thorbus gleeful that the OV pilot counted six bodies floating in the river. Who were those people? Another innocent family on its way upriver to visit relatives or taking goods to market?"

"Intelligence in Da Nang says that the VC are transporting arms and contraband rice in sampans along the river," Keilman said.

More Phantom pilots and RIOs came into the locker

room and unzipped their sweat-soaked survival vests and g-suits and hung them in the lockers. One or two glanced Bud's way and nodded to him while they unlaced their boots. The khaki shirt and trousers and cordovan dress shoes transformed Pritchard's appearance. Shedding the battle gear helped his frame of mind, and his spirits lifted, though the frustration was always close to the surface. He gave his flight equipment a quick check before closing the locker door and noted that one of the small bladders on the g-suit had been torn. If he was scheduled to fly tomorrow he would check the gear again. "I'm going over to the O-club for a beer," he said to Keilman and walked outside. He smoked a Kent half down and fieldstripped it. *I'm quitting these things.*

The sun was going down over the hills to the west of the Cung Mai Dong Marine base, and as Pritchard stood with his hands on his hips and watched the blood red eye stare back at him over the mirror-still water in the rice paddies, he thought of Marjorie's letter. He patted his pockets and found it in his pants, the plain envelope wrinkled and smudged with the red earth of Vietnam.

After he read the letter, his craggy features darkened and he wadded the paper into a ball and threw it hard against the wall.

"From your wife?" Dale Keilman walked out combing his straight black hair.

Pritchard thought he looked like a young Clark Gable, large ears included.

Dale put on his fore-and-aft cover—his cap—so that it angled down over his eyebrows, and he smiled broadly, stretching his narrow mustache. "Forget her—let's go have that beer."

An F-4 belching a thick trail of smoke from its twin exhaust pipes roared low overhead and banked into its final approach to Cung Mai Dong. The big Phantom made a slow aileron turn, and the pilot in the front seat and the radar intercept officer behind him were clearly visible.

"Ingram's wearing his white scarf," Keilman said.

Pritchard looked up at the jet. "He'll stuff it under the seat when he lands so the old man won't see it. If I was him I'd wear it all over the base." He opened the door for Keilman. "I think I'll start wearing a jockstrap around my neck."

Inside the O-club, happy hour was just beginning. Drinks were half price, and special goodies, Vietnamese appetizers, chao gio and bi cuon, were spread on trays for everyone to freely help himself to while they lasted. It was Friday and the "band"—a local Viet guitarist who did a bad imitation of Elvis Presley—had just arrived. The singer, a woman who could have been anywhere between twenty and thirty years of age and not too bad-looking if you ignored her half-starved figure, plugged in the amp and sat down. Her best songs were the dreamy Viet ballads and an occasional Ella Fitzgerald blues number that she had learned from a tape that someone had given her.

A pilot, a young lieutenant that Bud knew only as Herbie Babe and who had arrived only a few weeks ago, was already half zonked and arguing with the guitar player to let him sing the opening number with the girl. The guitar player smiled politely and said nothing; the girl looked at Herbie Babe with contempt.

Pritchard and Keilman elbowed room for themselves at the bar and each ordered a Coors. Bud drank half of his in one swallow and turned to survey the filled room. An F-4 driver in a group a few feet away was explaining how he had made two passes over a suspected truck park but couldn't positively identify it. On the third pass he rippled his load of 500-pounders and hoped that there was something under the trees other than a bunch of frightened villagers.

"Make another contribution to the Viet Cong toothpick industry?" Pritchard said.

The pilot looked Bud's way. "You do any better, Pritchard?"

"A sampan and a hooch."

"Terrific."

"Yeah . . . terrific." He drank the last half of the beer in one gulp and leaned back on the bar with his elbows. "I hear the Navy is bombing the runways at Kep, but they have to hold back if any MiGs are landing or taking off."

No one commented. It was more of the usual waste of manpower and machines handed down by the politicians who ran the war from their overstuffed chairs twelve thousand miles away.

The screech of amp feedback came through the speaker system and the band was off and playing. Herbie Babe, three sheets to the wind, had his arms around the skinny singer and was leaning well to starboard. After the first four bars of intro by the guitar, he croaked exactly three notes of "Hound Dog" into the mike, his baby-blue eyes rolled back into his head, and, clutching the girl's low neckline, he passed out, tearing the front from the girl's dress. The men applauded and turned back to their drinks and conversation, and the skinny singer sat down in the metal folding chair, holding her torn dress together, her lips pressed tight and her eyes narrow. The guitarist finished "Hound Dog" alone in a hip-swiveling frenzy.

Over the drone of voices and the clinking of bottles. Pritchard cocked his ear to a distant, reverberating and high-pitched sound coming from an unidentifiable direction outside the O-club. In less than a second the sound had changed to a shriek, cutting the air, and others in the room had turned their faces upward toward the ceiling.

"Rocket attack!" Bud Pritchard yelled.

Not everyone was on the floor when the 107mm Katusha rocket hit the outer wall of sandbags surrounding the officer's club. The ten-kilogram payload exploded with such force that a Yamaha motorcycle parked outside was blown through the building, decapitated the guitar player, and embedded two feet into the cinder block wall on the opposite side of the dance floor. The Viet singer, in shock, held tight to her torn bodice and stared with wide mascara-rimmed eyes at the head twisting and rolling past the unconscious Herbie Babe, unaware of the wide swath of hair that had been sandblasted from the back of her head. A trickle of blood ran down the back of her neck and into her dress.

The sharp raw smell of exploded TNT floated on the thick cloud of dust that rose to the ceiling and covered the men lying on the floor. The cloud was gray-black and swirled into the room from a five-foot-wide rip in the east wall.

The wall of sandbags had taken most of the rocket's force, and the only casualties other than the two Vietnamese (who were closest to the explosion) were a half-dozen men who had been peppered by grains of sand and bits of cinder block. They looked like they had been hit with No. 8 birdshot.

More shrieks followed, and the communist rockets arrived in wild rushes, two or three exploding together in the aircraft revetments along the runway, another bunch landing harmlessly between the barracks and mess hall, a single hitting the main gate and killing the sentries. The barrage continued for five long minutes and saturated the night air for miles around with their long trailing screams, then abruptly stopped.

"Are you all right, Dale?" Pritchard looked over a chunk of cinder block lying on edge between him and Keilman.

"Not a scratch."

Pritchard stood and used his hand to wipe some of the dust from his shoulders and hair, then walked around the bar and helped himself to the beer. With his forearm he swept away a spot on the bar and set two glasses up for Keilman and himself. "Looks like we won't be having any more music tonight," he said, glancing at the singer, who sat in the chair, staring down at the headless body. He poured the glasses full and drank his down. "Better take care of the wounded." He tore the medical kit from the brackets holding it to the wall and began administering first aid to the wounded.

After bandaging a pilot's face and neck, which were leaking like a sieve from many tiny holes, and carrying another man out to the ambulance, he saw the Vietnamese singer still sitting in the chair, her gaze welded to the corpse at her feet; her body trembled like a thin leaf in the wind.

When he got close to her he noticed the blood that had soaked into the back of her dress. She didn't know he was there; her arms were folded in her lap and she clenched and unclenched her fingers.

"You better let me take care of your head."

She said nothing, though her throat was quivering under the film of tears that had washed down over her chin.

Pritchard looked at the back of her head and winced. While he broke open a combat bandage and tied it to her scalp, he admired the straightness of her back and the perfect symmetry of her shoulders and neck, and thought that if someone fed her some pot roast and potatoes and apple pie for a couple of months she could fill out to be an attractive girl, though she would be partially bald for a while.

"What's your name, kid?" he said and tied off the compress after making two loops around her head.

Her eyes remained fixed on the body and she said nothing.

Pritchard walked around in front of her and looked into her eyes. They were stone hard and she shook all over. He touched her hands and found them to be uncomfortably cold.

"Come on, miss, I'm taking you to the ambulance." He motioned to a corpsman to bring a stretcher. He pulled her arm, but she was frozen to the chair and he couldn't budge her.

"My brother," she said. "I no want leave my brother."

"Good lord—he's your brother?" He took a deep breath and held it for a few seconds, then slowly let it out. "Senseless."

"What's going on here?" Dale Keilman looked down at the girl, then at Pritchard. He had a rolled-up stretcher balanced on his shoulder.

"That's her brother," Pritchard said.

"Oh, shit."

"Get me a body bag, will you, Dale? Someone's going to have to take care of this. She's in no condition to handle any of it."

"Yeah . . . it will only take a sec. Be right back."

"Want to tell me your name, miss?" Pritchard was on one knee.

"My brother" was all she said.

He saw her purse hanging on the back of the chair. "Mind if I look in here?"

She made no effort to stop him from rummaging through the purse. There was a comb, a small mirror, a few loose piasters (worth about two dollars at the current rate of exchange), a crumbled letter with much of the ink smeared on the cheap brown paper, the remains of what looked like a rice cookie, a piece of wrapped crystallized ginger, and a laminated card. A yellowed photograph of an old woman dressed in an *ao dai* with a man of the same age, along with a plastic toy car and half a pencil, were the only other contents.

"Take a look at this."

Keilman dropped the black plastic body bag on the floor and took the laminated card from Pritchard.

"It's her ID," Pritchard said.

"Is there an address?" Keilman was unable to read Vietnamese.

"Twenty-four Duong Tra in Cung Mai Dong. Her name

is Hai Van Phuong."

Pritchard and Keilman zippered Hai Van Phuong's brother into the body bag and carried him outside to an empty jeep. When they turned around, the girl was standing shoeless in the gravel path, the white, blood-soaked bandage wrapped around her head, and the torn front of her dress hanging loose and exposing her bra and small breasts.

"Damn war," Pritchard said. "What are we going to do with her?"

"She's sure a pathetic sight." Keilman picked up a handful of gravel and let it slip slowly through his fingers, the pebbles sounding like water splashing on the ground. "She's not our responsibility. The gooks can take care of themselves." He picked up another handful of gravel and let it spill through his fingers. "She's none of our affair."

Pritchard looked away from Keilman and at the girl. "None of our affair, huh? Then explain to me why her brother no longer has a head and why he isn't home eating a bowl of rice and *nuoc mam* duck like he should be if he hadn't come to the O-club to play his guitar for us. The rocket that took off his head was meant for you and me, not him; and you say it's none of our affair," he said with disgust.

"Could of happened to anybody."

"Oh, I see; he just got in the way, just like the family in the hooch this morning got in the way of our rocket. I suppose that was none of our affair either." The bitterness he had for the war and its waste of life rose out of his stomach and burned the back of his throat. "You talk about responsibility. That's the problem with this war—no one is willing to take responsibility for it. Well, in my small way I'm going to make a tiny contribution to righting a big wrong." He took the girl by the hand. "Let's go, kid. I'm taking you and your brother home."

He was sorry that he had taken his anger out on

Keilman, but he would apologize later, after he had gotten alone and talked himself down and no longer had to wear his rancor on his sleeve; and maybe he would buy his backseater a steak dinner and a bottle of Jack Daniels and they would go bomb the stars out of the Ho Chi Minh Trail again, or sneak out some dark night and drop an unauthorized load on Party Headquarters in downtown Hanoi—something to put on the back burner and stir up when it came time to make his final Vietnam contribution.

The girl was light in his arms, no heavier than a child, and she didn't resist—only stared at him with unblinking eyes—as he placed her in the passenger seat and climbed in beside her.

"Excuse me," he said and pulled the torn dress together to cover her exposed breasts, pinning the rip together with the silver pilot's wings that he wore above his left breast pocket. He adjusted the bandage on her head.

Dale Keilman stood beside the jeep rubbing his chin and shaking his head. A PFC ran by with an M16 slung over his shoulder. "Just a minute, Marine." He took the assault rifle from the young man and slapped it in Pritchard's hands. "You may need this."

Something of a smile formed on Pritchard's lips, and he laid the M16 across the girl's lap. He started the engine and nodded to Keilman, the jeep jerking a couple of times before it roared off toward the gate.

Chapter 2

The salvo of rockets that had hit the main gate had left smoking craters in the road and forced Pritchard to make a wide swing off the payment. The jeep bounced up to the wire where a squad of Marines was dug in around the demolished guard shack. An E-5 sergeant in camouflaged utilities and helmet cover stepped out of a hole behind the concertina wire and looked queerly at the jeep's occupants.

"You're not wanting out, are you, Captain?" He looked closely at Hai Van Phuong's bandaged head and the bloody, torn dress pinned together with Pritchard's wings.

"I'm taking this girl and her brother to their home in town."

The queer look on the sergeant's face deepened. "Her brother, sir?"

Pritchard pointed in the back of the jeep.

The sergeant unzipped the body bag and looked inside. His face screwed up ugly and he zipped the bag closed. "You sure you want to go into town, sir? I mean with the rocket attack and the sappers hitting the perimeter we can expect more trouble tonight."

Bud looked around at the young Marines in their flak jackets and steel helmets pulled down on their heads. The hot shards from the exploded Russian rockets smoked around them, and the remains of the guard shack were scattered over the red earth. Pritchard knew he wasn't making the wisest choice of his life. "Open the wire," he said to the sergeant.

The squad leader shrugged, pulled the concertina apart, and gave Pritchard a halfhearted salute, more of a goodbye-I-won't-be-seeing-you-again wave.

Going through the wire, Pritchard got a good lungful of the harsh, biting smell of exploded powder, and he coughed violently in an attempt to drive the bitter taste from his mouth.

Once through the wire and what was left of the main gate, he turned left and accelerated down the rutted road bordered by a stand of bamboo; it soon gave way to rice fields and paddy dikes and long stretches of trees lining the paddies. His gaze crisscrossed the shadowed paddies afire with long tongues of the evening gloaming, and he searched for anything out of the ordinary; if an attack was to come it would be from a well-concealed ambush.

Five minutes had passed since they left the base, and neither had spoken. His head was turned toward the Viet girl, and he hoped she would feel his look and say something, but she made no effort to move or talk and she kept her face averted so that all he saw was the classical profile of a Cochinese young woman whose smooth face was lined with tearstains and streaks of dirt and blood.

"Marjorie wouldn't approve of any of this," he said. He jerked his head toward movement along a paddy dike and saw that it was only an old man in rolled-up pajama bottoms with a mattock over his shoulder, stepping onto the dike. He relaxed again. "She's against the war—hates everything about it." He looked at the girl.

She stared straight ahead, her thin body vibrating like a taught spring, and he thought her a pitiful sight.

"She wanted me to go to Canada—bug out."

The jeep hit a hole and they bounced six inches out of their seats.

"Sorry; I better slow down."

The town, with its shabby wood-and-thatch homes and half-completed cinder block buildings, came into view through a screen of perfume trees.

"Got a letter from her today—same old crap—criticizing me for being over here and prolonging what she calls 'man's inhumanity to humanity.' She burns my butt, but I know if I were home I could straighten her out. She's a good woman, it's just that she got in with the wrong crowd—friends that she graduated with from Berkeley—and thinks America needs a second revolution. She calls it the 'greening of America'." He was sure the girl wasn't listening to him.

A chicken ran out from the side of the road, and he swerved into a line of muddy chuckholes. The girl fell over against the seat and made no effort to right herself. Her head lay against his shoulder and the M16 slipped from her lap and fell to the floorboards.

Her smell was mulchy, like forest humus, not too heavy, just enough so that he was aware of something new and different. No woman he had known ever smelled like this—earthy and primitive, yet unmistakably feminine.

"Your name is Phuong, isn't it? Saw it on your ID." He downshifted. "Sorry about your brother."

She lay motionless against the seat; only her hands moved, folding and unfolding in her lap. He felt strange—sort of like the sensation he remembered in childhood when Donna Wilms skinned both her knees playing tetherball and he helped her to the principal's office and stood by her side holding her hand while the school nurse brushed Merthiolate on the scrapes.

The principal didn't like him very much, thought him a maverick and a bad influence on the other boys in the sixth grade.

The trouble had started early in the year when the principal, Mr. James, had organized teams to play softball.

Young Bud Pritchard was used to playing hardball and thought softball for girls and sissies and told Mr. James exactly how he felt. Mr. James, of course, saw this as a challenge to his authority, and suspended Bud from participating in all school sports until he apologized and promised to join the other children in playing softball. This presented a challenge for Pritchard, who was loyal to his ideas, and he quickly persuaded his pals to come over to his side. He organized his own baseball team and set up a sandlot league with other schools in town to play on the weekends and after school. James was furious, but in the end he umpired the after-school games and went on to organize the first little league in Bellfield, which was created from young Pritchard's teams. Bud's reputation as a nonconformist followed him throughout his schooling and into the military.

A line of women and children carrying loads of bananas and breadfruit caught Phuong's eye, and she straightened up. Though the blank expression on her face didn't change, it was apparent that she recognized the file of peasants and wanted Bud to stop the jeep.

He pulled the jeep over to the side of the road near the grass edge of an irrigation ditch and waited with the motor running. Phuong sat quietly looking ahead, and when the group reached the jeep and began talking in excited voices, new tears began dripping from her eyes and she uttered not a word, but pointed at the body bag in the back of the jeep.

Pritchard watched with detached curiosity and wondered how many times a day similar tragic scenes were enacted throughout Vietnam.

The women threw down their bundles of bananas and breadfruit and wailed and tossed about and waved their arms, and Pritchard sat feeling dumb and out of place and thought this would be an ideal place for a Viet Cong to pop him. The children stared at him with their deep black eyes and waited patiently for their mothers to finish moaning and pulling their hair so they could go home to the hooches and build fires and cook the rice.

Brother was pulled from the jeep and held and passed around and laid in the grass and caressed, and it wasn't until the sun had disappeared and the air became damp with the threat of rain that the women placed brother back in the jeep and walked off holding to their bundles and crying loudly.

Phuong pointed to a track leading through the trees, and Pritchard switched on the headlights and put the jeep into low gear. After about a mile of nothing the headlights swung onto a two-room wooden shack with a thatched roof, set among banana plants and yellow-barked tamarind trees.

"This where you live?"

She remained silent, but put a leg over the side, ready to get out when he stopped the jeep. The night was very dark and filled with sounds of insects and frogs, and somewhere in the night he could hear the slow ebb of a river and the slapping of a branch hanging in the current. He had brought the jeep to a halt fifty feet in front of the shack, and when he turned off the lights, he was swallowed up in a black hole so dense that he couldn't see the steering wheel in front of him.

As his eyes became adjusted to the night, thin rays of light emerged from the cracks in the shutters and doors.

"Who lives here?" he said suspiciously and felt for the M16.

Phuong was no longer in the jeep; her fragile figure swayed across the open ground to the door, and he heard her hand quietly rapping on the rough wood. The door opened, and the light from a kerosene lamp illuminated an ancient, withered man squatting on the dirt floor and eating rice from a small bowl. He was looking up with a curious expression at Phuong and the middle-aged woman who stood in the doorway with her. A half-dozen children ranging from about five to twelve years old, all barefoot and wearing scanty clothing, hung back in the shadows.

An exchange of rapid Vietnamese followed, and Phuong looked to the jeep. The woman nodded and brought the lamp out into the yard, but not until she hesitated a moment when she saw Pritchard sitting in the driver's seat.

The older woman peered into the back of the jeep, and her expression didn't change when she saw the bag. The lamp was held high to get the maximum spread of light, and she looked for a long time, fascinated by the idea that a dead body was zippered up inside the slick plastic. She looked up at Pritchard several times as if to ask him a question, or maybe to accuse him.

All the while, the bandaged girl, Phuong, stood quietly beside the jeep, a thin hand supporting herself on the dull green metal, the blood on the back of her neck and dress still wet, and patiently waited for the woman to finish her inspection.

"Is there anything you'd like me to do?" Pritchard had no idea what the girl was waiting for, but it was apparent that she had a duty to complete and she was not going to allow the lengthening time nor the night to distract her.

She had not spoken to him since they had left the base. Now she turned to him, her eyes heavily lidded in the yellow light, and said in a small voice, "Please carry my brother." Her arm slowly rose, and she pointed a finger to the side of the house where an ox cart was sitting among the banana plants. One of the children was holding a lamp and stood beside the cart. The cart's gate had been removed, and it leaned against the wooden wheels.

Bud's curiosity was peaked by her request, and he asked her why she wanted the body put in the ox cart. Another child was leading the ox to the front of the cart.

She didn't reply right away, maybe thinking he didn't deserve a more detailed explanation, or possibly too tired to string the words together. "I must take my brother home to be buried," she said, her voice weak.

"I thought your home was here in Cung Mai Dong."

"My brother and I were born far away in the hill country. Our mother and father, brothers and sisters, and grandparents live there. I must return him to our ancestral home to be buried. My brother and I came to Cung Mai Dong to work, but our hearts are with our family in Quang Hoa village."

A chill beginning at the back of Pritchard's thighs ran up his body when he heard her mention Quang Hoa. His scalp tingled and once again he saw the rocket flash from under the Phantom's wing in the advancing light early this morning and explode into the defenseless hooch, and again the thick bile crawled from his stomach into the back of his throat and he was nauseated. Phuong's eyes widened for an instant at the change in his expression.

"Quang Hoa is far away," he said, "close to the Cambodian border; there are many North Vietnamese regulars and Viet Cong guerrillas between here and there."

"The NVA and VC will not bother me. Do I look American?"

Pritchard pursed his lips at the rebuke.

"Quang Hoa is three days by ox cart," she continued. "These people will rent me the ox cart for one hundred piasters. I do not have one hundred piasters. . . . Will you loan me the money?"

Brother will be pretty ripe after three days' travel in the jungle, Pritchard thought to himself, *and this girl is in no condition to survive a journey through the rough mountain terrain leading to Quang Hoa, especially alone. She belongs in a hospital.*

In the lamplight, Phuong's eyes were wide and looked like black, shining marbles. As always, she waited patiently, in no hurry for Pritchard to make a decision. She knew Americans always carried a lot of money with them and the hundred piasters she was asking was a very small sum to this Marine aviator.

"Hold the light up a little higher," Pritchard said to the woman who continued to stare at the body bag.

She looked at him, her face blank.

"Nhieu hon cao," Phuong said and pointed to the lamp.

The woman raised the lamp above her head, and Pritchard inspected Phuong's bandage. He frowned and took the lamp from the woman, holding it closer to the wound.

"Will you loan me the money for the ox cart?" Phuong said.

Pritchard slipped the bandage back over the wound and stood in front of her with the lamplight in her face. "Look, kid," he said, unlatching the medical box from the jeep's fire wall, "you've had quite a big shock in losing your brother, and the injury to your head looks nasty. You need treatment and some time to recover before you can think about a trip into the mountains by ox cart."

"I will leave tonight."

He could see that she was determined. He led her by the arm into the house, motioning to the woman to come along with the light, and opened the medical box. The steel box, in long disuse, needed a hard coax to open.

"Ask her to boil some water," he said to Phuong, nodding to the woman with the lamp.

While the rice straw and charcoal were placed in the earthen stove and lit, a clay pot of water was filled, and Pritchard laid Phuong on the table, removed the bandage, and opened the back of her dress. The wounds were not deep, but they were painful, and he could see grains of sand embedded in her scalp and in the encrusted blood. Her neck and upper shoulders were also pocked by the blast.

The children pressed close around the table and watched Bud pick out the sand grains with tweezers from the medical kit. The work was slow and painful for the girl, but she lay still and said nothing while he worked on her through the night, discovering that he had an instinct for doctoring and derived satisfaction from caring for her injuries.

After thoroughly washing the wounds in her head, neck, and shoulders with antiseptic, he dressed them in clean bandages. She looked exhausted and unable to walk ten feet without help.

"It's a good idea for you to get some sleep now." He dried his hands on his shirt and accepted a glass of homemade gin from the woman.

He sat down on a short stool next to the old man squatting on his haunches in the middle of the floor, and drank the gin, which tasted like liquid fire. There was a thump, and the flimsy wooden frame of the house trembled.

Pritchard looked up and shook his head. He drained his glass and walked over to the wall and gently pulled aside the woman and children who were trying to get Phuong on her feet. He lifted her in his arms and carried her back to the table. "You're really determined to start tonight for the mountains, aren't you?"

"You cannot stop me." She was breathing hard. "As soon as you leave I will go."

"You can't make it alone."

"I must try."

"I suppose you must."

He looked at her; she seemed so frail and helpless, and yet he had never seen anyone as resolute. There were courage and strength in the set of her eyes. He might regret it later, but right now it was important that he help her get to Quang Hoa. He wouldn't find peace unless he did.

Without saying anything further he carried her to the jeep and drove her and her brother back to the Marine base.

At regimental headquarters for the First Marines, Pritchard asked around and found that the second battalion had the AO for Quang Hoa. Across the complex of runways about a half-mile distant, men and equipment fought fires and tended the wounded. An F-4 Phantom burned in its revetment, and other aircraft parked near it were being towed away. The sweet smell of burning jet fuel swept over the base.

"Hey, Marine," Pritchard shouted, coming up alongside a PFC trotting with a heavy M60 and belts of ammo slung over his shoulder. "Where's the second battalion's area?"

The kid's free hand pointed down the gravel road; the other hand balanced the machine gun on his shoulder. "Straight ahead, Captain . . . hang a left at the motor pool." He disappeared off the road and down a ditch in the direction of popping M16s and AK-47s. Parachute flares illuminated the sky over the perimeter defenses and two AH-1 Cobra gunships twisted down the line of gun pits.

A huge explosion ripped out the fencing 200 yards down the road, and VC sappers, satchel charges strapped to their chests, poured through the ruptured wire and scattered over the runway, each one running to a preselected aircraft parked on the apron.

"My brother was a good boy—he never wanted to hurt anyone," Phuong said, unexpectedly becoming talkative. "He played with children in Cung Mai Dong and made them toy boats from padantas leaves and coconut shells. He was only two years older than me but he took care of me like he was my father."

Pritchard made a turn at the motor pool and drove down a line of ammo bunkers.

"When I was very young I got so sick no one thought I would live," Phuong said. "My brother carried me many miles to a village where a farmer had a white elephant, and my brother paid the farmer all the money he had so that he could put me in the elephant's mouth. I got well after that." She sat slightly slumped to one side and paid no attention to the three VC sappers running directly for the jeep.

Bud stopped the jeep and the Cong charged onto the road. It was plain that the VC were more interested in the motor pool across the road then they were in him or Phuong. The fact that he stood between the Cong and their target meant only that he was a nuisance and that they must eliminate him first before flinging their satchel charges into the fueled trucks and ammo bunkers.

Phuong was talking about the white elephant's healing saliva dripping over her while her brother held her in its mouth, when the AKs opened up. In a single motion, Pritchard scooped Phuong up in one arm and in the other caught hold of the sling on the M16 and rolled off the road into a shallow ditch. Immediately the dirt in front of the ditch blew apart in a burst of AK fire. Bud held Phuong down with his body over hers and drew the bolt back on the M16 and released it. He pushed the rate-of-fire selector to semiautomatic to conserve ammo (he had only one magazine). Phuong's delicate body shaking underneath him felt like it could be easily broken by his weight.

"Are we going to die?" she said without emotion. The idea of joining her brother was not an unwelcome thought.

It was difficult for her to breathe under Pritchard's body. She thought of her brother lying inside the ugly, so typically efficient American plastic, sanitized in his long sleep. She had to get her brother out of the bag, for it was suffocating him—he had no way to breathe.

Her scream startled Pritchard; he thought she had been hit and rolled off of her. She leaped out of the ditch and sprinted for the jeep, a line of bullets stitching the ground behind her feet. Another burst hit the windshield, and the glass sprayed across the back of the jeep in a wide plume.

Phuong's shoeless foot caught a rock jutting out of the ground and she went down, hard, hands out wide, headfirst, her head striking the hard rubber tire on the rear of the jeep. The impact did not knock her out cold, but she hit hard enough to keep her dazed and flat on the ground next to the wheel. She lay moaning forty feet from the ditch, her badly soiled dress now ripped from the bottom up to the middle of her copper-brown thigh as well as down the front where Pritchard had hastily pinned it together.

In one second the first Cong would be coming around the front of the jeep to kill her. His two friends were firing short bursts into Pritchard's position to prevent him from returning fire.

Marjorie Pritchard . . . where are you demonstrating tonight? Bud rolled twice to the right and rose to a knee at the same moment the VC, a skinny boy in his teens with big ears and a bad complexion, turned the corner around the jeep and in clear line of sight of stunned Phuong, who was struggling to rise. Pritchard jerked off a shot and heard it thud into the jeep's hood. It was enough to distract the sapper, and he turned to look for Pritchard. Bud's second round spun him into the jeep, the AK-47 pointed in the air and firing on full automatic. The Russian assault rifle dropped to the gravel, and the Viet Cong fell between the bumper and radiator grille, wedged in and hanging limp.

The remaining two sappers ran past their dead comrade and across the road to the regimental motor pool and its fuel storage tanks and bunkers. By the time Pritchard had climbed out of the ditch, the sappers were well down the slope and almost to the first trucks. He laid the rifle over the hood of the jeep—he had to brush aside the dead sapper's arm—and shot the VC on the right. Before he could switch the sights of the M16 the VC on the left prematurely detonated his satchel charge and blew himself into oblivion.

A cloud of heavy dust and acrid smoke drifted over Pritchard, who was unscrewing the cap of a canteen he had taken from the jeep. Sitting on the ground with his back on the rear tire, he supported Phuong in his arm and made her drink from the canteen, then soaked his handkerchief with water and laid it across her forehead.

"You've had a rough night, kid," he said.

"Where is my brother?" She gulped at the canteen he held to her lips.

Pritchard jerked his thumb over his shoulder. "Still in the jeep."

They sat in the shadowed light of parachute flares and star clusters and watched the Cobras wheel up and down the perimeter, firing Zuni rockets, and listened to the yells of Marine squads chasing down the sappers that had infiltrated the base defenses.

Fewer flares were fired into the air, and the bright night grew dark again, shouts of men weakened, and only an occasional M16 was heard firing. The Cobras had all landed and the VC sappers were either dead or captured. The fires still burned, and the main strength of the Viet Cong unit, the Cao Tren 303, melted back into the hills and villages and underground burrows.

It took Pritchard an inordinate amount of time to unravel the sapper from the jeep's bumper, and by the time he had pulled the VC through and dropped him beside the road, Phuong had lapsed into a taciturn mood and stared straight ahead into the night, looking through the empty windshield. The wet handkerchief had fallen into her lap.

"How does your head feel?" He poured more water on the handkerchief and placed it on her forehead. It stuck there for a minute, then fell back into her lap. "Hold it so it doesn't fall," he said and put her hand over the handkerchief.

He started the motor and pulled onto the road. The right front tire ran over the sapper's arm, and Phuong let the handkerchief fall off her head.

In the battalion area, Pritchard stopped the bullet-ridden jeep in front of a line of squad tents and Quonset huts; a sign planted out front said BRAVO COMPANY. Men were piling boxes of C-rations, ammunition, clean socks, five-gallon cans of water, and other supplies along the road. Infantrymen sat wherever they could—on crates, in trucks, on the ground—smoking, checking their loaded rucksacks, talking about the "real world," or just waiting and looking and not seeing. A few cleaned their weapons and others passed *Playboy* magazines around.

A second lieutenant glanced Pritchard's way and returned to chewing out a PFC standing at half attention, the contents of his rucksack spilled out on the ground. Bud turned off the engine.

"Where are your mines, shitbird?" the lieutenant said. "When you go on an assault you take two claymores just like everyone else."

"But, LT, I ain't got no mines."

"Shut up, shitbird." He tugged at the PFC's web gear and pulled him closer to inspect it. "Where's your grenades? You've only got two . . . and only one canteen." He removed the canteen and shook it. "It's only half full, shitbird. What're you going to do when you run out? Beg off someone else and make him short? Because you're a shitbird we now got two men without water."

"Top only gave me two grenades . . . said if he had his druthers he wouldn't give me any . . . and I didn't have time to fill my canteens when the word came to form up . . . and I got only one box of C-rats 'cause . . ."

"Shut up, shitbird. You'll learn when you get out in the bush, and then you'll never forget." The lieutenant kicked the PFC's gear. "Top," he shouted.

"Be right there, LT," the gunnery sergeant said. He checked off another box of RPGs being loaded in a truck and handed the clipboard to a buck sergeant. "Load the insect repellent and cigarettes next."

The lieutenant gave the rucksack a final kick and said, "Get this shitbird squared away by the time we jump off or I'm going to screw off his head, stand on his shoulders and shit down his neck." He spit tobacco into the red dust and walked away.

"He's a real hell-raiser for a youngster just out of TBS," Pritchard said to the Top.

The gunnery sergeant's face was deadpan. "The LT is all right. He may be young and this is his first tour, but he's got his shit together . . . no better mud Marine than the

LT." He looked over at the shot-up jeep and lifted his chin. He had acquired a new interest in Bud and looked him over more closely. "Seen some action tonight, have you?"

"There are three dead sappers back at the motor pool and I have a KIA and his wounded sister in the jeep. I'm trying to get them home to Quang Hoa." He pulled a Kent from a half-used pack and offered one to the Top.

They lit up with Bud's PX Zippo.

"Quang Hoa is our AO," the Top said.

"I figured. You resupplying in the morning?"

"Choppers should be here at first light. You and your friends can catch a lift if you want. Could be a hot LZ, though. Battalion reports a large force of North Vietnamese regulars moving into the area from up around the DMZ. Word is that the gooks are breaking out of the highlands and a major offensive is under way. Quang Hoa is right in their path."

"The girl has made up her mind."

"She doesn't look too good."

"She was singing at the O-club when a Katusha hit."

"That what did in her brother?" the gunnery sergeant said.

"Right; he played guitar."

"Too bad." The Top was just being polite.

"It was a waste." Bud was unable to say what he really felt.

The PFC looked down at his scattered gear and said nothing, though the side of his mouth twitched.

"Are you going to cry, *cherry?*" The Top said it with contempt.

The young Marine took his eyes off the dumped rucksack for a second, and his lips twitched more.

The boy was new, just in that day from Camp Pendleton or Okinawa, and was frightened about his first insertion and feeling lonely and unwanted jumping off with hardened veterans who had seen plenty of action and who had no patience or time for a cherry. He would be replacing another 0300, who had taken a shard in his spine from a 81mm mortar and would be coming out in a body bag on the same UH-1 Huey that the new kid was going in on.

His combat utilities were starched and his boots were new and shined and he had a growth of peach fuzz on his soft, untanned cheeks. His name, MCGARVIE, was stenciled over the breast pocket of his utilities. Cherry stuck out all over him.

It had been a long time since Pritchard had experienced the emptiness in his chest and the difficulty in breathing that came when he felt the helplessness of another human being. This kid, McGarvie, was going to die this morning on his first assault and no one even knew who he was. *In the name of all that's holy, why do we do it?*

There was a kid in my high school, Pritchard remembered, *who had the same dark blond hair, large sad eyes that belonged on a doe, and slim unathletic build as this boy. He always looked vulnerable and he always ate his lunch alone, an apple and a peanut butter and jelly sandwich. His mother must not have been very imaginative—or maybe he had to make his own lunch. If I had any kids I'd be sure they never had to make their own lunches and never ate alone.*

"Does this kid have a fire team partner?" Pritchard asked.

The Top looked at Bud's pilot's wings as if to tell him to go back to flying his kerosene burner and leave the real fighting to the grunts. "No one's been assigned to him yet—he just arrived in country." He ripped the wooden slats off a box, tossed two grenades to McGarvie, and pinned an extra one on his own web gear. The Top took Bud aside. "The truth is, Captain, that no one wants him. A cherry's life expectancy on his first assault is about sixty seconds and no one wants to be close to someone that only has sixty seconds to live. If he gets through the first day in the bush maybe somebody will talk to him."

The gunny spit tobacco juice into the dirt, and Pritchard knew where the lieutenant had learned. Phuong was watching the young Marine, a sad, faraway look in her Asian eyes. *She probably feels the same way he does,* Pritchard decided.

The Top cracked open a carton of C-rations and stuffed a two-day supply in McGarvie's rucksack. "Fill your canteens at the lister bag parked near the head," he said without looking at the PFC.

McGarvie double-timed to the lister bag, his big feet getting in his way and looking awkward and pathetic in his desire to obey, the way he had been taught in boot camp.

Pritchard couldn't take his eyes off McGarvie. There was something cathartic in being in the presence of innnocence, and he felt an atavistic urge to return to a gentler time when his ancestors settled their differences individually rather than with whole armies twelve thousand miles away from home.

"Say, Captain, mind if I ask you a question?" the Top said.

"What's on your mind?"

The gunnery sergeant looked toward the jeep. "What's the slopehead and her brother to you? They're none of your affair."

Pritchard hitched up the belt on his pants and walked to where Phuong sat staring blankly through the empty windshield. "I'm making them my affair." He stopped and turned back to the Top. "Ever see a rocket take out a sleeping family?"

Chapter 3

Dawn cracked through the gun-metal sky, unnaturally pale and melancholy. A squad of men, replacements for the KIAs and WIAs of Bravo Company, 2nd Battalion, 1st Marines, huddled under ponchos, the rain rapping on the green plastic and rolling down the folds to puddle around the thick, knobby soles of jungle boots that were supposed to be waterproof.

PFC McGarvie tucked the thump gun closer to him under the poncho and looked around with sad eyes and rain-streaked face at the piles of supplies and lumps of men squatting in the red mud. "Think the LZ will be hot?" he said to the man next to him, wanting to make human contact and stave off the fear that had worked into a hard knot in his belly.

The reply was a grunt and cloud of smoke from the opening in the poncho.

"This pack feels like it weighs a thousand pounds," PFC McGarvie said.

"Seventy pounds," the lump corrected. "Could be a hundred . . . more like seventy."

"We never carried anything this heavy in boot."

"This ain't boot, cherry."

McGarvie was quiet for a while. He hugged the thump gun and wondered if he should check his rucksack and ammo once more. He decided it didn't matter because he didn't know what to check for; no one had told him. Nervous and longing for companionship he coughed and said; "Ever been inserted into a hot LZ?"

"Shut up, man. I don't want to hear about no hot LZ. You wake me up again and I'm going to shove this between your cherry buns." A fist holding a grenade came out from under the edge of the poncho, remained motionless for a moment, the rain dripping off the ugly little bomb, then withdrew back under the poncho.

A hundred yards away, standing in the open door of a Quonset hut, Bud Pritchard unwound the red strip at the end of the Wrigley Spearmint gum wrapper and looked through the dawn rain and listened for the first whumps of rotor blades from the slicks.

"You'll need this." The Top threw him web gear with the ammo pouches stuffed with M16 magazines. It landed with a heavy thump on the floor next to Bud's feet. "Better get her ready," he said, jerking his head toward Phuong, asleep on a cot, a blanket pulled up under her chin. "The slicks will be here in a few minutes."

"I'll need someone to help me with the body."

"Get the cherry."

"Why him?"

"Why not him?"

The rain swirled into the doorway and Pritchard backed inside. He felt guilty using the Quonset hut as protection from the rain and cold while the grunts squatted outside with their butts hanging in the mud.

The radio on the Top's desk crackled and a garbled voice came through the background static. He keyed the set with his left hand and with the right drank what was left of the C-ration coffee in an oversized red-and-gold coffee mug emblazoned with the Marine Corps emblem. *Semper Fi* was engraved across the top of the mug.

"Hula Hoop . . . this is Grinder Four," the gunny said.

"We're ten-eight with Bravo resupply and a squad of replacement types and three hitchhikers."

More static and crackle and garbled voice.

The Top keyed the transmit bar. ". . . A kerosene burner, a Viet singer, and a body bag."

Garbled voice.

"The singer's brother," the sergeant said.

Static and crackle.

"Not on orders, Hula Hoop."

Static and crackle and garbled voice. End transmission.

The sergeant wrote on the clipboard and looked up at Pritchard. "You'll have to talk to the pilot of the lead Huey. Touchdown in five minutes. He wasn't too happy to hear you wanted a ride."

"Know where I can get an ox cart?"

"What?"

Pritchard said nothing and walked to the cot. It was a shame to have to wake her. She needed the rest, and she looked warm and comfortable and safe and so young and vulnerable. Her sleeping eyes were long slashes above her high cheekbones, and her lips, curved slightly upward at the ends as though in smile, vibrated from the exhaled air. A trickle of clear mucus drained from her small bridgeless nose and he wiped the stuff away with his finger.

The Top shook his head and shouted into the rain. "Hey, cherry—get your sweet buns over here on the double."

McGarvie sloshed through the mud, bent over under the weight of the heavy pack, his boots making loud splashing sounds in the puddles of rainwater. Behind him a line of three UH-ls painted in green and brown camouflage colors dropped down one by one and skimmed the treetops into the landing zone.

McGarvie stood just inside the Quonset hut and waited for the sergeant to tell him what he wanted.

"You're dripping on my floor, shitbird."

The PFC stepped back into the rain and to one side to

make room for Pritchard, who had thrown on a poncho and ran by McGarvie to the lead helicopter that had touched down.

The Top glowered at McGarvie. "Were you born in a barn, Marine? Don't you ever come into my home without asking permission first." He keyed the radio and called battalion: "Red Dog, this is Bravo . . . Hula Hoop is taking on supplies and replacements and will be airborne in a few minutes for Quang Hoa."

Pritchard jumped into the Huey, past the door gunner and boxes of supplies that were being strapped down on the deck, and leaned into the cockpit. "I'm Bud Pritchard and I've got a wounded girl and her dead brother I want to get to their home in Quang Hoa village. How about a lift?"

The pilot and copilot had turned around in their armored seats to look at Pritchard, whose rain-wet face was flushed with the exertion of running.

"You got authorization?" the pilot said. "Any orders?"

"I don't need any authorization," Bud said. He leaned into the pilot, his eyes snapping, and wiped the rain from his face with an edge of the wet poncho. "This girl and her brother were minding their own business in the O-club when they got hit by a one-oh-seven meant for me and some other guys. Her brother hasn't got a head any more and she wants to bury him at home. I owe them—you owe them—the whole friggin' Marine Corps owes them."

"No one owes them anything—they just got in the way." The pilot was frowning and his deep-set eyes were ugly.

"If I hear that one more time I'm going to hurt someone," Pritchard said. "I'm sick and tired of hearing that these people just got in the way."

"Screw you—get out of my bird."

The copilot tried to disarm Pritchard with an awkward smile. "There's a lot of action up at Quang Hoa—could be a hot LZ—we can't take responsibility. You get orders and we'll be glad to cooperate."

"If you don't take the girl," Pritchard said, "she's going to haul her brother to Quang Hoa in an ox cart. You know what it's like in those mountains. It will take her two, three days—if she stays alive. You can get her there in thirty minutes."

"I told you to get out of my chopper—now beat it," the pilot said, and he turned away from Pritchard and began flipping switches on the Huey's consoles.

Pritchard jumped out of the helicopter and ran back to the Quonset hut. McGarvie looked at him with unhappy eyes, ankle deep in water, and shifted his weight to help ease the discomfort of the rucksack straps cutting into his shoulders.

Phuong's hand was lying on her chest, outside the blanket, the red polish chipped on her fingernails. He touched her hand and gently woke her.

"What is it?" she said and sat upright in the cot.

"It's time to go," he said and snapped on the web gear and slung the M16 over his shoulder. "Got an extra poncho?" he said to the Top.

The old gunny threw him his.

Phuong stood by the side of the cot and accepted the poncho that Pritchard slipped over her head; it hung over her bare feet and covered the floor. She looked at nothing in the room except the body bag near the door. The bag was wet from the rain, and a puddle of water had formed around it on the floor.

She began shivering. Pritchard pulled the blanket off the cot and wrapped it around her shoulders underneath the poncho and thought he should ask the Top for a pair of boots to cover her feet, but decided that she was used to going barefoot and that the boots would be too large to be of any use to her. He lifted the end of the poncho and looked at her feet. They were small and brown and spaces between her toes were filled with dried red mud.

He hoisted her up on his back, piggyback fashion, and

picked up one end of the body bag. "Grab the other end, McGarvie."

The rotor blades were beginning the first turn on the lead Huey when Pritchard and McGarvie laid brother in the slick and strapped Phuong into a jumpseat. The two crewmen looked surprised, but Pritchard's eyes crushed any questions.

Before the pilot could shut down the engines and confront Pritchard, Bud pushed him back down in his seat. "Now you look like a sensible man, Lieutenant," Pritchard said and cranked a round into the chamber of the M16. He released the bolt, and the bang of metal against metal was loud inside the confined cockpit.

The Huey pilot's jaw was set like a block of iron, and Pritchard could see blood gorge into his neck and turn his face purple.

"There are some things that you just can't change." Pritchard was smiling while he stroked the barrel of the rifle. "You just have to accept them."

The rotor blades were turning half speed and the copilot was going over the switches. "We better get these birds to Quang Hoa before the weather gets worse. Those guys need these supplies." He looked at the pilot and then at Bud, and his eyes weren't hostile.

The pilot gave orders over the intercom to the crew and talked to the other chopper pilots for a few seconds, then applied power to the engine. The noise rose to a crescendo and the Huey lifted with a jerk, nose pointed low, and wheeled left and away from the Quonset huts and rows of tents, and the battalion area swept behind the chopper.

Within seconds they were scooting above the trees and out of Cung Mai Dong, and Pritchard watched with professional interest while the Huey pilot deftly worked the cyclic and collective sticks and used the directional-control pedals to apply anti-torque on the tail rotor.

The cockpit chatter between the chopper pilots was terse,

much like that which Pritchard used when he talked to fighter pilots, and the windshield wipers were having difficulty keeping up with the huge tropical raindrops colliding with the Plexiglas. The cockpit smelled of wet canvas and cracked leather.

Five minutes out of Cung Mai Dong the copilot pointed to two Cobra attack helicopters joining up with the line of Hueys, one on each side of the formation. They were loaded with rocket pods, rapid-fire miniguns and grenade launchers.

"We've got a hot LZ," the pilot said to Bud. He twisted in the seat so he could eyeball Pritchard. "I hope they blow your butt to hell," he shouted over the rotor noise and vibration.

Pritchard looked back through the hatch at Phuong belted in the canvas jumpseat along the side of the fuselage. He had never been able to figure out how he got into these fixes; trouble was always just ahead of him, standing in the road, waiting for him to stumble into the hole it had dug.

The crew chief announced that the landing zone was taking fire and that Bravo company had set up a perimeter around the LZ to protect the choppers coming in with the badly needed resupply. PFC McGarvie's large eyes became larger, and he stared out the open door, past the M60 gunner and out into the rain and clouds and the AH-1 Cobra flying escort. He was going into a hot LZ on his first assault and he had no idea what to do; all his training at ITR had left him. He looked toward the pilot's station and saw Pritchard motioning to him.

"What are you doing, you crazy cherry," the squad leader yelled, seeing McGarvie unbuckle and afraid that he had freaked out and was going to fall through the open hatch. "Get back in your seat and keep your seat belt on."

McGarvie, petrified by everything coming down on him, pointed at Pritchard. The sergeant let him go, but stood between the PFC and the hatch, and held onto a structural member to keep from being swept out into the slipstream.

"Squat down here, McGarvie," Bud said and pulled the boy down beside him. "I'm going to need your help with the girl."

"Yes, sir."

"This is my first insertion, too, kid, and if we stick together we just might make it."

"Uh huh," McGarvie said. At that moment he was willing to turn his life over to anyone who gave him a ray of hope.

"Listen closely to what I'm going to tell you." He had to put his mouth up close to McGarvie's ear so the PFC could hear him over the cabin noise.

The two door gunners standing opposite each other in the open doors talked to the pilot over the intercom mikes attached to their hard helmets. The large, dark green sun visors were pulled down over their eyes and streaked with rain that spewed in through the open doors, and they scanned the jungle rushing by underneath the Huey, their brawny, suntanned arms sticking out from the sides of the flak vests they wore.

Puffs of white smoke burst from under the nose of the Cobra gunships ahead, and the line of slicks banked to the left and began a wide, slow orbit to allow the AH-1s time to work over the landing zone.

"Better get back to your seat, kid," Pritchard said to McGarvie. "We'll be going in behind the gunships. Remember what I said and you'll be okay."

"Yes, sir." McGarvie stumbled back to his seat and sat stiffly with the thump gun locked between his knees.

Long silver lines arched away from the Cobras and ended in cotton puffs on a green carpet of elephant grass. One of the silver lines ended on a tall ceiba tree, and the top broke off and fell into the elephant grass.

"Get that friggin' poncho off, you shitbird." The buck sergeant had his nose in McGarvie's face. "Lock and load," he screamed over the engine and rotor noise, "and try not to kill us."

McGarvie got tangled in his poncho, knocked off his steel helmet, and dropped his weapon.

Phuong reached over and put a hand on his shoulder to stop his thrashing, and after he was quieted down, she pushed his head through the opening and lifted the plastic up over his shoulders. Very quickly the poncho was rolled up and she stuffed it inside the rucksack. The others watched her and said nothing.

Several thumper rounds spilled out of McGarvie's ammo holder and clattered to the deck.

"Dumb cherry," the man next to him said.

McGarvie placed a round into the thump gun's chamber and sat back, exhausted, feeling embarrassment and fright and the need to urinate.

The man next to him reached over and put the thump gun on SAFE. "Dumb cherry."

The two Cobras, their rockets and ammunition expended, pulled off the target, and the slicks—strung out in a loose line—swung out lazily from their orbit and started in, the door gunners hammering away at the jungle, their arms and bodies jerking from the recoils of the M60s in rhythm to the beat of the spent brass cartridges that spilled from the breeches and scattered over the deck, rattling and rolling in a confused pattern.

Muzzle flashes from the ground sparkled through the gray rain, and the ring of a 2.76mm AK round ricocheting off a spar in the Huey's cabin turned McGarvie's face white. The chopper began to fall, and he thought the slick had been damaged badly and was out of control and was going to crash (his stomach was in his mouth from the heavy g forces exerted by the rapid descent), but in reality the pilot was dropping into the LZ at a sharp angle to avoid ground fire.

The slick was quickly on the ground, and it settled on the skids. Men jumped out the doors on both sides, and supplies tumbled after them.

"Let's go," Bud said and was out the door with Phuong draped between him and McGarvie, her feet dangling above the ground and her arms wrapped around their necks.

The noise and confusion were unbelievable. The door gunner was rapid-firing his machine gun directly over their heads, and all around the cleared LZ, dug-in Marines from Bravo Company fired M16s on full automatic. Three M60s in fighting holes a few yards away pounded at the jungle. Enemy rocket-propelled grenades exploded into the U.S. positions, and AK-47 fire raked the ground.

Adding to the confusion and noise, the whining jet engines on the Hueys continued to churn the rotor blades and sprayed mud and water in every direction; and shouting infantrymen jumping from the slicks collided with men hauling the wounded and dead aboard and with those who were throwing the supplies out the doors. The door gunners paid scant attention to the rush of bodies and fired recklessly, swiveling their weapons back and forth on the pylon mounts.

"Get her into that cover over there," Pritchard said to McGarvie. He pointed to a defilade ten yards away.

"Aren't you coming, sir?"

"I'm getting her brother."

A wild AK round smashed into the metal skid next to Bud's boot as he lurched up into the Huey and tugged the body bag through the wounded, bloodied men; some were filled with morphine and stared zombielike at the overhead structure of the helicopter, and others yelled wildly for help, or for their mothers, or at the North Vietnamese. One Marine lay on his back with a smoking cigarette in his open mouth. He wasn't breathing. Next to him another Bravo man had a huge plastic-and-cloth bandage tied over a sucking hole in his chest. His left pant leg was torn open and the red stub of a leg showed through.

Pritchard jumped to the ground with the body bag over his back and ran to where McGarvie and Phuong were lying prone in the depression. As he went by the cockpit he looked up through the windshield; the pilot gave him the finger.

"It would have been better if you let me take the ox cart," Phuong said.

Pritchard dropped brother on the ground and crawled into the depression. "Right now I'm inclined to agree with you."

Though the LZ was under heavy attack and the sounds of exploding mortars and RPGs shook the earth around her, Phuong was remarkably calm and her face showed no signs of fear, only curiosity and excitement. She turned on her side and pulled the poncho tightly around her to keep the cold rain away.

McGarvie's steel pot was pulled back from his eyes and he was looking out over the berm of dirt in front of him; his thump gun was off SAFE and pointed into the treeline at the edge of the roughly circular LZ. His head turned sharply at every noise, and he grasped the thump gun to him for protection.

"Welcome to the war, kid," Pritchard said.

"I knew it was going to be something like this."

"We better lend a hand—start firing."

"At what?"

"Doesn't matter; just lob your shells into the trees—build up a base of fire."

"I didn't get a chance to write to my mother today. She's going to worry." McGarvie's fingers were twisting on the trigger guard of the weapon. "Sir . . . what's that going on over there?" He pointed at the treeline that came into view behind the first Huey that lifted from the LZ and slid away.

Pritchard watched for a few seconds. "That, PFC, is a squad of NVA working closer for a shot with their B-40s. They're going for the choppers still on the ground."

"What are we going to do, sir?" McGarvie said, his sad eyes unchanged in their compassion and innocence.

"You are going to kill them."

Pritchard at that moment wanted to huddle all the McGarvies of the world under his arms and protect them from the ambitions of misguided men that sent them to war. *Why is it that the McGarvies are always the ones that get the dirtiest part of it?*

A cloud of black smoke from an exploded 81mm passed over the three of them and was quickly broken up by the rain that came steadily down in fine drops. Phuong clutched the poncho for protection from the cold and wet.

There was pain in McGarvie's sorrowful eyes. He asked only how far away Bud thought the North Vietnamese were, and when Pritchard said "About a hundred yards," he adjusted the sights accordingly on the thump gun.

"Don't forget your windage," Bud said.

"I've taken care of that," the PFC said in a detached, clinical voice, "the way they taught me at ITR."

Phuong watched him without emotion, the rain washing the mud in long streaks down her cheeks and over her lips. She huddled under the slick poncho.

"Captain, that looks more like a hundred and fifty yards." He started to readjust the sights.

"Go for a hundred."

"I don't want to argue with you, sir, but on the range at ITR . . ."

"Shoot the gun, McGarvie."

Whump. The gun bucked against McGarvie's shoulder and his thin body jerked backward. Phuong watched, her curious almond eyes stretching to see where the round would explode.

"You were right."

"Hurry and reload—drop another on them. Come down about ten yards."

The PFC made a quick adjustment on the knurled knob.

Whump. The second round was off. A second or two later a puff of smoke rose close to the first explosion.

"Good shooting," Bud said.

Phuong screamed.

Bud looked at her. She had her legs drawn up underneath her, and the fingers of her left hand protruding from under the poncho were stuck in her mouth as if to stifle the scream. The long eyes, normally teardrop in shape, were round and wide so that the whites were clear and easily seen around the large black pupils.

At the same time Pritchard said "what happened?" he turned and saw the square face in the elephant grass twenty yards away. The curved magazine and red teak-colored stock of the AK-47 swung to the right and up with the twisting motion of the North Vietnamese soldier rising from his stomach to his knees.

Pritchard and Phuong were both down far enough in the depression to be protected from the soldier's fire, but McGarvie, who had risen to sight in on the NVA B-40 squad and had his back to the elephant grass, was completely exposed and directly in the line of fire.

"McGarvie" was all Pritchard could say. He saw the kid at school, eating his lunch alone on the long empty bench under the arcade in front of the home-economics room, Miss Shell's classroom; then he saw him in the team photograph in the school yearbook, standing in the last row and looking out of place, his thin shoulders sticking out of the basketball jersey that was too big for him; and he saw him in the school orchestra, sitting behind the bass drum that nobody else wanted to play, his sorrowful eyes big and thankful that he could participate. *McGarvie, your mother will be worried that you didn't write to her today.*

The square face was flat and brown and showed no hate, only determination. The man's cotton uniform had no markings, and he carried only ammunition pouches around his waist and a small pack on his back; he wore sandals and a green sun helmet. His black hair had been crudely cropped over his eyebrows with a knife. The soldier was a full-grown adult but looked no larger than an average-sized American twelve-year-old.

Phuong's small foot under the poncho tensed and stretched out at the bottom of the plastic, the rain licking at the toes and washing away the caked mud.

A second and third face appeared in the elephant grass and time slowed and the action was reduced to slow motion on the movie projector and Phuong's scream was long and warbled and it modulated into a higher key and the fire team close by in fighting holes stopped arguing among themselves and turned in her direction and the mortar explosions were muffled by the rain and mud, and all the world stopped what it was doing to watch PFC McGarvie take the AK rounds in his back.

The rain pattered on ponchos and helmets, and it soaked into the camouflaged cloth that covered the Marines' helmets, and when the covers were saturated the water collected in large drops that fell off the front lip in a steady line. Pritchard flashed on a scene some years previous when at Basic School in Quantico he rode in an open six-by during a Virginia downpour and he wondered how he would take to leading a rifle company in the muck and rain for days and weeks on end in some remote corner of the globe (where Marines always fought), and it was then that he decided to request transfer to Pensacola for flight training.

To die in a stinking rain-filled hole in Vietnam was not what Bud Pritchard would have chosen if he had been given a choice, but he gave it no thought as he threw himself at McGarvie's back and knocked him out of the hole and over the other side of the berm and down the incline, face in the mud, and the thump gun flying out of the PFC's hands.

It would be impossible to tell which came first, the collision of the two bodies over the berm or the enfilading fire from the AK-47s that tore off the top of the ledge. McGarvie was groping in the wet grass for his helmet.

"Throw a grenade," Pritchard yelled, "forget the helmet."

McGarvie dug into his pouch, a wild look in his face.

Bud was shaking him. "Hurry, kid, hurry."

"I can't get it out."

"Take your hand away—give me the pouch."

"Where's that fire coming from?" someone said down the line.

Another burst tore at the dirt and Pritchard and McGarvie pressed their faces down into the mud.

"Where do I throw it?" McGarvie had finally dug a grenade out of the web gear and was holding it in his hand.

"Behind us." Bud pointed.

"Where's my helmet?"

"You don't need your helmet . . . throw the thing."

The grenade arched out behind the berm and over the depression where Phuong lay hiding in its water-filled bottom, and hit with a wet thud in the grass.

There was no explosion.

"Did you pull the pin?" Pritchard said.

The Marines who were dug in fifteen yards away began cursing. "There's gooks behind us."

"How'd they get there? First squad is supposed to be covering our rear."

"First squad's on the other side."

"Frag the riceballs."

Bursts of M16 fire ripped through the grass, and there was a great deal of shouting, and then several fragmentation grenades flew out of the holes and shrapnel zinged overhead.

"Get some!"

Crump . . . crrrump . . . crump. Enemy mortar rounds fell with the rain, bracketing the LZ. *Crrrump . . . crump.* A Marine 3.5 rocket crew moved out of a hole and down the slope toward the NVA positions where the mortars were dug in.

"They'll never get 'em," a Marine said. "The gooks are firing from bunkers and tunnels and spider holes—we were down there yesterday. It's useless."

McGarvie looked at Pritchard, his face smeared with orange-red mud, the sad doe eyes with their long lashes blinking underneath the goo. He was lying on one side, and his dog tags had spilled out from under his utility shirt and dangled loosely across his chest. "Are we going to buy the farm, sir?" The mortars began to walk across the LZ.

From the south came the faraway throb of jet engines. Pulsing in the dense air, the sound reached into each Marine's hole at the same time, and a human roar rose above the barrage of mortars and rockets that shook and tore at the tiny hilltop LZ.

A small head looking out from under a poncho hood rose over the berm, and the voice was soft and childlike. "You are not hurt." The words were more an expression of curiosity than relief. Phuong looked away, toward the sound of engines.

"The fast movers," Pritchard said.

He turned over on his back and watched the four F-4s roll in between a gap in the mountains and make a high-speed pass over the landing zone, well out of range of ground fire.

"Hey, Captain," a Marine said, "why didn't they drop their loads?"

"Either they can't distinguish between the battle lines or the boss doesn't have the nerve to lead them all the way in. Who's calling your air?" Pritchard said.

"The LT."

"Where's he?"

"Who knows where anyone is in this circus," the rifleman said. "He should be down the slope thataway." He pointed with his rifle. "You'll never find him," he said and buried his head as another mortar exploded nearby.

The jets pulled up and disappeared into the rain, the

thrust from their engines trailing off into a distant moan as they orbited in the clouds.

Pinned down, the Marines couldn't move against the superior NVA force, nor could they move off the hill in a strategic withdrawal to more defensible positions. They sat in their fighting holes, waiting for the air support (the only hope of extrication), and listened to the enemy artillery increase in intensity and accuracy.

Pritchard crawled over the sloppy ground to the nearest hole. "You guys got a radio?" he said, looking in. "I'm a pilot."

"What are you doing out here in the bush with us grunts, sir?" The corporal squinted at Pritchard's captain's bars, smeared with mud on the collar points of his dress shirt. "Why aren't you with those guys?" He motioned into the sky with his thumb.

"We don't have time to discuss my intelligence." The earth heaved with the blast of two mortar rounds and Pritchard rolled into the hole with the corporal and another rifleman.

"We're not getting off this LZ without air support," the corporal said.

"Get me a radio and I'll talk those Phantoms right down into the gooners' mortar tubes," Pritchard said. "It's obvious that your lieutenant is having trouble getting them lined up on a target."

"He's new—just out of TBS. We're his first command and some of the guys are talking about fragging him next time he goes to take a shit. . . . No disrespect intended, sir, but he's a real dork."

"Get me a radio."

"Pass the word to get Rodriguez up here," the corporal shouted to the men in the next hole. "We've got a flyboy who's going to call in the air."

The word went down the line and in a few minutes a Puerto Rican kid with a bad case of acne crawled up to the edge of the hole. "Who wants my radio, mon?"

Pritchard reached out his hand for the set.

"You're old for a captain, ain't you, sir?" Rodriguez said.

"Are you up on the F-4s' channel?"

Rodriguez flipped the selector switch and nodded.

Pritchard keyed the set and got right down to business, ignoring radio discipline and call signs: "Who's the chicken boss of the four fox-fours over Quang Hoa?" he said into the transmitter.

There was a moment's silence as the grunts in the hole with Bud smiled at each other in respect for this weathered captain's irreverent style. They crowded closer, wanting to hear every word. Water ran over the top of the hole and joined the puddle in the bottom. A canteen cup used for bailing out the water sat on the edge of the hole.

"This is Flagstaff strike leader Sharkfin One. Identify yourself."

With his forefinger, Bud wiped away the rain running into his eyes. He blinked up into the depressing sky. "That you, Thorbus?"

A long silence.

"Who the hell is this?"

"This is Bud Pritchard, Major. What happened, did you run out of excuses for not flying and the Old Man got wise to you?"

A voice cut through the conversation, low, the words evenly spaced. "Bud . . . what the devil are you doing down there?"

"Like I told you outside the O-club last night, Keilman, someone's got to right the wrong."

"She and her brother there with you?"

"Roger that."

"Cut the chitchat," Thorbus said. "Put the FAC on, Pritchard. As far as I'm concerned you're AWOL."

"I'm controlling the strike now, bigshot; listen up good, Thorbus. We're going to be overrun unless you get your buns down here pronto and pickle your loads. The gooners have us zeroed in with mortars and B-40 rockets and we're taking casualties."

"I tried a pass and there's no way to line up. I'll have to wait for a big enough hole to open in the cloud cover before . . ."

"Can it, Major—I saw that chicken pass you made. There's no time to wait for the weather to break, because a company of Marines will be dead by the time you decide it's safe enough for your yellow ass."

"Whoever's on the radio, get off."

"Take it easy, Lieutenant," Pritchard said. "I'm an F-4 pilot and can call in the strike better than you. If you want your men off this hill alive you better let me do the talking."

"Who are you?"

"I'm Captain Bud Pritchard and I hitched a ride in one of your resupply choppers."

"Okay—it's all yours, Captain." The youthful voice sounded relieved. "You know where the mortars are dug in?"

"Some of your mud Marines are here spotting for me." He gave the names of the corporal, Rodriguez, and the other grunt. "You listen in on the freq and butt in when you got something."

A mosquito, unconcerned with the rain, buzzed Pritchard's nose, hovered in contemplation of using it as an LZ, then changed its mind and landed on his forearm to bury its proboscis up to the hilt. Pritchard slapped it hard.

Rodriguez, the radioman, felt for the insect repellent tucked into the band wrapped around his helmet. "Spray this bug juice on your skin, sir . . . it helps; and while you're at it give that leech a shot."

Sticking out from beneath Pritchard's rolled-up sleeve, the bloodsucking worm lay motionless on the underside of his forearm at the hollow of the elbow.

"I hate anything slimy," the corporal said, taking the bottle from Rodriguez and squeezing a drop of the repellent on he parasite.

The leech squirmed under the liquid and slid off Pritchard's arm, leaving behind a smear of blood and brown slime.

Cockpit chatter between Thorbus and the strike crews broke off when Pritchard pressed the transmit bar. "Are you listening, Sharkfin One?"

"I hear you," Thorbus said, restrained anger in his voice.

"Your first target is the mortars emplaced one hundred yards up the slope of the hill west of the LZ. Come over the saddle and break right in ten-second intervals. Roll up and out twenty degrees and you will be lined up for a quick pickle. Use your HE and save the white phosphorus for the gooner troops in the treeline. You copy that, Keilman?"

The reply was terse: "Got it."

"Stand on Thorbus's shoulders and don't let him break off once you've got him locked on the target, regardless of how hot the ground fire gets. The biggest stuff they've got down here is fifty-seven mike-mikes."

"Everything's cool, Bud—no one's going to break off," Keilman said.

The grass rustled and Pritchard and the others looked toward the sound of heavy breathing and bodies crawling over the ground. Rodriguez had a grenade on his chest; his left hand gripped it tight, and the index finger on the right hand strained on the ring attached to the safety pin. The corporal pointed his rifle into the grass and placed a full magazine on the edge of the foxhole.

Chapter 4

The movement of the grass was unnatural, not movement caused by the breeze that blew through the rain from down the slope up past the forward holes of the Marines who took most of the NVA attack.

Bud Pritchard's body was stone rigid, and he itched all over from the sweat that trickled under his collar and down his armpits and over his crotch and down his legs. Even the bottoms of his feet itched, and he longed to drop his trousers and give his testicles a good scratching.

None of the grunts spoke—they couldn't without giving away their position—but their eyes flashed messages to each other that were as good as words, a code that came naturally from the long months they had spent together in the bush.

The air blowing up from the bottoms chilled the rain, and Bud wondered if it was the fear or the rain that made him shiver.

Overhead, the afterburners on the Phantoms kicked in and a loud boom shook the air, louder than the exploding B-40s, but not as loud as the mortars. The grass waved back and forth in a jerking, swaying motion that reminded Pritchard of the grass skirts on the Hawaiian hula dancers that he had seen at the Kona Inn just a year ago. Was it only a year? It must have been, because it was Marjorie's birthday, when he met her at the Kona for that disastrous attempt at restoring to the marriage the vigor of those first years. He had felt stupid and a little sorry for Marjorie, and it was obvious from the first few minutes together that the feelings were no longer there and the distrust that they felt for each other was irreversible as long as they held opposite views concerning the U.S. involvement in Vietnam.

McGarvie's sad doe eyes looked out at him through the grass, not more than five feet away. Rain trickled down Billy's nose and dripped off the end.

"Hold it!" Bud yelled. "Put down the weapons."

The Marines relaxed and the tension went out of the air like a balloon deflating.

"Sir," Billy McGarvie said, "the hole we're in is filling with water and the girl is shivering. I think she's sick or something and she keeps wailing something in Vietnamese and points to one of the dead Cong that stares at her with wide open eyes."

"I'll be right there."

"I think you ought to come now, Captain, because she's in an awful mess."

Pritchard shook his head. "You have to take care of the situation—I've got my hands full."

Hanging back for a moment and with a lost look in his eyes, PFC McGarvie crawled back through the grass, the knobby soles of his boots looking back at Bud and his butt lifted high.

Thorbus couldn't be raised on the radio, and Bud experienced the sinking feeling that he and what remained of Bravo Company had been abandoned. He felt very old.

"Where are the fast movers, sir?"

"Gone," Pritchard said.

The Marines stared dumbly at him.

Without saying anything more, Bud crawled away through the trail of wet, crumpled grass that Billy McGarvie had left.

Up in the clouds, Ralph Thorbus circled for a few more minutes, then radioed Cung Mai Dong that the target was socked in (zero visibility) and that he was returning to base.

Slowly the North Vietnamese, a few here, a few there, slipped from their holes and probed for weaknesses in the Marine lines. The grunts instinctively pulled closer together and shrunk their perimeter, consolidating their forces, fire team with fire team, squad to squad, all along Bravo Company's circle of defense.

The ground shuddered and red mud sprayed over Pritchard. He looked over the edge of the berm into the depression and saw McGarvie and Phuong huddled together in the mud and water. Billy had dragged Phuong's brother down into the hole with them.

"McGarvie," Pritchard said.

The PFC looked up, startled. "Yes, sir."

"How's she doing?"

"I think she's unconscious; her eyes are closed."

"Put your ear on her chest and see if she's breathing."

Looking down at her lying on her side, Billy hesitated, then tugged on the poncho and rolled her over on her back and laid his head on her breast. His helmet fell off next laying to his M79 grenade launcher.

"Well?"

"I can hear something—I guess it's her heart." He wiped the rain from his face. "She isn't in very good shape—maybe she isn't going to last through this."

"Listen, McGarvie, we're going to leave her."

Billy's eyes looked sadder, if that was possible.

"There's nothing we can do for her except make her as comfortable as possible."

The ground shuddered again and the zing of shrapnel cut through the air and thudded into the mud bank.

In a few minutes Pritchard and McGarvie had Phuong out of the water at the bottom of the depression and up higher on drier ground.

"Wrap the poncho tight around her and get your gear. You and I are going hunting."

Billy McGarvie did as he was told and followed Captain Pritchard back through the grass to the fighting holes where the corporal and Rodriguez and the rest of the squad were dug in.

"Where you going, Captain?" Rodriguez put his arms through the PR-25 radio set and lifted it to his back.

"I'm going to find a way to get us off this hill."

Working along the back side of Bravo Company's foxholes and down the cut in the steep southern side of the hill, which was a tangle of roots and vines and branches, Pritchard stopped to get his bearings. The noise of battle was already diminishing, and the crash of B-40s and 81s sounded far away.

"Captain."

"What is it, McGarvie?"

"Look."

Behind them, strung out in spaced single file, twelve Marines, Rodriguez out front with the PR-25, picked their way down the slope.

"They're following us," McGarvie said.

Surprised that there was no enemy opposition, Pritchard pushed ahead cautiously, traversing the hill, feeling his way through the heavy undergrowth of the triple-canopy forest. He could be ten feet from an NVA soldier and not see him. He thought of Phuong in the elephant grass, wrapped in a poncho, cold and unconscious, her breathing so shallow that her small breasts never moved.

The newness of McGarvie's boots and utilities had vanished beneath the layers of red mud and the smell of decay and tropical rot. Innocence remained in his smooth cheeks, but the eyes had become sunken and lizard fast, and his lips were set in a firm, thin line. Both canteens were empty (he had drained them within the first thirty minutes), and his throat was burning for water.

Pritchard stopped among a tangle of roots and vines and was motioning for him to be quiet. The captain, head bent forward, listening intently, held onto a ropy liana with one hand, the M16 hanging by the strap from the other.

"Get Rodriguez down here with the radio," Pritchard said.

Ten minutes later, panting and sweating profusely, Rodriguez scrambled through the branches and over the aerial roots of the trees, and collapsed next to Bud Pritchard. He looked up and smiled. "Got a beer, Captain?"

By this time, because of the mud and rain, it was impossible to distinguish between Pritchard's class-A (dress) uniform and Rodriguez's jungle fatigues. Bud reached inside his shirt and tossed a can of Coors to the Puerto Rican.

"Hey, gee . . . great, mon; where'd you get this?"

"Compliments of the O-club."

Rodriguez chugged half of it down and held the can out to Bud.

"Drink it all . . . I've got another."

"You want a drink, Cherry?" Rodriguez said to Billy McGarvie.

"Naw," he said, embarrassed.

Rodriguez looked at him and frowned. He tipped the helmet back on his head. "You too good to drink with a spic?"

McGarvie shook his head and dropped his gaze. "I've never tasted beer."

The fierce look in the Puerto Rican's face turned to a contemptuous smile. "You *are* a cherry."

McGarvie took off his rucksack, sat on it and looked up at Pritchard to see if he would intervene.

"Get me your LT," Bud said to Rodriguez.

Quickly downing what remained of the beer, Rodriguez released the antenna band (it whipped upward), flipped the power switch, and keyed the set with a mud-caked finger. "Quaking Aspen . . . Pine Tree . . . Quaking Aspen . . .

Pine Tree."

He released his finger and some squawking came through, and Rodriguez used some of his Spanish and jive-talk encode to talk to Bravo Company's CP radioman. A few seconds passed and there was more squawking. Rodriguez turned to Pritchard. "The CO has been killed. The wimp is in charge." He handed the set to Bud.

"Yeah, this is the flyboy—we talked earlier."

"Where's your air?" The voice was anxious. "Over."

"They won't be coming to the party. Now listen up, Lieutenant; I'm no infantryman but it doesn't take much to figure out that we're in deep shit. I've got a plan and I need some intel. What's our strength and what's the gooks' ?"

The answer was quick in coming; the voice sounded relieved. "I've got about eighty men left, two platoons tied in a loose two-hundred-meter perimeter. I figure at least two companies of NVA on the hill opposite—north—and down on our forward slope. Over."

"I've got a squad down in the cut below you—south—and I've worked down behind the gooners. Another hundred yards and I'll be in good position to take pressure off your right flank. Over."

"What do you want me to do?"

Pritchard squatted on his haunches and looked at Rodriguez. "You're right, this is an inexperienced officer." He keyed the set, realizing that he had just been given the company. "Still there, Lieutenant?"

"Yes, sir."

"There's a highballer at the bottom of the hill, in a ravine; I can see it through the trees and I can see the gooners using it to haul supplies on bicycles and carts up to their lines."

Rodriguez was suddenly up on his feet, spreading the vines apart to look for the highballer, a crude road hacked out of the jungle, following the course of the watershed.

"I'm going to set up an ambush, kill a bunch of the

bastards and then attack up the highball toward the main force," Bud said. "When you hear us in the shit, you unass and *di-di mau len.*"

"You're going to do that with just twelve men?"

"You want to sit there in the mud like a bunch of wet hens waiting to get your heads chopped off or do you want the chance to fight your way off the hill? Over."

There was no reply.

"Pine Tree gone," Pritchard said and gave the radio to Rodriguez. "You and the corporal get the squad on line and work down to the bottom. I want everyone in position in thirty minutes, concealed along the highball, five yards apart, max. Got it?"

"Got it, Captain."

Rodriguez left, Billy McGarvie starting after him.

"You stay with me, McGarvie," Pritchard said.

At the bottom of the hill the slope rose immediately into another hill; the width of thirty yards between was the NVA high-speed supply trail.

"Don't screw up," Bud Pritchard whispered in Billy McGarvie's ear. "Do exactly what I tell you."

Billy nodded. His eyes were very wide and caked around the outside with a ring of red mud. The helmet cover was torn and hung down on one side, and an M26 fragmentation grenade was clutched in one smooth, almost feminine hand, the thump gun in the other. The undergrowth rustled and he jerked around.

"Just the squad taking up position," Pritchard said. "Relax."

Billy marveled at how easily and professionally each Marine did his job, knowing exactly what to do without being told. Each man used an entrenching tool, or E-tool, that he removed from his rucksack to dig a fighting hole well back into the undergrowth. While Rodriguez watched the highballer, the men concealed claymore mines along a length of 200 feet of the trail, connected by wire to handheld detonators.

The corporal, a twenty-one-year-old named Hank with eyes the color of a summer Wyoming sky (he was from Laramie) and legs bowed from the knees down, carefully and quietly chose his steps in the brown mush of decaying leaves underfoot, and leaned his bony body on a large buttress. "We're about ready, sir," he whispered. "Got the two hog-60s set up thirty yards apart—one in the middle of the line and the other toward the front. Mines are laid every ten or twenty yards and we got our foxholes dug far enough back into the bush to give us good cover. Anything else you want done?"

Rodriguez came up and kneeled in the brown soup and supported himself on his rifle resting butt-first across the instep of his boot.

Not taking his eyes off the trail, Pritchard smiled and said to Hank, "I don't know much about ambushes and jungle fighting, but my gut-feel is that you do. So if you say you're ready, then you're ready. What do you think, Rodriguez?"

He shrugged. "It's pretty much how we always set up on the L ambushes except we got an extra hog. We let the gooks all the way into the trap, they're usually bunched up pretty good—not strung out like we go—and then, *pow . . . !*" He quietly popped a fist into his palm.

"The mines?" Pritchard said.

"Yeah . . . the mines first, then we open up with the sixties and what's left over we chop down with the sixteens. Mostly it all comes down at the same time . . . claymores, hogs, and rifles."

"Better put the cherry with the M79 in the middle by the hog so he can blook the gooners up and down the line in both directions," Hank said. "Those spin-arm balls can really do a number when the thumper knows how to handle the weapon right."

Rodriguez put his cheek along the barrel of the M16 and scratched the beginnings of a beard, at the same time squinting at Billy McGarvie. "You get right out in the highballer when we get in the shit, Cherry, so you got a clear line of fire in two directions up and down the highballer. I want to hear that thump gun rock-and-roll."

McGarvie nodded and stroked the M79, holding it close to his chest. He thought about his mother at home cooking great northern white beans in the white enameled pot that had strawflowers painted on the side, and he remembered how she hummed "Pennies from Heaven" while she added the ham hocks and chopped onions.

The sound of high-pitched voices and many feet turned Pritchard's attention to the trail. Crawling to the edge of the highball he looked out at the well-packed red clay and saw a column of North Vietnamese infantry coming toward him. Leading the column were several carts and bicycles loaded with 81mm mortars, 3.5 U.S. rockets, and AK-47 ammunition.

"Get your men in position," Pritchard said, crawling back to Hank and Rodriguez. "A platoon-size group is coming down the trail."

Dug in at the top of Hill 506, his tiny command post in the middle of a rapidly shrinking perimeter, the brown-bar lieutenant fresh out of The Basic School (TBS) took the radio handset from Staff Sergeant George Huebner and looked out over the parapet of his bunker at the smoke and dust rising from his Marines' positions. They were getting butchered.

"Quaking Aspen one," Lieutenant Jerry Tatman said into the Prick-25. "Over."

"This is Flyboy, Lieutenant. Don't forget to take out your dead and wounded." That was all of Bud Pritchard's transmission.

Beside Tatman in the shallow bunker lay First Lieutenant Harold "Hal" MacGrath, the commanding officer of Bravo Company, 2nd Battalion, 1st Marines. He was dead. Tatman reached down and closed the lids of Harold Mac-

Grath's eyes and handed the radiophone to Staff Sergeant Huebner. "Be sure to take him with us."

"What's that, sir?" Huebner said, looking queerly at Jerry Tatman.

"We're moving out."

Staff Sergeant Huebner blinked and rubbed his muddy beard. No doubt the brown-bar from Quantico had gone over the edge.

"We're getting off the hill, Sergeant, and we're taking everyone with us—everyone—including Hal. Is that understood?"

Huebner searched Tatman's face and said slowly, "Yes, Lieutenant."

"Pass the word."

A chain of heavy explosions rolled up from below Bravo Company, at the bottom of Hill 506. Black smoke quickly rose, followed by the sound of machine gun and rifle fire and blooker explosions.

"That's M-sixty and M-sixteen fire," Huebner said. "Who's down there?"

"Get the men moving, Sergeant!" Tatman shouted. "Fire team by fire team, squad by squad, everyone bringing out their own dead and wounded. No one gets left behind."

The intense fire from the treeline forced Huebner back into the bunker. Waiting for a break in the fighting, he crawled over the parapet and ran hunched over toward two burning UH-1 helicopters that he planned to use as cover.

Not all the supplies had been offloaded the Hueys. Behind the dead pilot and copilot of the UH-1 that was split in half by a rocket-propelled grenade, a dozen wooden crates with rope handles were strewn across the deck of the forward fuselage. Cardboard boxes of C-rations and wool socks had already burned away and the wooden boxes were on fire. They contained the 40-millimeter spin-ball blooker rounds that Billy McGarvie used in his thump gun.

As Staff Sergeant Huebner ran to the first Huey he

stopped to rest behind its protection to catch his breath. He knew he was out of shape, spending too much time with the poguey Marines in the rear and patronizing the Shangri-la whorehouse in Cung Mai Dong, where he punched Trang or Linh almost every night and drank a half bottle of deadly Ho Chi Minh gin.

Up on one knee he looked through the broken fuselage and out the other side to the treeline. The NVA clustered together started forward, stopped—confused by the violent explosions behind them—and were driven back by the Marines throwing grenades and firing M16s in front of them.

Then Huebner's gaze fell on the dead door gunner draped over the burning crates of 40mm blooker rounds. That was the last thing he saw in this world. The explosion tore the helicopter and Staff Sergeant George Huebner into small pieces.

Second Lieutenant Jerry Tatman watched, horrified. He looked around for someone, anyone, but he was alone in the bunker. A piece of burning metal from the UH-1 spun through the smoke-filled air in front of him and landed in the mud, where it lay red-hot, sizzling in the rain.

Down in the ravine among the roots and branches and brown ground slop, Buddy Pritchard was busy with the squad of Marines that had chosen to follow him down the steep cut, not knowing where the old captain would lead them, rather than remain in their holes on top of Hill 506, where they were certain their fate was sealed.

"Get McGarvie on that thump gun," Pritchard shouted into the explosions.

Rodriguez hit Billy McGarvie in the helmet with his fist. "Get that thing in action."

PFC McGarvie, shocked by the swift violence and deafening noise, was knocked down by Rodriguez's blow. He lay on his face in the smelly soup of decay and rainwater and groped for the thump gun.

Rodriguez kicked the grenade launcher to him and continued to fire the M16 into the thick smoke. "Get up—get up," he screamed and jammed another magazine into his weapon.

Another explosion ripped the jungle, this one much louder and with much more force than the explosions from the Marines' claymore antipersonnel mines. The NVA ordnance in the cart and on the bicycles had exploded.

McGarvie had recovered from his shock and was standing in the middle of the highball, flak jacket open, firing the small grenades as fast as he could load.

"Get some, Cherry!" Rodriguez shouted. "Get some!"

Pritchard, kneeling beside Rodriguez with the radio, pulled the pin from a grenade, lobbed it onto the trail, and yelled into the handset, "Are you pulling out, Tatman? I've just killed forty of the slopeheads and I can see a lot of them coming down the break, leaving their positions on the hill. Get your ass moving."

Tatman left the handset dangling from the PR-25 and ran among the Marine foxholes. "Pull back . . . down through the cut . . . orderly withdrawal . . . fire as you go . . . cover each other . . . bring out the dead . . . and wounded . . . don't leave anyone . . . bring out all weapons . . . let's move it."

"Which way, sir?" a private said.

Tatman pointed behind him, through the burning Hueys. He grabbed the private by his flak jacket. "Stay with me." He stopped two more and another and another until he had a squad of men to cover the withdrawal. Second Lieutenant Jerry Tatman from Omaha, Nebraska, pulled men from holes, kicked butts, and organized his small force to pour withering fire into the NVA.

Bud Pritchard's ambush on the highballer had become a full-scale battle that caused the NVA commander, Major Nguyen Vo Toi to halt the offensive on Hill 506 and divert a large number of his troops to the highballer. Convinced that the Marines had slipped sizable reinforcements behind his lines and that he was risking entrapment if he remained on Hill 506, Major Toi made the only decision good Communist commanders make when confronted with what they suspect to be equal or larger enemy forces: withdraw from the fight and scatter into the jungle to regroup days, even weeks later.

"You hear that, Corporal?" Pritchard said.

"Yeah," Hank said. He lowered his rifle and listened.

Rodriguez smiled through the grime on his face. "The firing has let up."

"Sounds like the gooners mean to sky-out most rikky-tik," Hank said.

On the opposite slope, Hill 507, a line of NVA troops could be seen trailing up to the ridgeline, rocket launchers and mortar tubes and base plates on their backs. They disappeared over the back side of the ridge.

Sporadic firing continued on top of Hill 506 where Second Lieutenant Jerry Tatman covered the withdrawal of Bravo Company.

Rising unsteadily to his feet (he found it increasingly difficult to straighten up), Pritchard looked around through the powder smoke and sniffed the strong smells of battle. The air was still thick but he was able to make out the veiled forms of the squad. Some men cleared their weapons and reloaded with fresh magazines, others lay in their holes and watched for movement, and some crawled to new positions or to team up with a buddy. One M60 still fired, short rattling bursts.

Buddy Pritchard dropped his pants and vigorously scratched his crotch. He couldn't remember anything feeling so good.

"Shall we get a body count, Captain?"

Continuing to scratch, Bud watched through the trees and felt old and tired and not sure of what he had done. There hadn't been time to think. The North Vietnamese soldiers, the weight of their weapons bending their backs, filed north and back to where they came from somewhere in the triple-canopy rain forests of Cambodia and Laos.

"You want a body count, Rodriguez? You get a count."

Pritchard spotted McGarvie sitting in the middle of the highball, the grenade launcher resting on his thighs, the flak jacket pulled up over his head and his steel helmet lying upside down a few feet away.

Buckling his belt, Pritchard limped over to Billy McGarvie and pulled the flak jacket from his face. "What's the matter, kid?"

"I never killed anyone before."

"Forget it."

"No, sir . . . I won't."

The circulation was returning to Bud's legs and it was easier for him to stand. "Maybe you'll get used to it."

"No I won't."

"I don't think you will either."

"What about the girl, Captain?"

Pritchard was watching the Communist infantry silhouetted on Hill 507, snaking along the ridge. "What's that, McGarvie?"

"The girl's still back there."

"Yeah." He dropped a half-smoked cigarette into the wet leaves and kicked a detached arm laying next to his boot. "Come on."

It took them an hour to climb back up the cut to the top of the hill. McGarvie would slip in the mud and slide ten yards before his rucksack would catch in the roots and vines and stop him. Pritchard finally tied his web belt to Billy and pulled him to the top.

The rain had turned to a drizzle, and the fires at the LZ were still burning hot. The two UH-1 Hueys and what remained of Sergeant Huebner were what Pritchard first saw when he returned to the top of Hill 506. The only sounds were an occasional secondary explosion and the crackling of fires.

There were no Marines and there were no NVA. They had withdrawn in opposite directions, taking their dead and wounded. Boxes of C-rations, water cans, empty ammo boxes and M16 magazines, a steel helmet, a boot, ponchos, even a cassette player with a tape of Tina Turner still playing, were scattered over the LZ.

Inside the abandoned fighting holes, mixed with rainwater, was urine, defecation, and blood.

The smells of burning fuel, exploded cordite, and the ubiquitous jungle rot hung over the top of Hill 506. Rats had already come out of their burrows and were feeding on partly eaten C-rations and body parts.

PFC Billy McGarvie supported himself with one hand on the shattered hulk of a helicopter while he vomited.

"Where did we leave her?" Pritchard paid no attention to Billy's sensitive stomach.

"I'm not sure; everything looks turned around." He threw up another bellyful. "It's terrible, sir."

"Yeah." He looked around absently. "Could have been worse."

Pritchard walked among the debris and kicked ammo cans, looked inside foxholes, pocketed a set of dog tags and a Zippo lighter, and after walking the length of the landing zone sat down on the edge of Lieutenant Jerry Tatman's bunker and opened a can of ham and lima beans that he found in the ashes. It was warm, almost hot.

Tatman's PR-25 sat in the mud of the CP, the handset dangling from its cord, and squawked human noises. Buddy Pritchard finished what he wanted of the C-ration ham and limas and threw the can into the fire. The juice ran out and hissed and turned brown.

Keying the Prick-25, Pritchard spoke into the transmitter. "Quaking Aspen, over."

The voice from battalion was as near-hysterical as a battlefield commander's voice could get, high-pitched, rapid, and angry. "What the shit is going on up there, why haven't I been kept informed? There have been no reports since oh-nine-hundred and I'm going to court-martial your ass . . . who the hell is this?"

"Fuck you, Colonel." Pritchard let the handset fall into the mud and walked back across the smoking LZ.

When he reached the helicopter, McGarvie was sitting on his rucksack with a split APH-5 in his hands. He dropped the Huey pilot's helmet when he saw Pritchard and began tearing down the thump gun.

"Why are you doing that now?" Bud said.

"At ITR, Papa Sierra always told us to keep our weapons clean."

"Forget ITR. Let's find the girl."

"It's a mess up here—everything is blown apart. We'll never find her."

"Think positive, McGarvie."

Billy looked around at the devastation and carnage. "You've got a sense of humor, sir."

"Yeah, I'm a regular riot."

They traversed the LZ a couple of times (McGarvie's stomach went into spasms of dry heaves) and found nothing that reminded them of their last position on the hill.

"We must have been back there where the Hueys are burning," McGarvie said. "We didn't move far from where they unloaded us."

"Those Hueys aren't the ones that brought us in—ours got off the LZ—and there were choppers landing all over the area."

Pritchard looked down where the PFC was standing. McGarvie saw him and looked down also.

"What would you say those marks are, Billy?"

"Something heavy been dragged through the mud and grass. Could be a wounded or dead man being dragged on a poncho."

They saw that there were many such marks on top of Hill 506, all pointing in the same direction, south, toward the burning remains of the helicopters.

"You're right, Billy; that's where the choppers dropped us."

They followed the drag marks and came to the line of foxholes where Hank and Rodriguez and their squad had dug in.

"Okay—let's find her. This is the area."

Within a few minutes they had found the water-filled depression by back-trailing from the foxholes and through the elephant grass.

McGarvie stood on the edge of the depression and looked into it. "She's not here, Captain."

"And neither is her brother."

"Look here, sir."

Billy McGarvie was pointing to drag marks across the depression.

"That was caused by the body bag," Bud said.

For twenty minutes they trailed the drag marks, losing them several times where they crossed the grass or where they crossed over other drag marks.

The trail led in the general direction of Bravo Company's withdrawal, south, but when it reached the back slope of the LZ, near the steep cut where Bud and the squad had descended, the marks made an abrupt change in direction and turned east toward the village of Quang Hoa, not more than two klicks away.

On his knees, studying the trail, McGarvie looked uneasy. "What do we do, sir?"

"Follow the marks east."

"But that's away from the company."

"I know. It's the way she's going, so that's the way we go. How many blooker rounds do you have left in your pouch?"

Billy looked in. "About ten."

"That'll have to do." Bud checked his three magazines of

M16 ammo, took a swig of water from a canteen and gave it to McGarvie. "Go light. I don't know when we'll find more."

"Sir, can I say something?"

"What's troubling you, kid?"

"Shouldn't we be joining up with the company? We could easily get lost out here and never get back. And there are NVA and VC all over the place."

Billy McGarvie was probably right. The intelligent choice was to save their own butts. They had done what they could for Phuong and he had already placed Billy's life in danger enough times for one day. They turned back.

Neither talked, and once or twice Bud looked back. Billy did, too.

"She seemed very weak when we left her," McGarvie said after they had been walking for some time. "Hardly strong enough to pull herself that far, let alone her brother."

"She had resources down deep. Some women are like that; they can keep going when men can't."

"Kind of pretty, too, wasn't she?"

"Yeah, in a gook's way," Pritchard said.

Captain Bud Pritchard and PFC Billy McGarvie slowed down at the same time and looked back into the jungle in the direction they had come.

Phuong and the body bag containing her brother were a hundred yards from the point where they had decided to turn around. She was lying in a bed of acanthus under a banyan tree, her small muddy feet and part of her legs sticking out from under the foliage.

"You ever see anything so pathetic?" Pritchard said as he lifted her out of the acanthus.

Her dress was ripped in many new places and the big tear in the front was still held by Pritchard's pilot's wings. Red mud streaked her face, mud was caked in her hair, and her dress, which had been black, was smeared red.

Somewhere she had lost the poncho, though the large

bandage was still wrapped to the back of her head, and a swelling on her forehead the size of a goose egg was a reminder of where she had hit the rear tire of the jeep less than twelve hours before.

Phuong opened her eyes with difficulty, saw Pritchard and smiled. He uncapped a canteen and made her drink. McGarvie watched, amazed that she was still alive.

"It's back to Cung Mai Dong for you, girl," Bud said.

Knocking the canteen from his hand, Phuong screamed and her body went rigid and her mouth contorted. "I will not go back," she said, her voice falling to a hoarse whisper. "I will take my brother home." Her back and arms tensed to raise herself, but she fell back into Pritchard's arms.

Chapter 5

Quang Hoa was a villa of forty-nine hooches built fifty to a hundred yards apart, some as distant as a quarter mile to one half mile. The villa was located on the Cuu Long, more of a stream or large irrigation ditch than a river, and circled by twenty-five large fields of several acres each and cut into a checkerboard pattern of earthen dikes that separated the rice into paddies.

Banana and cashew and jackfruit trees grew around the huts, and dirt footpaths crossed the dikes and entered the villa from many directions. Vuon Chau grass six inches high grew on the edges of the footpaths.

Two hooches had hand-dug wells that were constructed of red clay bricks. The wells were about five feet across, and an iron windlass mounted on crude wooden supports above the well opening was wrapped with a hemp rope at the end of which hung a bamboo bucket caulked with black tar.

Sunburned peasants with red or blue striped cotton towels wrapped around their necks or heads and dressed in faded black pajamas planted young rice stalks in the paddy mud, men and women working side by side, while others used long-bladed *luoi liem* machete-like knives curved at the end to cut the already full-grown rice.

Broad-headed, thick-horned water buffaloes weighing a half-ton or more pulled plows ahead of whip-toting men and paid no attention to the cowbirds picking at the parasites embedded in their skin or at the white-and-black ducks foraging for food in their path.

Quang Hoa had been cut out of the jungle two hundred and twenty years before by wandering Meo tribesmen looking for fertile, protected land near water where they could plant their rice and begin life anew. They had been banished from their hamlet in the Valley of the Tiger (in what is now Laos) for stealing sweet potatoes from their neighbors' gardens. The six young founding fathers of Quang Hoa, not happy with the village chief's decision to cut them adrift, and needing women to make life more pleasant on the trail, stole the chief's three daughters and four others from prominent citizens, and set out in search of lands more conducive to their style of living.

Not only was Quang Hoa chosen because of its good soil and accessible water supply, but also because the exiled six were quick to notice that Quang Hoa was in a hollow between three mountains with only one entrance through a narrow gulch with steep limestone walls. Quang Hoa was a natural fortress.

In between stealing sweet potatoes (and anything else they could get their hands on) from their new neighbors across the mountains, and fighting off forays from distant villages, the founding fathers of Quang Hoa were able to keep the women pregnant and to propagate their redoubt. Quang Hoa grew to many hooches and prospered.

Captain Bud Pritchard USMC and PFC Billy McGarvie USMCR entered Quang Hoa through the same limestone pass that the exiled six had entered when first discovering the hollow. Pritchard's reaction as a military man was similar to that of the founding fathers: Quang Hoa was a natural fortress and a few men (as the founders soon discovered) could hold off a much larger force. Bud also noted what the exiled six could never know, that the village, because of its natural fortifications and inaccessibility, was no doubt a Viet Cong or NVA supply and staging point for the Northern Highlands and was probably infested with underground networks that connected Quang Hoa with other villages and could even serve as Headquarters for Highlands operations. He also noted that Quang Hoa looked much different from the ground than it did from the air.

Standing at the mouth of the pass, Pritchard carried Phuong in his arms and looked down into Quang Hoa not a day more advanced than it was two hundred and twenty years ago.

"It's kind of pretty, isn't it, Captain?" McGarvie hitched the sixty-pound rucksack higher on his back and shaded his eyes from the afternoon sun. He was soaked through with sweat and so thirsty that he would have run all the way down to the river and jumped in if Pritchard hadn't been there.

"I've seen it before," Bud said, unmoved.

"Sir?"

"Yesterday morning."

McGarvie squinched his nose and looked at Pritchard. Bud pointed with the hand that held Phuong's legs. "See that burned-out truck and the gutted hooch next to it back from the river about a hundred yards? Zuni rockets from my F-4 did that." He lifted Phuong to his shoulder and started down into the hollow, holding one end of the body bag, McGarvie the other, careful that the M16 slung over his shoulder didn't swing against Phuong, who was either sleeping or unconscious, he didn't know which. "Don't ask me any questions."

When they were within AK-47 range, about five hundred yards, Pritchard stopped and looked at the farmers staring at him from the fields. "Your thump gun loaded?"

"Yes, sir." His eyes worked rapidly across the fields.

"How many rounds did you say you got left?"

"About ten."

"And I've only got three magazines of ammo for the rifle."

"And we're out of water," McGarvie added.

"You know how to pray, kid?"

"Yes, sir."

"Start," Pritchard ordered. "And keep your thumper off SAFE while you're doing it."

PFC Billy McGarvie, a devout Baptist, began to recite a scripture from Isaiah 40:31 and 41:10-13 that he had learned as a youngster when attending Sunday School with his two sisters at the First Baptist Church of Windbreak, Nevada, population 250.

> "But they that wait upon the Lord shall renew their strength; they shall mount up with wings as eagles; they shall run, and not be weary; and they shall walk, and not faint.
>
> Fear thou not; for I am with thee: be not dismayed; for I am thy God: I will strengthen thee; yea, I will help thee; yea, I will uphold thee with the right hand of my righteousness.
>
> Behold, all they that were incensed against thee shall be ashamed and confounded: they shall be as nothing; and they that strive with thee shall perish.
>
> Thou shalt seek them, and shalt not find them, even them that contended with thee: they that war against thee shall be as nothing, and as a thing of nought.
>
> For I the Lord thy God will hold thy right hand, saying unto thee, Fear not; I will help thee."

The farmers returned to plowing and planting the rice, no longer curious, determined to look as inconspicuous and disinterested as possible, which was always the case whenever troops—either U.S. or NVA—appeared in Quang Hoa.

Brother had become heavy, and Bud and Billy McGarvie stopped to rest as they had every few hundred yards since deciding to carry Phuong and her brother's corpse to the illage.

The small detail moved along the length of the paddy like and crossed into the first jackfruit trees without taking ire, and McGarvie was greatly relieved, though not yet onfident that he wouldn't be killed outright. He marveled at Pritchard's lack of concern and wondered if all men who lew Phantom jets were as nervy.

By the time they had reached the second hooch and he vas still alive, McGarvie decided it was likely that there were no hostile gooks in the villa; and when a snaggle-oothed hag of about seventy or eighty or maybe a hundred years old rushed from a hooch and began jabbering in gook and pulling at Phuong, who was obviously someone she knew, Billy was sure the captain would do the intelligent thing and dump Phuong and her brother into the hag's custody and split for Cung Mai Dong.

His hopes fell, however, when he saw Pritchard refuse to give Phuong to the old lady and begin to argue with her and the crowd that had grown to a dozen people.

"Why don't you just give her over to them, sir? We've done what we came for. If there are VC and NVA around here we could get greased any second."

"I want out of this as much as you do, but I'm not going to leave her without knowing she's going to be properly cared for, not after all the trouble I've gone through in the last twenty-four hours to get her here."

The faces staring at McGarvie looked to him to be no different from the ones he'd been shooting at a few hours earlier on Hill 506. He was confused and frightened and wanted to get out of Quang Hoa; he began to shiver.

Billy McGarvie had only been in country for less than thirty-six hours and more had happened to him in this short time then he had expected to experience in this whole thirteen-month tour.

The death, the smells, the trees, the flat faces, the unbearable heat and humidity were all so alien to Billy

McGarvie and had hit him so suddenly that his senses had overloaded and he was coming apart. The shivering increased and he felt both hot and cold all over.

"What's the matter, Billy?"

"I don't know, Captain; I can't stop shaking."

Though Bud Pritchard had never seen this condition in others, he had come to the edge himself several times and had no difficulty in correctly diagnosing the onset of battle shock in the exhausted PFC.

Pulling McGarvie by the straps of the rucksack, Pritchard forced the crowd apart with the barrel of his rifle and made Billy lie down on one of two wooden plank beds in the nearest hooch. On the other bed he deposited the girl, who was immediately crowded around by several women.

"How do you feel, Marine?"

McGarvie tried to answer the way he thought a Marine should answer, but the words didn't come out so bravely. "Not so well, sir."

"You'll be all right after you rest."

He wanted water, but he didn't ask for it, and he knew that he was losing control of his bowels.

Pritchard lifted the rucksack from Billy's back and placed it under his feet so that the blood would tend to stay in the upper part of his body.

"I'll get you some water as soon as I can," Bud said. "I can't leave you and the girl right now."

"Watch out for these dinks, Captain. I don't trust them."

The snaggletoothed hag and the other women had Phuong stripped of her clothing and were examining the wound in the back of her head and the scratches and bruises over her body.

Pritchard held an empty canteen up to a middle-aged man (young, military-age males were noticeably absent) with deep creases in his face and pointed to McGarvie. The Viet's eyes showed contempt, but he took the canteen from Bud and disappeared.

McGarvie continued to shake and sweat, and his skin had turned cold. Pritchard was worried but said nothing. When the man returned with the canteen filled with water, Bud made him drink first.

The Viet looked long and hard at Pritchard then tipped the opening of the canteen to his lips and took a healthy swig. Bud then lifted the PFC's head and let him take a half-dozen swallows from the canteen, and soaked McGarvie's olive-drab towel with the cold well water and draped the towel over his forehead.

"That'll fix you up," Pritchard said and winked.

"Thank you, sir." Billy took a long breath and sighed and tried to wipe his lips with a hand but gave up the effort.

The women were bathing Phuong, carefully washing her wounds. Rather than stay in the hooch and fight the temptation to look at the girl's nude body, Bud stepped outside onto the dirt and smoked a cigarette under a cashew tree.

The body bag he had dropped in the path was gone—where, he had no idea—and across the way, past a grove of banana trees and on the edge of a dried-up rice paddy, was the burned-out truck. Twenty yards from the truck were the charred skeleton remains of a hooch.

The thought of Thorbus targeting him on Quang Hoa and the deuce-and-a-half gave him an ugly feeling down in his belly where fear always lay, cold and hard.

A drone far away and high up came down to him through the coconut palms edging the rice paddies. Looking through the cloud cover into patches of sky, he saw an Arc-light formation of B-52s driving north to drop their bombs on targets in Laos or up around the DMZ and the Ho Chi Minh Trail. They'd be there in a few mintues—hell, they were already there.

"Ba Muoi Ba?"

He turned around and saw a mahagony-skinned boy, more the color of a Jarai Montagnard from the Chu Dle Ya mountains than the color of a Vietnamese national, smiling with big white teeth (the only smile Bud had seen in Quang Hoa) and holding an open wet bottle of Viet beer.

"Good lord, it's even cold," Pritchard said as his fingers curled around the *Ba Muoi Ba* and he shoved the neck into his mouth, not caring that the kid may have poisoned the beer. "How did you get it so cold?"

The boy pointed to the well.

"Bic?" You understand? Bud said.

The kid nodded and showed his big white teeth. The Arc-light bombers droned overhead and Bud finished half the bottle and confirmed once again to himself that this was a strange war.

Even though there was danger all around him, Pritchard felt at ease. The skinny kid with thin sticks for arms and legs protruding from the handmade shirt and shorts, the sheds filled with bamboo and reed baskets overflowing with winnowed rice, the strange wet heat and equally strange cold, the lithe women with folds of hair tied on top of their heads, the odd smells, and the constant peril exhilarated him beyond anything he had ever experienced, and he felt more alive in Vietnam than he had ever felt anywhere else. He realized in a repugnant way that he belonged in this war regardless of what he thought about people like Thorbus or McNamara or Lyndon Baines Johnson or whether or not what he was doing here was right or wrong.

"Your friend?" The boy pointed to the hooch and then to the beer. *"Bic?"*

"Bic," Pritchard said. *"Ba Muoi Ba."*

The boy ran to the well and brought up another beer, which Pritchard took into Billy McGarvie.

"This is better than the water around here, kid, and it's cold." He poured a swallow between McGarvie's swollen lips, and the private first class drank without changing his expression.

"That's my first taste of beer, Captain," McGarvie said through chattering teeth. "It's not too bad."

A half bottle later, PFC Billy McGarvie was resting easy. McGarvie gave the mahogany-colored boy a five-piaster note that softened the stare of a woman who was no doubt his mother, finished the rest of his *Ba Muoi Ba,* and went outside under the cashews to think of how he was going to get a dustoff chopper to medevac Billy and Phuong.

The facts were becoming undeniably clear to him. He was three or four days' march from the Marine base at Cung Mai Dong through some of the most inhospitable jungle in the world. A young Viet girl for whom he had assumed responsibility was wounded and suffering from exposure and could very well die. Billy McGarvie, the kid from Windbreak, Nevada, whom he had more or less kidnapped from Bravo Company, was exhausted and in shock and in need of medical attention. And on top of all this he was hung up in what was no doubt a Viet Cong village where he would have to spend a long and sleepless night.

The sky darkened and the rain began to fall again and the unbearable heat turned to a bone-chilling cold and the clouds swam down from the mountain peaks and filled the hollow called Quang Hoa and Billy McGarvie began to shake and shiver.

"The slicks are here, Captain," McGarvie said. "We've got to board . . . we're going on another CA." He tried to rise. "Don't let them take me."

Pritchard held him down. "Easy, Marine. You're not going on another CA, you're staying right here and have another beer with me."

The young EM, sweating heavily in the chill of the hooch, lay back on the planks, his doe eyes hollow and frightened. "Let's go fishing, Nester. Come on, get the poles and the dog and Betty-Jane and we'll go catch a mess of them small catfish Dad likes, not the big ones that he says taste like the river mud, but the small ones he likes in the creek."

"Sure, Billy—sure, kid," Pritchard said. He didn't try to

take away the PFC's hand that held tight to his shirt.

"Hey, Rodriguez, tell me where to shoot, I can't see through the smoke." McGarvie sat up, his eyes closed, his head swiveling, a hand held tight to Pritchard's shirt. "Papa Sierra taught me how to shoot the thump gun real good, Rodriguez . . . at ITR . . . the smoke . . . come on, Rodriguez, I can't see . . . the gooners are all around us." He pulled at Bud's shirt.

"Easy, Billy."

PFC Billy McGarvie's trigger finger was working rapidly, and he was breathing like a long distance runner. "Hank—where's Hank—tell me where to shoot, Hank." His hand went up to brush away the imaginary smoke. "I've never killed anyone before." Tears ran from his dirt-rimmed eyes, down his soft cheeks, and onto his chin.

None of the Viets showed concern for McGarvie; not as much as a look came his way.

Thunder rolled across the mountains and rumbled over the rice paddies and into the hooch. Lightning flashed, and the people in the hooch said nothing, some squatting on the floor, others eating rice; a few women remained with Phuong, whom they had dressed in clean cotton pajamas. Her wounds were freshly bandaged and her eyes were open.

No one offered Bud any rice to eat or water to drink.

"How do you feel?" Pritchard said to Phuong.

The women moved away from the bed as though the American were carrying a disease.

Phuong didn't answer.

"Someone took your brother away."

She turned her face to the bamboo wall.

"After Billy gets some rest and when the rain lets up I'm going to tray to find Bravo Company and call a medevac chopper in."

He touched her shoulder and she turned to look at him. A tear was curling down her face. The soft rain pattered on the palm thatch roof and dripped off the edges and collected in red puddles.

"My family is all dead," Phuong said.

The few remaining people collected themselves in a corner of the shack and looked out of their huddle, eyes hostile.

Through the doorless opening, Bud could see the blackened hooch, rainwater running down a portion of the collapsed roof that had not completely burned away.

"An American Phantom jet killed them," she said. Her face was toward the opening and there was no anguish in it except for the tear.

The hard, cold pain in Pritchard's stomach made him sick and he got up from the bed and walked to the opening. He could feel the hate in the stares that followed him.

Rain-slick and black, the hooch stood alone and silent, but Bud Pritchard could hear sounds inside—crying, screams, the crackling of flames, and the sound of jet engines passing overhead.

Phuong was carried away and Pritchard and Billy McGarvie were left alone. The hooch slowly turned dark inside and Bud sat in the darkness listening to McGarvie breathe. A bit of sky opened up and the last ray of daylight came through a window cut in the wall and fell on the table in the middle of the room.

On top of the table, which was made from discarded boards, sat Bud's empty beer bottle looking lonely and cast off. Nothing else was on the table. Nothing was in the room except for the few pieces of crude furniture and a hole in the dirt floor that led to an underground bunker.

Bud watched the little glimmer of gray light disappear, and he was wrapped in complete darkness, the only sounds being that of Billy's labored breathing and the rain.

In the blackness of the hooch Bud sat on the floor next to McGarvie and watched Marjorie appear in the middle of the room. Her Carole Taylor high-heel patent leather pumps peeked out from under the king-sized bed at the Kona, and her stockinged long legs were curled up under her tight bum on the blue satin spread.

"All I could think about on the plane coming over was making love to you." Her face was turned slightly away from him sitting in a Queen Anne armchair (which he detested and thought the ugliest chair he had ever seen). "But now that I'm here I don't know."

The sinking feeling in the pit of Bud's stomach made him angry and he tried to fight it off, but it stayed there, spreading and eating away his hope.

"You have no right to do this to me," she said.

That took him by surprise.

"You didn't have to wear your uniform. If you had any concern at all for my feelings you wouldn't have worn your uniform."

"Why does my uniform bother you?"

She turned her eyes on him and they blazed with an intensity he had never seen before. "You know why: because it reminds me of everything I hate."

For a minute he could not find anything to say, and he sat in the Queen Anne chair wishing he had never arranged for Marjorie to meet him. The way it was turning out he would have done better by spending his ten-day R&R in a Bangkok brothel. She said nothing.

"You knew it was going to be like this when we got married. I was already a Marine and you admired my uniform then."

"People change, Buddy, and times change. When we got married there was no Vietnam."

"But there was Korea."

She sighed. "Look at you—you're an old man and you're still only a captain. When are you going to wake up?"

"Knock it off, Marge."

"You're an anachronism—time's passed you by—and you have no one to blame but yourself. You don't fit in anymore."

"I said knock it off."

She was off the bed and putting on her shoes. "It was a mistake for me to come."

"Yes, it was."

"You're not a man, you're an animal, a beast—big tough Marine killing innocent Vietnamese." She picked up her unopened suitcase.

"I'll take you to the airport."

"Don't bother."

The door slammed, hard. . . .

For several hours he sat in the blackness of the hooch listening to Billy's fitful breathing. A few times McGarvie yelled and mumbled about the choppers coming to take him on a combat assault or he talked to Rodriguez and Hank in desperate quick sentences, begging them to locate the gooks for him through the smoke. Once he threw off the poncho with which Bud had covered him to ward off the mountain chill, and he jerked his body as though the grenade launcher fired and he screamed at Rodriguez not to make him kill anymore.

After Billy collapsed and Pritchard was sure that the PFC was resting again, he picked up the M79 grenade launcher and Billy's pouch of 40mm rounds and walked outside into the cold rain, being careful to stay low and in the cover of the bushes and trees.

Finding a concealed spot in a vegetable garden next to a night-soil collector and shithouse (composed of a slit trench and half partition of bamboo), he hunkered down with a poncho pulled up over his head and Billy's loaded thump gun across his knees.

The rain pattered on the rubberized plastic, and occasionally he would wipe the drops from his eyes. The rain helped to suppress the smell from the slit trench.

Pritchard tried to think like a Viet Cong. The front of the hooch was open ground with few trees and bushes, and the best approach would be from the treed rear. It would be easy to sneak up on the Americans, who would presumably be asleep, and drop a grenade through the window.

He watched the shadows grow into people then back into shadows. Bushes would walk and the trunks of trees would move a few feet at a time. The rain fell steadily but not hard, and he waited. The attack wold come in the early morning hours when sleep was more seductive and the mind becomes less alert.

As the hours slowly (ever so slowly) passed, Pritchard's aging bones became stiff and his muscles cramped and he realized that if he had to move fast, he would be in big trouble. The rain had accumulated in a puddle underneath him, and he tried to arrange the poncho under his butt so he could sit on it and not get soaked in the process.

Nothing worked, and he got soggier and soggier in the vegetable garden, and he wanted the Viet Cong to attack and the night to come to an end.

A cigarette. He needed a smoke—just a few drags and he would be all right. Several times he fumbled in the breast pocket of his shirt just to be sure they were there, dry and ready to be smoked. That helped to reduce the desire.

His thoughts went to Marjorie and Hawaii and he wondered if he and his wife would ever be able to settle their differences about this war, about his career in the Marines. She had made it clear that if this was his last tour and he came home without the uniform she would be waiting for him and do the best she could to make the marriage work.

"I love you, Buddy, and I'll always love you, but you've got to meet me partway. Is that unreasonable?"

"It is if partway means that I have to leave the Corps."

"Then there is no hope for us."

"There is another way," he said. "You try to understand my life."

She took her eyes off his and turned away. "I'm sorry; I've already tried that. I detest the military and everything it represents. Your involvement in this Vietnam *thing* is unacceptable to me."

The sky began to lighten to a lead gray, and the rain had stopped. The burned-out hooch and the truck were visible in the dawn, and Bud Pritchard was inclined to agree with Marjorie.

He had killed Phuong's family and now he must learn to somehow live with the memory of that. When this tour was over he wouldn't extend for a third as planned. He would go home and retire from the Marines, shed the uniform as Marjorie wanted and do what he could to become a dutiful husband, maybe get a job—doing what, he didn't know—or just go fishing, join some service clubs, catch up on learning how to be a civilian again.

And there was Phuong. Somehow he would have to take care of her. He owed her family that. Maybe an annuity or something. He thought about telling her that it was he who had pushed the button that wiped out her family, but he couldn't see where that would do any good. He could bring her to the States, but there was a mess of red tape and a long waiting list and he would need Marjorie's cooperation, which would require a detailed explanation and more pain. No—it was best that Phuong stay in Vietnam, and if the war ever ended maybe he would come back to see her. In the meantime he would provide for her financially.

The Viet Cong never came and Bud stood up the best he could and walked out of the vegetable garden, careful not to step on the cabbage and rau and bok choy and the long, funny-looking eggplants.

"You go on without me, Captain," Billy McGarvie said. "I'll be all right until you get back with the chopper. Just leave the thump gun."

"Too risky—I figure the reason the gooners didn't make a try for us last night was because Phuong put in a good word for us. Tonight's another night, however. I don't want to push our luck. Read me?"

"Yes, sir—I'd like to do what I can to help." He tried to get up from the plank bed, but he fell back, dizzy and nauseated, the room swirling.

Bud lashed the bamboo cross members together to the two long side poles of the travois and laid in some palm thatch and a poncho. The primitive vehicle used by the Plains Indians was ready, and Bud picked up McGarvie and strapped him in with his web belt.

The rucksack on his back and M16 over his shoulder, Bud Pritchard dragged the travois out of Quang Hoa with McGarvie bouncing gently on the bamboo contraption, the thump gun held in his hands and resting on his chest.

"I should be walking, sir."

"Shut up and keep your eyes open. If you were walking I'd be picking you up every ten feet. This way we save time."

The two trailing poles of the travois left deep grooves in the wet earth as the two Marines passed the blackened remains of the hooch and truck. Fifty feet down the dike, Pritchard stopped and looked back over the dried paddy, now filled with two inches of water, at Phuong, who had been brought to the edge of the coconut palms by the village women. Their eyes met and held, and Bud thought he saw a small smile form on Phuong's lips

He waved, but she didn't wave back, and Bud turned north and in a few minutes was across the paddies and into the treeline.

Using a compass that he always kept on a chain with his pocket survival knife, he plotted a course down through the ancient pass and into the triple-canopy rain forest, back-tracking to find the trail of Bravo company.

One hour out of Quang Hoa the rain resumed, and Bud covered PFC Billy McGarvie with the remaining poncho, cursed Ho Chi Minh and the Marine Corps, bent his back to the travois and pulled with the determination of a Sioux pony.

The blackfaced monkeys no longer chattered in the canopy, driven to cover by the rain, and the parrots, normally squawking loudly when the sun was high, now were silent and hiding from the mountain cold.

"How you doing, Billy?" Bud put down the travois and came around to check the PFC.

"It's easy to get lost when you can't see the sun," McGarvie said. "Does it always rain like this?"

"It's the monsoon season—bookoo rain." Bud tucked the poncho closer around Billy and felt his rain-wet face. It was hot with fever.

The deer eyes looked up at Pritchard and said that it never rained like this in Windfall, Nevada, and that when it got cold he always had the flaming mesquite logs in the native stone fireplace to keep him warm and when he was sick with fever there was always the big feather bed with the goose down pillows and comforter and mother's hot mint tea sweetened with honey from the hives out back of the barn.

"Hungry?" Bud said.

"I'd rather have water."

Bud poured water between Billy's lips and said, "You should get some chow into your belly."

McGarvie shook his head. "Not hungry."

Finding a tree that offered some shelter from the rain, Bud pulled Billy under it, and using his body as a shield he lit the sterno fuel and heated a can of beans and franks.

"Open up," he said.

McGarvie obediently opened his mouth, and Pritchard fed him a plastic spoonful of the C-ration chow. Two more swallows were all Billy could take.

The tea that Bud made in the canteen cup was hot and Billy took a few swallows. For himself Bud made coffee; it tasted like the aluminum canteen cup, but it was hot and warmed him for a few minutes from the cold mists.

He ate the rest of the beans and franks, checked Billy again, shouldered the ruck and rifle, and cut trail down the compass line he sighted.

"Just like navigating an airplane," he said to McGarvie to keep a conversation going. "Ever think of what keeps an airplane in the air?"

"I didn't pay much attention in school."

Bud noticed the drop in McGarvie's spirits and he tried to put some enthusiasm into his conversation. Kids like Billy McGarvie could easily give up and die. He had seen it happen in Korea in the POW camp at Pyongyang. The young ones refused to eat and curled up in a corner and died without a whimper. Others collaborated unashamedly with the North Koreans, and some remained behind at the end of the war to become Communists. That was a strange war, too.

"Why did you join the Marines, Kid?"

Billy didn't answer right away. Bud struggled over the roots of a peumo tree and up a knoll clustered with red-berried mutisia.

"The other boys in school felt good about themselves," Billy said. "I never did. They played on the football team or in the band or got good grades or won 4-H projects. I didn't have anything so I joined the Marines. I thought they would look up to me."

At the top of the knoll, Pritchard stopped to rest. He heard explosions and the crump of mortars and didn't think much about it for they were not close enough to be of concern. The explosions got closer and closer, and finally he could see 81mm mortar flashes west of the broad, lazy valley that cut between the steep jungle-covered mountains. The flood plain below was checkered with green rice paddies, and a slow-moving river, the Vui Bong, ninety feet across at its widest point, meandered at the north side of the plain, close to Pritchard and McGarvie, who looked out at the Vui Bong through the mutisia.

Cloud mists floated above the river and paddies, and Vietnamese voices could be heard down in the valley on the near side of the river. Small-arms fire broke out and geysers of water erupted in the river.

"I think we found the company," Bud said to Billy.

Billy tried to look strong. He tried to get out of the travois but found that he was tied in. Bud was on one knee, studying the situation in the valley, and Billy fumbled with the belt.

"I can hear gook talk down there," Pritchard said. "I'm going to ask you to help out with the blooker." He loosened the belt from the travois and checked the grenade launcher in Billy's hands to be sure it was loaded.

Then came a sudden firing of small arms and mortars, unrelenting, from the edges of the flood plain. A red flare floated down through the mists and the morning light took on a strange pastel cast, like in a dream.

McGarvie was shaken by the intensity of the firing and his hands trembled around the thump gun. "This can't be real."

"Wish we had a radio," Bud said, "so we could make contact with whoever it is down there." He felt his throat drying up, and the unmistakable bad taste of bile filled his mouth.

Billy was sitting up, propped against a peumo tree. A rivulet of rainwater snaked under his boot. "Who's doing all the firing—our guys or theirs?"

"Hard to tell; sounds like most of it is from the gooks."

McGarvie turned to look at Bud, his eyes frightened. "I think you're right—that's the charlies firing."

So close were they to the enemy that they could hear the quick hiss of Communist mortar rounds leaving the tubes.

Looking north, Bud saw a flat-topped hill that was denuded of trees and had been leveled by artillery fire. "The LZ," he said. "Hill 506. We're back in the nightmare."

Across from the hill at which Pritchard was looking was a larger and steeper mountain, Hill 507, on which he had watched the files of NVA and VC withdraw. Evidently, Major Toi had massed his force on the back side of Hill

507, out of sight, and made an end run down the highballer and counterattacked Bravo Company's left flank, catching them in the open when the Marines attempted to cross the flood plain. Bud Pritchard could see flashes from enemy rockets at the base of Hill 507. The range was about one mile and the barrage was steady and accurate.

"They're getting the shit kicked out of them," Billy McGarvie said. "I don't understand it."

Pritchard was leaning on the same tree that McGarvie was propped against; the M16 rested in the crook of his arm, and one hand held the banana clip protruding from the underside of the rifle. Very seriously he said: "Son, I don't understand it either." But of course he did.

Upriver in a banana grove only fifty yards from Pritchard and McGarvie, a concentration of enemy 7.92mm heavy machine gun and AK-47 automatic rifle fire raked Bravo Company's flank and prevented the Marines from escaping from their pinned-down positions. The stand of banana trees was so thick that Pritchard was unable to see the machine gun and riflemen. They were somewhere along the near bank. Fortunately, the North Vietnamese soldiers could not see Pritchard and McGarvie, either.

Second Lieutenant Bradley Cummings from Portland, Oregon, First Platoon's leader, had taken command of Bravo Company after Second Lieutenant Jerry Tatman was killed covering the withdrawal on Hill 506. The new commander had done at least one thing right. His troops were dug in along the protective cover of the river bank and most of the 7.92mm fire, though heavy and concentrated, was thudding into mud and dirt and not into Marines. The perimeter was tight and Bravo Company was well dug in, but the only way out was to cross the river behind them. No one knew how deep it was, and, of course, anyone who tried to cross it would be fully exposed to the murderous fire coming from the banana grove.

Chapter 6

At the same time Captain Bud Pritchard USMC and PFC Billy McGarvie USMCR stood on the knoll of peumo trees and mutisia bushes and watched what was left of Bravo Company, 2nd Battalion, 1st Marines, take the full force of Major Nguyen Vo Toi's reinforced battalion of North Vietnamese Army regulars, Hai Van Phuong sat cross-legged among the ashes of her family's hooch in Quang Hoa and burned incense and offered a large bowl of fresh mangoes, papayas, and bananas for the safekeeping of the souls of her departed loved ones. Around her head was wrapped a band of white muslin tied in a knot. She was barefoot and dressed in the white *ao dai* that she had worn as a schoolgirl.

Hai Van Phuong's back was bent forward, and her head rested on her crossed legs in a position of prayer and subservience. Tears ran from her eyes and her small, full lips moved in prayer. For several hours she sat in this punishing position; when she rose two women approached her, the ones who had cleaned and dressed her wounds and given her clean clothing to wear.

"What will you do now?" Tran Thi Hoan said.

Phuong wiped at her tears. "I have no place in Quang Hoa to live."

"You can live with my family," Nguyen Ngoc Manh said. "Your mother and father were kind to me and I loved them dearly."

"I cannot do that," Hai Van Phuong said. "Another mouth to feed is too much for you now that your man is fighting with the Viet Cong. There is barely enough rice for you and your children."

Nguyen Ngoc Manh said nothing. She had made the offer as an expected courtesy, knowing that it would be rejected.

"I will go north . . . to Song Xanh," Phuong said. "I have relatives in Song Xanh." She wasn't sure she had relatives in Song Xanh, nor anywhere else for that matter. All her living relatives had perished in the hooch as far as she knew.

"When will you leave?" Tran Thi Hoan asked.

"Before the sun sets."

"I will give you some rice to take with you on your long journey," Tran Thi Hoan said.

"That is kind of you." Phuong smiled and bowed politely, her arms folded across her chest.

Upon the mound of earth in the center of the burned hooch where her brother's body and the ashes of the rest of her family (both parents, grandmother, grandfather, two sisters, an uncle and aunt and three cousins) were buried, Hai Van Phuong placed the bowl of fruit and the ten-inch burning joss sticks. She kneeled one last time and with her palms pressed together, touched the mound with her forehead.

In Tran Thi Hoan's hooch, a board was removed from the floor and Tran Mai Lan, the eldest daughter, crawled into the tunnel and handed out a brand new, never-fired 7.62mm Mat-49 submachine gun (SMG). The French 9mm weapon had been converted to take the Soviet 7.62 cartridge by fitting a longer 7.62mm barrel. The MAT-49 was so new that some of the cosmoline used to preserve the metal still adhered to the receiver piece and fold-up stock.

Phuong took the submachine gun and bandoleer of ammunition magazines. The SMG was light and compact and easy for her to handle. She also took the rice (wrapped in a slingbag made from U.S. parachute silk) and hung it with the bandoleer around her neck and over a shoulder.

"I am grateful," Phuong said.

The girl, Tran Mai Lan, replaced the board over the spider hole and patted Hai Van Phuong on the shoulder. "I will walk with you until the sun darkens the mountains. Then you are on your own. The Viet Cong and North Vietnamese Army have begun a TET offensive that we expect will rally the country to our cause and the people will rise up against the Thieu puppet government and the American invaders. I personally hope to march on Saigon."

Phuong's eyes were distant and her face blank. She could not hear Tran Mai Lan because she was listening to the voices of her family. There would be no TET New Year for them—not ever again. No more comforting words, no earth cakes or sweet rice, no lucky money wrapped in red paper, no gifts of duck eggs and salty pork and lemon grass candy and lotus seed candy and squash candy, and no bags of red watermelon seeds and no visiting friends to wish them good luck and long life.

"The north Vietnamese Army is moving south very quickly," Tran Mai Lan said, "and the government forces are fleeing ahead of them. It will be dangerous for you." She looked closely at Hai Van Phuong and then at her mother. "Did you hear me?"

Phuong smiled politely and looked at the submachine gun in her hands. Tran Mai Lan showed her how to operate the MAT-49, then took her by the arm and led her out of Quang Hoa, through the pass, and into the jungle.

For all their murderous power, Major Toi's 81mm mortars and 107mm rockets were unable to dislodge the Marines of Bravo Company, who remained tenacious and well dug in along the forward bank of the river. Their foxholes were so close to the water that some of the deeper dug positions were slowly filling with seepage. Lying on ponchos and huddled behind the protective three to four feet of red clay bank were the dead and the wounded.

Second Lieutenant Bradley Cummings had accurately assessed his condition and now turned to Staff Sergeant Freddy Bowman from Waco, Texas: "That heavy machine gun has to be put out of action. Got to get the men across the river before the gooks circle in behind and cut us off completely."

"We can't get a fix on it, Lieutenant. It's too well concealed."

"We've got to knock it out. Send a fire team after it."

The four-man fire team got exactly ten yards from the river and its protective bank before they were pinned down and could not advance another foot.

Watching all this from the high ground, Bud Pritchard had also accurately assessed the company's predicament. "They'll never take the machine gun—we're going to have to do it for them," he said to Billy McGarvie.

Down the river about five hundred yards where the bank made a wide cut through a thick stand of bamboo and the river bent around it, Pritchard could see a bunch of North Vietnamese soldiers in their brown uniforms and green sun helmets and packs, milling around looking for a shallow place to cross. Five hundred yards was not a difficult shot for a Marine infantryman, but Bud, though he qualified on the range at Quantico, hadn't fired a rifle in years. He opted not to reveal his position just yet.

Then came one of those strange incongruities of war in the Nam that seemed so remote and detached from reality that Bud questioned his sanity. The village of Vui Bong was in front of the Marines, and its herd of water buffalo, spooked by the explosions and gunfire, had broken from their pens and were charging toward the river with their owners in pursuit. When the animals and farmers broke through the treeline and galloped over the bank and through Bravo Company and into the river, churning the water into a froth (accompanied by great bellowing from the buffalo and shouting by the farmers), the battle became confused and the firing abruptly fell off.

Lieutenant Cummings, a quick and alert young man, stood in the confusion and shouted his men into the river: "Move it—out of your holes—across the river!"

Marines, buffalo, and farmers spilled into the river in bewildering disorder.

"Okay, Billy," Pritchard said in an even, quiet voice, "start dropping blooker rounds into the banana grove."

With steady precision, PFC Billy McGarvie fired the 40mm spin-ball antipersonnel grenades into the thick trees where the heavy machine gun and the concentration of AK-47s were hidden, while Bud Pritchard crawled down the knoll with the rifle and magazines of ammo and four hand grenades and a claymore mine from McGarvie's rucksack.

The bushes moved and Bud turned his head. A brown foot clad in sandals made from truck tires shoved through the mutisia and Pritchard fired a burst which was followed by a grunt and the fall of the body.

Quickly planting the claymore under the leaves next to the dead VA, Bud crawled behind a fallen tree and waited. He fired a burst in the air. Billy's blooker rounds came in one at a time on schedule.

When the enemy soldiers found the body, Bud was ready for the explosion. Four men lost arms and legs and squirmed and screamed on the ground, six were killed instantly without a sound from their mouths. The rest, dazed and bleeding, stood in a shocked stupor and looked directly at Pritchard walking at them through the gray smoke while he shot them one by one.

Inside the banana grove, McGarvie's M79 thumper rounds had killed the 7.92mm machine gun crew and seven riflemen. A dozen more lay wounded. Pritchard pulled the pin on a grenade, shoved it under the machine gun and ran out of the grove.

Breathing heavily, Bud reached the top of the knoll and looked down into the flood plain. The last of the buffalo had disappeared into the treeline on the opposite side of the river, and Second Lieutenant Cummings had his men digging in behind the coconut palms and heavy timber. He had brought his dead and wounded with him.

Forty-five long minutes after the last man from Bravo Company got across the river and was dug in behind the treeline and had his rifle pointed at the far bank where Major Nguyen Vo Toi was massing his battalion for the final attack on the beleaguered Marines, a hole opened in the fog behind the company and the Hueys were able to land in a rough LZ that the Marines had blown open in the forest.

Fire team by fire team, squad by squad, the men of Bravo Company, Second Battalion, First Marines, were lifted from the Vui Bong Valley and carried back to Cung Mai Dong. They brought their dead and wounded with them.

On the last chopper out, the last man aboard was an old captain in torn and muddied dress greens and oxford shoes. Over his shoulder was a young, doe-eyed, smooth-cheeked PFC.

The gaggle of UH-1 Hueys dropped rapidly over the trees and one by one, in a line, flared and landed. Aid tents had been set up in the battalion area to recieve the wounded. Later, the worst cases would be flown to the Navy hospital at Da Nang.

Adjacent to the aid tents was a smaller tent in which poncho-covered lumps were placed. This was the morgue.

The men of Bravo Company didn't jump out of the choppers. They offloaded in a controlled fall, first throwing out their mud-soaked rucks (many stained maroon and black with blood from the wounded), and then supported by a buddy or a skid, dropped loose-legged to the pad and to one knee or both.

Back on their feet, rifles hanging from their hands like sticks, they shuffled like bent old men (rucks held by a strap over one shoulder or dragged by a hand) to their squad tents where they collapsed on their bunks without removing their torn and mud-covered utilities and flak jackets, too tired to be offended by the stench of death on them or to quench the enormous thirst in their caked throats. The beer and soda rations that were covered in melting ice and stacked outside the tent flaps went untouched.

Carrying a bleeding and unconscious Billy McGarvie (he had been shot in the upper leg when crosing the Vui Bong River), Bud Pritchard stumbled into a pilot stepping down from his Huey. Bud looked into the clean-shaven, healthy face of the flight commander whom he had forced to take him to the LZ at Hill 506. He was still wearing his chicken-plate.

"Enjoy your trip, Captain?" The pilot laughed loudly and walked away.

Pritchard stood for a moment, the ugliness and pain and frustration of the last thirty-six hours bursting in his head, and he would have laid Billy McGarvie on the ground and smashed the pilot's face and groin had not someone called him.

"Say, Captain Pritchard," the gunnery sergeant said.

Bud spit and turned his head slowly away from the helicopter pilot, who was now around the nose of the Huey and chuckling to himself. "What you want, Gunny?"

"That the cherry you got with you?" His sleeves were rolled up, showing his burly arms, and the clipboard was clutched in a bear paw the way it had been when Bud last saw him.

"You can call him by his right name now."

The gunny looked surprised at Pritchard's ugly tone. "Your CO wants to see you *bookoo rikky-tik.* He sent word down that if you were on one of the Hueys coming in he wanted you to report to him straight away. How did he know you were out there with Bravo?"

"An AC named Thorbus."

The gunny lifted Billy McGarvie's head off Pritchard's shoulder. "Better get him over to the aid station right away, sir, while he's still alive. Friggin' war." He wrote something on the clipboard and walked to the next chopper to help the bandaged second lieutenant, Bradley Cummings, to the aid station.

Hunched over and back aching, Pritchard placed Billy on a stretcher in the aid tent. Two Navy corpsmen took the stretcher to a table, where a nurse cut away McGarvie's pant leg and examined the dirty wound. Throwing the plastic and gauze field dressing into a bucket that had rapidly filled with blood-soaked bandages, she looked up at Pritchard and said "You wounded, Captain?"

"No—I'd like to stick around if you don't mind; the kid is a friend."

"Hold this." She gave him a bottle of clear plasma she had taken from a refrigerated white box and thumb-screwed a quarter-inch aluminum rod to the table. "Hang it there," she said and pointed to the hook at the top of the three-foot-long rod. She unraveled the polyurethane tubes and inserted the end with the needle into the large vein in PFC Billy McGarvie's arm.

"Will he make it?"

She washed away the mud and dirt from the leg and gave Billy a shot of something. "This one's ready," she said to a doctor bending over a corporal with a head wound.

The tent smelled of antiseptic and body waste and sickly sweet blood. Men on stretchers waited on the tarp-covered ground, crowded near the operating tables. The rolled-up tent flap hadn't been secured and it fell, darkening the inside of the tent.

"Get some lights in here," a doctor yelled, "and roll up the side of the tent."

"You better find a place to crap out before you fall down," the nurse said. "You want me to give you a shot of something?"

"I've got to see if the cherry's going to make it."

"Better stay outside where you can breathe better." She was genuinely worried about him. "You sure you're okay?"

She was preparing another wounded kid, this one a private with only half an arm. McGarvie had been moved ahead in the line, to another table.

"I'm okay."

The nurse, a blond with short-cropped hair and a pixie nose, worked rapidly on the private and applied thumb pressure to the artery on the inside upper left arm. With her free hand she struggled to tie a tourniquet.

"I'll do that." Bud took the strip of rubber tubing and tied it off around the private's stub.

The kid was doped up on morphine and only slightly aware of what had happened to him. He mumbled something about a guitar he had left at the LZ.

"Thanks," the Navy nurse said. She was a lieutenant, J. G.

"What do you do when you're not patching up these kids?" Bud hadn't seen a white female in months.

"I read paperbacks." She didn't look up while she worked. PFC Billy McGarvie was on an operating table and a doctor worked on him. The nurse walked over to the doctor and said something, and the doctor looked at Pritchard and motioned for him to come over to the table.

"If you're interested in better company than your paperbacks, stop by the air wing officers' club tonight and I'll buy you dinner and a drink," Bud said as the nurse brushed by close enough so her upper torso pressed into him.

"It's not there anymore," she said.

He had forgotten that a Katusha rocket had put the O-club out of business.

"Your young friend is going to make it," the doctor said.

Pritchard wondered why the doctor was wearing a surgical mask. Mud and dirt and germs covered every inch of McGarvie.

"But I'm going to have to take his leg," the doctor added.

Very evenly and through mud-stained teeth, Captain Buddy Pritchard USMC said in a low, controlled voice, "You cut off his leg and I cut off your head." To emphasize, Bud grabbed the Navy doctor's collar points under his operating smock, thumbs and index fingers pressed on each of the railroad tracks, and pulled him to within an inch of his own face. "The kid keeps the leg, Lieutenant."

"I'll do what I can."

"See that you do."

Bud Pritchard limped to the door of the tent and shouldered McGarvie's rucksack.

"How about the regimental O-club?" The nurse said as she lifted one end of a stretcher.

"What's your name?"

"Janice."

"I'm Buddy." He studied her for a second. "See you for dinner."

Colonel Jerome Davidson was a bull of a man, 210, six foot three, and a neck as thick as a pine tree. He was from Missouri—no town, just a farm and a route number— and had to be shown, but when he a was, that was the end of it and you would be assured justice.

"You look like hell, Pritchard."

"The grunt gunny over at First Marines said most *rikky-tik.*"

Jerome Davidson smiled, then quickly cut it off. "You should have cleaned up first."

"Yes, sir."

"All right—stand at ease and tell me what the devil happened to you. You're AWOL, you know."

Pritchard spread his legs twelve inches, favoring his right leg and folded his hands at the small of his back in the prescribed at-ease posture. The colonel waited and the scar over his eyebrow tightened.

"I take it Major Thorbus was the one who reported me AWOL."

"Forget Thorbus and let me hear your version of this fairy tale."

Starting with the NVA 107mm rocket taking out the west wall of the O-club and killing Phuong's brother, Captain Bud Pritchard told Colonel Jerome Davidson how he procured Marine air transport for the girl and her brother and personally escorted her to her ancestral village at Quang Hoà, and how en route he had been delayed with Bravo Company, 2nd Battalion, 1st Marines, on top of Hill 506 and then delayed once more on the return in the Vui Bong Valley. He left out the firefight with Rodriguez and Hank on the highballer and how he and McGarvie had taken out the heavy machine gun on the Vui Bong River.

Colonel Davidson snapped his teeth together, making a loud click. "You talk to Thorbus over the RT?"

"Yes, sir—he aborted and a lot of Marines died. We needed that air."

Rubbing his chin, Davidson put his boots up on the desk and looked Pritchard between the eyes. "You should have been leading that air strike, Captain, but because you decided to play nursemaid to some slopehead, I had to put Thorbus in command". He brought his boots to the floor with a thump and he leaned forward across the desk. "Could you have brought in those aircraft and delivered the ordnance?"

"Yes, sir, I could have."

"Then you are just as responsible as Thorbus, if not

moreso, for those dead mud marines. Take the plank out of your own eye before you try to remove the sawdust from someone else's eye, Captain. That's what the Nazarene said, Matthew 7:3, and that's damn good advice. You might read John 3:16 while you're at it." He scratched at the scar. "You know how to pray?"

"I'm not very good at it."

"Well, you better learn because I'm going to fly your old tail off every day just to keep you out of my hair." Colonel Jerome Davidson was on his feet and his body was thrust forward at Bud Pritchard. "You're the best pilot I got but you're the oddest duck I've seen in my twenty years in the Corps."

The phone rang. "Davidson here."

As the second minute passed without Jerome Davidson saying a word, the frown lines deepened in his forehead and his lips sagged at the corners. He shook his head and hung up. "That was Colonel Proctor, the commanding officer of First Marines." Davidson sat down and sighed. "Battalion just finished their INTEL and debriefing of Bravo Company, the survivors of Hill 506 and the Vui Bong Valley. Some crackpot is putting you in for the Navy Cross."

Pritchard looked down between his feet and counted the cracks in the wooden floor. "Are they giving anything to the cherry?"

"Who?"

"Billy McGarvie."

"If that's the PFC that was with you, then they're decorating him, too."

Davidson looked down at the desk as if attempting to grasp the significance of what had happened out there with Bravo Company. It was quiet in the Quonset hut.

"Will that be all, sir?"

"Yes, Captain, that's all. As of right now you are on permanent flight status and don't get any ideas about taking any more vacations. Do I make myself understood?"

Pritchard came to attention. "Perfectly, sir."

"Fine." He smiled, against his better judgment. "Now get your old ass out of here before I call Colonel Proctor and tell him all the reasons why I don't think you deserve that medal."

"One more thing, Colonel."

Davidson was already sitting and back at work signing letters his aide had typed. "Make it quick, there's a war on . . . or maybe you haven't heard."

"It's about the girl."

"What girl?" The colonel didn't look up from the letters.

"Hai Van Phuong—the Viet girl I took to Quang Hoa."

Jerome Davidson stopped signing letters and returned to a D-3 report he was completing on a rescue mission. The radar intercept officer of a downed F-4 spent twelve days in the jungle south of the demilitarized zone. In attempts to extricate him, three helicopters were shot down by AAA fire and an OV-10 was destroyed by a direct hit from a Soviet SA-2. Seven aircrew were killed, one was captured, and one was rescued after ten days on the ground. "Hai Van Phuong, huh? The slope that started this mess you got into?"

"That's correct, sir."

"What about her?"

"I killed her family."

Colonel Jerome Davidson USMC dropped the pen he was writing with and held his head between his hands and shook it back and forth, moaning obscenities.

"Thorbus fragged me on a mission to Quang Hoa— a sampan and a truck. One of my two-point-fives missed the truck and hit a hooch. Her family was in the hooch. They're all dead."

"So what do you want me to do about it, for heaven's sake?" He looked at Pritchard with exhausted eyes. "This is war, man. Innocent people get killed all the time."

"I feel responsible for her. Isn't there something I or the

Marine Corps can do for her?"

Fighting for control, the colonel spaced his words and quietly said, "Get out, Captain. Go take a long hot shower, burn your greens or what's left of them and stop by sick bay and ask to see the shrink—or maybe the chaplain will listen to your problems, but leave me out of them—and the Marines will take no responsibility for the girl. She, her brother, and the rest of her family just got in the way, unfortunately."

Pritchard's teeth were set hard against each other and his jaw tightened. "Yes, sir." He did a brisk about-face and walked out of Colonel Jerome Davidson's office.

In his quarters, a hastily constructed building put together with sheets of quarter-inch plywood that housed six pilots each, Bud Pritchard flopped on his bunk without removing any of his clothing.

"I never thought I'd ever see you again," First Lieutenant Dale Keilman said. He pulled up a chair next to Pritchard and sat down. "You smell bad, Buddy." He pinched his nose closed.

Bud's eyes were already flickering into sleep.

Looking at Pritchard's grim appearance, Keilman said, "Where did you spend the night?"

"In a Quang Hoa shitter and vegetable garden. Stow the questions, funny-man; I'm beat."

"Yeah . . . sure. We can talk later."

"Wake me at chow time."

"What for? Why don't you just sleep through. You can eat anytime."

"I've got a date," Bud said.

Dale Keilman's eyes widened. "If it was someone else I'd laugh, but knowing Bud Pritchard . . . Who is she? . . . not a Viet broad in town?"

"Her name is Janice—a Navy nurse with the First Marines, a lieutenant, j. g. Now let me get some sleep."

"You're unbelievable. Okay, get your winks—no one will

bother you."

"Be sure to wake me. If you don't, Keilman, I'll throw you out of the backseat tomorrow—at forty thousand feet."

"Holy Ho Chi Minh—you're flying tomorrow?"

"Davidson wants me up every day . . . thanks to my friendly guardian angel, Major Ralph Thorbus."

"I tried to square it for you with wing but when Ops posted the aircraft for the strike and Thorbus had your name on the board as leader, there wasn't anything I could do to cover for you. Ralph shit his pants when Davidson said he had to take your place. And then when he heard you transmitting on the Prick-25 with Bravo Company he went out of his mind." Keilman stopped and looked at his clenched hands. "I think the real reason he aborted was because you were down there. He didn't want you to come back. That's why when you just walked in I said that I never thought I'd see you again." He looked down at his hands again. "I'm sorry about this mess . . . I wish there was something I could have done."

"Forget it. There wasn't anything you could have done."

"I could have gone to the Old Man and told him what I thought and maybe got another pilot and gone up there again and found a hole in the clouds and dumped a load and gotten you guys out."

"Forget it, I said . . . it's over and I'm back and I'll deal with Thorbus in time."

Keilman pulled the chair away from the bunk and slid it under the small desk with the OD gooseneck lamp and government-issue stationery. I'll wake you at oh-five-hundred."

"Thanks, Dale . . . and don't worry about what happened." He rolled onto his side and was immediately asleep.

The regimental officers' club was crowded, as it was every

night. Bud was wearing a freshly cleaned and pressed set of tropicals, a polished pair of Keilman's Chukka Florsheim Imperials, brassoed belt buckle and captain's bars, and a clean fore-and-aft cover to go with the khakis. He had also scrounged a new set of wings to pin above his Korea and Vietnam ribbons. It was the first time in country that he had looked spit-shined and Colonel Davidson would not have recognized him if he walked in.

"How does a pilot get a purple heart with two clusters?" Lieutenant, J. G., Janice Elderberry said, and pointed to the bluish red ribbon with white stripes at the ends on Bud Pritchard's chest.

"By not paying attention."

"No, seriously—I'm interested. You don't see many pilots walking around with purple hearts."

The Vietnamese waitress stood beside Janice, and Bud glanced up. The Viet had the slim, sullen features of Phuong and for a second he thought that he was seeing her again. "Chivas and water for me." Pritchard tried to smile.

"Martini, dry," Janice said.

The girl walked away and her *ao dai* brushed Bud's shoulder. He smelled her musky unperfumed body and he wondered how he was going to get a chopper out to Quang Hoa to get Phuong.

"Well," Janice Elderberry said. "Are you going to tell me?" She had an engaging smile.

"The first heart came when a MiG-15 shot an F-86 out from under me up near the Yalu in Korea. Fortunately, I got the plane back over our lines before I had to bail out."

The strains of a haunting Viet ballad were coming from the trio on a small plywood and cinder block bandstand, and Pritchard listened to the childlike female voice and he thought back to two nights ago when he waited for Phuong to sing. Those two nights seemed like two years.

"I got the second one near Hue on my first tour. Must have been a shoulder-fired SA-7 Grail missile that got me; I was pretty low. Fragments blew through the port side of the canopy—killed my RIO and wounded me in the neck, shoulder, and upper left arm."

Janice Elderberry was silent and listened carefully. The waitress placed a dry martini on the table in front of her, but she didn't notice. "And your third?"

"You don't want to hear about it."

"But I do."

Bud took a long drink of Chivas and water and smiled like a boy who had just been caught looking through the bathroom keyhole at his sister sitting on the pot. "I was coming in on a slick at Kontum for two weeks TDY as a FAC for a grunt company. The chopper pranged and I fell out and sprained my ankle. Spent five days in the hospital at Pleiku."

Her elbow bumped the martini and the ice tinkled in the glass. She still didn't notice the drink, her eyes fastened on Pritchard.

"I don't like how you're looking at me, like I'm a guinea pig or something—like in an experiment," he said.

She looked surprised and reddened. "I'm sorry—I was just too interested, I suppose. I tend to get involved in people's experiences, kind of like I'm living them."

"Your life that dull that you have to use other people's experiences?"

"I've never admitted it but I think it's true, until maybe I came to Vietnam. Life is pretty intense over here." She put a hand into her short blond hair and gave it a quick ruffle. "It was like putting glasses on for the first time and suddenly realizing that the world doesn't look fuzzy all the time. Being sent to Nam made a big impact on the way I think. I found that not everyone lives boring lives like mine. Back home I took it for granted that life was tiresome and uneventful for everyone."

Bud looked at her with new interest. "You're honest."

"There's nothing to hide; like I said, there's been nothing

worthwhile in my life to protect."

Janice Elderberry wasn't what you would call a good looking woman. It was easy for Buddy Pritchard to envision her staying home on Saturday nights.

"Aren't you going to drink your martini?"

She noticed it for the first time, but didn't touch it. "I ordered the drink because I didn't want to seem weird. Martinis seem to be what people order before dinner. I'm not much of a drinker." She looked at him, worried that he wouldn't approve.

"You look anxious," he said.

"Does it bother you that I don't drink?"

"Of course not, why should it?"

"It would be easier for you to get in my pants, wouldn't it, if I was loosened up with a few drinks?"

"Is that why you thought I asked you to dinner?"

"I don't care. I planned to let you anyway."

Bud swallowed another mouthful of scotch and sat all the way back in the chair to get a better perspective on Lieutenant, J. G., Janice Elderberry.

"You're looking at me the way you accused me of looking at you." She smiled. She had a nice mouth.

"Are you always so honest with your private feelings?"

"You mean like letting you get in my pants?"

"Yes, if you wish to be specific."

"You see, I've never wanted anyone to do it to me, at least not right off, so I never had any private feelings in that regard one way or another."

Bud felt like asking why him, but he waved the slim, sullen waitress over instead. They both ordered steaks: Janice's, medium well; his, rare.

"After working on the wounded all day, you must be pretty tired," Bud said.

"You weren't out on a picnic either, Captain." She smiled with her nice mouth. "Did you get any rest?"

"A few hours. How's the cherry?" Bud's face darkened.

"Does he still have both legs?"

"It's going to be touch and go for a few days. The doctor took a big chance. The kid could die, you know. If we had amputated he'd be out of danger."

"What's his chances?"

"Fifty-fifty. That might be optimistic. The doctor's keeping him here instead of sending him to Da Nang with the rest of the wounded. He knows they'll take off the leg in Da Nang. You made a big impression on that doctor—he really believes you'll kill him."

"Maybe I should have let him amputate Billy's leg. I was pretty tired."

She leaned toward him. "I'll monitor his condition closely and if there is no improvement in twenty-four hours or if he takes a turn for the worse I'll let you know. If that happens you'd be wise to tell the doctor to go ahead."

"He's a good kid. He doesn't deserve to lose the leg."

"None of them do," she said.

Rubbing his smooth face (he had shaved close) he appraised the nondescript Navy nurse who sat across from him with her arms folded across her small-bosomed chest, her brown eyes alert and watching him closely. "I like you, Janice Elderberry."

"And I like you, Buddy Pritchard."

The hot steaks arrived. The potatoes and lettuce and beans were as fresh as found in a Los Angeles Safeway supermarket, just flown in via the miracle of MATS C-141 Starlifters from Norton AFB in San Bernardino, California. The milk was powdered, however, but the Milkmaid tasted almost like fresh. It was cold. And the bread was the freshest you could get, baked by the Marine cooks for the officers' mess just a few hours earlier.

"Tolerable," Bud said.

Janice cut a small piece of the porterhouse and chewed it thoroughly before swallowing. "Yes . . . tolerable." She smiled at Pritchard bolting down large hunks of the steak.

"You must be very hungry."

"If all you had to eat was C-rat ham and lima beans for two days you'd be hungry, too."

"Agreed—enjoy yourself."

Chapter 7

Hai Van Phuong, her eyes blank and distant, sat cross-legged on the dusty roadside. She had been walking for three days and she was exhausted. Her few possessions were wrapped loosely in a shabby bundle resting securely between her legs, and with sad eyes she quietly watched the long lines of stunned refugees blindly shuffling down the road, packed together, herding south.

Two of the dispossessed, a small boy and a girl, stumbled out of line and stood at the edge of the road, tattered and alone.

The girl, no more than five years old, held tightly to her brother's hand. The boy was only two or three years older than the girl. Tears trickled down sister's cheeks, cutting tiny riverbeds through the red dust on her honey skin. Small bare feet stuck out the bottoms of black cotton pajama pants. Her flat nose was running and she was thin and frail and frightened.

The boy had a distant and resigned look in his troubled eyes. He kept a constant watch on the stream of people filing past paying him no mind. He was dressed as his sister. Over his thin shoulder he carried a stick with a bamboo cage tied to the end of it. A small bird was in the cage.

The children, paralyzed by the enormity of their personal

tragedy and the swirling confusion around them, stood transfixed, uncomprehending, waiting for someone to help them. But no one even looked their way.

The little girl began to whimper, looking at Phuong.

"Stop crying," her brother said. "You must be brave."

"I'm hungry and thirsty."

"So am I, but we have no food or water."

Sister whimpered louder, "I want to go home."

"We don't have a home anymore."

"Yes we do, it's back there." She pointed north, from where they had come.

"We can't go back."

"Why can't we go back?" She rubbed her flat runny nose.

"Because mama and papa told us we can't go back. They told us to run away with the other people." He frowned at sister. "That's what they told us before they went to sleep, remember?"

"Are they still asleep?"

"Yes."

"Won't they wake up?"

"I don't think so."

"Never?"

"No, never," brother said.

She looked up, her wet cheeks glistening in the sun. "What will happen to us?"

"I don't know." He stared into the dusty road.

Phuong opened her bundle. "Children," she called. "Come here."

The girl released the boy's hand and rushed to Phuong. Brother hung back, shy and afraid.

"Would you like something to eat?"

Sister nodded her head.

Phuong smiled. "How about some rice and dried cuttlefish?"

The girl took a peek into the open bundle and the boy ventured a few cautious steps forward.

"Go ahead," Phuong said. "Help yourself."

The girl reached in and her little hand came back with a white rice ball. She quickly sat down beside Phuong and began eating it. Phuong placed a stringy piece of cuttlefish in sister's mouth. "Good?"

She nodded, and reached for another rice ball, but the boy would not come any closer.

"Come, child, eat." Phuong pointed to the food.

He looked at her sullenly.

"Where are you and your sister going?"

He pointed south.

"Saigon? It's a long walk. You will need your strength, so you better eat some rice."

The boy's face remained blank and he rubbed his foot into the red dust.

Phuong motioned to the cage. "Can I see your bird?"

The boy's face suddenly came alive; he took the pole from his shoulder and placed the cage on the ground in front of her. His eyes were very bright and animated. "His name is Tan."

"Well, Tan, would you like something to eat?" She put a grain of rice on her fingertip and put it between the bamboo bars. "It's a long trip south and you'll need a full belly."

The bird quickly ate the rice.

"Would you like to feed him?" Phuong gave brother a rice ball.

The boy fed his bird a grain at a time until it was no longer hungry. "Can I eat the rest?" he asked Phuong.

"Of course you can." She smiled warmly.

He immediately wolfed down the remainder of the rice ball. Phuong gave him another and that one quickly disappeared with several pieces of cuttlefish.

"You are a nice lady," sister said.

Brother chewed slowly on a third rice ball. "Will you be our mother?"

Phuong's gaze dropped to the red dust. "You have no

parents?"

"They're asleep and won't wake up," the girl innocently said.

"Oh, I see."

There was a long silence. She gave them water to drink.

"How about some sour plums?" Phuong said cheerfully.

They clapped their hands happily. "Sour plums! Sour plums!"

"Yes, sour plums for two good children." Phuong placed two of the shriveled red fruit in each of their outstretched hands.

"Mmmmm." They smacked their lips and laughed happily.

Phuong put one into her mouth and sucked it. "I'm going into the mountain country to wait for the war to end. Do you want to come with me?"

Brother's face suddenly fell and he looked afraid. "The bad soldiers are back there—mother told us to run away from them."

"We always do what mother tells us," sister said sucking on her sour plum.

"But I'm sure your mother would approve of you coming with me; I will protect you and you won't have to be afraid anymore."

The boy thought for a moment. "Who will protect you?"

Sister's eyes went back and forth between the two of them.

Phuong put a dried plum into sister's mouth and patted the 7.62mm MAT-49 submachine gun. "This will protect me."

The boy didn't look comforted. "The soldiers don't like us."

"Brother is right," sister said matter-of-factly, not really understanding.

"I wish you would come with me to the mountains. You can keep me company and there are people there who will take care of you. Won't you please come?"

The boy stood, pulling sister up by the hand. "We must go south with the others. Mother told us. She said our aunt will take care of us."

"And where does your aunt live?"

"In the capital city."

"The capital city is very big with many people living there. Will you be able to find her?"

"We will try." He put the bird cage on the pole and raised it to his shoulder.

"Here, take this." Phuong tied most of the rice, cuttlefish, and the last of the sour plums into a cloth and handed it to sister. She gave brother the water bottle. "I will pray for you."

Hand in hand the two waifs stepped back onto the rutted road and were soon swallowed up by the river of fleeing people. Sister looked back at Phuong and waved goodbye. Brother looked straight ahead. The bird cage swung from the pole.

Phuong watched the children vanish, feeling a sense of sorrow. The sun traveled westward into Cambodia and Laos where the sky was pale white and relentlessly hot; not a breeze or breath of fresh air stirred on the baked land. A pair of redheaded vultures circled in the dead air, following the hordes of flesh rushing south, away from the advancing North Vietnamese Army. It was the first day of the New Year celebration, TET.

An ox cart filled with a family and their belongings trundled past Phuong sitting at her spot on the roadside. The cart was piled high with rough, handmade furniture, bags of rice, tied bundles, ducks and chickens, and a pig. Children sat on top of the furniture.

"Young woman!" the man leading the oxen shouted. "Young woman!"

Phuong looked up and squinted against the piercing sun. She remained sitting.

"Are you tired?" He stopped the oxen. A swarm of black blowflies swirled around the heads of the beasts, filling their eyes and noses. "Give me ten piasters and I will allow you to ride for a few miles."

Phuong looked at him with disgust. "There is no room in the cart." She turned her head.

"I will make one of the children walk."

"You should be ashamed of yourself," she reprimanded. "No matter. I am not going the same direction."

"Five piasters," the man said, spitting a large fly from his mouth. He ran a skeleton-thin hand through his matted hair.

"We will ride your ox cart," interrupted the leader of a band of South Vietnamese soldiers. "We are very tired and need the rest." His laugh was wicked.

"Can you pay?"

The leader slapped the man across the face. "There's my payment."

He motioned to his men, who long ago had thrown away their weapons, and they pulled the family from the cart.

"Stop! Stop!" the man yelled, waving his hands. "Don't do this to us. You have no right."

"There are no more rights," the soldier said, throwing the furniture down. A table broke into pieces with a loud crash. "The country is lost. We make our own rights."

The matriarch of the family, a toothless ancient, sat in the middle of the dirt highway screaming like a banshee. The children stood around her with bewildered looks on their faces. More soldiers jumped on the ox cart. The road was filled with soldiers.

The cart wheeled into the middle of the road, crammed with its jeering barbarous passengers. Sullen-faced refugees scarcely looked up, keeping their eyes to the dirt underfoot.

The family, resigned to its fate, soon gathered on their backs what few possessions they could salvage from the strewn wreckage and slipped unnoticed into the river of flesh.

Phuong sat rooted to her spot for hours watching her blank-faced countrymen silently shuffle past. They followed each other down the road to a vague destination that to most seemed worlds away—south to Saigon.

The big guns boomed in the distance and Phuong grew nervous. She listened to them get closer. Puffs of black smoke blossomed across the tops of the low hills miles to the north, and she shivered in the intense heat.

The sun was at its zenith, paling the land in its silver blaze. Chorus lines of undulating heat waves danced upward from the sweltering paddies and spread their transparent sheen over the tassels of limp rice.

"It is as if the very life was cooked out of the country," Phuong murmured. She stood and pulled the wide conical peasant hat over her eyes. Some of the palm thatch was missing. "The will has drained from the land. It is only a matter of time now—only a matter of time."

She glanced once more at the smoking black flowers springing out of the hills. Tying the grass thong under her chin, she lifted the bundle to her shoulder and looked back in the direction of Quang Hoa. *So be it . . . it is the way of things.* A trickle of perspiration ran down her nose. *Who will harvest the rice now that the people are leaving their farms? The fields are full to bursting. The grain is rotting. Ahhhh, why am I worrying; there are troubles enough of my own to worry about.* She scanned the torpid sky one more time, shading her eyes from the blinding sun.

From the rise where she was standing she could see the thousands of panic-stricken people crawling over the rice paddies. Men, women and children were everywhere, funneling into the road from the ravaged highlands, exhausted, terror in their worn faces, praying that they would live to see just one more day.

She adjusted the bundle on her shoulder. *The Communists will be here soon,* she thought to herself. *Who knows what will happen when they get here.* She looked north. A pall of black smoke covered the hills where the NVA barrages pounded the fleeing government army. Tears wet her dusty cheeks. *There is nothing left for me.* She stepped onto the road and its bedlam and began walking north toward the firing guns, against the human tide of refugees swarming down from the hills.

"Would you give a bite to eat, a small portion of rice for my children?" a tired mother said to Phuong. A sallow-eyed infant gnawed at her dry breast. Two more clung to her leg.

"There is rice in the field ready to be picked," Phuong chided. "Cook them some."

"We cannot stop to pick rice. The Communists are right behind us; we must keep moving."

"You should have brought rice for your journey."

"There was not time."

"You are a fool. You should have stayed on your farm. There is nothing but starvation waiting for you in the south."

"And the guns of death wait for us back there." The woman waved blankly at the rising smoke. "You are the foolish one. You are walking into the mouth of the dragon. Turn around and come with us."

"The Communist soldiers are not going to harm the common people. They are only interested in the politicians and the army."

"They will rape you, then torture and kill you." The woman waggled a thin finger at her.

Phuong ignored the woman and walked on, staying on the higher side of the road where there was more room. The soles of her sandals left tread marks in the dust.

"You are going the wrong way, sister," another woman shouted, limping along the refugee-choked road. "Freedom is south."

Phuong didn't answer. *Freedom for who, from what?*

"Freedom is south," the woman repeated.

"Who is to say where freedom is," Phuong said under her breath.

"Come with us. The army will make its stand in Da Nang."

Phuong looked around at the weaponless South Vietnamese soldiers pushing their way through the refugees, wild stares in their eyes. "Freedom is lost. We never had freedom," she said softly.

"What? What did you say, sister?"

Phuong walked, eyes fixed to the ground. The sound of so many feet on the packed dirt was the sound of rolling thunder, and she wished for rain to relieve her from the oppressive heat.

She glanced into the gleaming sky. Clouds building in the South China Sea were moving inland—hope for an afternoon refreshment.

The road dust rising from pounding feet sifted into her nose and mouth. She coughed and wrapped a muslin cloth from the bundle around her face. She stopped and gave a rice ball to a paralyzed old man pulling himself along the edge of the road with his hands.

Phuong's strong legs carried her north. She walked for many hours, head down, hat pulled over her eyes, ignoring the curious looks and cynical words.

Toward nightfall a magenta sunset streaked the western sky, and she stopped to watch the artillery flashes on the hills. The yellow and orange blooms bursting along the ridges held a bizarre fascination for her.

Increasing numbers of ARVN soldiers walked out of the treelines and took their places on the road alongside the refugees. Only a few carried weapons. Many tore the uniforms from their bodies, discarding them in the rice paddies.

Phuong turned off the red dust-covered road that led down from the highlands, and left its depressing wretchedness behind her. It carried the stuff nightmares were made from.

As she struck out westward through the fragrant rice fields, the suffocating feeling left her and she felt a new buoyancy in her spirit. The farther she got from the road the more the sense of freshness grew in her bosom.

Reaching a path, she followed it along the lines of coconut palms to the banks of a lovely green river. She collapsed against a tree, took off her sandals and soaked her tired feet in the cool, refreshing current. The curtain of night was falling on the land.

In the shadow of the palms she stripped nude and slowly slipped between the sheets of wetness, glorying in the river's sweet touch. She dove deep, her long black tresses trailing behind her, searching out the cool holes where the fish rested.

When she was completely refreshed, she came out of the water and lay in the soft grass, enveloped in darkness. She opened the bundle and unwrapped a paper package. She ate some rice and dried squid.

Inside the open bundle was a small picture of her family. Though it was too dark to clearly see the photograph, she was able to make out the faint outlines of the figures. The memories flooded back like the melodic notes of a bamboo flute. Fires were ignited in the deserted corners of her mind, burning away the torment, purging the hurt and the hate and the fury of a girl possessed with a singular flaming passion.

She picked up the worn picture and held it gently in her hand. A finger caressed the faces. The hurt ran deep, down into the quick of her soul, and she longed with all her heart to hold them all close to her breast. She sang to the picture, touching it to her lips:

"The stretch of the sea
As far as east from west
My kin you play

On a distant shore.

I send you my love
Wrapped in waves of blue
To keep you warm through
Winters of our parting.
Rejoice with me my
Blood—I sing songs of
Gladness, for you are
Alive in Heaven and
Pain is departed."

She lay down in the bank grass under the coconut palms and cried herself to sleep with the photograph held to her breast.

Through the long night, soft whimpers rose from the grass. The moon dipped below the palms, and toward morning no more sounds came from the bank where she slept.

Phuong dreamed of her mother and father, strong vivid dreams filled with joys that they shared. The thick rice waved in the cool night breeze drifting down from the northern highlands and she slept the sleep of the exhausted.

The night began to pale and the river frogs took up their dawn chorus, croaking dissonant melodies inside the ground fog. The mists crawled from the river and sent gossamer veils over the banks, across the paddy dikes and into the golden fields.

The yawning sun chinning on the crest of the low hills shined on Phuong's face and gently stirred her. The warbling voice of a brilliant yellow ki-bird perched on a flowering tamarind chased away the drowsiness and brought her fully awake. She rolled over and rose from the bank grass, stretching full length in the warm rays.

There was a small splash as her lithe body cleanly knifed into the river. She played in the current for a few minutes, then returned to the bank for a breakfast of rice balls and squid.

Retying the bandage to the back of her head, she shouldered the bundle and walked west following the river, her body swinging to and fro like young bamboo swaying in the wind.

The morning was delightfully cool and refreshing. She walked briskly and hummed songs to keep her attention off the deserted rice fields and pervading sense of loneliness. Missing were the usual early morning scenes of children riding water buffalo and farmers plowing the paddies. Occasionally she would come upon small groups of women planting new rice. There were no men. She walked faster, crowded by her emotions, fear nipping at her heels. Her limp became noticeable again.

Crossing the meandering green river, the well-worn path narrowed into an obscure brush-covered trail and left the rice fields and open land behind. The trail climbed through green rain forest, and within a few hours Phuong recognized the cleft in the Ba Den Mountains that marked the entrance to the Song Xanh Valley, where she hoped to find her father's oldest brother still living.

Without warning a strange reedy music drifted from the thick foliage, not exactly from the jungle itself, but partly from the humid, fetid air and partly from within the forgotten recesses of Phuong's memory. She froze in the middle of the trail, afraid to move. No birds sang; the air was still and very hot, steamy hot. She tried to move her legs, but like in a nightmare, her legs wouldn't respond, unwilling to catch up with her mind.

It was all so familiar yet so mysterious, a frightening déjà vu that caused her skin to crawl. The look of the sun's rays filtering through the forest canopy, the smell of the rotting leaves, the feel of the damp trail underfoot, the fluty music playing around in her head, all screamed at once for her to remember.

Suddenly she was overwhelmed with terror and she opened her mouth to scream. A black presence blanketed her, choking off her scream at the back of her throat. Her almond eyes, lizard fast, raked the undergrowth. She had been here before—a long time before—and she struggled with cues crowding her senses.

All at once a metallic roaring reverberated in the sky and she threw her hands to her ears, covering them tightly. But the sound persisted, growing louder. She saw the burned-out hooches, then the burned and broken tree trunks, bare and naked skeletons still grotesquely stark and threatening within the stands of new growth, a grim reminder of the horror that had happened here.

At the edge of the crematorium, seen through the charred tombstones, a dry riverbed snaked across an open stretch protected by a cliff on the high side. She pressed harder on her ears but the thundering noise wouldn't go away. It was hot—very hot. Rusted hulks lay where they died.

A ghostly form rose from the blackened graveyard and floated toward her. Petrified with fear, she tried to cry out while the mysterious emanation came slowly to her. She tried to run from it; her head spun and the rain forest became an echo chamber of violent sound.

Somewhere in her memory the Phantom jet came out of the sun in a long, screaming dive, arching over on its back, plunging for her hiding place. She saw the silver rockets fire from stubby wings.

The apparition was closer and she could see that it was a man. She trembled all over and her legs gave out at the moment the figure reached out for her. She collapsed into unconsciousness.

Phuong passed an eternity swimming in a swirl of colors of whites, reds, and grays. She listened to the throb of distant drums. When she regained consciousness the man was standing over her.

"My family," he said.

She blinked her eyes at him and looked at the young woman and child in the photograph that he thrust out for her to see.

The man was thin and dirty, and he held a bamboo flute in his bony hand. His coal black hair was matted and he had a scared, crazed look in his eyes. He wore no clothes except for baggy underwear that was held up by a string tied around his waist.

"You are pretty, like my wife." He was looking at the photo, and he stood straddle-legged and breathed hard over her on the ground. He leaned her MAT-49 against the trunk of a teak tree.

Phuong inched backward.

"Don't move!" he commanded, his lips curling down at the corners.

"What do you want with me?"

The curled lips changed into a lascivious smirk, and he tucked the worn photograph into his underwear.

She tried to will herself to stop trembling. The man's eyes slowly molested her and she cringed.

"Go away." Her voice sounded weak and childlike. "You are an army deserter, aren't you?" She regretted saying that.

The man's face became purple and the large veins in his temples stood out. "Deserter, you call me . . . deserter from what? From certain death? From officers who run ahead of me? From corruption and wickedness?"

"I am thirsty," she said, trying to divert his attention. "Do you have water?"

The purple drained away from his face. "You are a pretty thing; you shouldn't be traveling alone—evil can befall a pretty girl traveling alone." He looked suspiciously around. "You are alone, aren't you?"

"No, I'm not alone," she said quickly. "There are others behind me."

"You lie." He began to play a mournful tune on the reed flute.

"No, I tell the truth. They will be here very quickly."

He bent over and slapped her in the face. She twisted her head away and threw up an arm, warding off a second blow.

"Don't make me out a fool." His face was livid again.

"I mean you no harm. . . . Why are you doing this to me?"

"Because you are here—I need no other reason. There are no longer any rights or wrongs."

He slapped her across the mouth, and a trickle of blood oozed from the corner of her lip while her eyes glared back at him in hatred.

Suddenly she was on her feet. "Your mother was a whoring toad!" she screamed, lunging at him. In one motion she got hold of his scabby arm and sank her teeth into it.

"Aiiiii!" he yelled, forcing his hand into her face, unable to unlock her sharp teeth from his flesh. "Aiiiii!"

She swung her foot in a wide arc and cut loose at his groin. He twisted at the last moment, taking the kick on his thigh.

"I'll feed your poison bones to the wild dogs," he bellowed, wrenching his bloody arm from her teeth.

She slapped back and turned to run, but he caught hold of her long hair and threw her to the ground like a rag doll.

"You jackal!" she screamed, and clawed at him with her fingernails.

"Give me your money," the soldier said. He kicked her lying on the ground.

"I don't have any money."

His skinny leg shot out and he caught her again with a kick. She recoiled in pain.

"Please don't . . . I don't have any money," she cried. "I'm poor."

"Where are you going?" he demanded.

"To the village—Song Xanh—I have a relative there."

He pulled her up by the hair; she tried to jerk free.

"At the village you can get me money."

"No." She spit at him.

He wiped the drool from his face. "I need money." His eyes bugged from their sockets and he grabbed her by the throat and shook her wildly. "You will get me the money," he demanded.

"No," she gasped, stubbornly refusing, her hands struggling with his wrists, trying to free herself from his tight grip.

"You will." He bent her backward, choking the air out of her.

She couldn't speak, she couldn't breathe; she stared helplessly into his cruel, blank eyes. He tore his right hand away from her throat and slapped her hard again, knocking her to the ground.

She lay stretched on the dirt, her chest heaving, gasping for air.

All of a sudden he saw Phuong's bundle cast aside, poor, lonely, and lying in the dirt. He rushed to it, mumbling to himself, and quickly ripped it open.

Phuong leaped on his back. "Leave my property alone—you have no right!" she yelled.

"Shut up." He swung her off his shoulders and pulled at the bag, scattering its contents in the dirt. His eyes lit up like flares upon seeing the food.

"You filthy animal!" she shouted, struggling to decide whether or not she should try to reach the French submachine gun in a last effort to save herself.

He ignored her and grasped the strewn rice and dried fish in his shaking hands and shoved in into his mouth, dirt and all. He ate hungrily, squatting on his haunches like a starved dog while Phuong stared at him with fear and disgust.

"What are you looking at?" he said, eyeing her malevolently, rice dropping from his mouth. He spit out a rock.

"You are eating the last of my food." She clenched her small fists.

He threw his head back and opened his mouth wide, giving out a loud obscene laugh, spewing granules of wet rice all over her. He pointed a threatening finger at her.

She shrank back from him, crawling up against a tree. "What are you going to do with me?"

"Do with you?" He laughed wildly, sending cold shivers through her. He stuffed more rice into his mouth and bolted the mess down his throat without chewing it. "I have a surprise for you."

"My kin will hunt you down like a turtle and tear out your liver if you harm me."

"Pah!"

"Like a turtle they'll hunt you."

His evil eye flicked at her. "Pah."

"What are you going to do with me?" she insisted.

"You are going to find out—what's your hurry?"

She threw a rock at him, missing his head by inches.

"Life is cheap." The evil, dark eye wandered over her, but he didn't move.

"Why do you just squat there in the dirt looking ugly at me, you son of a pig?" She held tight to the tree trunk.

"Keep your foul mouth shut."

"Finish my food and be done with me. I wish to wait no longer. If I am to die let it be now."

He looked at her through narrowed eyes. He grinned sinisterly and saliva dripped from his mouth. "You will die, that's for sure, but first . . ."

"I'm not afraid," she said boldly. But her heart pounded wildly and she recoiled behind the tree.

"It will go better for you if you don't resist." He rose up from his haunches.

"I will fight you to the end." She picked up another rock and flung it at him.

He took a step forward and the rock hit him square in the

chest, stopping him in his tracks. A surprised look jumped into his eyes, then quickly turned venomous. "Whore."

"Your mother was a crawling snake," she shouted back at him.

He leaped at her, arms stretched out wide, but she skill-fully ducked under him and raced away, twisting through the burned trees, her feet quickly carrying her far ahead of the ARVN deserter.

She ran like the wind, forgetting the limp in her leg, past the burned-out hulks of amtracs and the eerie skeletons of charred trees. She ran and ran and ran, her leg hurting, not looking back, the soldier's black spirit lapping at her heels, driving her on. Already she could feel his hot, rancid breath on the back of her neck.

Her heart pounded hard against her ribs, trying to escape from her chest. The jungle was a blur of greens and browns as she fought her way through the tangle of growth. *I must get away, I must get away,* she told herself. *I will run fast, very fast, and he will not be able to catch me.* Her lungs burned for air. She wanted to lie down and rest, but she kept running and running.

Maybe it was the way the wind felt on her face as she careened through the forest, or the smell of jungle, or the look of the sun filtering through the trees that triggered it. A child running, the village children chasing her, a stranger not wanted. "I must get away." *Bang . . . Bang.* They shot at her with pretend guns. "Go away, you don't belong here," they shouted at her.

"I came to visit my uncle. My mother brought me." She ran fast. "Go away, we don't want you here," said the chil-dren.

She tripped and went down. The children fell on her, beating her, and they shouted their hate, and all the time she clawed and kicked them, forcing them back. *I must get away.*

The children formed a circle around her and shouted

taunts; the circle grew tighter and she lashed out, knocking one child to the ground. The chase was renewed and she fled through the forest, breathless and frightened. *I must get away.* Running, running, a crazed maniac chasing her. *I must get away.*

Suddenly she was out of the burned trees and she ran across a clearing of abandoned rice hooches. Over the next rise and she would be in sight of Song Xanh village. If she could just make the top of the hill maybe someone would see her; just a little more time, and a little more strength.

But it was too far. Already she knew it. Her leg hurt and she didn't have the endurance; it seemed like miles away and maybe it was. She couldn't make it—it was too far. The soldier would catch her before she could reach the rise and she was going to be killed and no one would see it; the madman was going to rape and kill her and no one would know.

The slap of the soldier's naked feet on the packed, damp earth reached her ears, and she ran faster even though she knew that she must collapse. Her body ached from oxygen starvation and she wanted to turn around to see how close the soldier was, but her eyes were fastened on the rise beyond where safety lay.

Then very quickly his hot sweaty hands were sticky on the back of her neck and she was screaming wild animal howls that cut the humid air and rolled up the valley and into the trees and vanished into the low-hanging cumulus. Only the birds heard Phuong screeching her death knell.

He knocked her to the ground, and she valiantly fought back, but her strength had been drained by the long run and she was quickly enfeebled. She lay on her back, chest heaving, drawing in sharp convulsive breaths.

"Outstanding . . . performance . . . my dear." His breath was short. "You have . . . the instincts . . . of a wild . . . animal." He stood over her; the sweat dripping from his face and body made tiny mud balls in the red dust.

Her eyes flamed at him, and her tongue was thick and dry in her mouth.

"Your . . . great lust . . . for life . . . excites . . . me," he said.

She cringed and covered her eyes with a limp arm.

"And now . . . my lovely little mango . . . the time has arrived to please your master. To the conqueror . . . go the spoils of victory." His breathing was returning to normal.

Phuong lay motionless, thinking hard about what she should do. *I have to keep my head. I can't panic again.* She knew she was doomed. *Let the end be quick,* she prayed.

The soldier began a low chuckling. He picked up her foot and started back across the clearing, dragging her by the leg.

"Stop! Don't do this to me . . . I beg you."

He paid no attention to her.

"Your bones will be scattered on the hills to poison the wild dogs and your spirit will wander in a thousand hells forever," she cried.

He dragged her limp body back through the trees and dropped her by the scattered remains of her poor belongings.

"You will be smote with giant boils over all your body for this. God will surely punish you severely."

He threw his head back and laughed with great contempt, then flopped hard to the dirt, breathing heavily. His wicked eyes bored into her, cutting off her stare.

Phuong had never seen shark dead eyes like this man's. They made her shrink in horror, and they curdled her blood. Her body became cold as though the very marrow of her bones had been frozen, and she was unable to move any longer; the starkness in his face paralyzed her.

It was evident that the deserter was crazed by fear and hopelessness that made him desperate, and that he would stop at nothing to get what he wanted.

He remained hunched over and sat on his heels to catch

his breath. His eyes, black ice, stabbed her soul and drove more terror into her heart. She knew that she only had minutes to live.

"Stop crying," he demanded.

"I will not."

"I can't stand a whimpering female."

She didn't realize that she was crying. A beam of yellow sunlight shot through the jungle canopy and splashed on her cheeks and reflected back a glistening wetness from her tears.

"I said stop crying."

"I can't stop." She cried harder.

I can't rape a crying woman."

After a moment he noticed a photograph lying in the jumble of her poor things, and he cautiously picked it up, not wanting to but compelled by some inner need. He handled it gingerly and looked from the picture to Phuong and then back to the picture again. He attacked the picture with his eyes, and then slowly, after a long time the tenseness went out of his body and his shoulders suddenly drooped. He ran a thin hand through his black hair.

A golden leaf, high in the mahogany tree under which they sat, loosened from its branch and spiraled down, and it turned slowly in the heavy air. As it spun, packets of sunbeams shimmered from its turning surfaces and it gently settled on the photograph. The soldier picked the leaf off the picture with his rough fingers.

"Your family?" he asked, and pointed to the picture. His face softened.

Phuong's eyebrows shot up, and the hairs on the back of her neck vibrated and prickled her skin. She lifted her eyes from the ground and wiped the tears away. The soldier's attention was fixed on the photo.

"Yes, my family," she said carefully and watched his reaction.

"This is a good-looking family." He removed the photo of

his own family from his underwear, studied it for a few seconds, then put it back.

She didn't answer; she was afraid and bewildered. There was a long silence between them.

"This one child looks to be less than a year old," he said.

"My baby sister is three years old now."

"You have no recent photograph?"

"No." She didn't want to explain further, alarmed at the sudden turn of events, wondering what he was up to.

"I see." His eyes grew cloudy. He looked south and sighed.

"Do you . . . h-h-h-have a child?" she stuttered.

"Yes, I have a child."

Phuong leaned forward and sat up. She tried to make her voice sound normal. "Is your child a boy or a girl?"

He didn't hear her. She waited a minute then asked him again.

"A boy," he answered. "I want my next child to be a girl."

She twisted her fingers nervously. "A girl will be helpful for your wife."

The deserter had not taken his eyes from the photograph.

"Is the boy with your wife?" she said.

His face twitched. "Yes," he said quietly. "They are in Saigon." His voice was just above a whisper. "I haven't seen them for two years."

"I'm sorry," she said.

"My wife is having a very difficult time without me. She lives alone, without help, and there is not enough to eat; she needs me and I must go to her." He looked south again and his eyes glazed over with memories.

"It is a difficult time for all of us." She eased away a few inches.

"My wife was a beautiful woman until . . ." He drew in the dust with a long finger. "My child . . . my child . . . he . . ." He didn't finish.

"You must miss them."

"I'm lonely for them . . . I miss them very much." His finger wandered in the dust. "The government is the cause of all this trouble. I hate the government." He spit into the red dust and watched the drool lie quivering beneath a pencil ray of sunlight.

"Everyone in my family is gone," she said.

He looked at her, startled, as if seeing her for the first time. His face had relaxed and he looked years younger. "Where is your family?" He raised himself up and took a few steps forward. "Where is your family?" he said again, sitting down beside her.

"Dead." She turned her head from him and she began shivering.

"Why are they dead?"

"An American warplane killed them."

He listened while she told him her story, all the while looking at the picture. When she had finished he handed her the picture and stood up; she held it protectively to her bosom.

"Why have all these terrible things happened to our country? Why must we suffer like this?" The flames leaped once more and set fire to his eyes. "The Communists deserve to win. We have all been fools. We trusted the government and the Americans—a pack of dogs!"

"Yes . . . a pack of dogs," she said, appeasing him.

He gathered her possessions together and mumbled epithets to himself and tied the bundle tightly; he placed it beside her and his eyes briefly met hers. She pulled the bundle to her and smiled weakly.

"Good luck," he said. He disappeared into the jungle, passing among the skeletons of charred trees and destroyed armored vehicles. She blinked a few times and rubbed her eyes. Had this all been something she had imagined? Was she losing her sanity? The strange reedy music returned and she heard screams far away.

Phuong reached the crest of the rise above the Song Xanh

Valley; in the middle of the valley, scattered along a broad river, was a village. Shading her eyes from the sun, she could see children who played in the water while old men and women worked the rice fields and water buffalo plodded ahead of plows that turned up curling slabs of paddy mud.

She hadn't been in Song Xanh since she was a child. Now she was back and a heavy weight seemed to lift. The pain of her past had been too much for her mind to bear, and she now withdrew from reality into a private world of childhood dreams. Here in Song Xanh and in the surrounding mountains she would honor the dead, herself a surrogate to atone for the sinful armies who took the precious lives of the innocents.

Chapter 8

The door gunner, PFC Malcomb Dresser, his monkey-strap holding him securely in the side hatch of the Huey gunship, watched for movement along the treeline. The M60 machine gun mounted on the pylon fitting in front of him was charged and ready for action. The rotors on the UH-1 turned slow enough so that the individual blades, though blurred, could be discerned (the pilot had throttled the engine down to idle), and PFC Dresser, nervous but in full control, flexed the fingers of his right hand that gripped the trigger guard. The butt of the stock was pressed into the small of his shoulder, and his left hand held the forearm piece that was ahead of the receiver group and below the barrel.

Quang Hoa was quiet, and though the rice paddies in which the gunship sat, its skids sunk in the mud, were freshly cultivated and ready for planting, no farmers worked the fields; nor did PFC Malcomb Dresser see any of the ubiquitous Viet children who ordinarily played about the hooches, nor were any water buffalo present or pigs or chickens or ducks, a sure sign that the villagers had pulled out.

"Looks creepy," Dresser said over the gunship intercom. "I've lost the captain—he's in the treeline somewhere."

First Lieutenant Bob Holcomb's left hand rested on the

collective pitch control, his right on the cyclic control stick between his legs, ready to rock the Huey out of the paddy mud at the first indication of trouble. "Any sign at all of the village being occupied?"

"None, sir," Malcomb Dresser said. "Nothing moving."

Captain Bud Pritchard lay prone beside the smelly outhouse and listened for human sounds, but all he heard was the hissing of the gunship's jet turbine and the swish of its blades coming to him from the middle of the rice fields. No mangy dogs barked, no pigs squealed, and no ducks quacked; no smells of cooking *nuoc mam;* no smoke.

He crawled through the vegetable garden and up to the side of the hooch where he had spent the night with Billy McGarvie, pressed his ear to the ground, and waited. Hearing no movement he go to his knees and peered through the thatch. Empty.

Inside the hooch everything was the same as when he was there last—the cracked porcelain rice bowls stacked on the plank table, the clay water jug in a corner, the rice straw piled absently against the earthen stove—but gone were the baskets of cabbage and sweet potatoes and the bag of rice and the strings of chom-chom and tamarind that hung from the rafters.

Every hooch that he searched was the same. The villagers had advanced warning of the TET offensive and chose to hide in the jungle rather than remain in the path of the attacking NVA. Those that were hard-core Viet Cong, like Tran Mai Lan, who kept a cache of weapons in the tunnel under her hooch, joined Major Toi's battalion and overran three ARVN outposts between the Vui Bong River and the Marine base at Cung Mai Dong.

"It's the TET offensive, Captain." She laughed low, a laugh of derision. "All the villages are empty—the people will be back when things quiet down."

"Damn!" Bud turned around and looked into the muzzle of a Russian AK-47 pointed at his heart.

"Don't be embarrassed," the girl said. She wore black pajamas and the red scarf and wide-brimmed soft cover hat of a hard-core Viet Cong. "There is no way you could have known I was here."

Bud saw the spider hole in the dirt floor; the heap of straw he had paid no attention to when he first walked in was cast aside.

"Drop the M16 and the ammo belt," she said.

"You speak good English."

Kanh Hai Thuy kicked the rifle out of Bud's reach with her foot. "Compliments of USAID in Saigon and Da Nang," she said. "Very good teachers, you Americans."

She had a hard smile and her face was flat like a Korean's and her eyes looked like Phuong's, long and narrow and slightly tilted toward her bridgeless nose; and long hair, black and straight, was pulled together and tied with a red string and hung to the middle of her back. On her feet were the usual sandals with straps made from rubber inner tubes.

Over her shoulders hung full ammo pouches made from duck canvas, and a small butt-pack made from the same brown material was strapped to her waist, below the small of her back.

"It was stupid of you to come back for Phuong," Kanh Hai Thuy said. "You were lucky we didn't kill you two days ago."

"Why didn't you? Because of Phuong?"

"Partly. We knew if we let you go you'd be back for her and we would be able to destroy a helicopter and kill its crew and capture much-needed weapons." She laughed at him.

Nothing Bud Pritchard could think of was more humiliating than being openly captured by the enemy without a fight, and by a girl at that. The patience and cunning of the Viet Cong he had not understood. He had, of course, heard the usual stories from a few mud Marine officers with whom he occasionally shared a beer at the O-club or in town when looking for a short-time, but until now he had never given a second thought to the notion that a Viet Cong would wait in a smelly, wet hole for two days for his return in order to ambush him.

"The girl, Phuong . . ." he said and looked at the spider hole.

Kanh Hai Thuy laughed quietly, kind of out the sides of her mouth with her lips parted slightly. "No—she is not down there. Phuong has left the village and will not return. She has gone north into the far mountains to live out her grief, far beyond your reach, Captain." Her smile turned contemptuous. "Your sentimentalism has been your undoing. You would not make a good Viet Cong."

"No— I suppose not." He looked out through the screen of bamboo and jackfruit but could not see the helicopter. The slow swish and whump of the blades turning on idle let him know that it was still there, however, and he would have given his left gonad to hear the engine gain in pitch and the rotor beat wildly at the air and lift the Huey and Malcomb Dresser and Bob Holcomb out of the paddy, and with nose low, tail rotor high, he would watch them swiftly pass over the treeline and disappear into the safety of the mountain passes.

"Lai day mau len." Come up quickly, Kanh Hai Thuy said.

A second Viet Cong, a peasant barely twenty and carrying a B-40 rocket launcher loaded with an armor-piercing RPG round, crawled out of the spider hole and gave Kanh Hai Thuy a length of communication wire.

"I take it you think you're going to take me prisoner." He nodded at the gauged wire.

"Lay down on the dirt—on your stomach," the VC girl said.

"No way—may as well shoot me and get it over with."

The paralyzing blow was quick and decisive and came as

a total surprise to Bud Pritchard. Kanh Hai Thuy took one step forward and swung the butt of the Kalashnakov into Pritchard's solar plexus. He dropped to his knees, then onto his face. Kanh Hai Thuy pressed a knee into his back and expertly wired his hands to his ankles. She kicked him over onto his side and spit into his face.

Biting his lip so hard that it bled and so that she wouldn't get the satisfaction of hearing him moan with pain, he looked up at her flat face and never hated anything as much.

She said something in Vietnamese and the Cong kid checked the RPG and looked out through the thatch toward the screen of bamboo beyond which sat the UH-1 in the paddy mud, its blades turning slowly in the hot wet air and the rice bent flat underneath.

The Viet Cong girl, Kanh Hai Thuy, was in no hurry. She squatted next to Bud Pritchard, her legs wide apart and her bottom resting on the back of her ankles while she steadied herself on the AK-47 that she had planted upright on its butt plate. There was a long tear in the crotch of her pajamas and he could see her vaginal opening surrounded by a few scant pubic hairs, very black and shiny.

The kid said something and pointed to the fields.

She held a hand up to quiet him, her eyes not leaving Bud Pritchard. She watched Bud stare at the tear in her pajamas, her eyes excited, and her lips moving involuntary.

She sat like that for a full two minutes; a smile broke out for a second or two, but otherwise her face remained hard with a sheen of perspiration on the flat cheeks. She shuffled closer on her truck-tire sandals, the red dust rising in puffs, so that Bud could get a better view; then with an easy and natural motion she moved forward the remaining two feet and sat on his face.

When she was finished she urinated in his face and rose, her cheeks flushed and wet; and she was smiling now and she looked very young, schoolgirl young, and if she were mixed in with a group of students in Hue or Da Nang or Nha Trang she would have fit in quite nicely and no one would have known the difference.

The three-round burst of 5.56mm hardpoints from PFC Malcomb Dresser's AR-15 caught Kanh Hai Thuy just above the waist and didn't kill her right away.

"Choi Oi!" My God! she screamed and fell on top of Bud Pritchard. Her long narrow eyes had opened wide with the shock of the hammer blows and her small, tight mouth was agape. Her total countenance was one of surprise and terror.

The Viet Cong with the B-40 had, within the few seconds it took Dresser to switch the AR-15 onto him, gotten turned around when the bullets hit him in the head and neck. The RPG that he squeezed off went through the thatched roof and exploded a hundred yards away. He died quickly.

Kanh Hai Thuy lay on her chest, unable to move and talking in Vietnamese. Dresser rolled her off Pritchard and she moaned unintelligible words and looked up at the thin pencil rays of sunlight that shone through breaks in the thatched roof.

"We better get out of here *rikky-tik,* sir. No telling how many Charlies are in this village." He was having difficulty unwiring Bud's hands from his ankles.

The moaning words from Kanh Hai Thuy were slow and steady. She had lapsed into repeating a long wearisome phrase.

Standing up and covered with red dust, Bud Pritchard rubbed his wrists where the wire had cut into his flesh, and then retrieved the M16 and magazines of ammunition. "What's she saying?"

"Don't know. Sounds like some kind of prayer. Gooks chant like that when they pray."

"Yeah—that's what it is," Pritchard said. "She's praying."

Without breaking the chant, the girl turned her head to the two Americans, who stood only a few feet from her, and looked up. Her face looked small and harmless and her flat cheeks were already turned waxy color. The chanting went on.

"What shall we do with her, Captain?" Dresser wanted no responsibility for the Viet Cong girl.

"She won't last long."

"Shall I waste her?" Malcomb Dresser raised the AR-15.

Kanh Hai Thuy's eyes were filled with pain and she nodded at Bud Pritchard.

"Yeah—waste her." He turned away and picked up the VC weapons.

The blast of the AR-15 on auto shattered the air inside the hooch.

On the way out Bud pulled the pins on two grenades and dropped them into the hole.

The blown-out wall that had been made by the NVA 107mm Katusha rocket was covered with a green tarp, and chairs and tables were scrounged to replace those damaged by the blast. Part of the dance floor was no longer usable but that didn't bother First Lieutenant Bob Holcomb and Janice Elderberry. They just danced around it.

"You fly today?" she said.

"Yeah—I went out to Quang Hoa with Bud Pritchard, a favor I owed him for a case of Chivas."

A thick finger tapped Holcomb's shoulder. "I'm cutting in, Holcomb," another lieutenant said.

"Screw off."

"Come on—you gotta share."

"Butt out."

The officer grumbled something and left.

Holcomb tried to pull Elderberry closer but she stiffened. "When's Buddy usually get here?" she said.

"He may not come tonight."

"I heard that he comes in every night."

"It's only a rumor." He looked down at her nice mouth. "What do you see in that old fart, anyway?"

She didn't know why she was attracted to Bud Pritchard; it might have been the gaunt, worried look about him when he walked into the battalion aid tent, carrying the cherry PFC, or the soft concern in his voice, or the offbeat confident go-to-hell manner that he waved like a flag on display.

"Bud's married, you know." Holcomb looked at Janice Elderberry out of the side of his eye as though she were now privy to classified information.

"Yes, but I was told that his wife wants out of the marriage and that he's not overjoyed being married to a middle-aged hippie who is doing everything she can to make him as miserable as possible while he risks his life every day for something he believes in." She had stopped dancing and stood with her hands on her hips.

"Hey . . . don't get mad at me."

"Sorry—the thought of what that man must be going through irritates the hell out of me."

"You've learned a lot about Pritchard, though I don't think you learned it from him—he doesn't talk about his personal life."

"He does to the man he flies with."

"Dale Keilman?"

"Don't you dare mention it to him."

Bob Holcomb smiled. "No, of course not."

Bud Pritchard had been at the bar for a few minutes when he spotted Janice Elderberry. He was glad to see her, but he wasn't too happy that she was dancing with First Lieutenant Bob Holcomb. The Huey pilot was a good friend and he had no right to begrudge him a dance with one of the few white women at Cung Mai Dong. He shrugged off the irritation and turned back to the bar. "Give me a *Ba Muoi Ba,*" he said to the bartender.

"I don't know how you guys can stomach that gook beer."

Pritchard took a couple of swigs. "It's not bad after you

get used to the chunks of fish floating in it." He looked in the mirror and saw Janice Elderberry standing behind him.

"I've been looking for you," she said. She was wearing Navy utilities, and they fit her too tight and revealed her plump figure more than regulations would allow.

Bud Pritchard twisted the bottle of *Ba Muoi Ba* in one hand and said without interest, "Say you're looking for me—what for?"

Hurt inside that Pritchard didn't show that he was glad to see her, her nice mouth pursed into a tight ribbon and she tilted her head at him. "After last night I thought you'd be friendlier than that." She turned and started back to Bob Holcomb.

"Janice."

She stopped.

"It's been a number ten day," he said, "Sorry."

"Want to get a table?"

He ordered a Shirley Temple for Elderberry, her favorite, and told the bartender to leave the lemon peel in the drink after rubbing the rim of the glass with it, and followed Janice to a table a few feet from the tarp-covered wall.

"Bob Holcomb said he flew you out somewhere in the bush today. Don't you get enough flight time in your jet that you have to tour Nam in a chopper?"

"That's what I like about you." Bud looked directly into her big wide eyes and smiled. She had been good last night.

She took a bite out of the lemon peel and smiled back. "What is it you like about me?"

"You talk the language and you're rough enough around the edges to be approachable. You're no threat."

"What you see is what you get," she said.

They touched glasses.

"Want to tell me what happened while you were playing mud Marine out in the bush today?" She started to touch his hand, then decided that he wouldn't like an open display of affection. Her hand stopped halfway across the table.

"She wasn't there," he said.

"Who wasn't there?"

After a few seconds he clicked his teeth. "Phuong wasn't in Quang Hoa. She left for the north and won't be coming back."

Janice Elderberry saw the concern in his face and the faraway look in his eyes. "Buddy, who's Phuong and what happened out there today?"

"It all started right there." He pointed to the blasted-away wall and said no more.

There was a long silence and they listened to the Viet singer who could hardly be heard above the raucous noise of aviators shouting at each other across the room and telling jokes and laughing at each other's war stories, and the breaking of beer bottles and the thrust of jet engines launching for the night flights.

"I think the kid is going to make it."

Bud looked up from the beer bottle.

"The cherry," Elderberry said. "His temperature is going down and the antibiotics are working on the leg."

He was on his feet and almost to the door.

"Hey, Buddy, where you going?"

"To see Billy."

"Wait for me."

"Well, come on, Elderberry—you got to learn to keep up."

PFC Billy McGarvie had been moved from the emergency aid station to the base hospital, a small building of twenty beds and a staff of two nurses besides Janice Elderberry. Billy and one other Marine, an ambulatory case, were the only patients. The rest had been flown to the main hospital at Da Nang. McGarvie was drowsy but awake.

"How you doing, kid?" Bud sat down on the crisp, faded blue sheets, next to the heavily bandaged leg with the clear plastic tubes running in and out of it.

"My mouth tastes terrible and I feel like vomiting all the time."

"The anesthesia," Janice Elderberry said.

The big, soft doe eyes looked around the empty room. "Where're the other guys?"

"Da Nang," Elderberry said. "You'll be going there in a few days. Then home."

PFC Billy McGarvie's eyes turned wet. "Home?"

"That's right, kid," Bud said. "And the Navy hospital in San Diego for a while, at least until that leg heals up so you can go out and play basketball again and whatever else eighteen-year-olds do."

"Can my mother visit me in San Diego?"

"Everyone in Windfall, Nevada, can visit you."

"Hey—that'll be great."

But reached into his shirt. "Here—I brought you these."

"*Spiderman* and *Superman* and *Wonderwoman,*" Billy said. "That's great, sir . . . thanks." He leafed through *Wonderwoman.* "My first CA and I got dinged. Ain't that something, Captain? I did okay, though, didn't I?"

"The colonel said you're getting a medal," Bud said.

His big brown eyes got bigger, and through the anesthesia-induced dopiness a proud smile spread across his face. He looked at Janice and then back at Bud and then over at the bed with the other Marine in it. "Hey, Lester, they're giving me a medal."

"Good—you can hock it when you get home."

"Naw, I'm going to give it to my mom." The smile returned and he reached for *Spiderman.* "How's the girl, sir?"

When Bud didn't answer right away, Billy looked up from the comic book, concern fixed in his soft eyes, and Pritchard knew for sure how sensitive a kid Billy McGarvie really was.

"I couldn't find her, Billy."

McGarvie stared at Bud Pritchard for a few seconds, the *Spiderman* comic limp in his hands. "But, sir, you got to find her. She ain't got nobody now that her brother and all her family is kilt. Who's going to take care of her?"

How do kids like this get into a war? Pritchard looked uncomfortably at Janice Elderberry, who was checking Billy's chart and replacing a drainage tube in his leg. *They have no business over here and should be left to grow up in places like Windfall and Eloy and Bend and North Fork. If the old had to fight the wars there wouldn't be any wars.*

"I did what I could . . . she's gone and no one knows where she went . . . somewhere farther north . . . maybe into Laos . . . who knows."

Bud said goodbye to Billy McGarvie and promised to drop by again before he was taken to Da Nang. He and Elderberry got in the jeep he had borrowed from Sergeant Major Dorsett at Operations and drove down the same road he and Hai Van Phuong had driven when they had been attacked by the sappers.

When they came to the motor pool and the burned area where Bud had shot the sappers, he pulled off the road and parked behind an ammo bunker, the walls of which were made from sandbags piled around and on top of partially buried fifty-five-gallon drums filled with dirt. The roof of the bunker was made from two layers of corrugated tin supported by timbers, and on top of that was piled a foot of dirt and more sandbags.

Captain Bud Pritchard USMC helped Lieutenant, J.G., Janice Elderberry USN over the four-foot-high opening in the bunker and down into the room that had been dug out of the red dirt of the ancient flood plain that was now Cung Mai Dong.

"Can't you find something more comfortable than this bunker, Captain? My back is still sore from laying on those cases of sixty-millimeter mortar rounds."

"Elderberry, I told you last night that I'd book us into the Hilton first chance there's a vacancy; but for the time being you're going to have to get along in the bunker."

Janice Elderberry was a little butterball, tight and firm with enough baby fat in the right places to round her out and make her exceedingly soft and comfortable. In the magnesium glow of the parachute flare that was slowly floating to earth, Bud watched her remove the faded utilities with the name tag over the stamped *USN* on the left breast pocket and stand before him with nothing on except her brown oxfords and the white cotton regulation underpants. She never wore a bra. She looked like a chubby white ghost in the soft flare light.

The little butterball melted in his arms and he removed the Navy-issue underpants, smelled them (they were lightly perfumed) and tucked them in his pocket.

Holding her under the armpits he lifted her onto a box of 7.62mm ammo so that she was eye level and kissed her, not a passionate kiss, more of a kiss that you would give a friend. Her tummy quivered against his belt buckle and she sighed down deep.

"I brought a sleeping bag for you to lay on tonight," he said.

"Good for you."

"It's in the jeep."

"I can't wait that long." She kissed him with her nice mouth, long and tender and wet, and the magnesium parachute flare sputtered its last and went out five feet before it hit the ground.

"It'll just take a sec."

"Promise?"

"Elderberry, the jeep is only parked thirty feet away."

"It's just like you to leave me in here with no clothes and only the mortars to keep me company while you decide to go back to the O-club for a bottle of champagne or a couple of *Ba Muoi Ba*'s and a plate of *cho gio* to bring back so we can celebrate afterwards, or maybe you would decide to go off as a *turista* again with Bob Holcomb and never come back."

Her small bosoms were deceptive—firmly upright, rubbery and sensuous—and felt much larger than they looked. He wanted to take her again as he had last night, over the ammo cases, raw and primitive.

"I promise I'll be back." He bent over and pushed through the bunker opening and climbed over the dirt parapet and stood beside the bunker, one hand on the oil drums and sandbags, the other shading his eyes against the brightness of a flare that had just popped. This one was a starburst and it was directly overhead. He thought that odd; it wasn't the usual illume he was used to seeing.

At the jeep he unzipped his pants and relieved himself while he watched another starburst explode, and he listened to his stream spatter on the ground. A far-off, familiar warbling sound came out of the night, beginning in the hills to the west and traveling over the river and rice paddies, and then changed to a high whistling shriek as it entered the still, black air over the Marine base at Cung Mai Dong.

The first Katusha hit inside the perimeter 100 yards from the flightline and the F-4 Phantoms parked in sandbagged revetments. Bud couldn't tell from the first hit where the NVA were aiming, but he assumed it was the flightline and the parked aircraft, including the UH-1D and CH-46 helicopters.

When the second Katusha screamed in several seconds behind the first and crashed not into the runway but on a line to the bunkers, Pritchard got worried. His bladder was full from the O-club beer, however, and he was still whizzing when the third Katusha exploded just outside the motor pool. The Charlies were walking the rockets right into the bunkers.

Pants unzipped and his leg dripping wet, he met Elderberry halfway back to the bunker, running toward him, stark naked except for her brown oxford shoes. The illumes and starbursts were popping all over the perimeter and in the hills and over the paddies, and Bud smiled at the comical sight of Lieutenant, J.G., Janice Elderberry's white roly-poly body caught in the light of the flares.

"What shall we do?" she yelled.

Bud looked around. There were no slit trenches or other places to hide except under the jeep or in the bunker with the mortar rounds.

"Six of one or half a dozen of the other," he said. "It's either under the jeep or in the bunker."

She ran back into the bunker.

The next incoming was delayed and fell out of the line of the previous explosions, but close enough to make it obvious that the Charlies knew what they were shooting at. Elderberry pulled Pritchard down between the ammo boxes, and he had the vision of having this immense orgasm at precisely the same moment the bunker took a direct hit.

As the attack intensified, Janice Elderberry became proportionately more aroused.

"You're just going to have to wait, Elderberry," Bud said.

"What difference does it make?" she said impatiently. "A little noise isn't going to make any difference and we aren't going anyplace. Do you realize we could be making history tonight?"

Not having much of a sense of humor, Bud looked at her and frowned. "What are you talking about?"

"The Navy and Marine Corps copulating in an ammunition bunker at the height of a VC rocket attack is sure to get into the *Guiness Book of Records*."

"Very funny, Elderberry."

She ignored his dourness and laughed. In fact, she laughed for a full minute, unable to control herself. Bud figured it was more from fright than anything funny. He had seen scared-to-death kids on Hill 506 laughing their asses off when they knew they had little chance of getting off the hill alive.

Elderberry was crying now, her butterball body shaking against him, her voice small and down somewhere far away.

"Easy," Bud said. "We're going to get out of here."

A Katusha shrieked in and exploded only a few meters away, and hot shards burned into the sandbags, and the ground shook so hard that the heavy cases shifted and Bud and Janice could hear the mortars bang against each other inside the boxes.

"Make love to me, Buddy, please," she whimpered.

Bud figured it wouldn't hurt any, and even though he was tense he found the Navy nurse desirable and was able to perform well enough to shift her mind off the pounding they were taking, and she even stopped crying and moaned instead with pleasure, little catlike purrs that came out of her nose, and she was very good and affectionate in a way that she could not have been if she hadn't been frightened out of her wits.

"Elderberry," he said.

"Why do you call me Elderberry and not Janice? What happened to the sleeping bag?"

"I call you Elderberry because it sounds more military than Janice, and if you roll off me I'll get the sleeping bag."

"No way—not until Charles finishes his party and goes home."

Those were the magic words, or so it seemed, for either Victor Charlie decided to call off the party or he ran out of rockets, in which case the effect was the same—deafening silence.

"What happened?" Janice said.

"It's over—Charles has gone back to the *nuoc mam* and rice he left cooking in his tunnel. Let's go before he decides he was having too much fun to leave."

"What's that noise?" she said, frozen to his chest. "Sounds like someone scratching." Her chubby body became rigid and her nails dug into his shoulders. "There's something in this bunker with us."

"The shelling shook them out."

"Shook them out?"

"Janice . . . your nails."

"Shook what out?" she demanded.

"The rats."

The noise that came from Janice Elderberry's throat was something between a scream and a strangle, and it took her no more than three seconds to claw her way out of the bunker.

"Elderberry—your clothes!"

Chapter 9

The massive prow of the USS *Coral Sea* cut through the dark oily waters of the Gulf of Tonkin in the South China Sea, and Captain Bud Pritchard USMC stood in the open bay of the hangar deck and caught the spray in his face.

"Thorbus really did it to me this time."

"Don't bitch, Bud, carrier duty isn't all that bad," Dale Keilman said. "The chow's great."

Through the open bay they watched the first light of dawn break over North Vietnam, the land mass only a black outline against a sky that had changed to lead, and the wind rushed through the hangar deck and it was warm and damp.

"Having us transferred to sea duty wasn't too difficult for Thorbus, not after he found out about you and Elderberry," Keilman said. "And you can't blame the Old Man—he had to go along with Thorbus and get you out of Cung Mai Dong; it was either that or be busted back down to a second lieutenant. Janice and the unauthorized flight to Quang Hoa were the last straw."

"How was I to know Thorbus had the hots for Elderberry?"

"Would it have made any difference?"

"No," Bud said.

"Then stop your bitching and get your head into flying

again. Maybe we'll get us some MiGs."

The wind whipped at Pritchard's face and he leaned forward against the heavy guard chain to take full advantage of the refreshment. "Too bad you had to get caught up in this with me," he said to Dale Keilman.

"Don't worry about it. Thorbus isn't one of my favorite people, either, and you need someone in the backseat who knows how to deal with the crazy way you fly. Put a newbie back there and there's going to be problems."

Bud's big hand grabbed Keilman by the back of the neck, and he gave his RIO a shake. "We've been through a lot, haven't we, partner?"

The smile Dale gave Bud was more than an ordinary smile in response to a friendly gesture, but spoke of the months of putting their lives on the line together and reflected the warm feelings the young aviator had for the old one.

Pritchard looked out to sea. "At last we'll be flying with a squadron of jarheads and not a bunch of swabbies. If Colonel Davidson had transferred me to the Navy pukes in VF-94 on the *Constellation* to fly noncombat photo recon missions like Thorbus had recommended, I would have loaded up with thousand-pounders, dumped everything on Ho Chi Minh's Party Headquarters in downtown Hanoi, then landed at Kep and voluntarily spent the rest of the war at the Hanoi Hilton. I'd do that before I'd fly with a bunch of women."

"The Navy pukes fly well."

"I know they do—but they're still a bunch of wipes." He took a last lungful of salt air. "Let's go get some MiGs."

On the way past the crews readying the F-4s and A-6s and A-7s for the morning strike, Bud saw his Phantom, Alpha-Charlie-Nine, carried up on the elevator to the flight deck, where it would wait for him to launch against the radar installations and SAM sites at Chuc Luc. The F-4 was hung with 500- and 1000-pound iron bombs on the hardpoints, and the missile rails were loaded with radar-lock AIM-7 air-to-air Sparrows and heat-seeking AIM-9 Sidewinders.

"What are you going to do about Janice?" Dale Keilman had reached the ladder that led to the pilots' ready room. He turned to wait for Pritchard, who was a few steps behind watching Alpha-Charlie-Nine slowly raised to the flight deck.

"She checked out fine, didn't she?" Bud said.

"Who—Janice?" Keilman looked surprised. "I only talked to her a couple of times."

"No—our F-4. There were no problems other than that thing with the steering bug on the VDI and the hydraulic leak in the nose landing gear?"

"Right, and the crew took care of that—I checked it out at oh-one-hundred." Keilman was a light sleeper and was known for his early morning wanderings. "What about Elderberry?"

"Our orders said TDY on this bucket so I think the Old Man may recall us; and if so and if Janice is still around, maybe I'll work something out with her. If not . . . well, that's the way it goes. I won't worry about it."

"TDY could mean anything—whatever temporary duty Davidson chooses—could last to the end of our tours."

"He could have sent me home—but he knows I want to stay in Nam. I'll give him credit for that." He turned away from the elevator that had reached the flight deck and followed Keilman onto the ladder. "I liked Elderberry; I'm going to miss her."

"Thorbus is probably drinking to that."

As Bud Pritchard and Dale Keilman made their way to the ready room to be briefed on the morning strike, Navy Captain Josh Billington stood on the bridge of the USS *Coral Sea* and pondered the threatening weather. Rain or shine the strikes would continue, but he didn't like the monsoon season, hadn't liked it since the typhoon caught him in the slot off the canal and he lost his torpedo boat. That was back in '42 but the memory was still clear and it haunted him.

"Want me to get another check on the weather, sir?" Jack Hunter, the officer-of-the-deck, was sensitive to Captain Josh Billington's preoccupation with weather, and being an alert young man eager for a good fitness report and an upcoming promotion, was always ready to go beyond what was required of him.

"Precisely my thoughts, Mister Hunter." Billington watched the radar screen. "Call the Combat Information Center and see if they can be more definite or at least expand on the oh-three-hundred report. When I turn *Coral* into the wind I want to know exactly what my pilots are going to face up there." The mass of black land outlined off the port side was already edged in a purple-blue light, and he was becoming nervous about the launch.

"Aye-aye, sir," Hunter said. "And, sir, the two DEs are exactly where they should be, thirty-five hundred yards off port and starboard, and a third, the *Jebson,* is taking up position ahead of us when we turn into the wind."

"Good, Mr. Hunter—we can cover every contingency in the event of an aborted launch if we put our minds to it, isn't that right?"

"Yes, sir." Jack Hunter rang the CIC and confirmed that the weather was worsening and that the target over North Vietnam would be socked in by the time the strikers got there. He told the captain.

Billington shrugged. "That's why we have the A-6s. Damn good airplane. Best all-weather bomber in the world."

Even in the early morning hours Josh Billington's shirt clung to his skin and he felt the sticky wetness of the tropics creep into his crotch and armpits; there was no escaping it. From the bridge windows he looked down on the flight deck at the aircraft parked together, some coming up on the elevators from below, their folded wings bent upward and looking in the red lights like broken birds.

"How long have we been on Yankee Station this time, Mister Hunter?" The coming rain would be good for the aircraft, he thought; it would wash away the dirt and salt, a constant corrosion problem with aircraft aluminum.

"Three months, Captain."

A long silence followed.

"Why do you think I asked you that, Mister Hunter?"

"I don't know, sir—you know better than anyone aboard how long we've been on Yankee Station."

"I asked you because I'm bored, the South China Sea bores me, Mister Hunter."

"Yes, sir."

"A captain of an aircraft carrier shouldn't say that, right?"

Hunter didn't know what to answer and he realized that Captain Josh Billington had purposely trapped him.

The belly laugh unnerved Jack Hunter and he struggled for an answer. Billington let him off the hook: "Go down to Strike Operations and find out how they're dealing with the latest weather forecast." He laughed loudly. "And, Mister Hunter, just once forget the fitness report and tell me what you think—from the gut." He smiled so the young man wouldn't think he was too serious and added, "When you're in Ops find out if that new Marine F-4 pilot, Bud Pritchard, is scheduled to fly the morning strike."

"And if he is, sir?" Hunter said in his always thorough manner.

"Then send him up to see me, Mister Hunter, send him up—most assuredly, send him to me."

After the officer-of-the-deck rushed out on the double, the captain of the *Coral Sea* sat down on his elevated bridge chair and chuckled to himself. The Jack Hunters would continue to please their superior officers, become well-liked team players, and feather their career nests in their usual servile, attentive manner while men like Captain Buddy Pritchard, the one Pensacola flight student he would never forget, never popular with their superiors because of their overbearing confidence and unorthodox ideas, did the fighting and dying.

Colonel Jerome Davidson USMC, his old Annapolis classmate, felt the same way and was equally frustrated, Billington knew, that the best warriors seldom survived long enough or played the game well enough to fill the leadership billets that determined military policy. They were always filled by the Jack Hunters and their clones. The Jack Hunters were the ones who early in their careers sat in places like the Strike Operations office beneath the *Coral Sea*'s flight deck and scheduled men and assigned aircraft and drank coffee and smoked cigarettes and made decisions based on maps spread before them and consulted each other's wisdom and created the strike plan and sent the warriors like Bud Pritchard out on some of the most incredibly dangerous and ridiculous missions imaginable.

The windshield wipers were on low speed, and they flung away the first drops of rain that struck the bridge windows, and Billington had settled back to think through the launch and wait for the first aircraft to mount the steam catapult. At the same time, Captain Bud Pritchard USMC sat down in the wardroom to a plate of bacon and eggs, hash browns, toast with strawberry jam, and a cup of black coffee. First Lieutenant Dale Keilman sat across from him. The ready room was down the passageway a few feet.

They were both dressed in baggy blue-green flight suits and hard-toed boots and carried .38-caliber Smith and Wesson revolvers on their chests.

Keilman put a strip of bacon in his mouth and followed it with a bit of buttered toast and a swallow of coffee in a white mug. "I always get a lousy shave when I use your razor," he said as he rubbed his chin.

The wardroom door opened. "Captain Pritchard."

Bud looked at Jack Hunter and put the coffee mug to his lips. "That's me." He swallowed some coffee and stuck his fork into the mound of scrambled eggs.

"Captain Billington wishes to see you on the bridge."

Bud looked at Keilman and continued to eat. "That so?" He swallowed the forkful of eggs and lifted the coffee mug.

"Right away."

"I'll be there as soon as I finish my breakfast."

The OOD scowled. "The captain wishes your immediate presence. He's not accustomed to waiting."

"That so?" He drank from the coffee mug and smiled at Keilman, who grinned back. "Tell the captain I'm on my way." He took his time buttering his toast and spreading jam over it.

Disgusted with Pritchard, Jack Hunter turned away in anger and went through the wardroom door to the ladder that led topside.

"I don't think he's none too happy with you." Dale Keilman finished the last strip of bacon and started on the eggs.

"And I don't think Josh Billington is none too happy I'm aboard his precious *Coral Sea.* He was my flight instructor at Pensacola and if he remembers me as well as I remember him, then I already know what he wants to see me about."

"Your reputation do follow you around."

His breakfast finished, Bud pushed the empty white plate away (not a speck of food remained, the plate wiped clean with the last morsel of toast) and stood with the coffee mug in his hand. "You'll have to take the briefing." He finished the coffee and winked at Dale. "Don't be surprised if someone else is in the front seat when you climb aboard Alpha-Charlie-Nine. Billington is a hardass, though I always found him fair. We'll see what he has on his mind."

"Good luck," Keilman said as Pritchard disappeared into the passageway. He grabbed five more pieces of bacon from the galley tray, laid them between two slices of toast, and headed for the pre-strike briefing.

* * *

Captain Bud Pritchard USMC had the good sense to come to attention in front of Captain Josh Billington USN. Billington eyed him closely from the pedestal bridge chair.

"Captain Pritchard reporting as ordered, sir."

Josh Billington swiveled the seat around to face Pritchard squarely. "You've gotten older, Marine."

"And so have you, sir; it's been twenty years."

"That long? And you're still a captain, I see."

"Does that surprise you, sir?"

"No—no, it doesn't surprise me, Pritchard, not in the least, but I am curious. Tell me, how does it happen that an officer stays in the Marine Corps for more than twenty years and never gets above the rank of captain?"

"By being an asshole, sir."

Billington smiled, "Stand at ease. Coffee?"

"I've had my cup, sir, that's my limit before I fly."

After filling his cup, Billington returned to the seat and looked long and hard through the windshield wipers. "Nasty weather—never got used to the monsoon season, regardless of all this fancy technology I'm surrounded with." He turned back to Pritchard. "Still fly by the seat of your pants?"

"I suppose so—don't think much about it anymore; twenty years is a long time."

"Yes . . . twenty years is a long time." He drank from a cup that had Navy gold wings painted on the side. "You and I are more alike than I wish to admit, Pritchard, and that's why, I suppose, I didn't wash you out at Pensacola. Another instructor would have, you know."

"More than likely. I've never heard of any other flight student graduating after inviting his instructor to take off his bars and step behind the hangar."

"We beat the piss out of each other," Josh Billington said. "Who won?"

"I don't rightly recall that either of us won."

"Sure you won't have a cup with me?"

"No, thank you, sir; but if the Captain wishes to invite me back to the bridge at another time I will be happy to oblige him."

"Fair enough—and next time I'll have more than coffee to offer you. Still drink Chivas?"

"Never stopped, sir."

Billington smiled and turned back to the sea. "Give 'em hell at Chuc Luc, Pritchard. Good luck."

Dale Keilman looked up from the padded theater-type lounge chair and nodded to Pritchard, only briefly taking his eyes off the closed circuit TV on the wall. "How'd it go?" he said not too loud and jotted down the launch time on the screen given by the briefing officer, Lieutenant, J.G., Mitchell Jones from Combat Operations. He offered Bud a slice of orange he had peeled.

Pritchard waved the orange away. "Don't you ever get enough to eat?"

Mitchell Jones's face was replaced by an Intelligence type, a lieutenant commander who was explaining the kind and number of weapons they would encounter at Chuc Luc.

"You didn't answer my question," Dale said.

"I'm still flying."

"He remember you?"

"Vividly."

Most of the pilots and RIOs in the room were slouched in their chairs, showing no tension, hands locked behind their heads or dangling over the armrests, as if they were watching a Disney movie on Channel 7 back home in their living room. Any nervousness or fear was effectively masked and held down deep in that special someplace that each man kept reserved for his private moments in hell.

While the other men wrote on clipboards they held or on kneeboards mounted on their legs, Bud Pritchard wrote what data he needed on the back of his hand. He wasn't inclined to need much info and what he did need he wrote in his own brand of shorthand.

The weatherman was on, Jasper Cole, an ensign who looked too young to be anywhere but in the tenth grade at Hamilton High and who put so much animation into his report that you got the impression that he was bucking for a slot on the CBS evening news. "The best you can expect is a possible corridor over Mig Ridge from the deck up to about fifteen hundred feet and some big winds maxing at sixty knots. Clouds top out at fifteen thousand at your ingress point south of Haiphong and when you egress at Loc Ninh you'll have to climb to nineteen thousand for visibility. Tides will be a minus two-point-five . . ."

The ensign's voice drifted away and Bud lost it on the way back to Quang Hoa and Hai Van Phuong. If she had stayed for just a while longer (he couldn't have missed her by but a few hours) how different her life would be—and maybe his. She had no right to deny him the chance to assuage his guilt, to provide for her future, remove the insecurity, give her a new life. Where had she gone—what would become of her? Where she was going it would take a person three days to penetrate a mile, unless she took a coast route through the lowlands where most of the attacking NVA were. If she made it through the TET offensive there was a chance she could reach the safety of the mountains; but what then?

He tried to shake her from his mind, but his guilt was big and the image of her small figure and bandaged head and desperate lost look persisted. How does a person deal with a loss of such immensity? What is the limit of human reserves? And who will pay for this atrocity? He? Thorbus? Davidson? McNamara? Johnson? And how many more would be committed? Maybe this morning at Chuc Luc . . . and tomorrow and the following tomorrows?

The ensign was smiling; he had just told a joke and his mouth was big and wide and he was obviously pleased with himself.

"What a dork," Keilman said.

Someone laughed.

Pritchard stared at the screen.

Lieutenant, J.G., Mitchell Jones was back on the screen going over the targets again, the map of Vietnam behind him stuck with red and blue pins, and he tried to say something funny to top the weatherman, Jasper Cole. The same person laughed again and someone threw a wadded-up sheet of paper at the screen just as it went blank.

"How you feel?" Keilman said.

Pritchard contemplated him for a second and then looked back at the dead screen. "What is this—you my doctor?"

"Just checking before I gave you this." He took a letter from a zippered pocket in his flight suit. "I stopped by our mailboxes."

After glancing at the return address, Pritchard folded the letter and shoved it into a pocket.

"I'm going to pick up a little snack in the wardroom. I may get hungry over Chuc Luc. Want something?"

Bud gave him a disgusted look and took the maintenance log Dale held out for him. "Says here that a split o-ring was the cause of the hydraulic leak in the nose landing gear. The crew replaced it."

"I told you I checked on it."

"Right, Keilman; right—just like you said. Go stuff your face again and I'll see you in the locker room." He noted that the steering bug problem had also been corrected. He signed his name next to the aircraft number, AC-009, and went to his and Keilman's stateroom to read the letter from Marjorie.

The sound of heavy boots coming down the gray-painted steel ladder (Navy-Marine designation for stairs) caused Bud to look up at two eager young Marine aviators.

"We haven't met, sir," one of the first lieutenants said. "I'm Bradford Collins, call me Brad. Welcome aboard."

"And I'm Jess Moskowitz," the other lieutenant said.

They shook hands with Pritchard and exchanged a few words about Quantico and Pensacola and other duty stations. Brad was from Sacramento and Jess from Chicago.

"Your backseater, Dale Keilman," Jess said, "was in the class ahead of mine. Saw him a few times at Trader Vic's."

They talked to Bud as if he were one of their contemporaries, but he knew little of what they talked about; the places and names were unfamiliar and a generation away. Had he ever been that young?

"See you topside," Bud said, wanting to get away from their youthful exuberance.

"Good luck on your first mission," Brad said and banged down the ladder after Moskowitz.

Resentment boiled up inside Pritchard. *First mission! I've got more stick time in Vietnam than any twenty of you young puppies combined.*

He kicked open the door to his quarters, fell on his bunk and tore open the letter from his wife. His hand had a slight tremor again, the same tremor that Ralph Thorbus had noticed at the debriefing the day he found Phuong in the O-club and the rocket blew out the wall and . . . He closed his eyes and pressed his balled fists against his head. *Maybe I should see the doc like Thorbus said.* He looked at his hand and willed it to stop shaking.

Marjorie said that she hadn't yet filed for divorce and would wait for him to come home before she did because it seemed to be the right thing to do, though she wasn't sure why. She was moving and would send him her new address when she got settled. There was a hint that she had found someone interesting, a man she had met at a campus protest and who no doubt was younger than she.

There was a bang above his head, an E-2 early warning aircraft landing on the flight deck, and he looked at his watch. Time to saddle up.

Most of the pilots were already in the locker room and dressed in g-suits and survival vests when Bud came through the door. His own locker was at the end against a bulkhead, and he got a few nods as he walked down the line of men stuffing flying bags with helmets, oxygen masks and manuals.

Dale Keilman laced his boot and looked up. "Thought you might have fallen overboard."

"You old woman—always worrying."

"Someone has to; you sure don't."

Pritchard opened his locker and pulled out a load of flight gear and began sorting it. "Met a friend of yours on the ladder—a first looie named Moskowitz."

"Jess Moskowitz—used to hang around Trader Vic's at Pensacola. We dated the same girl for a while . . ." He stopped to think and then zippered the survival vest. "Thelma Tatsugawa—a little Jap broad whose father owned a noodle shop on Okinawa. Thelma gave me his address and I stopped to see him when I passed through on a C-one-thirty on the way to Nam."

Pritchard heard little of what Keilman said. He checked the bladders on the g-suit, looked through the pockets of the survival vest to be sure that the two hand-held radios were there along with the flares and carbon dioxide cartridges and checked the Mae West and all the rest of the gear that would help him stay alive if he got shot down. He hoped he wouldn't have to use it again.

"Not thinking about Thorbus, are you?" Keilman noticed that Pritchard hadn't been listening to him. "We've got a whole bunch of flying to do and there ain't no room for anyone but you and I in Alpha-Charlie-Nine, so leave Thorbus and Davidson and Phuong and Janice Elderberry on the ship. You and I are going for a little drive into North Vietnam to visit Uncle Ho and when we get back you can pick up with Thorbus et al, again."

"I read Marjorie's letter."

"Oh, joy—I knew I should have hid it until we got back. She going ahead with the divorce?"

"Yeah, but she's going to wait until I get home."

"That's real big of her." He picked up the helmet bag and adjusted the holster on his chest. "Bud, why don't you marry Elderberry? She'd marry you in a minute if you asked her—she's what you need, no kidding."

Pritchard laced the g-suit tight around his legs and waist. "She's only a kid."

"Sure she is." Keilman shrugged and closed the locker door. "You could do worse, Pritchard, a lot worse."

"Maybe." He strapped on the torso harness and stuffed the flight manuals and maps and oxygen mask into the helmet bag and checked the Smith and Wesson for cartridges and pulled at his crotch for a more comfortable fit in the g-suit and shut the door of the locker. In two minutes he was on the flight deck.

"We're over here," Keilman said and pointed to AC-009 parked on the starboard side of the flight deck, near the aft elevator. Two other Fox-4s were in front of Alpha-Charlie-Nine.

Bud stopped near steam cat No. 2 and looked up at the superstructure. On the bridge of the *Coral Sea,* Captain Josh Billington USN stood with legs apart and arms folded; he looked down on his kingdom from three stories up, his chin elevated slightly, blue baseball cap with gold scrambled eggs on the visor squared away on his head, and saw Captain Buddy Pritchard USMC. The two men watched each other for a moment; then Billington gave Bud the thumbs-up sign and Bud trotted off through the crewmen preparing the aircraft for launch.

To the east the waters of the Gulf of Tonkin were an oily green under the dawn sky, and Bud frowned at the heavy overcast that had blown over Yankee Station from the South China Sea. No sight in Vietnam compared to the early morning rain clouds during the monsoons. Foreboding and oppressive was a good description, yet they carried a beauty that could inspire poetry.

While Keilman (in his twenty-five pounds of gear) climbed up the ladder that hung over the canopy rails and settled into the rear seat of the F-4J Phantom, Pritchard walked around the outside of the aircraft for the preflight check. First inspecting the nose landing gear for leaking hydraulic fluid and satisfied that the maintenance crew had fixed the problem, he shook the ugly green 500- and 1,000-pound bombs hung from racks on the wings and fuselage, checked the AIM-7 and AIM-9 missiles in the fuselage well and on wing launch rails, and checked for the telltale red fluid on the bottom of the airplane that could indicate more serious problems internally.

The wind came up and blew stinging water droplets across the flight deck and into Bud Pritchard's face. In the next aircraft, Bradford Collins and Jess Moskowitz were already strapped in the cockpit. They waved to Bud and he waved back and pulled on the black gloves, the ones with the ripped thumb seams.

Finished with the outside inspection, he climbed up the ladder, seated himself in front of Dale Keilman, and began the cockpit check while his crew chief, Sergeant Douglas "Happy" Hedrick, strapped him into the ejection seat.

Bent over Bud, his head inside the cockpit, Happy cinched up a loose harness strap. "Too tight, sir?"

"It's fine."

"The targeting radar tested out okay, and the squawk you wrote up on the six-forty after your checkout hop yesterday was fixed," Happy said. "You've got an active steering bug."

"So I've no excuse if I don't get a MiG."

Happy grinned through his waxed handlebar mustache. "No one from the *Coral* has gotten a MiG this time on station. Some pilots never even see one their whole tour."

Bud held his temper. The crew chief, like Collins and Moskowitz, made the mistake of assuming that Bud was new to the skies over North Vietnam. "Where you from, Sergeant?"

"Bishop, California."

"Hunting and fishing country."

"You been there, Captain?" Hedrick took a rag from his back pocket and cleaned a smudge from the inside of the windscreen Plexiglas.

"Caught an eight-pound brownie just north of there out of Convict lake."

"Yeah—sure, that's close to Mammoth Mountain, just off Highway Three-Ninety-Five."

"That was a few years back," Bud said. He opened a fresh pack of Blackjack gum and offered Happy a stick.

"Thanks, sir." He peeled off the wrapper and folded the gum into his mouth. "You and Lieutenant Keilman give it to them up there this morning and I'll have the red paint ready to put a big star on the splitter when you get back." He saluted and climbed down.

"How you doing back there?" Bud said over the intercom.

"Hey, man, fat city. Everything works."

"Want the canopy down?"

"Leave it up—a little rain ain't going to hurt; better than cooking in your own steam."

Pritchard completed his checks and sat staring into the wet wind and thought about the catapult shot. Flaps, throttle, max burner, ditch procedure, stick rotation. Ahead and off the bow he could see the dark hulls of the two destroyer escorts taking up position, and then he turned his head to the pounding of rotor blades and saw a Navy Sikorsky leave the deck to take up its orbiting watch in the event a pilot and RIO had to be fished from the sea.

High up on the island superstructure, Josh Billington waited with the pilots, Jack Hunter now beside him and assuming the pose of his commanding officer.

The hard-helmet was hot and uncomfortable, and sweat trickled down behind Pritchard's ears and down his neck to be soaked up in the collar of the flight suit. Removing the helmet and setting it on top of the windscreen, he closed his eyes and leaned back against the olive-drab seat (it had a two-inch tear in the headrest) and tried to think about nothing, especially the cat shot, which was the most unnerving part of a carrier mission for him. The landings he could deal with all right, nearly always catching a three wire, but the cat shot he had never gotten used to and nearly pissed his pants on every one. He double-checked to be sure that the red-flagged safety pins had been pulled from the ejection seat, and looked at the gauges on the instrument panel, noting the ones that he would only have seconds to read and analyze in the event of a launch emergency. Should he jettison the stores? Would he have enough time to get the landing gears up? *So what are you doing this morning, Marjorie?*

The flat red glow from the deck lights had all but faded in the slate-colored dawn. The strobe lights from the other aircraft winked at him, and beyond the catapults and parked aircraft was the 200 feet of empty deck—and at the end, the oily sea.

Hearing his name called from the port side of the flight deck, Pritchard turned and saw a big blond New York German, Steve Heink, giving him the bird from the cockpit of his F-4. Heink had been his RIO for a few months at El Toro Marine Air Station in Orange County, got in some trouble over a bar girl in Laguna Beach with a couple of ensigns from the *Constellation* and spent a week in the hospital recuperating from the fight.

Bud smiled and waved back. He wasn't surprised to see Steve Heink; the Marine Corps was a small outfit and the chances were good of bumping into someone you knew, particularly in an air wing, and when you had been around as long and stationed at as many Marine posts as he had been, pretty much every career man in the Corps knew who you were.

"Another one of your admirers?" Dale Keilman said.

The enlisted men who a few minutes before had been charging around the parked aircraft, setting bomb fuses, pulling red-flagged pins, checking for leaks, strapping in pilots and RIOs and talking to the air crews from mikes plugged into aircraft bellies, now stood around in their different-colored vests with stenciled letters and numbers on the backs, helmets and noise attenuators under their arms, looking out at the dark, oily sea and low clouds. They waited as the pilots and RIOs waited, in the hot wet morning, and wondered which of the air crews would not return.

The boredom and strain increased proportionately with the length of inactivity, but they didn't have long to wait this morning, for Josh Billington had ordered the *Coral Sea* into the wind, and already Bud Pritchard could feel the monstrous aircraft carrier shift into her turn and feel the waves crash into the steel-plated hull and feel the bow rise and fall with the swells.

As the *Coral Sea* came around, the wind lashed straight down the deck and into the faces of the men who sat in the F-4s, A-7s, and A-6s. It was raining now, big tropical raindrops that pounded down on the aluminum wings and Plexiglas canopies and on the enlisted men in their yellow and orange and red and green vests gathered in groups of twos and threes, huddled against the superstructure or squatted under wings that had not yet come unfolded and downlocked for flight.

Josh Billington watched it all, proud and uncommon, one of the remaining old salts, an aviator boat captain, a legend like Buddy Pritchard, both of whom followed the drum beat (unheard by others) from some distant band on a distant parade ground and thinking everyone less fortunate than they.

In the backseat, surrounded by the best and most complex avionics anywhere in the world, First Lieutenant Dale Keilman pondered the difficulties of getting Bud Pritchard through the rotten weather and through the North Vietnamese antiaircraft artillery, SAMs and MiG fighters to deliver the bombs on target at Chuc Luc. Then he had to get him back to the *Coral Sea.*

Forward of the planes came a hissing explosion. The deck crew had fired one of the steam catapults, a practice shot before the first A-7 Corsair would be loaded into it. The attack planes would be shot first, hit the tankers and form up for the dash into North Vietnam. Pritchard and Keilman and the others in the F-4s would rendezvous with them and fly fighter protection (MIGCAP). They would be the last to go in with their bombs.

Now with planes fueled, bombs loaded, and catapults charged, a voice boomed over the loudspeaker: *"Start your engines."* Good morning, Vietnam.

The tension now broken, activity resumed on the deck as one by one the aircraft commanders kicked over their APUs and started engines. The deck crew was everywhere, using hand and arm signals to talk to each other and the pilots. The noise and heat were fierce.

"Let's get this show on the road, Captain Marvel," Dale Keilman said. "Ah—the smell of jet fuel in the morning."

Bud could see him through the space between the canopy structure and seatback, bouncing up and down on his rear.

"Keep it in your pants—we're last on the cat."

"Get with the program *pog,* the little man down there says otherwise."

Pritchard looked over the nose of Alpha-Charlie-Nine at Sergeant Happy Hedrick signaling him to pull out of line and to taxi to the bow catapult. Without hesitation, Bud followed Happy, figuring he'd know soon enough why he was to be launched ahead of the attack aircraft. His left hand pushed the throttles forward, and the two General Electric J-79 engines eased the big jet forward.

After the routine roll call and readiness report, Pritchard heard the F-4 leader, Major Benjamin "Benny" Sanchez from Tucson, Arizona, call him on the RT. "Touchdown Dash One, Touchdown Dash Two . . ."

"Touchdown Dash Two," Bud said.

"We're going in first to take out the hundred and hundred twenty mike-mike batteries," Sanchez said. "You got them circled on your map?"

"Affirmative, just south of the radar installation and barracks." He looked at the map clipped to his kneeboard with the photo recon pictures. He darkened the circle with a grease pencil from a sleeve pocket.

It was going to be tough finding a hole through the overcast to the target. The A-6s, equipped with an all-weather bombing system, would end up doing the job alone if Sanchez couldn't find the hole, and most of them would be nailed if the AAA wasn't knocked out.

"You're first up on the cat," Sanchez said. "Then Dash Three and Dash Four. I'm last. See you upstairs."

Josh Billington, Captain USN, had brought the *Coral Sea* full into the wind and he steamed east (toward China) to produce 20 knots of airflow down the flight deck to help lift the aircraft off the carrier. He hadn't changed his position on the bridge.

"I wonder what Cookie's got for lunch," Keilman said. He was looking at Billington on the bridge.

"Leftovers from breakfast," Bud said.

"I don't think there was anything left or else Cookie lied to me when I went back after the brief."

"So you didn't get your snack?" Bud said.

"He gave me a piece of mince pie from last night. No one likes mince pie. I've got it tucked away in my survival vest."

"You're crazy, Keilman, if you think I'm going to fly down on the deck all the way into Chuc Luc just so you won't need to wear your oxygen mask and can eat that stale mince pie."

"Wouldn't think of it; I'll get most of it down after I turn the bird over to you on the bomb run, and then I can finish the rest off when you come off the target."

Bud grunted and rolled the Phantom up to the catapult, unfolded the wings, downlocked them into position, and dropped the flaps all the way.

As soon as Pritchard closed the canopy he began to sweat profusely. The perspiration ran down his neck and legs and he could feel it trickling from his armpits and down his sides; he used a gloved hand to wipe his face. It was hot under the locked canopy, but most of the sweat wasn't from the heat.

The tanker was launched ahead of Bud and Dale, and then the catapult crew signaled them forward. With the brakes released he gave the engines a blast and eased up onto the cat; plane and catapult clashed together, locked in position, and Dale Keilman set the ejection sequence.

A river of sweat continued to pour from Bud, and he watched the bow rise and fall with the sea swells. As the *Coral Sea* took a large swell and dipped forward, he caught a long look at the rolling dark waters capped with white.

Off to the right, wings not yet spread, three parked A-6 intruders waited, the bombardier-navigator in the right seat in the closest aircraft looking sullen that the F-4 flight would be going first. Pritchard worked the control stick and rudder pedals and checked in the mirror and out the side of the canopy for the corresponding correct movements of the aircraft's control surfaces.

Pointing directly at Captain Bud Pritchard with his left hand (index finger aimed like the point of a dagger), the cat officer signaled for full engine RPM. Bud gave the Marine jet 100 percent power, planted the back of his head firmly against the seat headrest, and asked Dale Keilman if he was ready.

"Let's go, Captain Marvel—*Shazam!* It's getting late."

Alpha-Charlie-Nine shuddered along its airframe, every rivet and seam trembling under maximum power from the terrible thrust of the twin tail pipes, a first-class thoroughbred from the best bloodline, straining at the jockey's hold on the bridle, impatient for the gate to crash open.

The gauges swirled and danced and surged, engines running smooth and in the normal temperature range, hydraulic pressure stable, surface controls operating normal, and the air conditioner (thank goodness) was blasting away, cooling down the two men.

The catapult officer now signaled for full afterburner, and Captain Bud Pritchard USMC pushed the throttles over the detent and past the stops and the Phantom shivered and shook and the two Marines vibrated in their restraining seat harnesses.

A highly trained eye—all in the flash of three seconds—studied Alpha-Charlie-Nine, a final inspection and approval. The catapult officer saluted and Bud returned the salute and the cat officer's hand circled in an arc to the deck; then his hand came up and the fingers pointed straight ahead toward the bow and the open sea.

The squirrel cage in Bud's mind raced and he clenched his teeth and held in his gut and waited and cursed at the catapult that didn't fire, then it fired and he raced down the catapult track, his vision blurred and the skin on his face pulled back, the g forces tugging at his body and pinning him against the seat.

Chapter 10

It was 1:00 P.M. in Berkeley, and Marjorie Pritchard mounted the steps outside Sproul Hall at the precise moment her husband, Captain Bud Pritchard USMC, was hurtling down the catapult track of the USS *Coral Sea.*

"This will be beautiful, Marjorie," Goodwin J. Rapshir said, "absolutely beautiful. We are very proud of you."

"It's nice to know that you feel that way, but I'm doing this not for recognition."

"Yes, I know that, but it's people like you, with the courage to speak out, that will bring this war of Johnson's to an end."

The microphone and speaker system were in place; feedback from the preamps screeched and the students down front held their ears and yelled. Then they saw Marjorie, and about a dozen of them stood and clapped and gave the peace sign and Marjorie smiled and returned the sign with both hands extended high and others stood and began shouting: Ho . . . Ho . . . Ho Chi Minh . . . Ho . . . Ho . . . Ho Chi Minh . . . Ho . . . Ho . . ."

"Beautiful," Goodwin purred into her ear. "It's going to be perfect." He pointed to a CBS camera crew that emptied from a van with their equipment, and pulling up behind them was NBC. Reporters from the *San Francisco Chronicle* and UPI and the underground press were milling around in the crowd on the lawn and steps, and a local media helicopter circled over the trees. The campus police were nowhere to be seen, as was expected, and many of the university professors, the younger vocal ones, well-known for their antiwar position, were holding court on the steps.

Marjorie Pritchard, dressed in torn and faded blue jeans, leather strap sandals, and a baggy University of California football sweatshirt, looked closer to the age of the students than she did to her thirty-nine years. A red bandanna was tied around her head, and a heavy bronze peace medal hung on a chain from her neck. Her fingers were covered with hand-tooled Navajo Indian rings. She wore no makeup except for black eye liner that exaggerated the largeness of her eyes.

The television camera crews ran across the grass and the photographers snapped pictures as the crowd parted for Marjorie Pritchard to ascend the steps. The rock band blasted out on electric guitars, and Goodwin J. Rapshir smiled and waved to the crowd that rocked and chanted, "Ho . . . Ho . . . Ho Chi Minh . . . Ho . . . Ho . . . Ho Chi Minh . . . Ho . . . Ho . . ."

Marjorie squeezed the younger man's hand, and her eyes seemed to glaze over. "I'm intoxicated by it all."

"It's important, dear," Goodwin J. Rapshir said. "The revolution is coming and you're making it happen."

"The greening of America!" she shouted.

"The greening of America," he answered and held her hand tight. "Your husband will thank you in the years to come," he said over the chanting and singing and loud rock music. "He just doesn't understand yet the conspiracy, but he will and he will thank you for the role you played in freeing America."

She leaned over and hugged him. "We will win—we will. Look at them," she said, waving to the crowd. "How can we lose?"

Goodwin J. Rapshir stepped to the microphone and motioned for quiet, but no one paid any attention. The band continued to play loud, and the chanting and singing became obsessive. "Ho . . . Ho . . . Ho Chi Minh . . . Ho . . . Ho

. . . Ho Chi Minh . . . Ho . . . Ho . . ." Then came: "Hey, hey, LBJ, how many kids did you kill today? Hey, hey, LBJ, how many kids did you kill today? Hey, hey . . ."

Rapshir gave the microphone to Marjorie. "Go ahead and speak. They'll quiet down for you."

As soon as she had the microphone in her hand the students stopped their chanting and singing and gave her their attention. Someone yelled, "Marjorie, we love you." The rock band played, but not as loud, for background.

"Fellow revolutionaries," she began.

There was applause, more chanting and then quiet again.

"Many of you know me—we have been working hard together to stop the carnage in Vietnam. This illegal and immoral war of Johnson's has got to end. I'm here today to publicly condemn the actions of one of the participants of this war, someone who I have spent the past twenty years of my life with and who I loved as much as anyone could love. I am doing this in order that the people of America can know the depth of my outrage."

Applauding and chanting. The TV cameras rolled. Everyone waited for her to say what they already knew she was going to say. That's why the press was out in force.

"My husband is United States Marine Captain William 'Bud' Pritchard, who has spent the past two years in Vietnam killing innocent people, including women and children. For these crimes our government has awarded him the nation's second highest honor, the Navy Cross—and I will reward him with a divorce."

The crowd went wild—Marjorie hadn't disappointed them. "Ho . . . Ho . . . Ho Chi Minh . . . Ho . . . Ho . . . Ho Chi Minh . . . Ho . . . Ho . . ." The band blasted with the amplifiers up full, and the students, five thousand of them, danced and sang, passed around speed and joints, took off their clothes and copulated on the grass and in the bushes.

* * *

Lieutenant, J.G., Janice Elderberry USN, sat in the jeep, reading the *Stars and Stripes,* her nice mouth pursed in thought.

"Just thought you might be interested in this latest development with our hero," Major Ralph Thorbus said. "Seems that he's been just as unsuccessful in his married life as he's been in his military life."

Janice Elderberry looked up from the front-page article about Marjorie Pritchard's speech, which had taken place three days before. "By your logic, earning the Navy Cross is not being successful." One eyebrow was cocked at him, a habit she had when irritated.

"Oh, come on, Janice . . . one achievement doesn't make the man . . . it's the cumulative total. The sum of it all is that Bud Pritchard's life is a shambles, and this business with his wife at Berkeley and her rocket to the top of the heap of antiwar protesters is just another piece of trash in the long trail of debris he leaves behind wherever he goes."

"I don't see it the way you do."

"He's a problem."

"For you he's a problem; for those men on Hill 506 and at the Vui Bong River he's a hero," she said.

"You can't seem to get him off your mind; I thought that after he had been transferred to carrier duty you might see things differently."

"You mean between you and I?" She folded the *Stars and Stripes* and gave it back to him.

"Well, since you mention it, yes, I thought we might get back to the way things were before Pritchard interrupted our relationship."

"We never had a *relationship,* Ralph. Your only interest in me was my underpants and it just burns your buns that Buddy Pritchard got to smell them and you still don't know what color they are."

He took a deep breath and looked away. "Don't be crude."

"Does it really matter? You may have been successful in getting Bud out of Cung Mai Dong, but what has that done except force you to fly his missions? You're not too smart, Major; and Bud Pritchard will be back."

There was a long silence with Ralph Thorbus looking straight ahead over the steering wheel.

"Believe it or not I'm not angry with you, Ralph. What you've done is stupid and I don't put you in the same league as Buddy, but I'm not angry. I'll go on seeing you if you want, just for the companionship."

"Nothing more?"

"Nothing more, Major. If I'm not worth that to you, then . . . well, I'm sorry. I've got the duty for the next couple of nights at the hospital." She stepped out of the jeep and waited for a second, her hand on the edge of the windshield.

"Thanks for not being angry," Thorbus said. "Pritchard is a lucky guy, even though he's an ass."

The jeep drove away, red dust rising from the tires, and turned down the line of sandbagged bunkers behind the hospital. Janice Elderberry watched Thorbus until the jeep was out of sight and then walked to her quarters, adjacent to the hospital.

"You and Ralph back together?" Betty Lanterno said.

"Suddenly I'm very tired." Elderberry sat on her bunk with the gray blanket that had *USN* stamped on it and looked up at Betty who was the same rank as she, lieutenant, junior grade.

"Maybe this will put some energy back into your young bones." Lanterno dropped two letters into her lap. One was from her brother in Fredericksburg, Virginia, and the other, addressed in an awkward, poor hand, was from PFC William McGarvie. The return address was U.S. Naval Hospital, San Diego, California. Her name was painfully printed in large letters, the kind a child makes when he is learning to write: MISS (OR SIR) LIUTENENT J.G. JANIC ELDARBARY.

The letter was written on Navy stationery and filled with

misspelled words and no punctuation, but Janice Elderberry was blinded to all that from the tears that filled her eyes and ran down her face and spilled onto her uniform. "Oh, my, oh, my . . ," she murmured over and over.

Lanterno said nothing and sat on the edge of her bunk and watched and bit her index finger.

"Oh, how nice; what a beautiful kid," Elderberry said. She folded the letter and placed it under her pillow and dried her tears with a lace handkerchief she kept tucked in a sleeve cuff. She blew her nose. "He wanted me to know that the doctors saved his leg and that he's starting to use it a little and that his mother wants to thank me for taking care of him when Bud Pritchard brought him off the helicopter." She began to cry again. "And he wanted to tell me that if he ever gets married he hopes that the girl is just like me. Oh, what a sweet kid, Betty."

"They're all so young and they're sent over here not knowing much," Lanterno said.

"Not all of them are like Billy McGarvie; Billy is one that should never be sent to fight anyone."

"Have you had chow?" Lanterno said.

"I'm not hungry; you go ahead." She went to the small window and looked out across the complex of Quonset huts, bunkers, gun emplacements, red dirt roads, barracks, and a mile and a half away, the two five-thousand-foot runways and the aircraft revetments running the length of them.

Betty Lanterno adjusted the cap on her head and looked back at Janice. "Sure you don't want to have chow?"

"I'm really not hungry."

"I'll bring back something if you like. Salad? Bowl of soup? Dessert?"

"That's nice of you, but I couldn't eat a thing."

"What's troubling you, hon?" She walked to the window and put her arm around Elderberry. "Is it the letter from Billy McGarvie?"

The window frame shook from the engine thrust of two

Phantoms in afterburner passing overhead. They left a long trail of black smoke from their tail pipes, arching up into the clean blue sky.

"It's all of it—all of them," Elderberry said. "They keep coming in with missing arms, missing feet, holes all through their bodies—and what for? It all stinks."

"Take it easy. Don't think about it."

Janice turned her head to look at Betty Lanterno. "How do you deal with it? Are you able to stuff it away somewhere?"

"Maybe I'm just not as sensitive as you, or I've temporarily been blinded to what is really happening. It gets me through. I don't think about it like I used to." She patted Elderberry's shoulder. "How long have you been in country?"

"Five months."

"If you stay for two years like I have you get a little crazy and part of you goes to stone, a good part of you, the best part maybe, like it did with Buddy Pritchard."

The roar of the F-4s faded away and only the black smoke, now thin and transparent, remained to mark the jets' passage.

"I shouldn't have told you about Bud Pritchard and me. That was private."

Betty Lanterno shrugged and pulled at her light brown hair, which was cut short according to Navy regulation. She was a plain-looking girl like Janice Elderberry, but not plump like Janice; she was thinner and lacked the matronly soft round curves that Elderberry had. "Your secret is safe with me. Who am I going to tell, Ralph Thorbus?"

"He already knows."

"Precisely."

Elderberry's mouth dropped open. "You knew that? How?"

"He told me."

"That rotten . . ."

"Easy—you forget that you've only been here a few months. Ralph Thorbus and I have been here almost five times that."

"You and he haven't . . .?"

"It's been a long war, hon, and there isn't much to do once you've seen all the movies and read all the paperbacks and been to the O-club for the ten-thousandth time."

"You and Ralph?"

"It was short-lived—nothing to get jealous over."

Janice Elderberry turned back to the window and watched a group of Marines roll a 105 howitzer into a gun pit they had dug and begin stacking sandbags around it. She laughed and said nothing.

"If you're thinking that maybe Buddy Pritchard and I had something going too you're mistaken," Lanterno said. "I never knew who he was until you told me."

"It doesn't matter."

"Oh, yes it does—it shows all over you."

"Go to chow."

"Mad?'

Elderberry turned and smiled with her nice mouth. "No—of course not. Bring me a piece of chocolate cake if it looks good."

After Lieutenant, J.G., Betty Lanterno left for the officers' mess, Lieutenant, J.G., Janice Elderberry went back to watching the mud-Marines sandbag the howitzer. A young PFC just out of high school, thin and bare-backed, lifted a heavy sandbag off the six-by and nearly fell from the weight of it.

"How long will it be before he comes in like Billy? How many hot LZs will it take? On which patrol?" A tear trickled down her nose and dripped onto her hand folded under her chin resting against the window. She left the window and sat at the small desk and began a letter to Captain Bud Pritchard USMC aboard the USS *Coral Sea* somewhere in the Gulf of Tonkin.

She thought of telling him how sorry she was that he was married to such a bitch and that his wife's Sproul Hall speech at Berkeley didn't mean anything, but she knew that it did and maybe it would be better that she didn't say anything about Marjorie Pritchard's antiwar protests and spare him the embarrassment.

Then she thought that she would tell him again about how much she had enjoyed the wild night in the ammo bunker, at least until he told her about the rats, and that she wished he was still at Cung Mai Dong because she missed him more than she had ever missed anyone.

She wrote a whole page in her flowery feminine script and part of another before she decided that he didn't want to hear from her and tore the letter to pieces and cried for a minute, quietly, and thought of Billy McGarvie in the Navy hospital at San Diego and about the PFC outside in the red dust who was stacking sandbags around the gun pit.

If Bud Pritchard were here she could deal with the fear and frustration; and though she had never talked to him about how she felt, she wanted to now, before Betty Lanterno returned from the officers' mess with a piece of chocolate cake that she wouldn't be able to eat.

She took out a fresh sheet of stationery from the drawer of the desk and without holding back she wrote out her frustrations about Nam, signed the letter and sealed it just as Lanterno walked in with a big slice of chocolate cake. Janice Elderberry ate every crumb and walked over to H and S company to mail the letter to Bud Pritchard and feeling better than she had for a long time.

While Lieutenant, J.G., Janice Elderberry USN posted her letter in H and S Company at Cung Mai Dong Marine Base, and Marjorie Pritchard in Berkeley, California, discussed plans with Goodwin J. Rapshir and the Anti-Vietnam War Coalition for her next speech, Hai Van Phuong, the third woman in Captain Bud Pritchard's life, sat under the ancient yellow-barked tamarind tree that grew twenty feet from the community well in Song Xanh village ten kilometers from Ba Den on the Laotian border.

The Ba Den Mountains were heavily forested with triple-canopy jungle dominated by teak, mahogany, and ceiba trees and interspersed with small open plains and clearings of elephant grass and low-growing thorny shrubs in the river valleys and in the saddles of the steep limestone mountains.

In Song Xanh village the mornings were chilled by the mountain mists and a man could stand on a ridge and see for miles only island peaks floating in a sea of white fog.

By noon the cold fog would burn off and a hellish heat would cook the jungle, a steam heat from which there was no escape and that penetrated deep into the viscera, and not a breath of fresh air could be found until the sun went down; and several hours later the first mists carrying cooling breezes would drift down from China and settle in the valleys of the Ba Den Mountains.

Hai Van Phuong sat with her legs crossed and a bowl of rice in her lap. The rice was untouched and had been so for several hours. Flies sat on the rice and buzzed around Phuong, who stared at the dust or at the children standing around staring back at her while they picked their noses and snickered. Empty tamarind pods and rice husks were scattered about in the dust under the old tree, and a wrinkled woman squatted next to the well and tossed rice in the air from her winnowing basket.

"Come away, child," a mother said as she led away a five-year-old girl. The woman was dressed in a black cotton wraparound skirt that hung to her ankles, and she was bare-chested. Her breasts were large, firm, and brown.

The Montegnard girl accepted her mother's hand, but all the while she was being pulled to her family hooch she looked over her shoulder at Phuong, who sat in the dust.

"That woman will bring bad luck to us," the mother said. "Stay away from her—her mind is filled with a sickness."

"She won't eat her rice."

"Even animals eventually get hungry and must eat," the mother said. "Each morning the rice bowl is empty and the Old Woman of the Well fills it again."

"Maybe the dogs eat it."

The hooch was built up on stilts, and a narrow plank with bamboo ribs led up to the porch. A man dressed in nothing but a loincloth sat in the doorway whittling an arrow for his crossbow.

"What is going to be done about that Vietnamese under the old tree?" the woman asked her husband.

"She is doing no one harm," he said. "Maybe she will bring the village good luck."

"Crazy people bring bad fortune, not good."

The man stood and brought the shaft to his eye so he could sight down the length of it. "It is a good arrow—one of the best I have ever made. I will use it to kill an animal for you to cook." He stood and raised the child in his arms. "Would you like to go hunt for an animal to shoot?"

"Don't take her hunting with you. Only boys hunt with their fathers—she must stay with me."

"Pah! Girls should learn to hunt like men; they need to be made more useful instead of sitting at home all day cooking rice."

"It is traditional."

"Pah! for tradition."

The man's wife squatted next to the open circle of fire ringed with stones in the center of the bamboo-and-thatch house, and removed the heavy lid from the blackened kettle that hung by its handle from a wire attached to the center-beam pole in the roof. "If you had to go one day without rice you would find another wife to do your cooking," she said. "No man will do his own cooking, not in this village or any other that I know of."

He came to the fire ring and looked through the smoke and into the kettle that was filled to the brim with white puffy rice. The child began coughing from the smoke in the room.

There was no escape for the rising smoke except for a small hole cut in the roof. The man and woman paid no attention to the coughing girl. She always coughed and so did the wife.

"Let me have a bowl of rice before I go hunt for the animal for you to cook."

"Yes," the wife said. "You will be gone until the sun sits on top of the roof of the last house in the village and you will need a full belly." She filled a bowl made from teakwood, mounding it high with rice, and with her fingers she placed a heavily salted fishhead on the rice.

He cracked and chewed the fish head and made hungry sounds and smiled at his rice. He ate with his fingers.

"We must go into the lowlands soon and trade with the government Vietnamese for rice," she said. "We have only one basket left."

The husband pushed a ball of rice into his mouth with his fingers and didn't look up. Some of the rice spilled from his mouth, but he was careful to catch the precious grains in the bowl. "I hate the government Vietnamese. I would just as well kill them as kill the Viet Cong."

"The Americans pay you to kill the Viet Cong and not government Vietnamese."

"Pah! It's all the same to me."

"Tomorrow take cinnamon down to trade with the Vietnamese and bring back as much rice as you can carry," the wife said.

"It will be four days before I see you again."

"It is always four days. If we could grow rice in the mountains you could stay home and work in the rice paddies like the Vietnamese and not have to hunt."

"Pah! Growing rice is woman's work. Only men hunt."

"Then go hunt and let me hear no more of your babbling."

The husband finished eating his salted fish head and rice and took his crossbow and quiver of short arrows and walked down the plank and ribbed bamboo and into the village, where the old woman winnowed rice beside the well. "Good morning, Old Woman of the Well," he said.

"Good morning." She looked at the crossbow and arrows and rotated the flat shallow basket and tossed the rice into the air. The hulls floated away and the grains fell back into the basket. "This morning are you hunting animals for your wife to cook or do you hunt the Viet Cong?"

"It makes no difference—whichever first comes my way."

The old woman laughed (a cackle) and showed her toothless gums.

"How is the crazy one?" he said.

"She has been digging."

He sat beside her and looked at Phuong sitting under the tamarind. "How do you know she has been digging?"

"She has dirt and mud on her pajamas and hands and under her fingernails; she sits under the tamarind all day and at night she digs."

"Where does she dig, old woman?"

"I do not know; I only know that she digs and sits under the tamarind and eats the one bowl of rice that I give her each day."

"The rice is untouched."

"She eats it where she digs. In the morning it is always empty in her lap when I fill it."

"Strange."

"Maybe it is strange, maybe not," she said.

"Where does she come from?'

"No one knows—far away, I would think; she is Vietnamese, not Montegnard."

"Does she speak?" he said.

"Not a word. If she did I wouldn't know what she said; I don't speak Vietnamese. Do you?"

"A little."

The old woman rotated the winnowing basket and tossed more rice into the air. The hulls floated in Phuong's direction and a few caught in her snarled hair.

The sun moved across a silver-blue sky that was filled with streaks of yellow light and wispy long clouds. The Old Woman of the Well squatted with her back to the well stones and hummed ancient hymns with her scratchy voice and licked her toothless gums and recited poetry from the Chinese poet Lao Lin; the winnowing basket never rested, its twisting rhythm keeping time with the hymns and poetry and Calcutta bamboo that swayed in the hot breeze.

The hours passed and the old woman left the well and the sun came to rest on the roof of the last house in the village and the husband returned home with a small deer over his shoulder, the short arrow embedded deep behind the shoulder. The wife butchered the small deer and hung the carcass inside the hooch and cut off a haunch and laid it on the coals to cook. She coughed from the smoke and scooped rice into three bowls.

When the sun disappeared behind the mountains and the village was cast in darkness, Hai Van Phuong rose from under the ancient tamarind tree and walked into the jungle. To the calls of the night predators she paid no mind, nor did she search for a way through the thick, black, wet forest; she just walked.

An hour passed, possibly two; Phuong had no watch nor would she use one if she had it. There was no moon this night, and if there had been she would have been unable to see it through the triple canopy.

When she arrived at the spot where she had been digging, she sat on the pile of dirt and ate the bowl of rice that the Old Woman of the Well had given her. Then she crawled down into the hole and brought up the bundle with her possessions and took out the photograph. There was no light by which to see the picture, but she looked at it for an hour, maybe longer, before returning it to the bundle. She crawled into the hole once more and began to dig with her hands and a stick, the jungle night noises all around her and the fogs rolling through the forest and between the trees and covering her with its blanket.

Hai Van Phuong worked all night and into the morning. When the fog turned the color of slate she came up from the tunnel and lay down next to the pile of earth and slept, hugging her bundle.

The dreams this morning were the same. The family sat peacefully, but not talking, around the table in their hooch in Quang Hoa. The table was set with many good things, sour fish soup, *cho gio, nuoc mam* chicken, thick ban, roast pork with ginger, and several different dishes of rau. There was hot green tea and coffee and bowls of lichees and mangos and melon. No one smiled, all were silent, and the elder brother sat with a full bowl of rice in front of him and no head with which to eat it.

Mournful Viet music and the sound of a jet airplane filled the dream and a red, flickering glow came through the cracks in the bamboo walls. There was the dim smell of smoke.

"You and elder brother have decided to go to Cung Mai Dong to work?"

"Yes, Father," Phuong said. "I can get work sewing in a shop and brother will work in a restaurant as a cook's helper."

"In the evenings we will play music and sing for the Marines at the Cung Mai Dong base," Elder Brother said, though he had no head with which to say it.

With his chopsticks, Father picked a string of rau from a plate and ate it with a scoop of rice. "It is settled then. The extra money will help the family and we will be able to buy another plot of land to add to the land of our ancestors."

The glow reddened, but no one showed concern, except Phuong, who wanted to warn them but was unable to because each time she tried to speak of the danger her voice became a whisper drowned out by the roar of the jet airplane. In the corner of the hooch her grandmother tended baby sister asleep on the palm mat covered by mosquito netting.

"It is a long journey to Cung Mai Dong," her mother said,

an aging woman whose beauty had not yet been taken from her. "Many days."

"We will worry about you," Father said.

"And we about you," the headless elder brother said.

The other children remained silent and looked at their food, not eating. The crackling of the fire was near and smoke now became visible in the bright red glow. Hai Van Phuong tried to warn the family but her voice was only a distant whisper and the louder she tried to speak the farther away her voice sounded.

"You must be good children in Cung Mai Dong and not do anything our ancestors would be ashamed of," Father said.

The dream ended with the faraway sound of a jet diving and a Marine captain sitting beside Phuong in a jeep. His face was clear and she wanted to touch him while he bandaged her head; then she woke.

The slate color was gone and the dark green jungle was visible in the morning light filtering through the canopy. Long pencil streams of bright sun shot through the jungle, but none of it penetrated to the jungle floor where Phuong lay on her back looking up at the yellow beams.

Tired and weak, she touched the pile of dirt and was comforted and wanted to stay hidden down in the tunnel where she felt safe and secure, but something deep in her bruised mind urged her to return to the village and the children who stood around and watched her and to the old woman who looked like her grandmother and who brought her food.

The face of the kind captain was before her as she walked through the undergrowth wet with the early morning mist. She smiled at the memory of him but didn't know who he was or whence he came; only his face and its vivid recollection remained with her.

Patches of fog clung in the hollows and when she walked through them her hair became wet and held tightly pressed to her face and neck and she felt hidden and safe and she wished that the fog would stay with her wherever she walked and was saddened when she came out of the hollow and she could see the dark green jungle; she became afraid again.

High in the teak and mahogany trees and in the giant ceibas the blackfaced monkeys fought with each other and screeched at her intrusion into their private world and broke off branches and threw them down at her.

Again, far off, came the sound of a jet airplane and her weak body rebelled and quivered and she hid behind a tree and waited for the swoosh of rockets, but nothing came and she cautiously looked out from behind the tree and when she saw that there was no explosion and no fire she again took up the path that she imagined led back to the village.

At the well the old woman sat with her back against the stones and listened to the hot breeze rustle the feathery leaves in the tamarind tree and to the crank and creak of the windlass hauling up the water bucket from the bottom of the well. The children laughed and played with their stick guns and with the tamarind seeds that had hardened in the sun.

The Old Woman of the Well looked at the empty spot under the tamarind and was worried that Hai Van Phuong was not there. Usually when she came to the well to winnow the rice, the crazy girl was sitting as she had left her the night before.

As the sun moved higher in the sky the old woman became more concerned and went to the husband and wife that lived in the fourth hooch from the one where the sun rested on the roof before disappearing behind the mountain. She stood below the plank with the ribbed bamboo steps and clapped her hands.

The wife came to the porch and looked down. She was wearing her wraparound skirt and a bright red scarf around her long silky hair. Her breasts were bare as usual except for a necklace of tiger teeth that hung in the cleft. "What do you want, Old Woman of the Well?"

"Call your husband. He must go look for the unfortunate

one."

The husband walked onto the porch and stood behind his wife and chewed on a leg bone from the muntjac he had killed the day before.

"She did not come back to the tamarind tree this morning," the old woman said.

"My husband has no time for crazy women who walk off into the jungle and get lost. He has work to do in my house."

"Pah!" the husband said. "I have no work to do here and there are no Viet Cong about to kill and we have enough meat from the muntjac to last two more days. I will help you find the unfortunate one."

The wife gave him a disgusted look and disappeared into the house.

The Montegnard husband traced the steps of Hai Van Phuong from the tamarind tree into the jungle and trailed her to the tunnel diggings. There he found her bundle and replaced it after looking at the photo of her family and examining her meager belongings; he then followed her trail back toward the village.

A short distance from the diggings he found her in the fog hollow where she had heard the jet plane and collapsed in the wet leaves. Laying her roughly over his shoulder he located an animal trail back to the village and within an hour was back at the well, where he deposited her next to the old woman.

Along the way he had killed another muntjac with his crossbow and he laid this beside the old woman. "The unfortunate one is weak from hunger. The rice you feed her is not enough. Give her meat every day."

Chapter 11

Alpha-Charlie-Nine dropped out of sight below the *Coral Sea*'s bow, and the catapult officer stood erect and stared at the spot where the F-4J had slipped away. Three long seconds passed and the bow plunged over the back side of the ocean swell and the Phantom's anticollision light came into view. The cat officer relaxed and waved the next F-4, Touchdown Dash Three, onto the catapult.

The sweat poured from Bud Pritchard's body and his flight suit soaked it up as though he had stood in the rain all night.

"Friggin' cat shots," he said.

"It wasn't so bad, Captain Marvel." Dale Keilman watched the *Coral Sea* slip behind Alpha-Charlie-Nine, the black hull bright with phosphorescence from the swelling sea. "You did real good this time—feet to spare."

The altimeter wound up to 100 feet, and Bud Pritchard brought the jet around in a climbing turn to the northeast and passed over the picket ships. Alpha-Charlie-Nine, loaded heavily with fuel and bombs, climbed sluggishly into the sunless morning sky to take up an orbit around the carrier and wait for the three other jets of Touchdown flight to form up.

Banked at forty degrees, the F-4J climbed and turned in a wide circle, and the two men watched as one by one Dash Three, Four, and One were hammered into the sky over North Vietnam and climbed for Alpha-Charlie-Nine's tail pipes.

In less than a minute Bud and Dale had reached the bottoms of the clouds and they were into the gray, cottony wet world that strike pilots have learned to accept as a way of life though never fully overcoming their fear of it.

"Weatherman was right on for the bottoms," Pritchard said. He watched the altimeter swing through 1,500 feet. "Let's see how well he did on the tops."

The farthest Bud could see was ten feet beyond the blinking red anticollision light on the end of each wing. Beyond that was gray dishwater.

On the open frequency, Bud listened to transmissions between the pilots getting shot off the carrier; and then he heard Benny Sanchez call him.

"Touchdown Dash Two, Dash One."

"Go, Dash One."

"Where's the top of this crap, Pritchard?"

"I'm at base minus four and all I can see is my nose."

Another two minutes passed. The pea soup thinned and streaks of light came through, then closed again; then came a dull blue glow, like the one a painted lightbulb gives off over the bandstand in a cheap bar, and finally Alpha-Charlie-Nine broke through the cloud tops and Bud and Dale looked into a bright orange ball chinning on the eastern horizon.

"Good morning, Vietnaaaam!" First Lieutenant Dale Keilman said from the backseat. He laughed loudly and keyed the radio. "Touchdown Dash Two is in the clear at base plus five. Congratulations, Ensign Jasper Cole USN."

The Phantoms from Touchdown flight hit the tanker

and topped off their fuel tanks and wheeled west at 550 knots to find the corridor over MiG Ridge.

The four F-4s sailed in the pristine air high above the clouds, nothing but rich, warm, energizing sunlight beaming through the front of the cockpit Plexiglas and into the welcoming faces of the pilots and RIOs. The Phantoms, way out ahead of the A-6 and A-7 attack planes, would find the ingress corridor, probe the NVA defenses, and bring the attack planes in behind them.

At this point there wasn't a great deal for Bud Pritchard to do but keep on Major Benjamin Sanchez's right wing, 100 feet behind and a few feet below, and feel the warm sun and sweat beads on his face.

The scenery consisted of the most intense cobalt blue sky imaginable and a fierce yellow sun ringed in silver, and below the planes, an endless carpet of snowy cotton. Other than that there was nothing for Pritchard to look at except the olive green Mark-82 500-pound bombs slung on racks beneath the wings of Sanchez's jet and the AIM-7 and AIM-9 air-to-air missiles poised on launch rails.

Beneath the F-4s and hung on hardpoints on the white bellies was the 2,000-pound centerline external fuel tank. Over Haiphong these ran dry and the aircraft commanders jettisoned the tanks after moving echelon right to avoid collisions.

All alone, Touchdown flight, directed by its radar controller in a cruiser designated Red Crown that lay off the coast in the Gulf of Tonkin, passed the coastline and dashed into North Vietnam.

"Touchdown is feet dry," Benny Sanchez radioed to Red Crown.

"Roger, Touchdown. Turn to two-eight-zero and steer for three minutes. You are alpha-three, bravo-one, at Bull's-eye-sixty."

"Rogerrrr, Red Crown—alpha-three, bravo-one, at

Bull's-eye-sixty and turning to two-eight-zero; will steer for three minutes. Go to strike frequency, Touchdown—we are on scramble."

Sanchez began the slow turn, and the other three jets followed him through the turn, maintaining position, and leveled their wings when the compass needle on the instrument panel below the gunsight came around to a bearing of 280 degrees magnetic.

"Dash Two, are you up?" Benny Sanchez said.

Bud Pritchard clicked the mike button twice on the control stick as a signal that he was on the strike's assigned frequency.

"Dash Three?"

Clicks.

"Dash Four?"

Clicks.

"My system shows guns locking on at three o'clock," Dale Keilman said on the ICS.

"Roger that—we'll be getting into a world of hurt if Sanchez doesn't get us down soon, like right now."

"SAM launch," someone said.

"Pick it up as it comes through the cover."

"Wish we had chaff."

"Let's get down on the deck," Bud said.

Red Crown was back on the air: "Turn to two-five-five, Touchdown."

"Rogerrrr, turning to two-five-five."

Pritchard was getting impatient. "Dash One, Dash Two."

"Go, Dash Two."

"We've got guns and SAMS and we're sitting ducks up here. Let's get down below."

"Get off the air, Pritchard," Sanchez said.

Bud went to the ICS. "I'm going to drop my bombs square on his canopy if he doesn't get us on the deck where we have a chance."

"Right, Captain Marvel," Keilman said. "Why don't you take the flight in?" There was a quiet chuckle over the intercom.

Two more SAM calls came in.

Pritchard decided to take matters into his own hands. "Red Crown, Touchdown Dash Two."

"Go ahead, Dash Two."

"How far do you put us from target?"

"Bull's-eye and forty."

Bud consulted the map on his kneeboard. The long finger of MiG Ridge ran out from Haiphong toward Hanoi where the shadowed imprint on the paper ended at the MiG base at Kep. He quickly made the computations and got back on the radio with Sanchez. "Benny, the ridge is five minutes away on this heading, time enough to get down on it and make our run without detection. What do you say?

"The bottom of the overcast is two-grand, the top of the ridge, three. Do I have to draw you a picture?"

"Weather reports are never on the money," Bud said. "Jasper called it perfect off the carrier."

Pritchard could see there was no use arguing with Benny Sanchez. He switched to the ICS. "We're going down to take a look . . . alone."

"What kind of chow do they serve in the ship's brig?" Dale said. "This ain't right, Captain Marvel."

"I'll let you out and you can take a taxi home," Bud said and at the same time rolled the jet over on its back and pointed the nose down into the clouds, throttles pushed to the stops.

Alpha-Charlie-Nine quickly dropped out of formation and was lost in the clouds.

"Ease us down gently," Dale Keilman said. "I've got a bad case of hemorrhoids."

He figured that if Benny Sanchez ordered him back into formation he would go, but not until he had checked out the cloud bottoms. He had a feeling that Sanchez wouldn't say anything, at least not right away, giving Bud a chance to find the bottoms and the corridor or to hang himself good. Either way, Benny Sanchez was safe—Bud had not been given permission to leave formation, but neither had he been told to stay.

The altimeter unwound: 15,000 . . . 12,000 . . . 10,000 . . . 9,000 . . . He checked his map; MiG Ridge had a maximum elevation of 3,100 feet. *Now, if the map-makers haven't made a mistake.* There was no call from Dash One.

Easing back on the throttle, he also started the stick back. The altimeter read 7,000 and began to unwind at a slower rate. Alpha-Charlie-Nine eased down to the cloud base—7,000 . . . 5,000—and still no indication of clearing.

"Feel any scraping yet?" Dale Keilman said, then added, "We don't have to worry about MiGs in this pee."

At 4,000 feet glimpses of the ridge came up through the broken cover, craggy outcroppings of dark stone and strewn rock, and were quickly lost once more in the dense clouds.

Feeling for the cloud base, Pritchard gently pushed the stick forward and throttled back more and dropped another 500 feet. The Phantom broke into the clear, skimming the top of MiG Ridge.

"*Mama mia,*" Dale Keilman said. "Shazam! and Captain Marvel does it again."

Off the right wing was a narrow trough that ran along the ridge, deep and protected by high walls on both sides.

"There's our corridor, Dale. Let's go bring the guys down."

Pritchard called Red Crown and explained that the attack planes could ride the trough along MiG Ridge all the way into the target with nearly 1,000 feet to spare below the cloud base. When he powered through the overcast, Touchdown flight was three white dots in the cobalt sky.

"Touchdown Dash One, Dash Two."

"Where are you, Pritchard?" Benny's voice was sharp.

"Two miles behind you. Did you copy the transmission to Red Crown?"

"I did. Get your buns in formation . . . you had your little sightseeing trip for the day."

"We've got it knocked down there: a thousand-foot-deep canyon below the cloud base—a clear shot into Chuc Luc. What more could you ask?"

"My equipment is going bananas. . . . We've got SAMs launched all around us," Dash Three said.

There were calls all around as six white telephone poles broke through the tops of the clouds and glistened in the intense tropical sun. Dash Four, trailing 300 feet aft of the flight, suddenly pulled up and rolled left, flames and black smoke rolling from the wing root.

"I've had it, Benny," Dash Four, Captain Dennis Mallory from Spokane, Washington, said.

The canopy blew away and the pilot and RIO ejected into the slipstream, the seats tumbling and twisting high over the vertical stabilizer.

"Better alert Rescue," Bud said to Keilman.

Dale pressed the mike button and gave the controller the coordinates of Dash Four's ejection. The crew's parachute beepers were strong in the earphones.

"Okay, let's take it down," Sanchez said, his voice not sharp this time. "Pritchard, get your aircraft up here and take the lead, and you had better be right about the cloud base or we're all just so much scrap metal."

Going to afterburner, Pritchard soon caught Dash One and Dash Three, checked his heading and corrected it a few degrees, then plunged the three jets into the rain clouds. In his earphones he heard Red Crown declaring an emergency for Touchdown flight. The A-1s and gunships were already in the air and vectoring for Dash Four's coordinates.

Captain Josh Billington USN, on the bridge of the USS *Coral Sea*, looked out through the windshield wipers and saw nothing but wind chop on the black, oily waters. "It's senseless."

"What is, sir?" Jack Hunter, officer-of-the-deck, said.

"That we take out a few SAM sites that will be replaced tomorrow by twice their number and the cost to us next time around will again exceed the payback." He looked down at the flight deck, which was empty except for a few recon Vigilantes and four BARCAP Phantoms on alert. "I've got sixteen aircraft heading toward potential disaster. The weather is rotten, chances are they won't even bomb the target, maybe a few rice paddies and farmers, an ox or two, and get clobbered going in and out. We've already lost one Fox-four." He shook his head and turned away from the windshield. "This is one of those missions that I have bad dreams about—the one that no one comes back from."

The bow of the carrier plunged thirty feet into a swell and the steel cables that held the tied-down Vigilantes strained in their eyebolts anchored to the deck.

"I'm going down to Mission Control, Mr. Hunter."

"Aye, aye, sir—and sir . . ."

Billington stopped at the inside door that led to the ladder.

"You might want to stop at CIC and listen in on the action over Chuc Luc. Might help to know just how the guys are doing—calm the nerves, maybe."

"Or snap them." Josh Billington descended the ladder and wondered why Jack Hunter always made him feel worse in a bad situation.

The mission planners bent over their charts spread on the tables. Lieutenant Commander Stanley Knudsen, a block-faced Annapolis graduate who had been too tall to fit in a fighter cockpit and was assigned multi-engines instead, stood alone at a wall chart that displayed the SAM sites surrounding Chuc Luc. The SAM rings were colored red, and many overlapped along the ingress and egress route that the strike aircraft would have to take. Stan Knudsen looked hard at those rings and massaged his face with the long fingers of his right hand and moved one of the multicolored pins to MiG Ridge.

"Think they'll get in?"

Knudsen was six inches taller than Billington and had to look down at him. "Don't know. Probably not; it's a real bitch this time. We've already lost one."

"I heard," Josh Billington said.

"Want me to recall them?"

"When in command—command," Billington said. "The mission is yours. I'm in command of the ship . . . you're in command of the strikes, and that's the way it's going to be on *Coral*."

A red-faced Marine second lieutenant handed Knudsen a message written on yellow paper. "CIC reports that Touchdown Dash Two found a hole in the weather and is bringing the strike force over MiG Ridge to the target. Benny Sanchez has passed him the lead and Red Crown has alerted the A-6s and A-7s."

"We have a corridor—what luck," Stan Knudsen said.

"Who's Dash Two?" Billington said.

"Bud Pritchard, the captain that came aboard TDY a few days ago," the second lieutenant said.

"Hmmmm." Billington studied the chart and rubbed his chin. "I don't think it was luck." He ran his finger down MiG Ridge and stopped at Chuc Luc. "I'm betting that the radar installation, barracks, and SAM and triple-A batteries will be ninety-percent destroyed. Any takers?"

He smiled and took two twenty-dollar bills out of his wallet. "We'll let the photos do the talking."

Everyone in Mission Control stopped what they were doing and looked at the *Coral Sea*'s skipper.

"Sir, you must have a lot of confidence in this Bud Pritchard," Stan Knudsen said.

Josh Billington placed the two twenties over Chuc Luc. "We've got that squadron of Marines aboard for just this kind of mission—on-the-deck bombing. No one in the world does it better, and I'm willing to take a gamble on Pritchard. If anyone wants some of that," and he pointed to the money, "we'll let it ride. I'll be in CIC if any of you want more."

After the captain left the planners, several men opened their wallets and dropped bills on Chuc Luc to cover the forty dollars and returned to studying the maps, charts, and tables and wondering who this Marine captain was that had suddenly raised Billington's confidence. No way would the target be destroyed. The strike force pilots couldn't find their ass with both hands in this weather.

Inside the Combat Information Center a red glow bathed the computer screens, instrument panels, communications equipment and the faces of officers and men. The room was compact, every foot of space efficiently utilized, and the men and officers monitored closely every sweep, blip, and signal generated by the electronics equipment.

When Captain Josh Billington entered CIC he sensed the tension. This was a *ten* mission and everyone knew there would be big trouble for the next couple of hours. Chuc Luc was heavily defended, the weather was shitty, and the planning had been hurried.

"Any MiG calls yet?"

Everyone recognized the skipper's voice and only a few heads bobbed up from the equipment.

"No, Captain, not yet," Lieutenant Nicholas Mancuso,

the communications officer, said.

"Radar coming up, Lieutenant," one of the *Coral Sea*'s threat receiver operators said. "S-band radar from the MiG base at Kep more than likely. Too powerful a signature to be from airborne MiGs. They have the strikers for sure."

"Would you like to listen in on the strike frequency, sir?"

"Thank you, Mr. Mancuso." Josh Billington took the headset and fitted it to his ears.

Nicholas Mancuso put on another set. They both listened over the discreet radio frequency to call signs being checked by the pilots and the usual background static, nothing in particular or out of the ordinary. Someone reported that the A-1 rescue planes had arrived on station with the Jolly Green Giant extraction chopper and the Huey gunships. Then the airwaves came alive with the action he had waited for, and Billington pressed the headphones tighter to his ears, his face wrinkling in concentration.

"Okay, I got acquisition, clouds breaking up," someone said.

"I can't see anything out my canopy," another voice said.

"Tomahawk One, this is Touchdown Two—you read me?"

"That you, Pritchard?" the A-7 leader said.

"Affirmative, Tomahawk."

"I understand you're going to walk me down through this shit."

"Affirmative, Tomahawk One; listen up. Give me your location and EDP."

The leader of the A-7s gave his position, course heading, and time readouts and Bud began talking him and the attack planes down through the overcast and into the protective corridor for the bomb run on Chuc Luc. The

A-6s, five minutes behind the A-7s, monitored the cockpit talk between Bud Pritchard and Tomahawk One and flew the corrected course to follow the A-7s down onto MiG Ridge and into the trough.

A few minutes passed in confusion because the strike frequency was garbled; then Red Crown (all cozy in his cubicle on the cruiser) came on with the warning that radar emissions had stepped up from the MiG bases, and the action picked up again as the strike force approached Chuc Luc.

"Tomahawk One, this is Touchdown Dash Two, your target is two o'clock, come around to two-seven-five, range now twenty miles. Keep your ECM systems on and watch for the hundred- and hundred-twenty mike-mikes at three o'clock and the fifty-seven and eighty-five mike-mikes at eleven o'clock. I'll be going in ahead of you with three Fox-fours to knock out the guns; at this altitude we'll all be looking down their throats. Good luck."

Captain Josh Billington USN removed the headphones from his ears and handed them to Lieutenant Nicholas Mancuso USN. "What makes them do it?"

Mancuso looked at Billington, puzzled by the remark. "Sir?"

"Where do we get men like that?" He stared at the communications officer, the red lights shadowing his face and the deep creases at the corners of his lips and in his forehead. He turned and headed for the hatch and the ladder and without turning back to look at Mancuso, muttered: "Every day they climb into their jets and go north to face death—where do they come from? Where do they get the strength?"

As the rocks and craggy surface of MiG Ridge swept past the wings of Alpha-Charlie-Nine, Captain Bud Pritchard USMC held the control stick firmly but with a sensitiveness that could be likened to a patient, experienced lover stroking the thigh of a woman in heat who was not quite ready but real close and any false move could cause her to change her mind. He sensed rather than controlled Alpha-Charlie-Nine, and every shimmer and creak in the jet's airframe, each surge in pressure on the controls and wiggle on the gauges, told him what to do to keep the F-4 tracking to the target.

In the backseat, Dale Keilman concentrated on his instruments, totally unaware of what was streaking by outside the canopy, counting off the time to target, giving course corrections, monitoring the North Vietnamese gun and missile threat display on the radar and operating the electronic countermeasure system.

"We've broken their lock-on, Captain Marvel, and I'm shutting down the ECM. No need to press our luck. I don't think the gomers have a clue as to where we are."

Unexpectedly the trough made a right turn and emptied out into the plain, and Alpha-Charlie-Nine thundered off MiG Ridge and down the alluvium fan and into the paddies and farmland.

"Target ahead," Keilman said in the dry stiff voice he always changed to when it was time to earn his pay. He was leaning forward into the radar, and his hands moved across the consoles in a flurry of activity.

Looking up, Bud estimated that the cloud base had fallen to 900 feet around Chuc Luc, and he radioed Tomahawk to tell him about the new bottoms. The A-7 leader was bringing his attack planes onto MiG Ridge when he got the call. He in turn notified the A-6 leader that the cloud base was as stated and that he should have no trouble getting down per Touchdown's instructions. The bomb run with Pritchard in the lead moved to the next phase.

"Okay, Captain Marvel, how many runs do I have to

set up? I recommend we pickle the whole load on the first and then we go MIGCAP *rikky-tik*."

"Two runs," Pritchard said, and his left hand lifted off the throttles and turned the ordnance selector switch on the control panel to pickle two racks of bombs, half of the sixteen 500-pound Mark-82s the Phantom carried.

On his kneeboard, Bud had clipped the bombing data which he now consulted; he made adjustments on the bombsight.

"Come four degrees left," Keilman said. "Two minutes to target."

The A-7 and A-6 flights had both made it through the overcast and were in the trough and thundering toward Chuc Luc. None of the aircraft had been fired on since coming down from altitude.

"Steer two degrees right—you should have visual any time."

"Roger . . . two degrees right."

Alpha-Charlie-Nine passed over a row of palm-and-thatch hooches and people scattered into the treeline. A farmer fell off a water buffalo he was riding and hid under the animal; a woman picked up a rock to throw.

Bud eased back on the stick to clear a treeline and then dropped down on the other side. The paddies were a blur and as the jet passed over, a rooster tail of water erupted and trailed the Phantom's twin tail pipes over the flooded rice fields.

Bud flipped a switch, and the piper on the sight glowed red on top of the instrument panel. He looked through to sight on the gun emplacements that loomed at him from the end of the long stretch of rice fields. "Benny—I'm taking the one-twenties on the right. You clean up on the one-hundreds."

"Rogerrrr, Dash Two—good luck," Benny Sanchez said, navigating on Pritchard's run. "Dash Three, you take out the eighty-fives on the left."

"Two runs," Pritchard said. "We'll take the SAMs and troop barracks on the second run and anything that's left of the triple A."

A black puff of smoke with a flash of fire in the center erupted out the right side of the canopy. Another at twelve o'clock, one at two, all high.

Sanchez's steady voice came over the radio: "The gomers onto you yet, Dash Two?"

"We're taking some flak."

"We're locked up," Keilman said. "Better maneuver."

"No room for jinking . . . we're steady on the target."

The three jets rocketed over a road and porpoised up and over another treeline and then down the paddy dikes and across the green, waving rice, over more hooches and a line of ox carts and farmers with mattocks over their shoulders. The Phantoms were fifty feet off the ground, and the NVA gunners brought the bores of the artillery down to the horizontal and felt for the range.

With the throttles advanced to the stops, Bud ignored the new muzzle flashes concentrated on the road crossing he was rapidly approaching. The red goofballs and tracers arched out like hot third rails of subway tracks and ranged for Alpha-Charlie-Nine. Keilman looked up from the radar in time to see the molten stuff lining out from the road crossing, and he involuntarily ducked behind the instruments.

Pritchard pulled RPMs off the engines and the nose dipped and the Phantom dropped the necessary ten feet and the white-hot cannon shells sailed over the canopy, trailing long tails of white smoke.

Then they were through the crossroads and gone before the gunners could get turned around. Another blur of treeline, up and over, and across the waving rice. The rain was blown from the windscreen as fast as it settled.

A herd of bullocks, their massive heads and heavy horns clearly visible, stood dumb and nervous in a rickety bamboo corral, hearing the scream of jet engines but not seeing the aircraft. The feeling of intense speed was intoxicating, and Bud Pritchard wanted to be nowhere else.

"Drop off a couple, Bud." Sanchez was having trouble keeping up.

"You got it."

"There's the one-twenty mike-mikes," Keilman said. "One near the radar van and the other about five hundred yards behind in the hillside."

"We're on final, Benny."

Bud looked at the gauges and discovered that he had pulled up to 100 feet. A large green-covered hill, at the bottom of which the gun pits were dug, rose slowly behind the Chuc Luc defenses and disappeared into the overcast of thick gray clouds less than 1,000 feet above him.

He scanned the gauges one last time, flipped the master arm switch that put power into the bombing circuits, and pressed the mike button: "Two's in hot."

"Right behind you," Benny said.

"We're dead on—can't miss, Captain Marvel."

The air was thick with flak and tracers; the plane rocked with the explosions, and the hot shrapnel sizzled and crackled around the canopy. A long line of muzzle flashes erupted off to the left, and the third rails reached for Pritchard.

Fighting to concentrate, he looked through the sighting glass and placed the glowing piper on the bottom of the gun emplacement directly in front of him. The jet rocked to the right with a flak explosion and he fought the controls to bring Alpha-Charlie-Nine back on line with the 120mm antiaircraft gun.

At the last moment Bud Pritchard decided to go after both 120mm guns on the same run and quickly changed the bomb selector setting. The last seconds stretched beyond real time, and Pritchard saw the action reduced to slow motion. The flak bursts became incandescent black flowers with beautiful streamers of petals, stamens and pistils unfolding before him, and the long white-hot silver stream of 23mm tracers was slowed to the flashing of Fourth of July sparklers. The rain falling on the paddies was so clear that he saw the splashes of muddy water rise from the surface as the raindrops hit. The tropical foliage seemed to curl back from before the hooches, and he could see the cooking fires and rice pots and big-bellied children sitting on the dirt floor with bowls in their hands, and he remembered Quang Hoa and the look in Phuong's long eyes when she learned that her family never woke on that fateful overcast morning.

His thumb rested on the stick pickle and the cross hairs were perfectly centered on the gun pit and he thought of Phuong's family and the A-6s and A-7s coming in behind him; the thumb hesitated a crucial half-second—and then mashed down hard.

The bombs kicked off two at a time, a fraction of a second between releases, and the aircraft vibrated across its frame as the ordnance dropped free. Looking down the nose, Bud passed over the battery and saw the faces of the crew looking up at him, their brown uniforms, brimmed pith helmets and sun-browned skin clearly visible in the rain. An instant later they were blasted into eternity along with their artillery piece, sandbags, and radar-controlled equipment.

Turning the plane a few degrees, Pritchard lined up on the second 120mm battery. The little men were in a confused state of activity loading and firing the weapon, pointing at the F-4 boring down their throats, jumping around each other and over the sandbags and into trenches dug near the pits.

Bud Pritchard didn't think of Phuong this time. He leveled the wings and centered the sight on a small brown man dressed in black pajama bottoms and a brown tunic with ammo pouches on the front who had for some reason jumped on top of the wall of sandbags in front of the gun. He might have had a rifle and might have intended to use it on Bud, but by that time Pritchard rippled his next load and flashed by at Mach 1 and felt the shock wave of the blast jolt Alpha-Charlie-Nine, and the man on the sandbags and all his buddies were vaporized in an instant.

The green hill filled the windscreen and the land began to rise quickly.

"Pull up, Captain Marvel," Dale Keilman said, "unless you want to share the cockpit with a grove of banana trees."

The needle on the altimeter climbed up the numbers, and the green carpet raced underneath and quickly disappeared in a gray mat of clouds.

"How you doing, Dash One?" Bud said.

"Right behind you."

"Dash Three?"

"Still here."

The clouds enveloped the three ships, and Dale Keilman, navigating in the backseat of Alpha-Charlie-Nine, brought the F-4s around to the east end of Chuc Luc for their final run.

Bud checked on damage. "How'd we do, Dash Three?"

"The two one-twenty mike-mikes are down and I think Sanchez got the one-hundreds. I don't know about the eighty-fives. Fires burning and plenty of smoke."

"What do you think, Benny? Shall we leave the barracks and installations to Tomahawk?" Bud said, not wanting to take all of Sanchez's authority away.

But Benny threw the ball back to Pritchard. "You've got the lead, Dash Two. You got everyone down through the muck and on the target so you might as well follow through. I'll take over when we go MIGCAP."

Keilman called the turns and read off the elevation numbers, and when they were ready to come down out of the clouds for the second run, Pritchard radioed the attack planes.

"Tomahawk, this is Touchdown. Our last man through reports heavy damage to the triple-A and Chuc Luc on fire and the target covered with smoke. We may have hit some fuel. We are commencing our final fire-suppression run." He pulled off five percent RPM on the engines and banked down. "Your run should be east to west with plenty of top cover, and you have no SAM threat."

Two large batteries were still firing when Pritchard pulled level, and small stuff along the treeline on the north side of the main defense pumped out shells in long lines. Knowing that Dash One and Three would take the artillery, Bud concentrated on the SAM site.

He went through the final setup once more (Keilman ticking off essential instrument readings), pulled off another two percent, tried hard to ignore the red and white streaks that came right at him and at the last minute flashed under the jet, checked the ordnance panel setting and scanned the gauges a final time and made the radio call: "Dash Two in hot on the SAM."

Six Russian SA-2 surface-to-air missiles sat on launchers out in the open and were pointed into the clouds, their radar control shack only 100 feet away. White-hot, smoking artillery shells crisscrossed in front of Alpha-Charlie-Nine's nose, and the little brown-uniformed men were everywhere, running in confusion and pointing at him. Why did they point?

As Bud rippled the last of the dark green Mark-82s and the F-4 jolted when the racks were emptied, Red Crown radioed that MiG-21s were airborne out of Kep.

Chapter 12

Captain Josh Billington USN drank coffee from the white cup with gold Navy wings painted on the side and hung up the radiophone. "That was COMSINCPAC," he said to his executive officer, Commander Darrel Seals from Little Chute, Wisconsin. "They want a full report on your Yankee Station operations since our arrival for the second tour. Seems some senator is making a stink about Bud Pritchard's wife and wants an investigation."

"Hope that call was on satellite scrambler," Darrel Seals said.

They both laughed and swallowed their hot coffee.

"No . . . we wouldn't want the gomers to see any more of our dirty laundry," Billington said. "I understand the State Department can't keep up with the number of U.S. types visiting Hanoi these days. What a dreadful mess."

"Pritchard know anything about this?"

"Couldn't. He's been too busy ducking punches his wing commander was throwing at him in Cung Mai Dong; and besides, the investigation is being kept under wraps."

"At least until some career-builder decides to leak it to *Stars and Stripes* or *The New York Times,*" Darrel Seals said.

The rain beat on the bridge glass, and the two men watched the weather worsen. Jack Hunter walked onto the bridge. Seals acknowledged his arrival but Billington continued to look into the rain.

"Not even ducks are flying in this weather," Hunter said. He hung his yellow rain slicker on a bulkhead hook next to the captain's dry gear and rubbed his wet hands together. "Weather's only fit for mad dogs and Irishmen," he said and smiled.

"That's mad dogs and Englishmen, Mr. Hunter."

Jack Hunter looked hurt for a few seconds, then quickly recovered. "Quite right, sir, sorry . . . Englishmen."

"No need to apologize, Mr. Hunter," Billington said. "A small matter." He looked at the radar to be sure the destroyer escorts had taken up their new positions. "A thousand yards out front—right on schedule." He signed the morning report after reading it and handed the clipboard back to Hunter. "Everything seems to be in order, Mr. Hunter, as usual. Now . . . as long as the North Vietnamese don't sneak a torpedo boat through our pickets and we recover the Marines all right, I'd say that we're going to have a good day on Yankee Station."

"Quite right, sir," Hunter said and left the bridge.

The phone on the bulkhead buzzed and Commander Seals answered. "Hmmmm . . . how many . . . yes, I'm sure the captain wants to be kept informed . . . thank you, Mr. Mancuso." He hung up.

"What does Nick have to report?" Billington said.

"Good news and bad news. They clobbered Chuc Luc. Your boy Pritchard got them in and we haven't lost any more ships . . . not yet, at any rate. The A-7s and A-6s are finishing up and the F-4s have gone MIGCAP. Fires burning everywhere."

"What's the bad news?"

"The entire North Vietnamese air force is up."

"A hell of a fight developing, huh?" Billington said. He

licked his lips and punched an open palm with a fist. "What an opportunity . . . wish I was up there with them."

"Touchdown hasn't reported contact yet. Shall I launch the Crusaders?"

"They'll never get there in time."

"How about the BARCAP?"

Billington rubbed his tight forehead and turned back to the storm. "Have to protect the carrier at all costs; keep the BARCAP in position."

The rain pounded the windows and the wipers were unable to keep up with the deluge.

"Go ahead and launch the F-8s," the captain said. "At max burners they just might get there to save Touchdown and the rest of those jarheads."

"Will they have fuel left to fight when they do get there?"

"That's a chance we'll have to take. Also, get all the A-6 tankers in the air and alert Sanders on the *Constellation.* Maybe he has fighters in the area around Chuc Luc that can lend a hand. Hell, get everyone in on this; send a CONSECPLN to the Air Force in Da Nang and Korat and tell them a turkey shoot is about to start over Chuc Luc and MiG Ridge the likes of which hasn't been seen since the Marianas and if they want to get in on it they better move fast. Every fighter jock in Nam will be kicking his ass for the rest of his life if he misses this one."

The three Fox-4s of Touchdown flight with Major Benjamin Sanchez USMC in the lead aircraft, AC-100, were spread in combat formation. Captain Buddy Pritchard USMC and his radar intercept officer, First Lieutenant Dale Keilman USMCR, were in AC-009 and spread

2,000 yards off Touchdown Dash One's starboard wing. First Lieutenant Henry "Mustang" Bronson USMCR, from Jacksonville, Florida, and his RIO, Second Lieutenant Buster Peck USMCR, from Cut-and-Shoot, Texas, were flying 2,000 yards off Dash One's port wing.

"Say altitude, Red Crown," Benny Sanchez said. "I didn't copy."

"Angels twenty-four."

"Roger." Sanchez quickly read the altimeter in the olive-drab instrument panel. "They're above us, Touchdown. Let's take it up a couple of grand."

The Phantoms raised their noses and climbed higher into the cobalt sky, three white fish in an ocean of blue air.

"Are we going head-to-head with them, Dash One?" Pritchard was anxious. He hadn't seen a MiG since the big fights of '66.

"Split 'em—keep the attack planes clear," Sanchez said. "Tomahawk . . . your people off the target yet?"

No answer.

"Tomahawk . . . Touchdown . . ."

"My last aircraft is off safe and egressing . . . A-6s going in. Smoke everywhere . . . fires burning . . . secondary explosions. Has to be fuel and ammo—can't be anything left down there. Tomahawk Three took hits in his tail and has control problems."

"Get out of there fast, Tomahawk. Red Crown has called fifteen MiGs heading for Chuc Luc and more heating up on the runways."

"Roger, Touchdown—we're gone."

Bud Pritchard checked the tones on his Sidewinders, and Dale Keilman watched the radar for the blips.

"Say range, Red Crown," Keilman said.

"Bandits Bull's-eye and twenty, turning to angels one-seven-five and closing. Speed one-point-two."

"Should see them soon, Dale," Bud said over the ICS. His head kept turning and he studied every patch of sky. *See them before they see you.*

"Bandits climbing to angels twenty-three, Bull's-eye and seventeen, turning to one-seven-one, speed one-point-two."

"Okay . . . I got 'em." Dash Three's RIO, Second Lieutenant Buster Peck, had picked up the lead MiGs on his radar. "Steer two degrees right, Dash One."

"Roger—we've made radar contact, Red Crown."

"We copy, Touchdown; watch for Fox-eights on cross heading to Bandits. Looks like you have help on the way . . . range, Bull's-eye forty, speed two-point-zero."

"They're hauling," Mustang Bronson said. "The Skipper made this decision. Mancuso doesn't have the balls."

"Okay—let's take it up another grand."

"How about a few more," Bud said. "Get the advantage."

No response.

"How's the fuel, Dash Two?"

Bud gave two clicks on the mike button.

As the F-4s climbed, long tails of exhaust smoke marked their position, an unavoidable condition of flying Phantoms in combat. The smoke could be seen for miles.

Pritchard's stomach twitched and he leaned forward to relieve the tension. It twitched several more times and he smiled. *Go ahead and do your flip flops.* He regarded it as a healthy sign and a good omen. Better to be nervous and alert.

The intense blue was cut through with long arms of thin clouds that looked like strings of small feathers laced together. They were all clustered at the same altitude, just above the Phantoms. Several dots appeared in the feathers and at first Bud thought they were MiGs, but they turned out to be only spots on the Plexiglas canopy.

"Let's start our turn," Benny said.

Clicks on the mikes; then nothing but the steady hiss and crackle of radio static. No one talked. Even Red Crown was strangely quiet.

They had turned away from the sun, and the sky took a silver-blue finish. Straight up over the canopy it looked almost purple. Bud breathed deeply to quiet his stomach, but it didn't stop it from twitching. The rubber smell of the oxygen mask was strong.

The white feathers floated by the jets and then there was a call from the A-7 pilot that had taken hits in the tail and he didn't think he was going to make it to the sea, but he had no choice but to try. His speed had dropped off and Tomahawk slowed to protect him—tough decision.

Then suddenly Pritchard had his own problems. RPMs on the starboard engine were no longer steady. The needle began to fluctuate.

"Did you feel any hits on the bomb run?" Bud said on the ICS.

"Nothing," Dale said.

"Some farmer must have gotten in a lucky shot." He reached forward and tapped the gauge glass. The RPMs steadied for a second then began to fall.

"Bull's-eye and five," Red Crown said. "Bearing one-seven-three, speed one-point-two."

The feathers drifted by the canopy and the sky turned hostile and danger crawled into the cockpit. Pritchard and Keilman strained to see the dots that should be there in the silver blue, but there was nothing, just the crisp, elastic ocean of air.

"Benny, I've got a rough-running engine," Bud said.

"How bad is it?"

"I've lost about five percent power and it's dropping."

"Dash Three—drop under Bud and check him out."

Clicks on the mike and Mustang Bronson slid out of formation and drifted under Alpha-Charlie-Nine.

"How's it look?" Bud said.

"You're losing hydraulic fluid from the wing root fairing—a steady stream."

"Better break off, Pritchard."

"Sorry—you're stuck with me."

"You didn't ask how I felt," Keilman said.

"You can get out and walk."

Bronson climbed back into position 2,000 yards off Sanchez's wing, and Bud turned inside on the other wing, one eye watching the sky, the other on the instruments.

Then they were there. Only dots, but unmistakably aircraft, less than 1,000 feet above him and at one o'clock, passing from right to left. Benny Sanchez had called the turn perfectly. The sun was behind and the intercept angle ninety degrees and closing.

The lead planes grew from dots in the windscreen to definite outlines. "Tallyho!" Bud said. "I've got MiGs; one o'clock and crossing to twelve."

"Got 'em," Benny Sanchez said. "Looks like four . . . no, six."

Clicks from Bronson's radio.

If the North Vietnamese pilots had seen the U.S. Phantoms, they gave no indication. They flew straight and in a shallow climb, the silver skins on the wings and fuselages reflecting brightly the morning sun.

The stomach muscles tightened and the adrenaline splashed into the bloodstream and Pritchard's face became taught and very wet. There was nowhere else for him to be—he had been born to it.

The mouth was cotton dry and the rubber taste was stronger than he remembered—a headful of sensations, all focused and pointed in the same direction. *Good morn-*

ing, Marjorie Pritchard, and what do you have planned for your day?

The MiGs began a slow turn into Touchdown flight, lazy and ballet-like, as though choreographed for the Marines' entertainment, a symphony in motion, silver fish in an ice blue lake; delicate, dangerous poetry—pound eternal heart.

Out of habit, Pritchard advanced the throttles, then remembered that he was not in the lead and it was his responsibility to protect Benny Sanchez. He retarded the throttles and glanced at the gauges. RPMs were falling steadily in the starboard engine. He tapped the gauge glass with the index finger of a gloved hand and the needle swung up to normal, and then began to fall back once more. *Weird.*

"Benny, better lighten up on the gas or we're going to overshoot," Keilman said. He was leaning forward, watching the dots retreat off the screen. "We need the angle, not the speed."

"Bring it in, Dash Two, keep me cleared."

"Roger—no sweat—everything is in front of you."

It was maddening; why hadn't the MiGs made their move? Surely they had seen the Phantoms. Pritchard felt himself reaching for the throttles again. Maybe the gomers were ignoring the MIGCAP because they wanted the A-6s and A-7s. The attack planes were more vulnerable, slower and not as maneuverable as the F-4s.

Pritchard waited, thinking; it didn't mesh. Something was wrong—he could feel it in the pit of his stomach, that feeling that came when a silent danger was hiding in ambush for him, what kept him alive at Quang Hoa, on Hill 506 with Billy McGarvie and at the river. He called the controller.

"Red Crown, Touchdown Two."

"Go, Dash Two."

"Say altitude of bandits."

"At your altitude, angels twenty-five, and at angels sixteen, range three miles, speed . . ."

Pritchard didn't hear the rest. *And angels sixteen,* he thought to himself. A second group, far below, in the soup, hidden from him at this moment . . . He flipped Alpha-Charlie-Nine over on its back and he looked down at the clouds and behind. Climbing fast into Benny's six o'clock, afterburners cooking, four silver MiG-21s, the red stars of their fuselages and wings bright in the heat of the sun, streaked in for the kill.

"Benny! Break right, now—or you're dead."

Major Benjamin Sanchez, a veteran of over a hundred combat missions, reacted instantly and broke hard, bleeding off energy and pulling more than 6 g's.

The North Vietnamese, booming through Mach 1, didn't have the strength to muscle their sticks over and couldn't stay with Sanchez.

Overshooting, the leader reversed his turn right in front of Pritchard and continued up into the metallic sky.

The leader of the attacking jets was the North Vietnamese Air Force ace, Major Nguyen Tan Hong, flying aircraft 4061, an unpainted Soviet-built MiG-21 Fishbed armed with four Atoll air-to-air missiles, copies of the U.S. AIM-9 Sidewinder. He was wearing a tight-fitting, ribbed black pressure suit made in Leningrad's Military Garments Plant No. 17 and an oversized white hard-helmet and attached green sun visor that slid over the top of the helmet when not in use. He had shot down *nine* U.S. Phantoms with No. 4061. One more and he would be a double ace.

When his force of twelve Fishbeds had been scrambled from their base at Kep, the thirty-four-year-old Hong had been sitting at a wooden table (made in the base furniture shop) with his pilot comrades, eating a simple breakfast of steamed white rice, cabbage soup (which gave him gas whenever he flew) and a small bony fish cooked in *nuoc mam.* His friends ate the same breakfast. There was seldom any variation in the meal, though occasionally pork was substituted for the fish, a privilege experienced by the officers over the enlisted men.

The rain pattered on the tin roof of the mess hall, and he contemplated the sensibleness of his participation in a war that had no beginning and as far as he could see, would never end. Vietnam had always been at war, and though Ho Chi Minh repeatedly encouraged the military and the civilian populace with his long-winded speeches that proclaimed, *Our struggles are nearly ended and our patience and determined persistence will see us through to a final and lasting victory of prosperity for all,* Major Nguyen Tan Hong would admit in private that the regime was too old and clung to outdated methods and beliefs that would in the end mire down the country in a morass of political bungling and economic disaster.

But Hong was a good Communist, and as he ran through the rain and mud to No. 4061, which waited in its concrete revetment hidden in the hillside, his mind geared up to meet the Americans on the blue aerial seas above the clouds, and by the time he had reached the MiG and placed his boots into the footholds on the fuselage of the delta-winged aircraft, he had already completed his mental checklist and formulated the plan to spring the trap for which he had been training his group over the past weeks. This morning had perfect conditions for success: high cloud cover with a clear sky above and at the altitude the Americans liked to fly.

He would be guided to the U.S. planes, as was customary, by a ground control intercept (GCI) officer and, as was also customary, employ the hit-and-run tactic that had gotten him his previous Phantom kills. Seldom did he or his comrades engage the Americans in their favorite tactic, the classical dogfight first employed in WWI and later perfected in WWII and Korea.

An educated man (a graduate of the National Institute of Aeronautical and Astronautical Engineers in Moscow, and one year at the Sorbonne in Paris), Major Hong had an active and alert mind and was curious about the lives of the men he met in combat. He sometimes pondered the possibility of meeting some of them after the war and discussing their customs, habits, and belief systems. Were their lives much different from his in Quan Lang, where he was born, obtained his early education and met his patient and loving wife, Ngoc, who had given him twin sons, Tan and Bao, now six years old, and a daughter, Hoa, who at thirteen promised to be one of the loveliest women in Vietnam? Did these American warriors eat nothing but meat as he had been told and did they fornicate with goats and sheep when women were not available?

Leaning into the cockpit of the single-seat MiG, No. 4061's crew chief, a small man with bony features and soft, dark brown eyes who was nearly as old as Hong, old by the standards of Americans, whose crew chiefs were often in their teens, strapped in the major and helped him go through the hurried check procedure.

"This morning will be good hunting, Comrade Tung," Hong said. The RPMs were coming up along with the familiar whine of the turbines.

"Number ten will be yours, sir; a double hero to be honored at Party Headquarters in Hanoi. They will be talking about you today in Moscow and Peking."

"You flatter me—but I do feel good about this one. Our ambush tactic has been perfected and we have had plenty of fuel shipments. We can mount a maximum effort this morning."

Tung smiled and tapped Major Hong on the helmet to indicate that he was secured to the ejection seat and plugged into the aircraft's electronic and life-support systems. "The war will soon end and we will be reunited with our countrymen in the south. I have family in Saigon."

"Ah, it has been a difficult and long war."

Tung climbed down to the ground and saluted. He pulled the wheel chocks and Major Nguyen Tan Hong throttled up and the Fishbed rolled out of the revetment and onto the runway, the cockpit descending to snap shut and seal in the major for his appointment with Captain Bud Pritchard USMC.

Long tails of condensation swirled off the tips of the MiGs' wings, and Benny Sanchez broke away from the North Vietnamese and looked back over his shoulder and saw that he was out of position to take them under attack. "Go get 'em, Pritchard."

"Roger—Touchdown Dash Two is engaging," he said not only for Sanchez's benefit but for all friendlies in the area. "We have contact with four MiG-Twenty-Ones and six others in sight."

There was static and crackle over the airwaves, and then a heavy Louisiana drawl broke through. "Where y'all, Touchdown? This is Air Force Dallas One and I've got four hot Fox-fours looking for some action. My Thud strikers are on their way home and we've got bookoo fuel to burn."

"Dallas One, Touchdown Two; we're six miles north of Chuc Luc. Come on down—the party's just beginning."

"Rog, Touchdown—save a few for us."

The radios began burning up.

"Where's the fight?"

"Over Chuc Luc."

"Jeez, and me low on fuel."

"We can lend a hand."

"Ident."

"Navy DF-100 from the *Connie;* I've got six Fox-eights on station over Cam Do."

"Ten MiGs at four o'clock . . . moving to three."

"Touchdown One, Tomahawk One. We've got MiGs eyeballing us on the deck."

"On the deck?"

"Repeat—on the deck."

"Get into the crud and scoot for home."

"Going to need help when we come out of it; the gomers aren't breaking off today."

Bud Pritchard shoved the throttles past the stops and lit the afterburner. Alpha-Charlie-Nine shuddered and leaped out past Mach 1, climbing fast after the North Vietnamese jets.

To Bud's surprise the four MiG-21s, almost as fast as the Phantoms, stayed together instead of splitting into singles or pairs. "These pilots are well trained, Dale; they're not going to avoid engagement."

As Major Nguyen Tan Hong brought his flight around in a wide turn, Bud tried to fly inside, but they had the advantage and were out-distancing him, so he slipped to the outside to keep up his speed. From experience he knew that if he kept up the tactic he could beat the MiG, but if he fell off below 400 knots he'd be an easy kill for the more maneuverable aircraft.

"Tomahawk, this is January leader." It was Josh Billington's F-8 Crusaders from the *Coral Sea.* "We are Bull's-eye and thirty, buster at fifteen grand and close to bingo, waiting to escort your attack planes home. Can you reach us?"

"There's five minutes between us, January."

That was like five years.

Major Nguyen Tan Hong kept the turn shallow, careful

not to bleed off energy, but tight enough so that the American could not pull the nose of his Phantom into his MiG and get missile lock-on.

Bud quickly went to the gauges and noted that the starboard engine was holding steady at sixty-percent power at full burner. The port engine was at 100 percent.

"How's it look, Bronson?"

"You're clear," Mustang said, flying his wing.

"Where's Benny?"

"He's got his own troubles. Two gomers jumped him after we engaged."

Bud could only hope that Benny Sanchez got away because he couldn't help.

"Big fight above us." Buster Peck said.

Pritchard shot a look through the top of the canopy and saw contrails crisscrossing the sky. "Must be Sanchez."

Suddenly the MiGs reversed left, went into a vertical climb 2,000 yards out front and split into pairs. Bud went up after them, taking the pair on the right. After a minute he was sure that the enemy aircraft had grown larger in the windscreen. He was gaining on them, not very much, but enough so that he had a slight advantage. They continued up, Alpha-Charlie-Nine gulping precious fuel.

"Bud, I hate to spoil your day but two twenty-ones are at three o'clock," Dale Keilman said.

"What!"

"Look left."

Two MiG-21s were climbing straight up with Alpha-Charlie-Nine, 1,500 yards off the left wing.

"The other pair," Bud said. "Let me know if they commit." He turned his attention back to the two that were ahead of him, convinced that he was going against a

MiG leader par excellence.

Orchestrating the performance with masterful skill, Major Hong brought Pritchard into position less than a mile behind him and began the loop back to tie in behind the U.S. pilots. The nose of his MiG pointed away from the sun and the angle widened off the vertical. He began to invert slowly, and he could clearly see Pritchard and Bronson through the top of his canopy (he had to arch his neck backward), in the vertical and climbing fast. He smiled behind the black oxygen mask and went to the gauges to watch the airspeed indicator rapidly bleed off.

Bud had two options. He could follow through the loop with Hong, losing precious energy, getting slow and vulnerable, or continue up into the vertical and break away with his speed intact. The first option would keep him in the attack mode and with a chance to gain a quick advantage that would put him at the MiG's blind six. The other option would be a disengage, and though putting him out of danger of the MiG scissoring him, he would have no chance for a shot.

Major Nguyen Tan Hong NVAAF was betting that Captain Bud Pritchard USMC would opt for the former and stay engaged. He was correct, and Pritchard came over the top inverted with Alpha-Charlie-Nine's nose pointed into the MiG's tail pipe. Dale Keilman couldn't hold lock-on and yelled over the ICS for Bud to bring the nose down farther and tighten down on the enemy aircraft. They were totally inverted and the g's were high, over six, and each time Bud pulled another degree down, Major Hong pulled more g's and Bud's vision would blur and the cockpit would turn gray and he would have to back off on the stick that he held tightly between his legs.

The two combatants had engaged at Mach 1.4 (just

under 1,000 mph) and rapidly bled energy from their aircraft as they climbed into the vertical, then watched their airspeed drop to zero at the top of the loop.

Now they were screaming down the back side of the loop, the airspeed indicators winding up again, and Bud was accelerating past Hong, a place he didn't want to be. Bud dropped the speed brakes but it was too late and the North Vietnamese ace turned his MiG's nose down into the Phantom and rolled to the left.

Knowing that the scissors was coming and helpless to stop it, Pritchard did the only thing that came to him. He pulled the Phantom's nose farther down into the scissoring MiG, which increased the g forces that stretched the skin back from his face and pressed him down hard into the seat as if a ton of concrete were sitting on top of him. He could feel the blackout edging up, but he tenaciously held on and forced the angle to open between the two ships.

Down from the heights they came, rolling around each other, each pilot fighting on the edge of blackout to gain the slightest advantage to launch a missile.

In the headphones Bud could hear his call sign being repeated, but the g's were too overwhelming and he couldn't see except for a silver blur in front of him and all he could think of was that he had to get the lousy gomer before the riceball got him.

"Where's Bud?" It was Benny Sanchez talking to Mustang Bronson.

"I lost him when he got wrapped up with a twenty-one."

"Look at three o'clock," someone said.

"What?"

"Look low at three. A Phantom and a MiG-Twenty-one. That's Pritchard."

"Why doesn't he answer? . . . Touchdown Dash Two—

Pritchard, where are you?"

"Two MiG-Seventeens at nine," Bronson said.

"Okay, let's take 'em. You're on your own, Bud."

Major Nguyen Tan Hong was worried. He knew that though he held the advantage he could easily lose it. The F-4 was gaining energy, and the longer the fight continued the greater the chance the American would turn the tables on him. This was a good Yankee pilot, one that knew well the performance characteristics of the new MiG-21 Fishbed and who was capable of using his own machine to its maximum potential.

Hong's wingman had broken off, as had Bud's, unable to keep up with the fight, and was nowhere to be seen. He was alone and there were more of the American's friends in the air and he was getting low on fuel. It was time to disengage and save himself and the aircraft to fight another day. No need to press his luck. There would be better opportunities. The sky was blue, his wife and children were safe in Quan Lang, and he would get leave soon to go home. He keyed the radio and called his controller. "Number Four-oh-six-one returning to base."

Chapter 13

Tran Thi Ngoc peddled her old Peoget bicycle down Gia Voi Street. Her daughter, Hoa, pedaled beside her with one of the twins, Tan, riding behind her and holding tight to her waist. The other twin, Bao, rode behind his mother and made faces at his brother.

The family all wore black cotton pajamas that Ngoc had made for them. Ngoc wore a straw hat, conical and wide and with a white string that tied under her chin, as did her daughter, Hoa. The boys were bareheaded, their short black hair wet from the light rain falling in Quan Lang.

Gia Voi Street was the only street in Quan Lang that was paved; as the two bicycles rolled across the asphalt a fine spray lifted from the tires, and in between making faces at each other the twins watched the spray with fascination. There was little else to hold their interest during the ride home.

"Mother, shouldn't we stop at the marketplace and get some extra food for father when he comes home tomorrow?" the pretty young teenager, Hoa, said. "It has been many months since we have seen him and it would be nice if we had something special for him."

"Money is scarce, child, and we must be careful with how we spend it."

"Can't we at least afford a bit of crystallized ginger candy and a bottle of beer or two?"

Ngoc smiled across the few feet of space between them and was cheered in her heart that her daughter would think it important that her father be given something special upon his return home. She was a good girl and she must remember to find her a good husband.

"Father promised to bring us a toy airplane the next time he came home," Bao said, "like the one he flies."

"You are not to ask him for anything," Ngoc said firmly. "Father mustn't be burdened with your whims. He is coming home for a much needed rest and we must not put undue pressure on him." She was quiet for a few minutes, then said: "You are right, daughter, we should buy him something special. We will stop at the marketplace."

Though the small job she had at the government rice-distribution center paid only twenty dong a week and Hong's military pay wasn't much more, she was able to manage well enough if she budgeted carefully. There was never enough for luxuries, though occasionally an extra ration of rice and a small amount of pork or duck would mysteriously arrive from the cadre leader (a government reward for Hong shooting down another American airplane). Also, because her husband was an officer, the children attended the Communist Party Academy and not the regular Quan Lang communal school that the ordinary children of the town attended.

"Can we ask him to tell us stories?" Tan asked. "Father tells good stories. Why don't you tell us stories, mother?"

"Because I am busy all day at the rice factory and after I pick you and your sister up from school and finish cooking dinner and help you with your homework and take care of grandmom, I am very tired and fall asleep. Now stop chattering and give my ears a rest."

They stopped at the marketplace, a large open-sided

building with a tin roof under which squatted several dozen vendors with their goods spread between them on the floor or hanging from the roof. The freshly butchered pig meat, ducks, chickens, and bullock meat were displayed with great care, though without much consideration for cleanliness.

Piled in bamboo baskets were sweet potatoes, cabbage, bean sprouts, onions, cauliflower, ginger roots, bitter melon, black stringbeans, and the usual assortment of herbs, spices and fruit (mangoes, breadfruit, bananas, duran, and green oranges). A few cages of live chickens, ducks, and piglets were for sale, as were tanks of frogs, turtles, and blackfish and carp and eels.

"Buy an eel, mother," Bao said.

"Father doesn't like eel," Tan answered.

"I do."

"Father likes duran," Hoa added.

Ngoc looked into her elephant-skin wallet and did some mental arithmetic, then selected a fat carp, which the pregnant vendor wrapped for her in wet banana leaves.

"Can we get him a duran?" Hoa asked again. "Or tamarind candy?"

"Tamarind candy; yes, tamarind candy," the twins said. "Get father tamarind candy." They hopped around on one leg then another and clapped their hands.

"All right," Ngoc said. "Get your father the best tamarind candy you can find." She gave the children some money while she shopped for a fat duck and a large, heavy breadfruit.

Finished with the shopping, they mounted their bicycles and pedaled off into the rain, the children happier and looking forward to the reunion with their father, and Ngoc feeling a hard ball of anxiety growing under her heart for the safety of her husband. Far away, high above the rain clouds, she could hear him call to her and she felt his danger, and shivered.

Major Nguyen Tan Hong NVAAF made one more turn in the vertical rolling scissors then broke hard left and pulled the stick all the way back. The nimble Soviet jet responded instantly and carried Hong up and away from Captain Bud Pritchard USMC.

Pritchard shook his head, amazed at the quickness of the maneuver.

"Good grief, did you see that?" Dale Keilman said.

"I'm going to try and stay with him."

"No way—he's gone. By the time you get this hog turned around he'll have finished his second beer at the Kep O-club."

"I'm going after him," Bud said.

The stick was laid over on the inside of Bud's left thigh, and he gave Alpha-Charlie-Nine full rudder. The big Phantom came around in a wide turn and passed through one of the thin cloud feathers that temporarily masked Major Hong's departure from the fight. In less than one minute they were through the cover and broke out into the clear blue again; but Hong was gone.

"Eleven o'clock," Keilman said. "Look high."

Already the MiG was only a dot in the silver-blue ocean of air with no chance of Pritchard catching it.

On the outside chance that there might be friendlies ahead of the MiG and they might turn him, Bud sent out a call. He gave the location, altitude, speed, and direction that the MiG was traveling, and continued to follow the enemy aircraft. He checked his fuel and decided that he could pursue for a while longer with the

5,000 pounds that remained before he would have to return to the carrier.

A flight of F-8 Crusaders from the USS *Constellation* were in the area when they heard Bud call out Nguyen Tan Hong's flight path; they climbed to his altitude and began searching. "No joy, bogy dope," the F-8 leader said.

Bud fed him more data (he still had the MiG in sight). "The gomer changed to zero-five-two, speed, point-nine."

"Roger, Touchdown Two. He's somewhere around here. You sure about that altitude?"

"I've got something, Tex."

"Where?"

"Look at three, low."

Ten seconds of silence.

"I think we have a tallyho, Touchdown," the F-8 leader said. "Your friend is just below us . . . and about two miles east."

"Can you turn him into me?" Bud said.

"Affirmative, Touchdown; we're starting in."

Anticipating the new flight path for the MiG, Pritchard cut across the great circle and pushed the throttles around the detents and the F-4 accelerated out to combat velocity. The adrenaline flowed freely and he urged Alpha-Charlie-Nine forward by leaning into the straps and thrusting his neck ahead so that his face was closer to the windscreen and the gunsight. He knew it was silly, but it gave him some release from the tension and for an instant he thought back to when he was a small boy and rode a toy stick horse and went galloping around the backyard as though he were Wyatt Earp in Tombstone, chasing the Clanton gang.

The MiG began a slow turn into Pritchard, and the distance between the two aircraft shortened considerably. Dropping down and behind Nguyen Tan Hong, Bud fixed Alpha-Charlie-Nine on the MiG's blind six and was quickly within effective kill range for the AIM-9 Sidewinders.

"I'm going boresight, Dale. Get me a setup."

"You're fine—keep her coming." Dale worked to get radar lock-on.

Off to the left and high, Bud caught a glint of reflection. The four crusaders were flying close formation with the sun behind them, sitting high above Bud and the MiG.

"Okay, Touchdown—we rounded up that little doggie for you, now rope it and put your brand to him," the F-8 leader said.

"We're bingo, Tex," the wingman said. "My pumps are sucking bottom. It's *Connie* time for me."

"Right behind you, Shorty," Tex said. "Sorry we can't stick around to watch you splash the varmint, Touchdown. Glad we could help."

"Much obliged," Bud said. "Where do I send the case of Chivas?"

"To T. Texas Risser, care of the Birmingham Jail."

And then they were gone, rolling over so Bud could see their white underbellies, thundering back to Yankee Station and the USS *Constellation.*

Hong applied more right rudder and turned away from the Crusaders that were fast slipping from view. He watched the American jets grow smaller and then vanish into the cloud feathers, and he leveled his wings, throttled back to conserve fuel and set course for Kep and home for his visit with Ngoc, Tan, Bao, and Hao. Over the long lonely months he had missed his family terribly. Tomorrow at this time he would be with them, and his heart swelled with anticipation.

There's an old axiom among fighter pilots: "See your adversary before he sees you." Major Nguyen Tan Hong not only didn't see Captain Bud Pritchard USMC first, he didn't see him at all, and worse, he wasn't looking for him because he had made a second error: he thought of home and family when he should have concentrated on his flying.

The MiG-21 had poor rearward visibility and a wide blind area existed below and behind the aircraft. It was here that Bud parked his F-4 and Dale Keilman locked on the missiles. The MiG flew straight and level.

"He doesn't have a clue we're here, Dale."

"You've got lock-on; cleared to fire."

Bud Pritchard selected the firing sequence for the launch and got a good tone on the Sidewinders. The Sparrows were armed for backup in the event the AIM-9s didn't guide.

The MiG bounced in the turbulent air, rising and falling and shifting right and left as though it were a small model undergoing wind tunnel tests. The glow of its tail pipe was easily seen in the thin high-altitude air, and the sun's rays spread across the fuselage and wings in a spray of silver light.

"You're cleared to fire," Dale Keilman repeated.

The pretty jet danced in the sunbeams and Bud Pritchard did not fire, his thumb resting on the launch button. He couldn't bring himself to shoot—there was something very wrong about shooting someone in the air when he didn't see you. Grunts could bag their prey any way they could get it, but old pilots of Bud Pritchard's ilk lived by a different code—a throwback from WWI.

It was an unwritten law among duck-hunter purists that a duck should never be shot while on the water, and

Bud always made certain that his quarry was well into the air (not just rising) before pulling the trigger on his double-barrel 12-gauge Fox Savage. MiGs or ducks, it was the same to Pritchard.

"He's not going to stay there all day, Captain Marvel."

Sometimes Bud would have to stand up from inside the blind or throw a rock at the cinnamon teal and pintails that snuck in unseen among his decoys or at the big green-head mallards that he found resting in the potholes in the Owens Valley up around Big Pine and Independence and Bishop.

"Hey, Bud . . . can you hear me up there?"

There was a time he had taken Marjorie to the ponds in Independence and she grumbled so much all morning about his stupidity of sitting in a bunch of weeds and freezing his buns off just to kill a few defenseless water-fowl that he finally packed her up and drove the 300 miles back home without saying a word to her until they got in the house and that was to tell her what a bozo she was and that the next time they were in a restaurant together and she ordered chicken or duck or any other bird he would take great pleasure in shoving her meal, plate and all, up her ass. He then turned right around and drove back to the wetlands and spent the most en-joyable three days of his life hunting alone, just him and the Tule elk.

"Bud . . . are you okay . . . hey, Bud . . . talk to me."

He thought of the bobbing heads in the river and the splintered bamboo and the water turning red and Thor-bus congratulating him, and he thought of PFC Billy McGarvie and his doe eyes and peach-face complexion and how he talked about his mother, who would worry if he didn't write her every day, and he saw the rockets smoke out from underneath the Phantom's wings and explode into Phuong's hooch and he saw the look in the Viet Cong girl's eyes when the bullets from PFC Malcomb Dresser's AR-15 cut her in half, and his thumb mashed down on the top of the stick and he watched the rocket motor ignite and the missile streak for Major Nguyen Tan Hong NVAAF, a devoted father and husband.

"We've got a hot one," Dale Keilman said. "Tracking true . . . fire two."

Bud mashed the red firing button again and the second heat-seeker missile launched, the plume of smoke chasing the rooster tail ahead of it.

The explosion was spectacular. A fireball erupted in the aft fuselage and the tail fell off and black smoke poured out in a great streaming cloud. The tail section fell straight down, billowing fire and smoke, and disappeared into the gray clouds thousands of feet below.

At first Bud thought that the pilot would eject, but after a few spins of the remaining forward section it was evident that Nguyen Tan Hong was either dead, badly wounded or disoriented and unable to free himself from the stricken plane. The front half of the MiG followed the tail section down, the sun rays glistening off the spinning wings, fuel spewing from the ruptured tanks in a spiral of white vapor.

It was Friday, late afternoon, and the sun was descending behind Marine Corps Headquarters, 8th and I, in Washington, D.C., and the Sunset Parade was getting under way. In the bleachers along the parade ground were several hundred spectators, a usual mix of tourists, Washington residents and political figures entertaining guests, who had come to see the taking down of the colors, an inspiring ceremony of military pomp.

In addition to the usual gathering of spectators, officer candidates from the 43rd Officer Candidate Course, Marine Corps Schools, Quantico, Virginia, were also in attendance, their greens freshly cleaned and pressed, shoes spit-shined and their shorn heads covered by carefully stretched barracks hats.

Seated in the front row of the officer candidates was the commander of Marine Corps Schools, Colonel Norbert "Iron Jaw" Keane USMC, and Senator Chester T. Newman. Between the Marine colonel and the U.S. senator, dressed in a simple blue cotton dress (she had planned to wear jeans, but at the last minute conceded to her better judgment and conservative upbringing), plain black pumps, no jewelry, and a sweater and coat she had borrowed, sat Marjorie Pritchard.

Turning to Iron Jaw Keane, Marjorie smiled pleasantly. "It's been a long time, Norb; good to see you again. You didn't have to go to all this trouble for me."

"No trouble." He smiled back and his block jaw and wide mouth made his smile swallow his face. "Just thought that by watching the Sunset Parade you may get a better understanding of what motivates Marines."

"Or more particularly," she said, "what motivates Captain Buddy Pritchard—right?"

"I admire a woman who cuts away the underbrush and right away gets down to the hardpan," Senator Chester T. Newman said.

Norbert Keane's blue eyes widened at the senator's frankness.

"I think Colonel Keane's idea to first bring you to Marine Headquarters from the airport to see this most patriotic of ceremonies rather than deposit you directly at your hotel was an outstanding suggestion." Chester T.

Newman looked smugly at Marjorie Pritchard and waited for her to respond.

Marjorie Pritchard said nothing and turned her attention to the stirring beat of snare drums approaching from the barracks. Marching down the arcade in immaculate dress blue uniforms, the 8th and I Marine drum and bugle corps and drill team color guard swung onto the parade ground and an electric tingling carried up the back of Marjorie's thighs as the military beat quickened and the tall young men marching in precision cadence, backs rod-stiff, eyes frozen front, made a column left and started down the middle of the intimate parade ground, flanked by WWI cannon.

"Impressive," she whispered.

For thirty minutes she listened to the strangely emotional tap-tap-tap of the parade drums and calling of the bugles, and watched the clean, flawless motions of disciplined men performing close drill exercises with M1 rifles and fixed bayonets, and listened to the platoon commander, a first lieutenant, tall and wiry and as handsome a young man as she had ever seen and who reminded her of Buddy Pritchard when he was twenty-five, bark terse commands to the men. It was exciting, rousing, and yes—as the senator had said—patriotic.

And when Colonel Norbert Keane, seeing the excitement in Marjorie Pritchard's face as the bugler sounded tattoo and the colors came down, leaned forward and said, "This is the esprit de corps that drives Bud Pritchard," she didn't resent him.

The ceremony was over and the people in the bleacher seats quietly filed out into the street and parking lot to the cars and buses, their backs straighter than when they first came, their heads held higher and their eyes brighter. They talked in low voices if they talked at all.

Marjorie was concerned with the way she felt—her belief system was tottering. "That was sneaky to bring me here," she said to Norbert Keane.

"Marines are known for their unorthodox style and ability to adjust under fire."

She decided that he was still a ruggedly handsome man and that he would be an absolute buffalo in bed. His large jaw fascinated her. "How long has it been since you and I and Bud got together?"

"Just before his last tour in Nam; we all got smashing at Exeter's in Dago, remember? You did a torch number on top the piano."

"How well do you really know him?" she said.

"When you share a foxhole and your rations with a man you get to know him better than his wife." He stopped on the sidewalk, under a bare silver maple, and looked back at the parade ground. "I asked you to come to Washington in the interest of our country and in the interest of a man we both have spent a lot of time with and have feelings for. Bud Pritchard isn't perfect, but he deserves a much better shake than he's getting."

"From the Marines?" Marjorie Pritchard said, a note of sarcasm in her voice.

"You know what I mean."

The senator cleared his throat. "Mrs. Pritchard, you must be hungry after your long flight and maybe a little tired."

"It's Ms. and not Mrs., Senator, and, yes, I would like to rest before dinner. I take it you have plans for me this evening?"

The chauffeur dropped Marjorie off at the Carlton Hotel, a few blocks from George Washington University, and Keane went in with her while Senator Newman waited in the car.

At the desk, Iron Jaw asked to see the hotel manager and when he arrived Norbert Keane said in his most command-presence voice that it would be greatly appreciated by the U.S. Marine Corps if Marjorie Pritchard was given the best of everything and that the bill should be sent directly to the Commander, Marine Corps Schools, Quantico, Virginia.

The manager smiled his best hotel-manager smile, which was no more than a break at the corner of the lips, and said that he would personally see to it that the beautiful lady was well cared for.

Norbert Keane took Marjorie's hand in his and asked when he and the senator could call on her for dinner.

She looked disappointed. "Must the senator come with us?"

"I'm afraid so; protocol, you know."

"To hell with protocol."

He smiled. "Would eight o'clock be a good time for you?"

At the car, the colonel sighed in relief and looked at Chester T. Newman. "Round one is over."

"How does it look."

"Too early to tell, but I think we have better than even odds."

"This whole affair is an embarrassment to us all, especially to the President," Chester T. Newman said. "How do these creeps time their moves so effectively?"

"Who knows," Norbert Keane said. He sat back in the leather seat of the Lincoln and removed his barracks cap and placed it neatly in the center of his lap. "All I care about at the moment is that Marjorie Pritchard be prevented from going to Hanoi. The consequences could be devastating if she goes ahead with her plans."

"Yes, that's something we all agree on."

Bud looked at the senator seated next to him. "Marjorie Pritchard is the wife of Bud Pritchard, a man who has won the country's second-highest military award and a host of other decorations. He's a real-life, old-fashioned war hero and it will be the worst kind of treason if Marjorie meets with Ho Chi Minh's crowd. Why, it could stir up the anarchists to the point of guerrilla warfare throughout America."

"She's not the first to go to Hanoi," the senator said.

"No, but she's the first to go with enough explosive power to rally the entire country against the military—and against the President."

"You should be in politics, Colonel."

"Not my cup of tea, Senator. But look at the effect her speech at Berkeley had on the people—and she hasn't stopped. She's rolling like an overloaded freight truck with burned-out brakes on a downhill grade."

"I think the investigation I started on Bud Pritchard only worsened matters," the senator said. "It has focused the nation's attention on the problem and put us in an unpopular position, to say the least."

"That it has, but more important, it's focused attention on her, precisely where we don't want it."

They drove down MacArthur Boulevard, along the Potomac River, with the windows rolled down and a cold wind blowing into the car. Langley was only a few minutes away.

"When I asked you to lend a hand because of your personal friendship with Bud Pritchard and his wife I didn't have a clue as to how to proceed." Chester T. Newman said. "I'm grateful for the direction you've given."

The colonel looked at the senator. "I know them as well as anyone, I suppose, and I can tell you that those two had a fine marriage until Marjorie entered a so-called midlife crisis and lost her identity. As long as she held onto Bud she was all right. His strength was all she ever really needed and with it she would have been able to work herself through to the other side. Bud would have helped her if she had let him, but she got mixed up with the university crowd and the activists and she made the mistake to think that in the antiwar movement she would find the meaning in her life that her childless marriage with Bud didn't provide."

Senator Newman yawned.

"She desperately wanted a baby and couldn't come to grips with the disappointment—felt guilty and inadequate that she couldn't bear a child."

"We have to do everything we can to discourage her from pursuing the course she's on. We can't afford another Martin Luther King."

The colonel shot him a sharp look. "I'm going to do everything in my power to discourage her."

"You know the only option open to us if you can't change her mind."

He took a deep breath and looked out the window. The Lincoln pulled into the concrete parking structure for the Central Intelligence Agency. "I fully understand and I am in total compliance," he said and looked back at the senator. "It is my duty as an officer of the military forces of the United States to carry out the orders of my superiors and I will do exactly that. What happens after I have carried out my orders is none of my affair and it will in no way play on my conscience."

"I'm thankful that you see it our way, Colonel, and I think that Captain Pritchard would also be grateful if we could tell him."

"You may have been misled about Captain Pritchard."

Colonel Norbert Keane USMC and Senator Chester T. Newman showed their identification and secret clearances to the guard and were waved through, and in a few minutes they were in the CIA director's red-white-and-blue decorated office and looking out the windows at the Potomac Valley.

While Norbert Keane and Chester T. Newman waited for the director of the CIA and looked out at the expansive view of Virginia's most famous river, Marjorie Pritchard sat alone on the bed in her small, comfortable, and expensive colonial hotel room and looked out her paned window, not at a famous river valley, but at the beeches and chestnuts and maples on the campus of George Washington University visible a few blocks away.

From the fifth floor she could see the students milling about in groups, walking along the paths or sitting on the walls and benches with their open books. She loved the academic world, the freedom of speech, the ideology of the students. During these difficult times of testing which way the country would spring, it was the university that would determine the methods and direction and would forge the tools to work the fields for the new revolution. It was with the young that she belonged, where she could find significance for her life.

Marjorie Pritchard picked up the phone and placed a call to California with the operator.

The telephone rang five times. "Hello, this is Goodwin."

"What took you so long?"

"Marjorie—I didn't expect to hear from you until tomorrow." Rapshir put a finger over his lips and frowned to keep the pale-faced freshman silent who lay nude in his bed.

The girl frowned back at him and rolled over to reveal

a tattoo on her backside that said, *LBJ sucks.*

"Miss me?" Marjorie Pritchard said.

"Enormously; how's it going?"

"I need inspiration; Keane and the senator have me thinking too much and I don't want to feel that way. Was it Sartre or Jung that said that logic will not budge emotion? How about emotion budging logic, because that's what they are doing to me. Norbert Keane is a clever man—he has me scheduled to see some more propagandists, military people, and the senator wants me to meet with a bunch of his hawk congressmen friends."

"Come home."

"I have to go through with this the way we planned."

"I don't like what's happening. How could they have you thinking second thoughts? This is ridiculous. We are on the threshold of the revolution and it's because of your efforts that we have come so far so quickly. Don't let us down; everything is in place and your trip to Hanoi and the speech you've written and the world press waiting, why, we can't miss—it's your destiny, darling."

"Do you love me?"

"Immeasurably," he said.

"That's not the way to say it."

"I'll say it a thousand ways, any way you like it, when I see you after your speech at the Lincoln Memorial. Can you hold on until then?"

"I'll hold on, Goodwin. Just be sure everyone is at the Memorial," she said coldly, and hung up.

The hot shower soothed her tired body, and when she crawled between the sheets after putting in a wake-up call for dinner, Marjorie Pritchard was instantly asleep.

In Berkeley, the young university dropout smoked his Indian hashish and stared at the floorboards of the old apartment. The girl with the tattoo on her bottom lay on her side and stared at the wall, stoned. The room was littered with half-eaten cans of food, old newspapers, discarded clothing, and toenail clippings. Books were crammed in the shelves and piled on the floor, and cockroaches crawled over the dirty dishes that had lain in the sink for ten days.

"That chick better not freak out on me," Goodwin J. Rapshir said.

"Screw her." The girl picked her nose and wiped her finger on the mattress.

Chapter 14

A half-moon was high over the Ba Den Mountains, high enough to send its light down into the Song Xanh Valley so that the elephant grass in the small clearing could be seen moving if you stood in the protection of the thick forest that grew at the edges.

Inside the forest it was very dark, the light from the moon and stars not penetrating beyond the first layer of triple canopy, but in the clearing where the trail had to cross, there was enough light for the point man to see across to the other side, fifty yards away.

The elephant grass came to the top of Corporal Melvin Spratt's steel helmet, and though he could see the dark outline of trees through the tops of the elephant grass, he remained concealed in the heavy foliage. He moved slowly ahead a few steps at a time and stopped every few seconds to listen for sounds that were not natural to the jungle night.

Behind Melvin Spratt, two fire teams of Marines stood in the trees and watched the top of the elephant grass move and stop, move and stop across the clearing. No one smoked. Each white Marine's face was blackened and a sock was wrapped around external metal gear that hung free from rucksacks and web belts.

Branches of foliage were held to the camouflaged helmet covers by a wide rubberband, and each man carried an M16 assault rifle, except for PFC Howie Mullen, who sat with his back against a teak tree, an M60 machine gun lying across his thighs.

In addition to the belt of M60 ammo that each infantryman carried for Mullen's hog (Mullen carried two), the Marines carried ten magazines each of 5.56mm ammo for their M16s.

The leader of the Lurps was Sergeant Nunzio Pellegrini, a Brooklyn Sicilian who was twenty-four years old, short, muscular, and had begun shaving when he was in the eighth grade. He had shipped over for a second tour of duty in the Nam and spent his entire pay bonus and three weeks' liberty in Bangkok with four bar girls he had recruited within two hours of hitting Thailand.

Sergeant Nunzio Pellegrini, his head still bandaged from the lacerations he received in a thirty-minute brawl with sailors from a DE parked in the Gulf of Siam who took exception to Nunzio and his Marine Corps pals calling them "deck apes" and openly soliciting the services of their women, who sat quietly sipping tea at their tables, peeled the wrapper from a stick of Dentine and stuck it into his mouth. He handed PFC Howie Mullen a stick without taking his eyes off the clearing and the trembling grass.

"Thanks, Sarge," Mullen said.

"Shut up," Pellegrini hissed through his teeth. "How many times I got to tell you to clam up. You're a pain in the ass, Mullen." He wadded up the gum wrapper and stuck it in the top of his boot, a habit he had acquired in boot camp at Perris Island.

The Long Range Patrol (LRRP) had been out for four

days in an attempt to make contact with elements of Major Nguyen Vo Toi's NVA regulars, the same crack battalion that Captain Buddy Pritchard and PFC Billy McGarvie had encountered at Hill 506 near Quang Hoa. The Communists had withdrawn far north into the rugged, thickly forested and difficult-to-penetrate Ba Den Mountains, where Major Toi was preparing for a second offensive into the Song Xanh Valley.

Sergeant Nunzio Pellegrini and his Lurps were not the only ones watching the moon-shadowed clearing. A squad of tired, hungry, sick NVA soldiers had been camped for days at the edge of the elephant grass, knowing that the Americans would send a scout party to make contact. They had set up an L-shaped ambush every night for the last five nights without any success. Tonight would not be the same.

The twelve men, sick with dysentery and festering sores over their bodies, and eating rations of only a few handfuls of white rice a day, saw the trembling blades of elephant grass in the moonlight and waited quietly with the years of patience borne by their ancestors. They would soon enough be filling their empty stomachs with U.S. C-rations.

Yet another person sat out of reach of the moonlight, just inside the forest canopy, and watched the elephant grass. When the NVA squad first arrived and set up camp, Hai Van Phuong stayed hidden inside her tunnels, venturing out only at night to observe the soldiers and to explore their camp while they slept. She went from hammock to hammock and peered into their closed eyes, looking for a familiar face, that of her mother, her father, brothers and sisters. She listened to their breathing and smelled their bodies and then went back to her tunnels and sat in the dark and talked to the faces, tears carving out paths down her dirt-encrusted cheeks.

Tonight the half-moon drew her out of the ground, for she was comforted by the soft light and dark shadows cast across the clearing. In Quang Hoa she had sat in the jackfruit trees on nights like this and watched the unharvested rice wave in the night wind, and her dreams didn't seem so far away. On some nights her elder brother would walk down to the jackfruit trees and sit with her and they would talk about the way it would be when there was no war and they could plant the rice without fear.

What Phuong saw around her was not a clearing of elephant grass and forest but a hamlet of hooches, gardens and groves of fruit trees—Quang Hoa as it had been when she was a child and when her life was filled with soft words from her mother, a belly filled with hot rice and rau and roast duck, and time to float toy bamboo boats in the water of the irrigation ditches with her brothers and sisters.

"We will grow to inherit this land," brother was always fond of saying. "You and I are the eldest and we must take responsibility for the others and learn all we can from mother and father so that when the land is ours we know how to take care of it; for it is all that we will have and without it we are nothing. People without land walk without heads. They have bodies only and they wander in circles."

When brother talked to her in the jackfruit trees she was comforted because she was a girl and no one talked seriously to girls. None of the girls she knew would be given property to care for; they would have to marry a boy who would inherit property.

From the rise outside the hidden entrance to her tunnels, Phuong scanned the edges of the clearing and she saw forms on both sides, but she was not alarmed. Quang Hoa was a peaceful hamlet and there was never trouble, only love, family security, and much hope.

Sergeant Nunzio Pellegrini looked at the radium dial of his watch and then at the clearing. No longer could he see the elephant grass moving. "Spratt must be pretty close to the other side," he whispered to his two fire team leaders. "Better move them out." He balled the Dentine gum between his thumb and forefinger and stuck it behind his ear.

"We been out four days, Sarge, and we ain't seen no VC." PFC Howie Mullen remembered to whisper this time. "You know what I think?"

Nunzio Pellegrini looked at the voice in the darkness. Mullen's black face was invisible. "Educate me, Mullen, tell me what you think. I won't be able to take another step until I know."

"I think the dinks is waiting for us. They know we coming and they just waiting to hit us. For four days they watching us." He pushed his six-foot body off the teak tree and stood next to the short sergeant. "We going to be in a world of hurt soon. Them dinks smart and is watching us. Four days—tell me they ain't watching us." He lifted the machine gun and edged up closer to Nunzio and bent his head down. Beads of sweat had popped out all over his face. "We going be in the shit, Pellegrini." He walked to the clearing and took up his position behind the others.

Nunzio Pellegrini said nothing, but he was thinking, *The dinks will hit us anytime.* He didn't want to go across the clearing; he should pull the men back and go around. Spratt was already across; the first fire team was moving into the elephant grass.

Corporal Melvin Spratt walked into the trees and listened, but all he heard were the usual sounds of buzzing and chirping insects and the croak of frogs, layers of monotonous static in the night. The air was dank and smelled of rotting leaves and dead things.

"Why are we going out at night?" Spratt had asked Pellegrini.

"Because we ain't seen anything during the day; the dinks like to move around at night . . . so we move around at night."

Spratt had been on night patrols before, but they had always been to a specific objective, mostly to ambush sites such as a trail junction or where Charlie had been spotted the day before. Never had he been out at night just nosing around; that was asking for trouble. You could stumble into an ambush and be in a world of hurt before you had any idea what hit you, and the chances of a react team finding you were about as good as finding a Subic Bay cathouse empty when the fleet was in.

Like Howie Mullen, Corporal Melvin Spratt was certain that he was going to be in the shit soon. He moved forward into the forest, the M16 off safety and held with both hands across his chest, the index finger of his right hand flexing on the trigger. He had difficulty locating the trail again and when he stepped on the branch and it made a crunching sound, he cursed audibly.

The blackness was total, and if the NVA had been standing in the open, Melvin Spratt would not have seen them. As it was he walked within ten feet of the twelve men lying prone in a line behind the trees and foliage. They let him pass through unharmed.

"Get your black ass moving, Mullen, and keep ten paces between you and Garcia in front of you." Sergeant Pellegrini had positioned himself and the M60 in the middle of the patrol. "If we get hit, you move fast to the front of the action."

"I know, I know, Pellegrini—how many months I been humping this hog with you? How many times we been in the shit before?"

"Just in case you forgot; your attention span don't impress me none."

Howie Mullen grumbled and slapped the blades of elephant grass away from his face. *He lucky I haven't greased his white butt with this hog. I may yet.* He stepped into the thick grass and listened for the first shots that would tell him what he was waiting for.

When Nunzio Pellegrini had worked the Brooklyn streets around Flatbush Avenue with his gang of toughs, he would smell the trouble a mile off before it erupted. He smelled that trouble creeping up on him now and he wanted to yell, get the adrenaline surge going, get the edges of his nerves cleaned off so that he could think straight, make the right moves.

The grass was too thick; he couldn't see anything but Mullen's back, and if he didn't stay close, Mullen would be swallowed up in the tall stuff. Each man was dependent on the guy in front of him to get him across.

Pellegrini figured you didn't have to be too bright to know that if the dinks were waiting, the patrol wouldn't have a chance in the grass—no chance at all. They couldn't see who to shoot at; they'd be more likely to shoot themselves than any slopeheads.

By the time Nunzio Pellegrini got halfway across the clearing he began to think that his animal instincts had overreacted. Spratt had to be well into the forest, and the lead men in the column were already walking out of the grass, and no shots had been fired and there had been no explosions from a mine that Spratt would have tripped on the trail if the dinks had wanted to get him.

No one ever had to tell Nunzio that the dinks were slick—he had learned that the first five minutes of his first CA into the Ia Drang. What bothered him now was the nagging fear that in his haste to cover the two klicks to Song Xanh by dawn, he had not skirted the clearing and if the NVA wanted, they could wipe out him and his seven men within minutes. Maybe they didn't want to; maybe they had something bigger up their sleeve, like thinking that his Lurps were only the advance elements of a much larger recon patrol and if they sat tight, bigger pickings would come along; or maybe they had let Spratt pass through so the rest of the patrol wouldn't . . .

Twelve AKs on full automatic opened up simultaneously and cut through the elephant grass like a scythe cutting wheat and left the first two men in the column dead, wounded the third, shot the M60 from PFC Mullen's hands, skipped Sergeant Pellegrini and wounded the two trailing Marines.

After the opening burst, Corporal Spratt ran back along the trail and was cut down immediately and died within minutes.

"Return fire!" Nunzio Pellegrini screamed. "Get your sixty working, Mullen."

Howie Mullen groped around in the grass with bleeding hands and finally found the machine gun; the receiver was shattered. "They busted the hog—I ain't got nothing to fight with," Mullen said over the noise.

"None of our guys is firing; why ain't they firing?" Nunzio said. The rifle bucked against his shoulder and he kept the trigger depressed, burning out the barrel and not knowing where to point the weapon except forward; all he knew was that the dinks were somewhere out front.

"Ugh."

"Mullen," Pellegrini said. He crawled to the black PFC and found a neat hole in the side of his head. The hole on the other side was not so neat.

"Garcia! — Leventhal! — Smitty!" No answers — only moans.

The AKs stopped firing and he heard the North Vietnamese soldiers' excited chattering, like a gang of mean little children that cautioned each other yet prodded the ones in front to go on. They came out of the trees, crouched over, rifles pointed straight ahead, and jabbered fast without letup, not concerned about the Americans hearing them.

Sergeant Nunzio Pellegrini realized now that he was the only one alive or not wounded and that he had two choices: play dead and take his chances or kill as many as he could before they got him. The first option was quickly eliminated when he heard a single shot in the grass, followed by another; then, a half-minute later, another.

Nunzio Pellegrini was not afraid of dying; he had it figured when he first joined the Marine Corps and volunteered for Vietnam that he was going to get it. He was surprised that he had lasted as long as he had. What ate Nunzio Pellegrini was that he came into the world nothing and he was going out a nothing. He hadn't even gotten the medal he wanted.

The sounds of the little children were close. The dinks were not careful and searched fast through the grass, looking for the Marines. They found the two wounded Marines behind Nunzio and quickly shot them in the head and tore open the rucksacks and argued over the C-rations.

Moving noiselessly, Pellegrini popped the empty magazine from the rifle and after fumbling in the ammo pouch, inserted a fresh magazine. The soldiers could come from any direction so he lay chilly where he was and waited.

The rucksacks were systematically opened and their contents scattered over the wet ground and picked clean of food, mines, medical supplies, clothing and whatever else was useful to the Communist soldiers.

The weapons and ammunition and much of the web gear was stripped and piled under the trees, and all the time the soldiers jabbered loudly nonstop. They left the steel helmets, flak jackets, and boots on the Marines' feet—they were much too large for dink feet.

Thirty minutes passed and the North Vietnamese soldiers searched the grass and ate C-rations and chattered, and then a soldier found PFC Howie Mullen's corpse and Sergeant Nunzio Pellegrini twisted quietly around in the grass and sat up, pointed the M16 with the burned-out barrel at the voices only a few feet away behind a wall of elephant grass, and pulled the trigger.

He was able to get off two magazines and killed three of the enemy and wounded two (one died three days later from his wounds) before a grenade was lobbed in on him. His last thoughts were that he never got the medal and that he was checking out a nothing.

Firebase Briggs was fifteen klicks south of the ambush, and Captain Patrick T. Slaughter, CO of Charley Company, was wakened from a troubled sleep.

"What is it, Kellar?" he said to the RTO. He was wide awake in seconds.

"Sir, the LRRP is an hour late in checking in. Thought you would want to know."

Slaughter threw the poncho (wet with night dew) from

him and sat up, feeling for the steel pot. Kellar kicked it over to him and walked back to the bunker and continued to try to raise the Lurps.

"An hour, you say?" Patrick T. Slaughter took a swig of warm canteen water and rinsed the sleep out of his mouth.

"Jeez—what's that?" Kellar pressed the receiver to his ear.

Slaughter snatched the handset from him and listened. "Get me the map."

Kellar spread it out and shined a flashlight on it.

"Cover the light, dork-brain."

Kellar threw a poncho over the light and lifted an end so the captain could see the map under it. The bunker was getting crowded—the news had spread.

"Lieutenant, we got any ARVN where Pellegrini is operating?" He listened to the radio.

"No, sir."

"Then we got eight dead Marines out there." He handed the receiver to Second Lieutenant Gary Hill from Ogden, Utah. "What you hear is gook talk and if we ain't got ARVN personnel in that area then what you hear is NVA jabbering."

Second Lieutenant Gary Hill looked blankly at his CO, the receiver pressed to his ear.

"Get the react team together, Lieutenant—you got some humping to do."

Dawn was breaking in the clearing and Hai Van Phuong walked down to the bodies. The North Vietnamese soldiers were gone and the elephant grass was heavily trampled and lying flat.

Phuong knelt beside each body and touched it lightly.

She smelled and looked, and talked softly to the dead men and then began dragging them one by one into the forest and hiding them under the trees and in the foliage. She had gotten Sergeant Nunzio Pellegrini and PFC Howie Mullen close to her tunnels and was back in the clearing taking the dog tags off Garcia's neck and taking the pictures out of his wallet when she looked up at the sound of the Huey whumping through the gray morning sky.

Inside the chopper Second Lieutenant Gary Hill removed the binoculars from his eyes, shook his head and handed the field glasses to Staff Sergeant Lawrence Stuckenburg, who sat next to him and the door gunner. "We found them."

Stuckenburg looked for a long time and then said, "There's no movement—just the dink broad. Looks like she took all the weapons and the rucks are torn apart. They're all dead." He was quiet for a few seconds. "What's that she has in her hands?"

Gary Hill took the field glasses. "Dog tags—she's got a string of dog tags hanging from their chains . . . and wallets; she's taken their wallets."

"Lousy bitch—see if you can pick her off," Stuckenburg said to the door gunner.

"I can't see her."

Hill put down the binoculars. "She ran into the jungle." He shook his head. "A whole patrol wiped out by one dink broad," he shouted over the roar of the wind and rotors.

The door gunner with the helmet headphones yelled to Second Lieutenant Gary Hill: "The pilot wants to know if you're ready to go in. It looks quiet—we're not taking fire."

Hill gave the kid a thumbs-up, and the UH-1 began a

sharp descent into the clearing. Two more choppers followed them down in a line.

The Huey pranged hard and the men were out both open hatches in seconds, Hill going out first and to the left, and Stuckenburg to the right. Hueys two and three dropped their troops and rose immediately out of the landing zone with Huey one.

Five minutes later the Marines were in the treeline and a rough perimeter defense was set up. Lieutenant Gary Hill and Staff Sergeant Stuckenburg walked among the bodies.

"Weird—all the dog tags are gone," Hill said.

"And the wallets." Larry Stuckenburg rolled Garcia over. "Shot in the head like the others—close range by the looks of it. Took a couple in the chest."

A PFC walked up through the trampled grass.

"What'd you find?" Hill said.

"We found Corporal Spratt's body about twenty yards down the trail. Still can't find Pellegrini and Mullen."

Stuckenburg rested on one knee and lit a Lucky Strike with his Zippo. "Weird—really weird."

The react team spread out through the forest and searched the rest of the morning for Sergeant Nunzio Pellegrini and PFC Howie Mullen, but never found them, though they came within twenty feet of where Phuong had dragged their bodies under the pteridium ferns and broad-leafed acetia.

Sweating profusely in the midday heat, Second Lieutenant Gary Hill sat with Staff Sergeant Lawrence Stuckenburg and ate a can of C-rat peaches. "What do you think, Larry?"

Stuckenburg swallowed the last of his beef and noodles and licked the white plastic spoon. His utility shirt was soaked a dark green, and a ring of salt had formed around each armpit. One canteen was already empty and the other nearly so. "I'll tell you what I think, Lieutenant, for whatever it's worth. The Lurps were ambushed by a squad-size NVA force and took Pellegrini and Mullen prisoner. The girl's probably a local Viet Cong who loots the bodies for whatever valuables she can get, gleaning what the regulars left. We just happened to arrive when she was finishing up. The gooks are long gone."

"What about the dog tags?"

"Just some kinky habit—collects dog tags like some guys carve notches in their rifle stocks. Who knows?"

Gary Hill yelled for the RTO and reported in to Captain Patrick T. Slaughter at Firebase Briggs. Slaughter decided to list Nunzio Pellegrini and Howie Mullen as missing-in-action (MIA) and ordered Hill to call off the search.

The Hueys returned, this time with a fourth chopper to carry out the six green plastic body bags, and as they lifted off and their rotors beat down the elephant grass and the roar of the engines rose to a crescendo, Hai Van Phuong stood on the rise next to the concealed entrance to her tunnels and watched the American helicopters fly away in single file, the noise of the rotors fading over the trees and the sun glistening hot off the dried blood on the elephant grass.

Using the entrenching tool taken from Howie Mullen's ruck, she spent the next hours digging graves. She buried the two Marines close to the tunnels, under the ferns, and placed a small pile of stones on each mound of earth to mark the graves.

Inside the main room of the tunnel complex, Hai Van Phuong built an altar out of wood and stone and dirt. This took her several days. When she finished, the altar stood four feet high and was three feet wide and in the center was a two-foot-high Christian cross that she had made from teakwood carved with a Marine K-bar.

On the cross, Phuong hung the dog tags of all eight Marines. Around its base she placed photographs from their wallets as well as other personal items (keys, pens, good luck charms, watches, rings, necklaces), and on the altar she burned candles.

As the days and weeks passed, more ambushes and battles took place around Hai Van Phuong's underground lair, and she would hear the shooting and explosions and see the smoke rise black in the sky, and she would walk to the battle and watch until it was over and then drag a body (American or Vietnamese, it didn't matter which) back to her tunnels, sometimes taking days to get it there, where she would bury it with the others and place their identification and mementos on the altar with her growing collection.

Her reputation spread throughout the northern provinces, and the Montagnards grew to fear her and became entranced by the strangeness of her bizarre behavior, though some of the Montagnards themselves were accustomed to performing bizarre acts of their own on the Viet Cong and North Vietnamese regulars.

The sighting reported by Second Lieutenant Gary Hill and Staff Sergeant Stuckenburg linked Hai Van Phuong to other ambushes and small VC force operations in the Ba Den Mountains and in border areas of Laos and Cambodia, and became the basis for a wide-scale search for the Dragon Girl of Song Xanh. A reward of 10,000 piasters was placed on her head, but the superstitious Montagnards, who by this time believed Phuong to be a special creature from beyond the great fogs of Pong Doi, and who had no use for the Vietnamese or their money, went to great lengths to conceal the girl's whereabouts.

She had become a good luck charm to the mountain people and was believed to be under the protection of Pong Doi himself.

Her reputation spread among the U.S. troops as well, and reports circulated that she had been seen as far as Pleiku and even Binh Hoa and Tay Ninh provinces. As far as the Marines were concerned, however, the Viet Cong broad or Dragon Girl of Song Xanh (or any of the many names given to her) was only an expected oddity in a psychedelic war that produced a number of strange people on both sides. None took the rumors of her seriously, though a pot of considerable size ($2,500) had grown for anyone who bagged her.

The girl, of course, knew nothing of her reputation, and went about her secretive search for the ones she loved and honoring those that had fallen under fire. She prayed before the altar throughout the day and burned splinters of wood (a substitute for joss sticks) and gave sacrifices of rice and fruit.

Often when she crawled among the dead and wounded or when she watched the battles from the top of a tree or from under a bush, she looked for the face of the tall, sandy-haired Marine captain that had brought her home to Quang Hoa village. The memory of who he was and their relationship had faded, but his face was still clear to her and sometimes all the soldiers looked like him.

On days, and especially on nights, when the rains came and the *drip-drip-drip* of water was heard in the tunnels and the rats were driven out of their burrows by the flooding water, Hai Van Phuong walked in the jungle with the Marine captain and talked to him about her home in Quang Hoa and about her family, which was looking for her. She would ask him to take her back as he had from Cung Mai Dong, but when they returned to the tunnels to pay respects to the brave soldiers who lived there with her, he always said that he had to go away and fight one last battle and that he would return for her at the next rain. She believed him and waited, and when the rains next came they went for their walk and made plans to return to her family in Quang Hoa, where the rice grew higher, the rivers ran clearer, and there was enough love for everyone.

Chapter 15

Captain Buddy Pritchard USMC had the red meatball centered for a full six seconds, and then the prow of the *Coral Sea* dipped twenty feet in the surging seas; Alpha-Charlie-Nine was suddenly too high above the decks, and the LSO gave Bud the wave off.

"Okay, Captain Marvel, get your shit together," Dale Keilman said. "Just because you're flying on one engine doesn't give you the authority to dump us into the ocean."

The *Coral Sea* already had a couple of bolters from the A-6 squadron, and the worsening weather promised difficult landings for all the returning jets. Alpha-Charlie-Nine, with only one engine, would be especially difficult to land.

"How's your fuel?" the deck officer said on the radio.

"I'm sucking wind."

"Let's hit the tanker, Captain Marvel," Dale Keilman said and raised the ejection seat so he could get a better view forward.

"I'm taking it around one more time."

An A-7 turned in front of Bud and the flaps and wheels came down. Bud slipped to the outside of the Corsair and began the long two-mile swing to bring the Phantom into the landing pattern again. His fuel read

100 pounds. He should be tanking up, not attempting another landing.

The A-7 came in high like Bud had and the pilot firewalled the bird and it roared past the island structure, thirty feet off the deck.

"Bad day in Black Rock," Keilman said.

Somewhere in the gray muck was the A-6 tanker from the *Coral Sea*. It orbited for returning aircraft low on fuel, but by the time Bud Pritchard could locate the tanker (if he ever did) he'd be out of gas; so the only option left was to make one last attempt to catch a wire.

With only one engine, the big Phantom handled badly, and with the loss of half its power, mistakes would not be forgiven. Alpha-Charlie-Nine had also developed a starboard yaw that created rudder and steering problems for Bud Pritchard.

In the backseat, Dale Keilman was yammering away as usual, and Bud, his brain overloaded with too many transmissions from the carrier, from other pilots, and from guard channel, went cold-mike and disconnected Keilman, though Bud's side remained open so his RIO could hear his orders. He also turned off guard channel; everyone seemed to have an emergency.

Dropping the left wing, Pritchard broke out of the downwind leg of the landing pattern and turned into final approach, nose high, flaps down, gear down, a long trail of black exhaust smoking from the one good engine, and the rudder flicking back and forth like the tail of a shark riding the surface.

The red meatball bounced between the horizontal lines as Bud came out of the bank and flattened out at 180 on an opposite heading with the *Coral Sea*'s massive prow, which was bobbing up and down like a cork in the ocean storm.

"Steady, sweetheart," Pritchard said to the jet that was approaching stall speed. "Deck coming up, drop the nose, meatball rising . . . steady . . . okay, a little more rudder . . . power, power, need more power . . . only one engine—got no more power to give . . . deck still rising . . ."

Tail hook hanging down, remaining engine whining, nose flared, Alpha-Charlie-Nine screamed over the prow as the deck reached the top of the swell, and Captain Bud Pritchard USMC cut the throttle and the Phantom dropped to the steel and caught number three wire.

Bud clicked Keilman back on the ICS: "There's a role of toilet paper under the seat, Dale."

"You're a funny man, Captain Marvel."

The canopy stayed closed so the rain wouldn't come in on them, and Bud followed Happy Hedrick, who directed him to a parking spot over the elevator that would take Alpha-Charlie-Nine down to the hangar deck.

Through the rain-streaked Plexiglas Bud saw a crowd of pilots and deck crew forming around his aircraft.

"Hail the conquering heroes," Dale Keilman said. "Our fans await us with gifts."

Bottles of champagne popped open and were poured over Bud and Dale when they reached the deck. Several cameras appeared, including that of the *Coral Sea*'s press and PR officer, and flashbulbs sparkled in the crowd.

"Nice job—congratulations, Bud," Benny Sanchez said and slapped him on the back. "Scratch one more gomer; that brings our kills to fifteen."

Pritchard held his revulsion and remembered the sick feeling he had when Ralph Thorbus congratulated him at Cung Mai Dong.

"Billington wants to see you when you're through with debriefing. Give yourself time to clean up."

Pritchard pushed his way through the men and left Dale Keilman to answer the questions and revel in his moment of glory.

The debriefer squeezed Bud for all the information he had in him, asking him to repeat the many details and go back over the kill until Pritchard saw only Ralph Thorbus' face across the table from him and he wanted put his fist into it. At one point Bud began to describe the attack on the truck and hooch at Quang Hoa and the debriefer looked oddly at him and Bud realized that what he was describing had occurred on a different mission. He became quiet for a while and looked down at his flight suit and survival vest soaked through with sweat and champagne and at his trembling hands, and he wondered if Hai Van Phuong would forgive him.

"I think we can terminate the debriefing, Captain," the officer said. He turned his eyes from Bud Pritchard's trembling hands and busied himself with the forms he had completed. "That will be all."

Pritchard remained seated and stared at the torn seam in the thumb of the glove he had not yet removed from his hand. The same silly notion that the glove was injured came back to him as it had with Thorbus and he wanted to take care of it in the way he would take care of the wounded hand of a child.

The debriefer continued to write on the forms and then stopped in the middle of a sentence and looked up at Bud, who had not moved from his chair. "I said you could go—we've got everything, don't we?"

"Not quite everything."

The man blinked and gently placed the pen on the

table, next to the forms. The room had become quiet, and the other pilots and debriefers looked at Pritchard.

"What did we forget?"

Bud Pritchard stood and looked around the room and then down at the officer. "We don't know where to send the flowers."

Before going to the bridge, Bud Pritchard stopped by his stateroom to dress in a fresh set of tropicals and to be alone for a few minutes. The shower in the locker room had partially revived him, but the dull ache in his stomach was still there. It felt like he had swallowed a shot-put.

He spent a long time shining his shoes and thought about what he had done over Chuc Luc and whether or not the MiG pilot might have gotten out of the broken and burning aircraft after it had disappeared into the overcast. At least the mission was significant and not a useless waste like rocketing hooches with families in them.

The trousers, pressed and well-starched, felt cool against his warm showered legs, and as he reached for the shirt he had laid on the top bunk (Dale Keilman's), he saw the envelope.

Not many things elated Captain Bud Pritchard these days, but when he saw that the letter was from Lieutenant, J.G., Janice Elderberry USN, he smiled and a very good feeling, warm and peaceful, passed through him. He sat down and spent fifteen minutes slowly reading the five-page letter.

While he read he thought of their night in the ammunition bunker and how Janice Elderberry's butterball figure gleamed in the light of the magnesium flares and he laughed at her sense of humor and he remembered what Dale Keilman had said—that she cared a lot for him and that she would marry him right away if he asked. *What would I do with two wives? Oh, yeah, Marjorie is going to divorce me.* He folded the letter and put it in the breast pocket of his tropicals, squared away in the mirror and left for the bridge.

A few feet along the passageway he met Dale Keilman coming down the ladder and headed for their stateroom; he had one of his raunchy black cigars in his mouth.

"The guys already got a red star painted on AC-Nine's splitter," Keilman said. He reached up to button Bud's breast pocket. "Messy, messy—won't do for your little tête-à-tête with the skipper."

The cigar was only inches from Pritchard's face and he fanned the smoke out of his eyes.

Keilman saw the letter protruding from the pocket. He buttoned the flap and patted the letter inside and smiled out one side of his mouth, the cigar sticking out the other side. "What did Elderberry have to say?"

"That she misses me and that she's confused and frustrated by the war and that Thorbus is putting the rush on her and that she's getting short and will be going home soon and that she'll stop at the Navy hospital in San Diego and see Billy McGarvie."

"That all?" Keilman grinned through the cigar smoke.

"She wants to know if it would be all right to visit Marjorie and shove a grenade up her ass."

Keilman laughed. "Lieutenant Elderberry has spunk. She's also intelligent, got a cute butterball figure, got a sense of humor and is in love with you. You ought to take her serious."

Bud faked a punch at Dale's chin and jogged past him up the ladder.

Captain Josh Billington USN turned the bridge over to Commander Darrel Seals and invited Bud into his stateroom. After dismissing his orderly he poured two stiff drinks from a bottle of Chivas Regal and held his glass up in a toast. "To a successful mission."

The two men drank, their eyes on each other.

"I told you that I would have something more than coffee to offer you next time you came up," Billington said.

Bud smiled. "It's mighty welcome after this morning."

Josh Billington sat quietly in the leather chair and thought about what he wanted to say. He tapped an ice cube and watched it sink and then bob up; he did that twice and then looked up at the oil painting of Admiral Chester Nimitz, his World War II mentor, and wondered how the Old Man would have handled this difficult decision. He took another drink from the glass and swallowed hard.

Sensing the uneasiness in Billington, Bud looked at his old flight instructor and set his jaw. "Sir, you were never one to beat around the bush. If it makes it any easier, I'd like to say that there's not much that will surprise me—too much has already gone under the bridge."

Josh Billington nodded to Bud in appreciation of the remark and drew a long breath. "Your wife Marjorie, as you know, has been a big embarrassment to the country, to our effort over here, and particularly to the President. She's meeting with Ho Chi Minh in Hanoi this month against the expressed wishes of Washington, and her speech at the Lincoln Memorial devastated plans for the President's reelection. It is the opinion of Senator Newman and other conservative members of Congress that her antiwar efforts have rallied a significant and powerful coalition of people that could not only force us to surrender South Vietnam to the Communists, but eventually, if allowed to continue, lead the country to anarchy." He paused and tapped the ice cubes and smiled at Pritchard. "I don't believe that for a minute, but what I believe doesn't count. What does count is that there's a wheelbarrow full of frightened and nervous people, all of them in Washington, who are crying for your wife's head."

"It's all a crock," Bud said.

"I'm glad you agree."

"She's not a leader—not that powerful—just an effective rabble-rouser, and she's always been an orator of sorts. When push comes to shove I don't believe all those millions that Senator Newman claims are behind her will support her and that crowd of donkeys that put her where she is."

"You think she's going to be out on the end of the branch all by herself?"

"And they'll cut it off behind her when they see she's no longer any use to them—and that will be when she goes to Hanoi."

"Interesting." Josh Billington got up from the chair and stood before Admiral Nimitz's portrait. "You never knew Nimitz, did you, Pritchard?"

"No, sir, not personally."

"Commanded Pacific Fleet operations throughout the Second World War, made Admiral of the Fleet—five stars—in 1944; Chief of Naval Operations, 1945 to 1947 . . ."

"You plan to follow in his footsteps, sir?"

"God willing," Billington said. "I'm not a modest man,

Pritchard." He returned to his red leather chair, sat down and crossed his legs. "Do you recall what I used to tell you when you flew in the backseat of my trainers at Pensacola?"

" 'See your enemy—kill him—get away fast.' "

"And that applies not only in aerial combat, but in political combat as well—and we've got plenty of that in the Navy. That never interested you, though, did it?—the political combat."

"No, sir—never had occasion to be involved."

Billington laughed a little. "You've been involved but never knew it, and now you have occasion to know."

"Sir?"

"You've become a political hot potato. You're one of the most decorated men in the Naval Service. You won the Navy Cross and Silver Star for gallant action against the North Vietnamese and Viet Cong forces, and will be decorated again for heroism, this time for this morning's action over Chuc Luc. This doesn't square with your wife's behavior back home, and the politicians find you a political liability."

"They want me out of Vietnam."

"Tucked away on a shelf somewhere, inconspicuous, where you will no longer be controversial or noticed," Billington said.

"Where I can't cause trouble by doing something silly like shooting down MiGs or killing people who are trying to kill me, doing what I'm paid to do."

"That's what I liked about you at Pensacola, Pritchard. I could never shit you. You always knew what was coming next."

Bud finished his drink. "So that's the end of it—no more flying . . . no more Vietnam . . . back to the world."

The captain tapped the ice cubes a couple of times and looked up at the portrait.

"Bull Halsey was more my type," Pritchard said.

"Entirely different man than Chester Nimitz." Josh Billington sighed and looked at Bud, his eyes softer than before. "Okay, so you're getting a rotten deal, but look at it this way. You're an old man for a fighter pilot, and though you might become an ace flying for me on the *Coral Sea* the chances are better that you'll get your butt flamed by some hotshot twenty-year-old Russian-trained gomer."

"I haven't anything but the Corps—nothing but my flying. Nothing."

"Listen, Bud, stop fighting the system, stop trying to make things over in your image. You've got many talents. There's still time for you to make something of yourself in the Marines even though you're thought by many to be a broken-down captain well past forty. Protect yourself."

"See your enemy—kill him—get away fast?"

"I'll back you; there are those who listen to me."

"Aren't you risking your career if you back a broken-down captain well past forty?"

"Only if you give up."

Bud thought for a moment. "You make sense. When you make Fleet Admiral I'll remind you of this conversation."

They both laughed.

Captain Bud Pritchard flew off the deck of the *Coral Sea* for two more weeks and shot down another MiG before his orders came through for him to report to the Third Marine Air Wing at the El Toro Marine Air

Station in south Orange County, California, where his new billet, yet undetermined, would be given to him. He could only hope that he would remain on flying status, though the possibility of that was remote.

"All I ever had was the Corps, Dale."

"You still have it."

"It won't be the same—I've never flown a desk before."

"There's more to the Marines than killing gooners."

Bud looked at the orders and deep down he wanted to tear them up and jump overboard and swim out to sea. All he knew was flying. Keilman was right, though; there was more, and he never had taken to war the way the old-line grunts did.

"I'll miss you, old buddy," Pritchard said.

"It won't be the same without Captain Marvel at the throttle." Keilman had an unlit cigar clenched between his teeth. "They'll probably assign me some young puke that's never seen a rice paddy and I'll have to start all over teaching him like I taught you."

Pritchard grabbed for one of Keilman's Clark Gable ears, but Dale dodged away. "You take care of yourself and keep in touch, ya hear. You know where you can find me."

"Why would I want to find you?" Dale threw a big bear hug around Pritchard, and when he released him his eyes were wet. "Get out of here before I make a fool out of myself, you crazy old man." He hooked the sling of the olive-drab seabag over Pritchard's shoulder and saluted him.

"Semper fi," Bud said and returned the salute.

"Semper fi." Keilman closed the door of the stateroom and leaned against the desk, staring at Bud's empty bunk. He would be like that for the next ten minutes

and then sit down and make the last entry for the day in his log: "Said goodbye to the best friend I ever had."

The twin-engine propeller-driven C-1 COD sat next to a Grumman Hawkeye E-2 early warning aircraft, its pilot reading a manifest on a clipboard and checking off the mailbags and personnel being loaded. Bud came out of the island and headed for the COD, the brown envelope containing his orders flapping in his hand from the salty wind that blew down the deck.

The pilot was about to motion him into the short fuselage when the bullhorn blared, "Captain Pritchard, report to the bridge . . . Captain Pritchard, report to the bridge. Hold the COD."

Bud Pritchard, his lined face looking up at Jack Hunter signaling him, muttered to himself, "What now—did Marjorie dynamite the White House?"

"Go ahead, Captain," the Navy pilot said. "I'll stow your gear."

Trotting back to the island, Pritchard clambered up the ladder to Josh Billington's nest atop the *Coral Sea*. When he entered, the captain of the carrier was grim-faced and held a little black box in his hand. It wasn't wise to try to read what was behind Josh Billington's expression, Bud had learned years ago in flight school.

"Captain Pritchard reporting as ordered, sir."

Billington thrust out his jaw, and his wide eyes fixed on Pritchard's deep-set ones. "There isn't enough time to do this in the proper manner, Major, the COD has a schedule to keep and I'm sure you'll forgive me if I dispense with the formalities." He opened the black box and took out the two oak leaves. The stern look was replaced by a smile.

Jack Hunter, officer-of-the-deck, beamed like a schoolboy whose teacher had just stuck a gold star to his forehead.

"Goes with the new territory, Pritchard. You deserve it." The grim look returned. "Long overdue." He ushered Bud into his private stateroom.

"Is this a reward for deciding to play ball with the good old boys, sir?"

"Don't sneer at good fortune, Pritchard."

"No offense intended."

"It wasn't easy getting you this promotion. You've been passed over more times than anyone could remember, and the popular choice was to drum you out of the Corps—elegantly, that is—for public relations reasons. I might add, however, that you have made some new friends in Washington and they came to your aid."

"Would it be improper to ask who these secret admirers might be?"

"Don't get snotty, Pritchard—I haven't pinned these leaves on you yet."

"Just curious, sir."

Josh Billington was as tall as Bud Pritchard and looked at him level-eyed. "There are places for mavericks like you, Pritchard, but it's in the seat of an F-4 or behind the iron sights of an M16 and not where you're headed. If you get rid of that chip on your shoulder and keep your brass polished, your new friends like Senator Chester T. Newman and some of your old pals like Colonel Norbert Keane will be happy to give you a leg up. And you can also include me in there among your supporters, though if you mention this conversation to anyone I'll deny it." He removed the captain's bars and pinned the major's oak leaves on Bud Pritchard's collar points.

"So old 'Iron Jaw' remembered."

"Scuttlebutt has it that you two go farther back than Pensacola when I had both of you. You also flew together in Korea, I understand."

"We flew F-86s off the *Hornet*. You were on the *Lexington*, weren't you, Captain?"

"I was," Billington said. "Best CV in the fleet at the time. Now it's the *Coral Sea*." He winked at Bud and finished pinning the brass on the collar points. "I appreciate the damn fine job you've done in the short time you've been aboard my boat, Pritchard, especially how you brought the strikers down on the target at Chuc Luc. Good piece of work. The two MiGs helped us close the gap on the *Connie*'s lead, and *Coral*'s stock has jumped a thousand points. Thanks, Bud, and the best of luck to you." He shook Pritchard's hand.

As Pritchard descended the ladder on his way to the waiting C-1, Josh Billington stood in the hatch and watched him go. When Bud emerged from the island structure and walked out on the flight deck, Billington called his name and Bud looked up at the bridge and the ensigns flying high above the captain's nest, the sky blue and clear.

"See your enemy—kill him—and get away fast," Josh Billington shouted down, and then disappeared behind the heavy armored glass.

How much Captain Josh Billington had to do with Bud's promotion, he didn't know, but it was clear that without his recommendation it would not have been possible. What Billington had to say gave Pritchard much to think about, particularly that Colonel Norbert "Iron Jaw" Keane USMC, after these many years, had reentered his life—this time as one of his backers along with the self-appointed leader of the hawks in Congress, Senator Chester T. Newman.

Pritchard suspected that Marjorie had the hots for his old high school pal, Norbert Keane, as far back as when Bud and Norbert were student pilots together at Pensacola, though he was confident that Iron Jaw had respected his marriage.

When Keane hit his jaw on the AT-6 trainer's instrument panel and cracked a couple of gauges and not his jaw (hence the tag "Iron Jaw") during a bad landing on one of Josh Billington's training flights, Marjorie expressed more than normal concern and rushed to the base hospital with flowers and a box of chocolates even though Norbert Keane was only kept there overnight for observation and released the next day for full duty.

The COD pilot checked Bud's name off the manifest, and Bud strapped into the seat and looked around the interior of the aircraft. There were two other Marines, a pilot and RIO, and a Navy Lieutenant who were being rotated back to the States. The trio looked happy, even ebullient, compared to Bud Pritchard's somber mood. The mailbags and a dozen empty parts crates were strapped down in the rear of the C-1.

The men tried to make conversation with Pritchard, but after a few attempts they lost interest and concentrated on discussing among themselves what waited for them back in the world.

The flight to Da Nang was bumpy and longer than Bud expected (in jets he was used to much shorter ETAs), and when the COD landed and rolled up to the operations terminal he was the last one out. Standing on the tarmac he looked out across the rice paddies and toward the green hills in the west and beyond where Cung Mai Dong, Quang Hoa, and Hill 506 and the Vui Bong were hidden. Specters raced through his mind and he saw the girl, Hai Van Phuong, her head bandaged, and her decapitated brother in the body bag, riding in the jeep, and he saw himself load her into the Huey, next to PFC Billy McGarvie, and then they were over the hot LZ and the smells of blood and urine and cordite crowded in on him and he knew that he would have to find her out there wherever she was and he could never rest until he did; his life would remain hyphenated with nothing following the hyphen if he didn't find her and bring her back. Dale was right after all—there was more to all this than killing gooners.

"Sergeant," Bud shouted.

The E-5 turned in the jeep and looked at Bud Pritchard, his thick glasses enlarging his eyes so that he looked bug-eyed.

Throwing the seabag into the jeep, Bud climbed in beside the E-5. "Take me to a chopper pad where I can catch a hop to Cung Mai Dong."

With some pain in his face the sergeant put the jeep in gear, wheeled around in the opposite direction from the one in which he had intended to go, and stomped down on the gas. Dirt and rock spit out behind the rear wheels, and Bud grabbed the corner of the windshield in time to save himself from being thrown out. "Am I keeping you from something important, Sergeant?"

"Yes, sir—you are."

In the old Corps, Pritchard recollected, *a Marine would never talk like that to an officer*. He decided to ignore it.

At the helicopter pad he had to snatch the seabag out of the jeep before the sergeant spun away with it still in the back. Dirt and rock flew from the rear tires and Bud Pritchard stood with the seabag at his feet, covered with red dust and his teeth on edge.

Dragging the seabag next to a young second lieutenant, he sat down on the bag and looked out over the runways and parked jets and the perimeter fence and barbed wire and gun emplacements of sandbagged 105mm howitzers, mortars, and 50-caliber machine guns.

"Gum, Lieutenant?"

"Thanks, Major." He took a stick of Blackjack from the blue-and-black pack held out to him and unwrapped it. "Where you headed?"

"Cung Mai Dong."

"Me, too." He folded the stick of Blackjack into his wide mouth and pointed to the low hills, which were covered with rich green foliage, and beyond them, blanketed by clouds, the damp mountains of Quang Hoa. "I hear it's pretty rough out there."

The butterbar LT couldn't be more than twenty-two, Bud Pritchard decided, and the protective feelings that he had experienced for Billy McGarvie surfaced. "Your first command?"

"Yes, sir."

"Damn."

"Sir?"

"Nothing, Lieutenant," he said and decided not to ask for the kid's name or to introduce himself. Bud didn't want to know who he was; he had enough to worry about without having to adopt another Billy McGarvie. Pritchard remained quiet for a long time and tried to ignore the officer.

"Don't mean to pry, sir, but I was wondering if you could tell me something about what it's like out there."

He jerked his head to the cloud-hidden mountains behind the gentle hills and rice paddies. He looked Bud over closely and noticed the arms and face that were roasted brown by the tropical sun, the deep creases around the mouth and extending up his face, the hollowness in his cheeks, the tightness in the eyes, the lean, near-starved body, and the tremor in his hands. "I take it that you've been out there."

"Yeah—you could say that." Major Buddy Pritchard USMC unwrapped the paper from a stick of gum and placed one end between his teeth and started to wipe some of the red dust from his tropicals, then decided it would be useless. He looked into the second lieutenant's eyes, and he saw Billy McGarvie all over again and wondered what would have happened to the PFC if they hadn't been thrown together on Bravo's CA that fateful, cold, rainy morning. "What I would say wouldn't help you none." He wrapped his tongue around the black gum, pulled it into his mouth and chewed, hard, not wanting to talk.

There was no shade at the chopper pad and they sat in the sun, chewing gum and not speaking. A four-man fire team sat in the dirt, one man sharpening a bayonet, another reading a Superman comic book; a third opened a can of C-ration fruit cake, took a bite and offered the rest to the lance corporal with the comic book. The fourth Marine, a peach-faced private with rosy cheeks and big, sad eyes, sat alone outside the group and stared at the ground between his clean new boots.

"A cherry," Bud said.

The second-john looked up. "What's that, sir?"

Pritchard jerked his thumb at the private. "He's a cherry like you; a newbie."

"Yes, sir."

"On second thought, Lieutenant, there is something I'd like to tell you." Bud turned his head to the familiar whump of Huey rotor blades coming at him over the rice fields. "Watch over the cherries; for God's sake and for their mother's." He stood and shouldered the seabag and held tight to the cap on his head, the rotor wash kicking up dirt as the UH-1 settled down on the pad.

The young lieutenant looked at Pritchard, puzzled by the advice, but his attention was quickly diverted to the body bags that were stacked inside the Huey. The fire team was already in the open hatch, and they began to unload the dead. The lieutenant stared, eyes wide when one of the bags dropped from the helicopter and split open.

"Welcome to the war, Lieutenant," Pritchard said.

Chapter 16

Bud Pritchard was not sure why he had come back to Cung Mai Dong. On the back burner of his mind was the nagging notion that someone would have news about Hai Van Phuong. He had two weeks before he must report in at El Toro MCAS, and he was none too anxious to get there; and, of course, Lieutenant, J.G., Janice Elderberry USN was in Cung Mai Dong.

"I missed you, Buddy Pritchard," Janice Elderberry said. She had not eaten much of her meal and she had lost some weight since Bud had last seen her, though she still retained a chubby, matronly look.

"I could say I missed you, too, Lieutenant, but I know you don't take to being bullshitted."

She looked down at the partially eaten T-bone in her plate, and Bud could see that he had hurt her. She poked at the green beans with a fork. The joke didn't fit her.

"Sorry, kid, I didn't mean to be so raw; it's a habit that I don't think about much. The truth is that I thought about you quite a bit and your letters were mighty welcome."

"Why didn't you answer any of them? That hurt, Bud."

Normally not a sensitive man, Pritchard felt a twinge of regret for not allowing himself to indulge his feelings with Janice Elderberry, who was as open with him as he was closed with her. "I'm sorry. I should have answered, but I'm not much at letter writing and I was busy with other things—like trying to stay alive—not that I didn't think about writing; but good lord, Elderberry, you wrote just about every day and I couldn't possibly write that much. I don't know where you found all that stuff you wrote about. I've exhausted everything to say after one or two paragraphs." He looked sheepishly at her. "My spelling is none too hot either."

She tried to smile, but it came out as a grimace instead. Her hair was ruffled in a cute bob and her little breasts were well-formed points pressed against the tight blouse of her uniform and her bare arms were smooth and tanned and she wore a dash of lipstick to bring out the natural rosiness of her nice mouth. She looked fresh and very young and edible.

Janice Elderberry would never be a beautiful woman, but there was a homeyness in her ordinary face and a sparkle in her round eyes that quickly invited you in, and she was quick to put you at ease with an easygoing, spunky manner. Her uniforms were always too tight and not as tidy as they could be, but she took two long showers a day (though the base was on water rations and restricted each person to one short shower every other day) and she always smelled like summer flowers.

So many things were swirling around in her mind that she didn't know where to start. The one question that she thought she dare not ask blurted out in the spontaneous way that was so characteristic of Janice Elderberry.

"How's your wife?"

Bud was cutting into his steak; he stopped and looked up at her. "Why do you have to ruin a perfectly good evening?" He looked around the O-club and recognized many of the men that he had flown with and who soon enough would come over to the table to share their scuttlebutt and to see how he liked it flying with the Navy. He finished cutting the steak and lifted the fork to his mouth. "She's going to Hanoi—haven't you heard?" The steak went down with some difficulty. "Thought you would from the comments about her in your first letter . . . something about a grenade."

"It's because of her you're not flying anymore, isn't it? And why the Marine Corps is sending you back before your tour is over."

"And it's because of her that I'm wearing these gold oak leaves."

"That doesn't seem to be a fair trade."

"It isn't."

She dug her fingers into his arm and leaned across the table to him. "Why do you make me squeeze everything out of you? You don't volunteer a thing. Can't you see that I'm worried about you?"

"You and Thorbus seeing each other?" he said, wanting to change the subject.

The long sigh from Elderberry helped to relieve the developing tension. She ruffled her short hair and reached for Bud's glass of draft beer. "We see each other occasionally." She drank from the glass, and when she replaced it on the table there was a thin mustache of white foam above her upper lip.

Bud reached up and wiped the beer away with a finger. He continued to look at her.

"Forget it if you think he's getting in my drawers, because he's not."

"Why should it matter?"

Janice Elderberry's mouth dropped open and her round

eyes got rounder and the openings in her small nose flared. She flushed red. "You mean you don't even care?"

The words he searched for weren't there, and he knew if he didn't say the right thing she was going to turn the table over onto the floor and make a scene. She was already talking too loud.

"We try to run a quiet, respectable place here, Pritchard."

Bud looked around at First Lieutenant Bob Holcomb, who grinned down at him. "Have a seat, Bob—how you been?"

They shook hands.

"You two having a spat?" He put his *Ba Muoi Ba* on the table and sat down next to Elderberry. "If this old fart has offended you, Lieutenant, I will be honored to come to your assistance." He cupped her hand in his and kissed it. "I think you should apologize to this fair child, Captain."

"He's a major," Elderberry said.

Holcomb frowned and bent forward to look at Pritchard's oak leaves. "Ahhh—miracles still happen."

"He shot down two MIGS and . . ."

"Okay, Elderberry—don't rub it in; I got the message. Sorry I interfered, but please be gentle with my heart. My love for you is deeper than the Gulf of Tonkin . . ."

"Oh, brother," Bud said and looked up at the ceiling.

"Corny, huh? I was the only one in the history of West Jordon High to flunk drama. By the way, Pritchard, I'm running out of Chivas. Want to take a cruise out to Quang Hoa resort or tour the Highlands or see the historic Tan Binh River? My helicopter is at your disposal." He lifted his bottle of *Ba Muoi Ba* to Bud.

"We may be able to do business again." Bud looked at

Elderberry, who seemed to have forgotten the incident. "I've got a debt to pay. You remember that Viet singer I was looking for when you took me out to Quang Hoa in your Huey?" He continued to look at Elderberry.

"How could I forget," Bob said. "If it wasn't for Malcomb Dresser we'd all still be there—buried in the paddy mud. Don't tell me you're still looking for that slopehead?"

Pritchard frowned when he heard Hai Van Phuong referred to so derisively. "Like I said, I got a debt to pay." He finally turned his eyes to Holcomb.

"This is the same girl, isn't it," Janice Elderberry said, "who you were trying to tell me about the last time we sat at this table, before you were transferred to the *Coral Sea?*"

"That's right—Bob knows all about her."

"Well, I don't."

"Tell her," Bob Holcomb said.

Pritchard looked down at his hands on the table. "Elderberry, sometimes you . . ."

"Tell her, Major—she deserves to know."

Bud Pritchard drew a breath and looked across the table at Lieutenant, J.G., Janice Elderberry USN. "I killed her parents—her whole family."

"Oh, Bud," she said. "How?"

With a great deal of reluctance, the tremor in his hands returning, Major Bud Pritchard USMC recounted the painful story for Janice Elderberry. When he finished she had tears in her eyes and Bob Holcomb sat silent and turned the half-empty Vietnamese beer bottle in his two hands.

"It's worth a case of Chivas if you can find out where she is," Pritchard said.

"She had a pronounced limp, didn't she? I remember she always had difficulty getting on and off the platform when she sang."

"Yeah . . . she had a limp. Why?"

"Malcomb Dresser was out at Firebase Briggs in the Ba Den Mountains near the Laotean border—flew door gunner in a Chinook that resupplied the grunts out there, who are getting shelled 'round the clock . . . just as bad as Khe Sanh, I hear. He came back with stories about that Charlie broad who's ambushing Marines and stealing their dog tags."

"What are you talking about?"

"You haven't heard about the Dragon Girl of Song Xanh?" Bob Holcomb said.

"He's been at sea," Janice Elderberry said.

"Anyway," Holcomb continued, "Dresser says that a sergeant by the name of Stuckenberg told him that he saw the girl."

"So what?" Bud said.

"She had a limp."

Elderberry looked down at Bud's hands. "Bud, you ought to let the doc take a look at your hands."

"How soon can you get me out to Briggs?" Pritchard said.

"I can work something out tomorrow. I'm scheduled for an ass and trash to Lai Khoi and can swing over to Briggs. No problem."

Dawn in Cung Mai Dong breaks across a U-shaped valley checkered with rice paddies separated by treelines. The first light comes through the opening at the east end of the valley through a break in the mountains called the keyhole, and it was in that direction that Bud Pritchard would fly with First Lieutenant Bob Holcomb and ten cases of mortar rounds and C-rats and six infantrymen from Echo Company, 2nd Battalion, 1st Marines. Out of the valley, they would turn north, fly along the Tan Binh River to Lai Khoi where a company of Marines and a company of Vietnamese rangers were to sweep north to Firebase Briggs in search of Major Nguyen Vo Toi's battalion of NVA regulars.

Holcomb gave Bud an M16 and 782 gear with eight filled magazine pouches. "The guy who last used these isn't in any condition to want them back." He pinned a couple of grenades on the web gear. "Think the girl is Phuong?"

"If it's Phuong I'll find her," Pritchard said.

Shallow, long rays—the first of the morning—cut through the treelines at the east end of the Cung Mai Dong rice fields, and Bud and Bob Holcomb gave the grunts a hand loading the last cases of mortar ammo and C-ration cartons. The copilot finished the exterior check of the UH-1, and the door gunner, PFC Malcomb Dresser, pulled on black gloves and nodded his recognition to Bud Pritchard.

"Good to see you again, Private," Bud said. "How you been?"

"Fair to middlin', sir. Charlie's been keeping me busy."

"Hope you don't have to pull my nuts out of the fire again—nice to have you along, just in case."

First Lieutenant Bob Holcomb USMCR, radio cord dangling from his APH-5 hard-helmet, shoved his left boot into the Huey's stirrup and swung up to the cockpit. "Okay, mount up—let's go find the war." He turned to the copilot, Second Lieutenant Leonard Malecki from

Battle Creek, Michigan, married two weeks before getting orders to Vietnam and leaving his wife, three months pregnant, with his mother. "And I don't want you to spit tobacco juice on the deck, Malecki. You do and I'll write you up on an Article-15 and make you lick up the mess, understand?"

The cud of tobacco bulging in Leonard Malecki's right cheek rolled to the left cheek, and he strapped the double belts to his waist and chest and plugged in the radio cord. "Turbines coming up—CLEAR!"

"Get Charlie-Tango," Holcomb said.

Leonard Malecki called the Cung Mai Dong control tower (a sandbagged perch set on top of a two-by-four stilt structure on which the VC would zero in their mortars and 122mm and 107mm Katusha rockets), and received permission to lift off and proceed through the keyhole. The choppers always left Cung Mai Dong from the light end, the east end.

Coming through the keyhole, the slick took a round from an AK through the cabin, turned north, found the Tan Binh River, and in just under thirty minutes settled into the red dust at Lai Khoi.

Bud Pritchard, Malcomb Dresser, and the second door gunner, a fat kid named Baby Huey, helped the grunts unload while Bob Holcomb and Leonard Malecki remained strapped in the armored seats and kept the rotor blades turning on idle.

The last of the crates and boxes piled in the dust, Dresser shouted into the mike fixed to his helmet, "Let's hump, Lieutenant."

Bob Holcomb pulled cyclic and throttle, and the slick, "light-light" with most of the load gone, jumped off the ground, heeled west and crossed the river.

Keeping treetop low and flying the nap of the earth, Holcomb weaved the UH-1 up the mountain canyons and over the ridges are back down into the canyons and along rivers, skirted the villages where he usually drew fire and within ten minutes (about 25 kilometers) Firebase Briggs, a red scar on a mountaintop, desolate and scraped clean of any form of plant life, came into view above the morning fog.

"Shangri-la," Bob Holcomb said to Pritchard, who was in the cockpit, leaning forward against Holcomb's seat to get a complete view of Firebase Briggs.

In a whirl of dust the Huey settled onto the mountain, among the debris of discarded ammunition boxes, C-rat cans, spent brass from the howitzers, heaped sandbags filled with red dirt, empty 55-gallon fuel and water drums, and scattered timbers and tin for constructing the bunkers dug out of the earth.

No sooner had Bob Holcomb chopped the switches and the rotors started their slow spindown than Captain Patrick T. Slaughter USMC crawled out of his command post dug into the back slope of the hill, and hitching up his pants, walked up to the knot of Marines that had collected near the nose of the UH-1 Huey. Slaughter was built like a Chicago Bears linebacker.

Holcomb was the first to see the CO. "How you doing, Slaughter? Still got both your testicles?"

"Screw off, Holcomb, or I'll set fire to your toy and you'll have to start earning your pay like the rest of us." He turned to Pritchard. "I'm Pat Slaughter, keeper of this zoo." He extended a dirty, callused hand. He needed a shave.

"I'm Bud Pritchard." He took the hand and returned Slaughter's hard grip.

"What brings you to paradise?"

"The gook girl," Holcomb answered for Bud. "We split a case of Chivas if we help him find her."

Slaughter tipped his steel helmet back on his head and took a pack of Chesterfields from the pocket of his flak jacket. He offered a cigarette to Pritchard. Bud unwrapped a stick of Blackjack instead and folded it into his mouth.

"This here isn't official military business, Captain," Bud said. "At least not yet."

The look on Slaughter's face was noncommittal. "What's the girl to you?"

"That's a fair question; the answer is not simple. Can we step into your office?"

Inside the bunker, Slaughter tossed out a pile of C-rat cans and pulled up a wood ammo case for Pritchard to sit on. Holcomb and Dresser stayed with the helicopter to check out any damage made by small-arms fire during their approach to the firebase. Dresser, a popular and talkative kid, exchanged war stories with some Lurps and artillerymen who were hungry for straight scoop from down below.

"That's a hell of a story," Slaughter said after Bud had finished telling him about Hai Van Phuong. "If the Dragon Girl and Phuong are the same person then she's a far piece from home. What're you going to do with her if you find her? She'll probably try and kill you."

"Don't rightly know; got to find her first." He took out the gum package and unwrapped another stick and offered one to the CO.

Patrick T. Slaughter took the gum from Bud and examined it in his big hand.

"I'll bring her out—that much I know," Pritchard said.

"Can't leave her out there."

Slaughter spit out the Blackjack. "That's bad stuff—I'd rather chew cow dung." He bit off a chaw of Bull Durham and offered the plug to Pritchard.

"Can you get me into the bush—into her turf—where I might be able to make contact?" He bit off a chaw.

"Our mission is long-range recon and I've got patrols all through the area . . . and I've got one going out tonight." He spit tobacco juice into the dust. "They'll take you right through the area where she and her pals wiped out eight of my Lurps. If you capture her, Major, don't bring her back through Briggs. I can't ensure her safety."

That evening, just before the rise of the strange magenta sunsets that streak the fog-laden Laotian border mountains, Major Bud Pritchard had a dinner of chipped beef on toast and canned peaches at the open mess.

"We jump off at twenty-one-thirty hours, Major," Second Lieutenant Gary Hill said. "Have your gear together at Captain Slaughter's bunker a half-hour early for the briefing." He swallowed a spoonful of the SOS and gulped down hot black coffee from a canteen cup. "It'll take us most of the night—a good hard hump—to reach the clearing where Nunzio Pellegrini and his Lurps were ambushed."

"That where you saw the girl, Sergeant?" Bud Pritchard said.

Staff Sergeant Lawrence Stuckenburg had his mouth full of peaches. "That's right—Lieutenant Hill saw her, too, right out in the open, picking Mullen's and Nunzio's bodies clean."

"Malcomb Dresser said that you saw her limping." Pritchard wiped up the chipped beef and white gravy with a piece of toast and pushed away the aluminum mess tray.

"Anything else you noticed about her that might be peculiar?"

"Yeah—she had a dirty bandage on her head," Larry Stuckenburg said.

"On the back of her head," Gary Hill added.

At 9:30 P.M., Major Buddy Pritchard, Second Lieutenant Gary Hill, Staff Sergeant Lawrence Stuckenburg, and fifteen Lurp enlisted men walked off Firebase Briggs and down into the night fog. Along the route they left men at two different trail junctions to set up ambushes. They would meet Pritchard, Hill, and Stuckenburg at the clearing the next day. Each of the teams carried a PR-25 field radio to keep in contact with each other.

It was an hour before dawn when Gary Hill's team reached the clearing and Stuckenburg set the Lurps in an L-shaped ambush at the intersection of two Montagnard trails, only a few yards from where the North Vietnamese had hidden in wait for Sergeant Nunzio Pellegrini's two fire teams.

"Might as well have breakfast," Hill said to Bud Pritchard when the first light of the sun broke through the trees and cooked away the ground fog. "Charlie won't be coming down the trail now."

The two officers ate in silence, and Bud looked around at the wet foliage and listened to the screech of monkeys and parrots. Stuckenburg walked over and reported that there had been no activity over the radio all night and that the other two teams would arrive in about three hours.

"Want to look around for sign of your girl?" Gary Hill said. "You're in the heart of her turf. There's a Yard village about three klicks west on the trail, though I doubt if anybody there would tell you anything."

A hundred yards away, standing in the trees near the hidden entrance to her underground home, Hai Van Phuong watched Major Bud Pritchard talk with the Lurp lieutenant and his sergeant. Around her neck hung Sergeant Nunzio Pellegrini's and PFC Howie Mullen's dog tags. Fear held her in the protection of the jungle—the fear that a wild animal experiences when it gets the scent of the hunter.

This tall man she knew. In her demented state she realized that he would help her, yet she was afraid of him. Her tortured mind struggled with what was psychotic and what was genuine, with what she was seeing through the disintegration of her personality and what fragments she was able to hang onto from her real world. In her state of mind she could not distinguish between the illusory and the authentic. The man in the Marine uniform that she was watching from her hideout was the same man that she remembered she walked with in the forest when the rains came and who promised to return her to her family, but there was something different about him now that she saw him with the other men and heard his voice at a distance and not close to her.

"It might be worth something to talk to the villagers. About three klicks up the trail, you say?"

"I'll give you a couple of riflemen, Major," Gary Hill said. "No telling what you might run into; if we hear any firing, I'll bring the rest of the men up fast."

"Much obliged." He looked back over the clearing where Pellegrini and his men had fallen. "Where exactly did you see the girl?"

Stuckenburg pushed the spoon down into the can of

beef stew and placed a round, dry biscuit cracker into his mouth. He chewed a few times and looked at the elephant grass, which was still and glistened with morning dew. "She was standing about midway in the grass, and when she heard the chopper she ran into the trees right over there."

Pritchard studied the forest where Larry Stuckenburg pointed. "She was alone?"

"As far as I could tell." The sergeant took another cracker from the can and swallowed it nearly whole. After digging around in the stew with the plastic spoon, he ate a mouthful and said to Bud Pritchard, "She couldn't move very fast because of her limp, but by the time we landed she was gone. Funny thing though . . ."

"What's that?"

"Well—we searched the whole area and penetrated pretty far into the trees. She didn't have much of a head start on us, and with that bad leg of hers she couldn't have gotten far ahead. She just seemed to vanish."

Shouldering the ruck and M16, Pritchard started out across the clearing to the point where Stuckenburg had said the girl had disappeared into the jungle, the two Lurp riflemen following behind him through the tall elephant grass.

Hai Van Phuong watched him approach and made no effort to conceal herself in the tunnel. She had a peaceful look on her face though her heart beat rapidly and her eyes were wide and she held her hands tightly together below her small breasts.

"Major," the RTO yelled to Pritchard who was well into the elephant grass and only the camouflage cover on his helmet could be seen.

Bud stopped and looked around through the break he

and the two enlisted men had made in the grass.

"Captain Slaughter is on the radio—says he needs to talk to you rikky-tik."

Hai Van Phuong, when seeing Bud Pritchard turn around and walk back, felt alarmed and made a step toward the clearing as though she would rush to him, but the fear held her and she stopped, her small hands gripping and ungripping together below her breasts.

Laying the M16 in the crook of his arm, Pritchard took the olive-drab handset (the paint chipped and cracked) from the RTO. "Pritchard here."

"You're wanted in Cung Mai Dong, Major," Pat Slaughter said.

"What's up?"

"Don't know; the message said to get you back immediately. I'm dispatching a chopper for you—should be there in twenty minutes."

"Roger," Bud said and gave the set back to the RTO.

On schedule, the Huey from Firebase Briggs landed in the clearing, and Bud Pritchard climbed aboard; the slick rose, pointed its nose low at Hai Van Phuong, pivoted, and banked away, fast, skimming the top of the elephant grass.

The panic that rose in Phuong's heart crumbled her to her knees, and her head bowed down and touched the moldering ground, and she wept. The thumping of the helicopter's blades, which faded slowly away, wrenched her stomach into a hard knot, and she put her hands to her face, the tears running out between the fingers and dripping to the jungle floor. She raised her face to the sky and screamed like a wild animal, then crawled on all fours through the spider hole and down into the tunnels, pulling the sod cover behind her over the entrance.

"What was that?" Sergeant Stuckenburg said, dropping the empty can of beef stew.

"Sounded like the howl of a wild animal." Lieutenant Gary Hill turned to look in the direction of the banshee-like scream and scratched his two-day stubble. "This place is weird—the whole Nam is weird. You never know what you're going to run into next—gives me the creeps."

"Want us to take a look?" Stuckenburg got up from the steel helmet he was using as a seat and reached for the M16.

"Don't waste your time; probably one of those black-faced monkeys in heat." He checked to see that his rifle had a full magazine, took a swig of warm water from a canteen and looked back one more time at where he had heard Hai Van Phuong scream. "Mount up," he said. "This place gives me the willies."

At 3,000 feet Vietnam looked like a peaceful tropical paradise resplendent with sleepy rivers that wandered in and out of a verdant carpet; there were sparkling waterfalls and foaming cascades and beautiful clear skies colored cobalt blue and so intense it hurt the eye to look at them.

The Marine helicopter took a direct heading to Cung Mai Dong and did not return to Firebase Briggs and Captain Patrick T. Slaughter, who had his hands full at that moment coordinating three fire missions in the area in which his patrols were operating.

As the Huey began to descend into Cung Mai Dong, a flight of four Phantoms, launch rails and bomb racks empty, flashed by the open door, and Pritchard turned quickly, but they were too fast and he was unable to catch their tail numbers.

The Huey pilot made his approach from the west, and as the aircraft banked, Bud got a good look at the long valley that led up to the twin mountains that guarded the entrance to Quang Hoa many miles away. The four jets crossed the deep valley between the chopper and the twin mountains, banked hard and headed into their approach to Cung Mai Dong. That view was the last Bud Pritchard would ever have of Quang Hoa.

When the helicopter landed, Pritchard remained strapped into the canvas jumpseat, staring at the deck, his body limp, one hand clasped to the rifle in his lap, the other dangling loosely at his side, his mind meandering between Phuong and Quang Hoa and the outback of Firebase Briggs. His eyes changed focus across the Huey's deck to pieces of 782 webbing, a canteen cover, a cracked helmet liner with a bullet hole in it, two banana clips of 5.62 ammo, a discarded rucksack and a torn and badly soiled flak jacket. Brass shell casings littered the deck. The last thing he remembered looking at before he heard Ralph Thorbus shout at him from the hatch was a pool of dried blood the color of a toy tractor he got from Santa Claus when he was a small boy.

"You coming out, Pritchard, or are you planning to camp in there for the rest of the war?"

When Bud didn't answer, Thorbus jumped up on the skid and looked inside. "You okay?"

Not taking his eyes off the deck, Bud said that he was all right and that he wanted to be left alone for a few minutes.

"Still as strange as ever," Major Ralph Thorbus mumbled and dropped down to the pad and stood off fifty feet from the aircraft and smoked a cigarette.

By the time Ralph Thorbus had smoked the Marlboro down to the filter, Pritchard had thrown his ruck out and was climbing down to the ground. The four Phantoms that had landed ahead of the Huey were parked in revetments, and the pilots walked along the wall of sandbags and looked over at Pritchard. He didn't recognize any of their faces.

"How have you been, Ralph?" Pritchard's voice was tired.

"I've been okay." He glanced at the oak leaves on Pritchard's collar points but said nothing; he had heard the rumor.

"How'd you know where to find me? I've got orders to MCAS El Toro."

"Your orders have been changed as has been your time in transit," Ralph Thorbus said. "Your new orders are waiting for you in Da Nang, where you would have picked them up if you had followed standard Marine Corps operating procedures and reported in to the base commander as ordered."

"Stow it, Ralph—just give me the straight skinny."

"I'll give it to you all right, but first you'll listen to what I've got to say. When I tied the can to your tail and washed you out to sea I knew you'd think I'd done it because of Janice. The truth is that I think Lieutenant Elderberry is too good a woman for you, but she's in love with you and not me and there's not a thing I can do to change that, though I've done my best to change her mind."

"Including getting me transferred to the *Coral Sea* where you hoped I would be killed."

Thorbus's face began to purple, and his lips contorted and his hands balled into fists. Pritchard wasn't worried.

He knew he could take Ralph Thorbus with little trouble and wished that the major would give him the excuse to clean his plow, but he also knew that Thorbus was too intelligent to risk an incident that would mar his record, and on top of that he valued his health too much to let someone punch out his lights.

"I may not like you, Pritchard, but I didn't get you fired from my squadron because of Janice Elderberry. I did so because you were endangering the lives of the men you were flying with and for your flagrant disregard of orders. I felt, and the Old Man felt, that the discipline of carrier duty would shape you up. I see that I was wrong."

"You know something, Thorbus, you always dish up a hot plate of bullshit when you're in a corner and sometimes it gets to steaming so much and smelling so bad that I'm surprised it doesn't melt the paint right off the aircraft parked along the runway."

To Bud's great surprise, Ralph Thorbus took a shot at him. All temper and no skill, the major was not a fighter, and Pritchard quickly had him in a double hammerlock and his head shoved up against the side of the UH-1. "You fool, Thorbus—what did you expect to gain by that?"

Ralph Thorbus grunted in pain and clawed at the fuselage with his free hand, his face beet red and contorted.

"And while I'm at it," Pritchard said, his breath coming hard, "I pray that every night you crawl in the sack you see the faces of those dead kids on Hill 506 whose lives you could have saved."

He gave Thorbus's arm a twist and the major's mouth flew open and his head bent backward and he yelled.

A jeep slid up in a cloud of dust, but Pritchard never noticed, so intent was he in punishing Ralph Thorbus for the months of abuse he had taken from the man. The parting words of Josh Billington came through the red haze: *If you get rid of that chip on your shoulder and keep your brass polished you can have a new life in the Corps.*

"Let him go, Bud, you're going to break his arm!" Bob Holcomb had Pritchard around the neck, his forearm pressed against the Adam's apple.

Bud twisted out of the hold and planted a left hook on Holcomb's jaw. The lieutenant went down as if he'd been hit by a sledgehammer. Ralph Thorbus slid down the side of the helicopter and collapsed on his back.

"You animal," Janice Elderberry screamed. She stood beside the jeep in her too-tight dungarees, hands to her face, eyes wide and staring at Bud Pritchard. "Look what you've done—look!"

Not bothering to retrieve any of the gear he had dropped, Pritchard pushed Elderberry roughly aside and climbed into the driver's seat, started the engine, and spun away in a choking dust that left Janice Elderberry alone with two battered men and near-hysterical with anger and frustration.

Chapter 17

The C-141 Starlifter taxied off of the parking apron and rolled onto the 5,000-foot runway. After a few minutes of waiting for clearance with engines on idle, the big four-engine transport groaned forward, picked up speed an inch at a time and climbed into the air like a slow, awkward reptile that belonged on the ground and not in the sky.

The Starlifter, loaded with seven-foot-long, two-foot-wide aluminum coffins strapped together in its hold, turned south along the strand of white sand beach with the green rice fields of Da Nang on one side and the turquoise blue of the South China Sea on the other, and passed through white towering gates of cumulus that began with their bottoms at 10,000 feet and rose to 20,000 feet at their tops.

Seated next to the coffins in the Starlifter as Vietnam slipped away underneath him was Major Bud Pritchard USMC, strapped into a jumpseat next to a small window. He fingered the brown manila envelope on his lap and stared at the shiny metal cases with the olive-drab straps tightened around them. Inside the envelope were orders for him to report without delay in transit to the Commandant of the Marine Corps, 8th and I, Washington, D.C. There he would be met by his old friend

Colonel Norbert "Iron Jaw" Keane USMC and U.S. Senator Chester T. Newman.

The frustration of not being given a chance to search for Hai Van Phuong in the jungles surrounding Firebase Briggs and the guilt he felt for punching Bob Holcomb cold and his quick departure without a word to Janice Elderberry gave Bud Pritchard a big empty feeling and a very large sense of regret.

At Clark Air Force Base in the Philippines he had a two-hour layover and took a bowl of soup at the officers' mess but was unable to finish it. Hours later at Guam he was able to eat a fried egg sandwich on toasted wheat bread. He left the coffee, which tasted like the bottom of a canteen cup. While he ate the fried egg sandwich two B-52 pilots sat down at his table with trays of food and the three of them discussed the war and shared their experiences bombing the Vietnamese.

The Air Force bomber pilots were very interested in Pritchard's encounters with MiGs, and afterward they took him out to the flight line, where they went aboard one of the Stratofortresses and Bud was given a brief familiarization course on the characteristics of the B-52.

In the Hawaiian Islands at Hickam Air Force Base, the Starlifter made a fuel stop only and then climbed back into the air and flew direct to Norton Air Force Base in San Bernardino, California, where the aluminum boxes and the men in them were offloaded and placed in cold storage pending delivery to the families.

Taking a chance that PFC Billy McGarvie was still in San Diego, Bud called the Naval Hospital.

"He's indisposed at the moment," the nurse said.

"What do you mean he's indisposed?" Bud said, impatiently.

"He's on the head."

"Well, why didn't you say so? Tell him to hurry up—I'll hold the line."

"Who shall I say is calling?" the nurse said in her most irritating voice, as though Pritchard were interrupting a meeting with the Joint Chiefs of Staff.

"Tell him Major Bud Pritchard is calling."

Her attitude quickly changed and she answered in a calm, pleasant voice: "Yes, sir, I will do that."

"On second thought," Pritchard said as he watched a well-endowed WAF with legs that came all the way up to her neck walk by the telephone booth, "change that to *Captain* Bud Pritchard."

"You know there are criminal penalties for impersonating an officer." The irritation was back in the nurse's voice.

"Just tell him . . . I don't have time to explain."

Less than a minute later Billy's excited homespun voice was on the line; he was out of breath. "Captain! How you doing? What you doing in Dago? Where's Lieutenant Elderberry? She wrote me a letter. How are the guys in Cung Mai Dong? And what happened to the girl? And—"

"Hold on, kid—calm down."

"When the nurse told me you were on the line I got so excited I forgot to wipe my ass and I tripped on the pants around my ankles and gee whiz what you doing back in the world?"

"It's a long story—too long—and I don't have but a minute; I'm between transferring airplanes in San Bernardino and took the chance that you were still in the hospital."

"Good thing you called today; tomorrow I leave the

hospital for Camp Pendleton, and then they're going to ship me back to Nam."

Bud Pritchard was dumbfounded.

"Sir . . . are you still there?"

"Incredible," Bud said. "How can they send you back, Billy? That was a bad wound you received—so bad it should disqualify you from active duty. You should be discharged and sent home to Nevada and finish your schooling or go to work for that Mr. Miller you talked about all the time, the fella who runs the Shell station in Windfall."

"The docs fixed me up real good—hardly have a limp. They say I'll be able to run as good as I ever did once I get to Pendleton."

Bud Pritchard wanted to put his fist through the glass door of the telephone booth. The waste—the idiocy of it all.

"Besides—I'm kind of looking forward to getting back to my battalion and Bravo Company; I feel like I let the guys down when I got hit so quick."

Bud's lips were squeezed tight and the lines in his forehead deepened. "They won't call you Cherry when you get back." His laugh was hollow. "Did you get your medal?"

"Yes, sir. A colonel from the base came over with a couple other officers and they had a little ceremony around my bed with some of the hospital staff after I'd been here for a few weeks. It was real nice and some of the guys in the ward came over in wheelchairs and on crutches and congratulated me. I guess you got yours—I been reading about you in the papers, all that trouble with your wife."

An Air Force master sergeant tapped on the outside of

the booth and pointed to a C-130 on the apron, its number four engine prop slowly turning over.

"Billy, I've got to go. I probably won't talk to you again before you ship out. Take care of yourself and remember to keep your flak jacket zipped and your head down and write to your mother every day."

"Sir, one last thing."

"Make it quick, kid—my aircraft is leaving."

"What happened to the girl—the Vietnamese girl and her brother we took to Quang Hoa?"

"After you got hit I went back to the village to look for her, but she had left—gone north—no one knows where for sure."

"Someone should take care of her now that she doesn't have a family. Too bad you couldn't find her; it's a real shame 'cause she was such a nice person and very sick and hurt."

Pritchard started to tell him about the Dragon Girl and his trip to Firebase Briggs and the patrol with the Lurps, but the master sergeant pounded hard on the booth and Bud had to hang up.

The flight across country to Bolling Air Force Base in Washington made a stop at Wright-Patterson AFB in Ohio to offload aircraft spare parts and six officers who were to report for new assignments at ASD/BILHT in the Technical Order Control Unit. Bud Pritchard had been in the air more than forty hours, smelled like a goat, had lived on coffee and Blackjack gum and an occasional old sandwich from a box lunch, and had slept a total of five hours (which he caught only in snatches while strapped in the webbed canvas jumpseats). When the C-130 Hercules rolled up to the terminal at Bolling Air Force Base in Washington, D.C., the only consolation to his red eyes, ugly-tasting mouth, and rumpled uniform was that he had complied with orders and was reporting without delay in transit (wilth the exception of the two days lost at Firebase Briggs, which he would explain).

The small washroom in the terminal was crowded, and rather than attempt to clean up—an impossible task—he decided to take a cab to Headquarters Marine Corps and check into the BOQ.

The cabbie, not used to seeing a Marine, let alone an officer of Marines, unshaven and so scruffy-looking, tried unsuccessfully to hide his curiosity and kept sneaking glances at Pritchard through the rearview mirror, the act of which caused him twice to slam on the brakes to prevent the cab from slamming into the cars stopped at red lights.

At 8th and I he reported to the officer-of-the-day and was given a billet in the BOQ, an old brick building with iron beds that looked as if they had been requisitioned for Tun Tavern during the Revolutionary War. The barracks was empty except for a second lieutenant in the head whose haircut was so short that Pritchard could see the moles on his scalp.

"Major."

"Lieutenant."

Bud undressed and dropped his sweat-stained uniform on the concrete floor and kicked it into the corner. He tossed the skivvies on top of the heap and dug at his crotch with both hands, enjoying the luxurious scratch.

"Just in from Nam?" The lieutenant examined his face with great care in the mirror and lathered up with shaving soap.

"Is the mess still open? I haven't had decent chow in

three days."

"Don't know, sir—just got in myself."

Bud looked at him closer and searched his memory. The young officer looked familiar. "Got an extra towel? I didn't bring one in the rush to get out."

"Take mine—I can get another."

"Thanks." Pritchard turned to go into the shower.

"You've been promoted," the lieutenant said, looking at him through the mirror while he scratched at his beard with a razor.

Pritchard looked back. "I thought you looked familiar, but I can't place your face."

"We met briefly. There wasn't time for introductions; we were too busy saving our asses."

Then Bud recognized him. He looked much younger without the steel pot on his head and a six-day growth of beard and the red mud of Hill 506 and the Vui Bong streaked on his face. "Bradley Cummings—Bravo Company's CO."

"Acting CO," he corrected. "Jerry Tatman was killed, remember? I took over when we came off the hill after you and Rodriguez and Corporal Hank and the cherry, Billy McGarvie, and the rest of that squad of crazies ambushed the gooks supply line and then counterattacked down the highballer from behind. Never saw you and McGarvie again until you showed up at the river and pulled our balls out of the fire again. We thought you were dead somewhere back at the hill."

"Had an errand to run in Quang Hoa." Bud turned on the hot water and steam rose in the shower.

"That right?" Bradley Cummings said. "Say, you had a dink girl with you. Saw you jump out of the resupply chopper with her; what was that all about?"

"I owed her a favor."

Cummings rinsed his face of shaving soap and picked up Bud Pritchard's uniform shirt lying in the corner and examined the rows of ribbons and saw the Navy Cross and Silver Star on the far right of the top row of decorations. *Good, they gave them to him. I guess the recommendation of a shavetail second lieutenant carries some weight after all.*

The spray of hot water full in Pritchard's face helped to wash the fog from his brain, and as he scrubbed the grime and tiredness from his body he began to think seriously about getting some food into his stomach. The official business could wait. "Hey, Cummings," he shouted over the roar of the water that he had on full blast, "How about you and I having some chow together?" He was feeling much better. "I don't like to eat alone."

"Sure, Major—be my pleasure."

The officers' mess was traditional Marine Corps and spotlessly clean and carried an air of authority and old military flavor. In fact, it was a lesson in Marine Corps history. The walls were covered with portraits of past Commandants, scenes of historic battles at Chapultapec, Tripoli, Belleau Wood, Iwo Jima, and Inchon, and pictures of Marines in uniform beginning in colonial times at Tun Tavern and coming up through WWII and the present.

"Think you can find some extra Cs in the back for a hungry grunt and an old kerosene burner?" Bud said to the mess sergeant, who was leaning into a couple of PFCs mopping the red tile floor.

The sergeant, his beer belly bulging underneath the white apron wrapped around his waist, pushed the fore-and-aft white mess cover forward so that it rested canted on his eyebrows. He looked over the two officers.

The permanent scowl in his face gave him a tough, leathered look and his eyes drilled into Bud Pritchard. "You two look like a couple of starved scarecrows. Looks like I'm going to have to put in another tour in Cung Mai Dong and get the chow straightened out. You're Major Bud Pritchard, aren't you, sir? Recognize your picture from *Stars and Stripes* and the *Washington Post.* Come on into the galley, both of you gentlemen, and I'll cook up your meal, personally." As he led Pritchard and Cummings into the spacious galley he looked over his shoulder: "Steak and eggs be all right?"

"That'll be just fine, Sergeant."

While the mess sergeant threw two porterhouse steaks on the four-foot-long griddle, he introduced himself as Ted Hauk and said that he had been in Vietnam for a thirteen-month tour in the early days when the Marine base at Cung Mai Dong was first built and the Viet Cong would steal food from his mess galley at night until he booby-trapped the pantry and refrigerators and blew the whole mess to hell including the VC.

Bud's stomach grumbled and his mouth filled with saliva and he came close to grabbing the porterhouse off the griddle and eating it with his bare hands. By the time he and Second Lieutenant Bradley Cummings each sat down with a plate piled with the cattleman's cut of steak mounted with two fried eggs, French fried potatoes and fresh corn on the cob dripping with butter, he was hungrier then he had ever been in his life.

"I'm putting you in for a Medal of Honor, Sergeant Hauk," Bradley Cummings said. "Best C-rats I've ever eaten."

"Gives me great pleasure to see my officers well fed and enjoying it." The scowl never left his face. "Don't mean to pry, Major, but how are things working out for you, I mean the newspapers have made a big thing about you being a decorated war hero and your wife a leader in the antiwar movement. Seems to me that a man's career could get pretty messed up from something like that."

Bud Pritchard kept right on eating, shoving a forkful of French fries into his mouth and cutting a hunk of steak. He took time to wash it down with black coffee, then said; "I'll find out about my career right after I finish this great meal, but I don't think there's much that can get messed up in that area."

"Sir?" Sergeant Hauk said.

"My career was messed up before my wife got hold of it."

The paneled oak door swung open, and Major Bud Pritchard USMC walked into the Marine Corps Commandant's office and came to a halt the regulation three paces in front of the general's desk and stood at rigid attention, hands along the seams of his trousers, cover tucked under his left arm, his eyes fixed at a point just above the four-star general's head, the regulation position. The adjutant quietly closed the door behind him.

"Stand at ease, Major," the Commandant said.

"Thank you, sir." It was the regulation response.

"I think you know Colonel Keane."

Colonel Norbert "Iron Jaw" Keane, commander of the Marine Corps Schools and longtime friend of Bud Pritchard and his wife, Marjorie Pritchard, stood up out of the black leather Angelus Brothers armchair. "Bud, how you been; good to see you." Norbert Keane grabbed Pritchard's hand and shook it vigorously. "Been a long time, old buddy."

"Two years, Norb." Bud studied his friend's face. It was the same rock-solid face with the strong, determined jaw that he remembered in flight school at Pensacola with Josh Billington and aboard the *Hornet* in Korea and at MCAS Cherry Point before he shipped out for Vietnam. There was something else there too, in the eyes, that wasn't familiar—a hardness, or was it something else, maybe insensitivity. It puzzled Pritchard because he remembered Norbert Keane to be a man quick to respond to the feelings of others, even soft-hearted at times.

The Commandant ran the palm of his rough infantryman's hand over the steel-gray sidewall of his GI haircut and leaned forward on the huge hand-polished teak desk that he had brought home with him from Subic Bay, in the Philippines at the end of WWII. "First, I want to congratulate you on your battle commendations, Major Pritchard. Your aggressiveness in the field is in keeping with the highest tradition of the Naval Service and the proud record of the United States Marine Corps. You've done a fine job in Vietnam, and there is no reason you shouldn't progress nicely after the long hiatus in your career, asuming that you carry out your new responsibilities efficiently and with the same enthusiasm that you have demonstrated on the battlefield."

In other words: play ball, Pritchard. He remembered what Josh Billington had told him just before he left the *Coral Sea.*

There was a short, effective silence, and the Commandant leaned back off his elbows on the desk and sat back comfortably in the chair and smiled; he revealed a row of clean white teeth, his own.

Pritchard cut his eyes over to Norbert Keane while the Commandant lit his Morlin pipe and noticed that Iron Jaw was staring with dead eyes across the room at nothing at all.

"My role in meeting you today," the general continued, "is to encourage you to carry out your new duties as expeditiously as possible and with the utmost force." He emphasized force. "Colonel Keane will fill you in on the details and provide you with the necessary logistic support and answer all your questions."

The Commandant stood and offered his hand, terminating the meeting. Bud shook the general's hand, came to attention and then walked to the door with Colonel Norbert Keane in front of him.

"Oh, by the way, Major Pritchard," the Commandant said.

Bud turned. Keane had his hand on the doorknob.

"Give my regards to your wife."

Once outside, Iron Jaw returned to the joking good-natured friend that Bud Pritchard knew. They walked across the parade ground and past the row of old cannon and out through a break in the silver maple trees to the curb on 8th Street where a new, green Oldsmobile with *U.S. Marine Corps* painted on the side waited with a staff sergeant.

"Take us to Capitol Hill," Norbert Keane said to the staff sergeant. He turned to Pritchard after they had gotten settled in the backseat, and the Oldsmobile pulled away from the curb. "We're going to see Senator Newman."

"What's this all about, Norb? I travel twelve thousand miles in a rush to get here because my orders are stamped 'urgent' and 'no delay in transit,' and I arrive red-eyed, hungry, and feeling stupid and meet the Commandant, who does nothing but shake my hand and tell me to give his regards to Marjorie."

Keane bent forward and examined Bud's eyes. "You're right, your eyes are red, but that could be from the unaccountable two days, probably in some unknown Asian port with a couple of long-eyed, flat-nosed lotus blossoms." He laughed and smacked Bud on the leg with his open hand. Then his expression changed and he got serious and that hard look that Pritchard had seen in the Commandant's office returned. "These are difficult times, Major—we are all being called upon to dig our foxholes deeper." He looked purposely away from Pritchard and watched the silver maples lining I Street go past the open window. The Oldsmobile turned right on 6th Street and drove south toward Pennsylvania Avenue.

A red squirrel scrambled down a tree and raced across the street; the driver put on the brakes and there was a screech of tires. "Sorry, sir." He got up to speed again and turned left on Pennsylvania Avenue. The Capitol was in view a half-mile away.

"The TET Offensive took the American public by surprise." Norbert Keane said, still looking out the side window. "Though it was a disaster militarily for the North Vietnamese and the Viet Cong, the initial force of the surprise attacks throughout the major cities of South Vietnam was overplayed by the liberal press and the hyped reports made all of us look like we got caught with our pants down. The Communists came out looking like they had won a major victory and many in Congress and elsewhere say we should pack up and go home while we have any face left to save."

Bud Pritchard unwrapped a stick of Blackjack gum and

curled it into his mouth. "We kicked the *nuoc mam* out of the gooners at TET. Anyone that was in the action knows that."

"Reporters—those with the biggest media pull—sleep in the Caravelle and Continental with sweet-smelling boom-boom girls and not in rain-filled fighting holes with sour-smelling infantrymen." He declined the gum Bud offered him. "The point is that the people over here believe the media and not the military, and to make matters worse, Westmoreland is crying for more troops and the antiwar protesters are putting extraordinary pressure on President Johnson to get out of Vietnam. We don't think he's going to seek reelection."

"I suppose you're going to get around to telling me how I fit into this," Bud Pritchard said.

"We'll be with Senator Newman in just a few minutes and we'll get down to business. I think you'll be pleasantly surprised what we have in mind for you. I might mention that I've invited Marjorie to join us."

Bud swallowed his gum and began a fit of coughing. The Oldsmobile pulled to the curb in front of the steps leading up to the Capitol, and the staff sergeant opened the rear door.

Marjorie Pritchard sat on a Clarence House contemporary love seat covered in dragon empress chintz designed by Jacquard. Her Benson and Hedges Filtertip Gold (extra long) lay smoldering in a crystal ashtray that rested on the Edgar B. cherry wood lamp table next to her. A soft lemon glow from the Frederick Cooper Buddha lamp lit the table.

Bud stood in the middle of Senator Chester T. Newman's office, and his eyes quickly took in the original oils, the Persian carpet, the hand-carved mahogany desk, and his wife. "Hello, Marjorie . . . thought you were in Hanoi." His voice was pleasant, but there was a firm set to his mouth.

"Hanoi was postponed." She looked at Norbert Keane and then to Senator Newman, who had come around from behind his desk and stood to the side of Keane. "I see you've been busy," Marjorie said, looking at Bud's new decorations and the rank insignia on his uniform.

Colonel Keane quickly defused the bomb Marjorie Pritchard had lit by introducing Bud to the senator, and then Newman asked Bud how his flight was across the Pacific, to which Bud answered that it was long and tiring but without incident (his eyes remained on his wife).

The faded and torn Wrangler jeans, Bud Pritchard decided, did justice to Marjorie's figure, though the sloppy blue-and-gold University of California sweatshirt (with a peace symbol painted on the front and back) did nothing for her big breasts except reveal that she wasn't wearing a bra. She looked totally out of place in Senator Newman's office, which, of course, was the way she had planned it.

Goodwin J. Rapshir sat next to Marjorie Pritchard on the Clarence House love seat, his fingers idly caressing the dragon empress chintz. He was not introduced.

After five minutes more of small talk, Norbert Keane set his jaw and turned to Bud Pritchard' "Bud, the Senator has an interesting proposal that we would like you to listen to."

Pritchard had purposely chosen a straight-backed Queen Anne wooden chair instead of a seat on the original Hepplewhite settee with Colonel Norbert Keane because it prevented him from relaxing. Senator Chester T. Newman remained standing.

"We would like you to accompany your wife to Hanoi to meet with General Giap," Chester T. Newman said. He folded his arms across his chest. "What do you think of the idea?"

"I don't like it," Pritchard said immediately.

Marjorie lifted the Benson and Hedges Filtertip Gold from the crystal ashtray and took a long drag. "Why not?" she said. The smoke she exhaled curled around the Buddha and rose into the lampshade. "You've never been happy with your little war; now's your chance to bring it to an end and get out."

"What Marjorie means," Norbert Keane said, "is that a peace overture to General Giap from both a military hero and a leader of the antiwar movement could go a long way in influencing the North Vietnamese to sit down with Henry Kissinger to negotiate the end of the conflict."

The smile that Marjorie gave Bud Pritchard reminded him of the too infrequent intimate moments he had experienced with his wife over the more than twenty years of marriage. He caught her looking out the tails of her mascara-rimmed eyes at Iron Jaw Keane, and he wondered if she was sleeping with him as he guessed she was with the wimpy kid sitting next to her on the Clarence House love seat.

"You're both internationally known personages and Hanoi cannot take you lightly," the senator said. "They'll have to listen."

"At least that much," Bud said disparagingly. "Do you think for a second that the North Vietnamese will settle for anything but total victory? They've made that clear from the beginning, with the French."

"I'd like to say something to Major Pritchard," Goodwin J. Rapshir said.

Everyone turned to him. Bud was surprised at the deepness and authority of the young man's voice and could see by the air with which he spoke why Marjorie was taken by him.

"It should be perfectly clear from the popularity of our efforts, especially after the great outpouring of support that followed Marjorie's last speech at the Lincoln Memorial, that America is fed up with the butchering of the Vietnamese people."

Bud Pritchard felt revulsion, the same kind he felt when he saw a stink bug crawl out from underneath an overturned rock.

"I would prefer that Marjorie go without you, Major," Rapshir continued, "free from the encumbrances of the U.S. government and the prejudices of the military command. There are many disadvantages to going to North Vietnam as official emissaries. There is little doubt that General Giap would give us much more attention and publicity if we arrived in Hanoi in direct violation of U.S. foreign policy. However, before any realistic end to the war can be worked out, official U.S. government representatives must sit down with Hanoi to discuss the POW issue and conditions of troop withdrawal, and we are in no position to do that, but you are. Now, doesn't it make sense that we cooperate for the good of the country?" Goodwin J. Rapshir leaned back in the love seat and waited, a thin smile on his lips.

They all stared at Bud Pritchard. Marjorie smoked her cigarette and rocked a long leg across her knee.

"How long will it take to work out the trip?" Bud said.

"A few weeks," Newman answered.

"All right—I'll go along with it, assuming that I'd be ordered to anyway; the Commandant said as much. I have only one suggestion, that Marjorie and I arrive and leave Hanoi together and that there be no separate meetings with the North Vietnamese for either of us. When the press photographs us we are to be together and any statements made to the press will have both our concurrences. In this way we will present an image of solidarity that the Communists will have difficulty exploiting."

"There won't be any objections to that, right, Marjorie?" the senator said.

She smiled. "Of course not." She tugged at the sweatshirt, her big breasts rolling like grapefruits underneath the material.

"Then it's settled." Senator Chester T. Newman clapped his hands together and smiled broadly. "Whether or not General Giap agrees to see you, which I believe he will, we have accomplished something here that will go a long way to heal the country. Thank you both."

After Marjorie and Goodwin J. Rapshir and the senator left the office, and Pritchard and Norb Keane were alone, Bud unwrapped a stick of gum and came directly to the point: "There's more to this, isn't there?"

The hard, insensitive look came into Colonel Keane's eyes. "I told Newman that you wouldn't be fooled. I don't have to tell you anything more, you know that, don't you?"

"The deal's off unless you give me the whole story."

"Doesn't matter what you do now—we got what we wanted accomplished."

The frown on Bud Pritchard's face deepened. "What the hell are you talking about?"

"Tomorrow's papers will announce the agreement we've come to with the antiwar people, and Marjorie will be made to look like a saint—no, that's not quite right."

"More like a turncoat?" Pritchard said, the gum, unwrapped, held between his fingers.

"Oh, you are quick, Pritchard; you haven't lost the touch."

"You bastard—you never planned for a second that there would be a meeting with Giap. All you wanted was for Marjorie to look like she sold out to the establishment."

"Marjorie and Rapshir were getting too powerful, I think you can appreciate that. The whole movement was taking on a cohesiveness and structure that would, in a very short time, develop into a monster that we could no longer deal with. We could very easily have a revolution on our hands. Something had to be done to derail the freight."

"Clever, Colonel . . . real clever, but it doesn't wash. I was set up from the start, wasn't I? When did you decide to use me—how far back?"

"When Marjorie began using you for propaganda—her first Berkeley speech at Sproul Hall."

"The transfer from Cung Mai Dong to the *Coral Sea* and the promotion and the medals were all part of your plan?"

"Let's just say that we exploited the situation and did what we had to do for the good of the country."

"You mean for the good of Norbert Keane."

"Come along with me, Bud. There's plenty of room at the top for the both of us. You'll have silver eagles on your shoulders in no time at all. Don't you think it's time that you do yourself a favor and stop going against the grain? The rewards are unlimited for team players."

"So this is what Billington meant when he said that I had acquired new friends and to keep my brass polished." He jammed the unchewed gum into the ashtray and started for the door.

"Bud, just another minute before you go. This wasn't my idea. It developed from much higher sources and I was brought in by the CIA because of my close relationship with you. I never thought you would take it so hard, believe me. If I had I wouldn't have agreed to do it."

"See your enemy—kill him—and get away fast," Bud Pritchard said and walked out of the office.

Chapter 18

The chuffing of helicopters landing and lifting off Firebase Briggs filled the muggy air while the 105mm and 155mm artillery pieces pounded at the North Vietnamese dug in the mountains miles away. The temperature was 102 degrees.

With one leg draped over his rucksack and the other dangling in a foxhole, and his back against a wall of sandbags, Major Bud Pritchard USMC ate a mouthful of C-ration ham and lima beans and looked up at the line of Hueys that approached the top of the red, scarred hill; he shaded his eyes against the brilliance of the silver sky. "Here come more wounded," he said with a heave of his chest and turned his attention back to the ham and limas. "This tastes terrible—you got anything better?"

Lieutenant, J.G., Janice Elderberry USN gave him her can of beans and franks. "Go ahead, I can't finish it—got to get to the aid tent." Her eyes were red and her nice mouth drawn and her white arms sunburned up to where the sleeves of her dungaree shirt were rolled above the elbows. Her hair was tucked under a blood-flecked utility cover, and she had trouble getting her chubby, matronly rump off the sandbags. "You going out with Lieutenant Hill and Sergeant Stuckenburg again?"

"As soon as Slaughter can decide what to do."

A 105 howitzer fired three rounds; red dust rose around the emplacement and drifted over Pritchard and Elderberry.

"There's another platoon from Cung Mai Dong coming in and he may want Hill and Stuckenburg to take them out." He dug the white plastic spoon into the beans and franks and looked up at Elderberry. "The dinks are dug in to stay—doesn't look good."

Elderberry attempted to brush off some of the red dust from her pants. The helicopters were much closer and she could see the wounded inside, arms and legs hanging out the open hatches. The bored door gunners leaned against the M60s mounted on pivot pylons.

"Think you'll ever find her?" she said.

"Have to—got no choice."

"How many more days do you have?"

He looked inside the bean can and was quiet for a while. "I'm not going back until I find her."

"Don't be foolish. You've got five days before you have to start flying again and if you don't report in, Thorbus will hang you." She bent down and patted him on the chest, and red dust rose from the utility shirt. "Take care of yourself out there, Buddy Pritchard. This war is for kids, not old men; see you when you get back."

"Maybe tonight."

"I'll have a can of ham and limas heated up for you." She ran off to the lead helicopter that had touched down.

He watched her attractive rump bounce between the ammo bunkers and 55-gallon drums and sandbags, and he laughed at himself for what had happened to him in the past weeks.

It would have been easy to go along with Norbert Keane and Chester T. Newman to secure his career: rapid rise in the ranks—making up for the lost years—command of an air wing and later a fat position in the Pentagon with Keane and shaking hands with the boys at Langley.

The whole setup stank as far as he was concerned, and he would probably never be able to wash the smell of Washington out of his clothes. Once Senator Newman and the CIA's version of what happened broke in the newspapers and on prime-time TV, Marjorie Pritchard's circle of power crumbled and the antiwar movement lost its momentum. It divided into leaderless, bickering factions.

Marjorie, of course, accused Pritchard of stabbing her in the back, and there was a big scene in San Diego before he shipped out for his third Vietnam tour. She filed for divorce and dropped out of sight and he never heard from her again.

Coming in behind the medevac choppers, the Hueys from Cung Mai Dong circled once and then came straight down onto the pad, their rotors whumping and chuffing and the red dust flying in a great cloud swirl.

The troops broke from the side hatches and ran stooped over for about twenty yards where they were safe from the rotor sweep, then threw off their rucks and lit up smokes.

The last Marine out of the second Huey carried an M79 grenade launcher and a pouch of blooker rounds hung from one shoulder. His big feet caught on the chopper's skid and he went down; the steel pot fell from his head and revealed a mop of dirty blond hair and a peach-skin face and doe eyes.

Major Bud Pritchard threw the can of beans and franks into the foxhole and rose slowly. "I'll be a pregnant whore!" He ran to the chopper. "Billy."

McGarvie rose from the red dirt, his gear twisted and spilling, and made a try at saluting, but his arm got caught in the sling of the thump gun and he got the hand only as far as his eye. "Hello, sir. I heard you was out here somewhere."

"They went ahead and did it."

"No, sir—I asked them to send me; I had to come back."

Bud Pritchard stood under the blades of the slick, staring at Billy McGarvie, the kid who should be back home in high school and working on weekends at the neighborhood gas station. The creases in his forehead and in his face deepened. "You figure you owe someone?"

"Sort of." PFC Billy McGarvie unwrapped his stuck hand from the grenade launcher's sling and picked up the spin-ball grenades that had spilled. "My squad leader says he'd put me in for lance corporal but I haven't been in the Corps long enough . . . not enough time-in-grade."

Pritchard continued to stare at him.

"I guess I was lucky to make PFC right out of ITR. The range sergeant said I did real good with the thumper, that's why they made me a PFC." He smiled, looking for approval from Bud.

Pritchard secured the cover of the pouch that held the blooker rounds and strapped it in place on McGarvie's web gear. "You're the best thump gunner in the Marine Corp, Billy; you've proved that."

Billy McGarvie brightened. "Thanks, sir. Well, I better get over to my squad and get formed up; don't want to screw up on my first CA."

"Your second," Pritchard said. "The first was worth a thousand." He watched the boy run across the pad to his squad, a noticeable limp in his leg.

More helicopters came in and unloaded infantrymen and supplies until Second Platoon—forty men from Bravo Company, 2nd Battalion, 1st Marines—had assembled at Firebase Briggs and waited for their orders to move out against Major Nguyen Vo Toi's force hidden in the limestone mountains of Ba Den and Song Xanh.

A powwow in Captain Patrick T. Slaughter's bunker took place between the officers and senior NCOs. Two platoons from Bravo Company were already in the bush and had made contact with the enemy. The NVA had withdrawn from their positions and were moving north and west. Second Platoon with Gary Hill in command would swing away from Briggs then abruptly pivot and at flank speed race to a point just south of the Montagnard village of Song Xanh and intercept Toi's reinforced battalion.

"The dinks have been using these mountains for a sanctuary," Slaughter said. "Now we have a large enough force to hurt them, and they're beginning to stir from their burrows." He described the terrain and the enemy's strength and what had been learned from the patrols. "For you new men, listen to Sergeant Stuckenburg even though he may be junior to you; he's been out here a long time." He looked at the two master sergeants and the master gunnery sergeant, who didn't appear too happy with what he said.

After Slaughter briefed the NCOs on their mission and told them that jump-off was 1400 hours, he dismissed them and pulled back a poncho that covered a hole in the ground. "Those men are going to wonder what a major is doing with them," he said to Pritchard and pulled a new bottle of Chivas Regal from the case hidden in the hole.

"No sweat," Second Lieutenant Gary Hill said as he held up a canteen cup to Pat Slaughter. "As usual he's an observer with secret orders from Westmoreland. No one cares. The men have gotten used to him; the new ones will, too."

Slaughter shrugged and poured.

Bud drank his Chivas in two gulps and left the two officers. He checked his gear to be sure that he had six magazines of M16 ammo, grenades, a box of C-rations, two full canteens, extra socks, first aid, map, K-bar, two claymores, and his kit of personal items. His ruck was as heavy as any grunt's.

From where he kneeled he could see through the open flaps of the aid tent to Janice Elderberry working over the wounded, her face away from him. He wanted her to turn around so that he could see her nice mouth and large eyes one more time before he left.

Billy McGarvie was thirty yards away reading a Superman comic, chewing bubble gum and looking like he was waiting for the school bell to ring so he could go to class.

"Hey, Billy," Bud shouted.

The kid looked up and swiveled his head around and finally found Pritchard.

"You checked your gear?"

"Uh—oh, yeah—yes, sir, I'll get right on it." He unbuckled the straps of the rucksack and searched inside with his hand and brought out a roll of comic books and a handful of candy bars.

Bud walked up and looked inside. "Where's your fragmentation grenades and extra ammo?"

"They're in here somewhere, sir." He tossed out five boxes of C-rations and two sets of utilities. "My mother told me before I left to be sure that I got enough to eat and to dress warm."

Pritchard smiled and nodded. Only one of the canteens he shook had any water in it. "What's this?" He picked up a crushed box at the bottom of the ruck and examined it.

"A cake my mother sent me. It's kind of broken up and mashed, but I don't mind. It'll taste pretty good still."

It took Pritchard almost an hour to get Billy McGarvie squared away, which included returning the two extra claymore mines (nine pounds each) that another Marine had given McGarvie to carry for him, and finding him an extra pair of socks (indispensable in preventing jungle rot).

"Saddle up!" Second Lieutenant Gary Hill shouted at exactly 1400.

The men moved lethargically in the heat, the rucks slowly being strapped to reluctant backs and heavy weapons shouldered.

"Hey, Cherry . . . I mean, McGarvie," third squad's leader, Corporal Hank, shouted. "Get your buns up here on the double—we're moving out. And don't get lost. Somebody keep an eye on McGarvie—that'll be you, Hillbilly."

Second Platoon trudged past Captain Patrick Slaughter's bunker—a few men glanced up at him standing on the roof without a shirt, the metal dog tags on his chest reflecting the sun—and kicked up a long line of dust as they filed off the firebase and headed down into the first valley. The spacing between each man increased to five-yard intervals and the platoon strung out along a line 200 yards long.

After checking out Billy McGarvie and satisfied that he could keep up with the other men and that Hillbilly was keeping an eye on him, Bud Pritchard worked through the long line of men to the front of the column and took up a position beside Second Lieutenant Gary Hill, the platoon commander.

"Think we'll make contact this time?" Pritchard said. He unwrapped a stick of Blackjack and curled it into his mouth, the black licorice juice quickly forming at the corners of his parched lips.

"Who knows? It's a strange game we play. We know they're out there . . . they know we're coming. A grown-up's game of hide-and-seek."

There had been no reports of anyone seeing the Dragon Girl since Bud had come back. If she was out there she had decided to hole up, or maybe she had been killed. No one could determine the truth behind the many rumors that had built up about her; she may have been dead or possibly never existed in the first place.

Bud was convinced, though, that Hill and Stuckenburg had seen someone resembling Hai Van Phuong on that morning when they found Sergeant Nunzio Pelligrini and his Lurps all dead in the clearing. It was no longer just an obligation that he had to find the girl, some sort of responsibility that he had to meet or a debt he owed to her family. The search for Hai Van Phuong had become an obsession, a lunacy and blind passion that besieged his every waking moment and haunted his dreams.

"What I'm afraid of is that the gooks will turn down to Cuc Mai instead of working their way to Song Xanh. If they do that we've lost the element of surprise and stand a good chance of walking right into an ambush," Gary Hill said. "The men are going to be out on their feet by the time we reach the Montagnards, Slaughter should have known that; and if the gooks know what I think they know—" He drew a line across his throat with a finger.

Second Platoon was in deep rain forest now. The triple canopy closed in on the Marines, and the interval between men shortened so that each one could keep the man in front of him in sight and not wander off into the jungle and get lost.

Pritchard dropped back to third squad and found PFC Billy McGarvie heaving under the weight of the seventy-pound pack. He was out on his feet and the sight of Bud Pritchard strengthened the boy for a few yards more, but he finally collapsed with a moan, the weight of his weapons and ammunition and rucksack driving him into the wet jungle floor.

Pritchard quickly removed the equipment from Billy's body, rolled him over on his back and elevated his feet. McGarvie's two canteens were empty so Bud used one of his own to pour water over the kid's face, allowing some of it to run into his mouth.

"Corpsman up!"

The sound of buzzing cicadas was everywhere and black-faced monkeys screeched from the top of the teak and mahogany trees. The smells were heavy with rotting humus and the air was thick, hot, and humid.

The eyes of Billy McGarvie were wide and frightened, and his face had lost its rosy freshness and had become pale and gaunt. The olive-drab utility uniform was a deep green from the sweat that saturated every inch of cloth, and his breath came in short, painful bursts, like that of a wounded deer.

"Don't be scared, kid, you're going to be okay," Bud Pritchard said.

Billy tried desperately to speak but the sounds were noises deep in his chest, quick and convulsive. The platoon halted for a breather while the corpsman gave McGarvie two salt tablets and a swig of sucrose water, and several men massaged his legs and upper body.

"Okay, get him on his feet," the corpsman said after a few minutes. "Got to get him up and moving or he'll crap out on us completely."

The RTO at the rear of the column was talking to Gary Hill, who was a hundred yards ahead in the thick foliage. "The lieutenant says we got to get moving."

"On your feet, Billy," Bud said. He took him under the arms and let the boy lean against him to steady himself.

The other Marines in the squad divided McGarvie's gear among themselves, and the RTO told the lieutenant that they were ready to move out again. He kept the handset glued to his ear. Slowly the column began to push ahead, snaking up the next hill to the top and then down once more into the next narrow valley and up another hill, doing it over and over until they reached Song Xanh five hours later.

The yellow light of cooking fires across the Song Xau River flickered through the trees, and the Marines of Second Platoon, Bravo Company sat in their fighting holes and ate cold C-rations and drank warm river water that tasted bitter from the little white halazone tablets.

"Three fingers of Slaughter's Chivas would go down nice right now," Second Lieutenant Gary Hill said. He pulled the OD poncho (slick from the light rain) up around his shoulders and watched the warm fires on the banks of the Song Xau.

The cold fogs from Laos flowed over the mountain ridges and down into the Montagnard village and chilled the rain. The Marines hunkered down in their holes and listened and waited.

"Give me your canteen cup," Bud Pritchard said. Reaching into his ruck he took out a canteen and poured some of its contents into the cup and handed it back to Hill.

The lieutenant sniffed the contents and smiled in the darkness, then lifted the canteen cup to his mouth and swallowed, slowly. "Smooth—real smooth."

"That'll build a fire in your belly," Bud said. He stuck a small piece of C-4 to the bottom of his own canteen cup filled with powdered C-rat coffee, pulled his poncho over the cup and lit the C-4. There was a flash under the poncho and the coffee boiled over.

Pritchard poured half the coffee into Hill's cup. They added a slug of Chivas and toasted each other.

"The privileges of rank," Bud said, and sipped the hot coffee.

The rain fell in a steady, cold drizzle and the men shivered in their ponchos and no one heard the North Vietnamese soldiers take up positions in the jungle around Second Platoon, Bravo Company.

The hours dragged through the cold miserable night and the Marines had difficulty remaining alert, most dozing under their ponchos, some sound asleep from the long hard march from Firebase Briggs. One of those that remained awake was PFC Billy McGarvie, who for the past thirty minutes had been troubled by sounds coming from the underbrush thirty yards in front of his listening post.

The effects of the heat prostration earlier were still with him—headache, nausea, and general body weakness—and his fear was great, but he was determined not to die tonight.

His partner in the LP, Lance Corporal Charles "Hillbilly" Green from Mobile, Alabama, was snoring—three or four quick vibrations of the palate followed by a long wheeze through the nose. McGarvie wasn't sure how to work the radio but was afraid to wake Hillbilly, who had told him that he would stuff a grenade up his ass if he woke him for nothing. The rain had not altered and a shallow pool of water had formed in the bottom of the fighting hole.

In Billy McGarvie's left hand was the clacker from which wires led to the four claymore mines that he and Charlie Green had planted in a crescent pattern directly ahead between the mahogany and teak trees. The M79 grenade launcher lay on the ledge above the foxhole, his right hand, wet and cold, resting on top of it. He looked at the glowing dial on his PX watch. It was 3:35 A.M.

PFC Billy McGarvie took a long breath and keyed the radio: "Mickey Mouse . . . this is Donald Duck."

"Go ahead, Donald."

"I've got movement out here."

"Have you had a bad dream, McGarvie? None of the other

Lima Papas have reported anything."

"I tell you I got something out there."

"Probably an animal. Stay awake. Out."

Billy McGarvie pulled the hood of the poncho away from his head and stared painfully into the black trees. The right hand came away from the thump gun and firmly grasped the clacker held in the other hand. *I ain't goin' get killed out here—not tonight I ain't.* He looked at the watch: 3:37.

The trip wire went off with a little pop and there was a second delay before the illume flare ignited, and Billy McGarvie stared wide-eyed with terror at the North Vietnamese soldiers frozen in the silver smoke-filled light.

"McGarvie! What's going on up there?" the radio squawked.

He smashed the clacker, but nothing happened. He mashed it again and again, pumping it as fast as he could, but the explosions never came. In the light of the flare he saw that there were no wires connected to the clacker.

The soldier coming at him was covered with leaves and branches hanging from his jungle helmet and ammunition harness and looked to Billy McGarvie like a demon from the pit of hell. Dimly on the periphery of his vision he could see other ghost forms, many, gliding between the trees and over the ground fog. Except for the hissing sound of the burning flare there was no noise, only the loud thumping of his heart and his hyperventilated breathing.

The sound of Hillbilly's M16 on full automatic shattered the stillness and McGarvie recoiled against the wall of the foxhole, his hands flying up in a quick reflex reaction to protect himself.

The rattle of an M60 came in behind Hillbilly's M16, but the forms continued to float ahead over the fog, the flarelight casting long, dim shadows against the trees and over the underbrush.

"Davis," Gary Hill said over the Prick-25, "what's the situation up there?"

"Gooks" was all that came back from second squad.

Rifles were firing up and down the Marine line, and Hill tried to get a disposition on the enemy force, but it was dark and the men were confused and all they could do was to pour fire into the jungle ahead of them.

A burst of AK-47 fire shattered the tree next to Hill, and the bark flew into pieces. The lieutenant fell to the ground and in the blackness two NVA soldiers camouflaged with shrubbery ran past him.

Running forward toward McGarvie's listening post, Bud Pritchard smashed into a North Vietnamese soldier and both were knocked to the ground and lost their rifles. The Communist found Bud first and reached around behind him with a triangle-bladed knife, tilted Bud's head back with the palm of his hand and drew the knife across his throat. Reacting on reflexes, Pritchard twisted his head and grabbed for the hand, forcing the blade to cut into the side of his neck just above the shoulder rather than through his throat.

Wrenching the knife free from the man's hand, Bud drove it forward, but all he caught was empty air, and the NVA soldier escaped into the din of battle.

"The gooners are pouring through on both sides," Sergeant Benjamin Davis from Topeka, Kansas, said. "We're having trouble holding."

"Stick in there, Benny," Gary Hill said on the PR-25. He gave the RTO a fleeting look and called Firebase Briggs. "Fire mission."

"Rog, Mickey Mouse." The artillery officer repeated the coordinates to Gary Hill then sent in one round to mark.

A few seconds later the HE 105 exploded in the trees.

"Left fifty, down seventy," Gary Hill said.

A second round whistled in over the canopy and exploded.

"Fire for effect."

The firebase hurled in a stream of shells, and the NVA troops recoiled and looked for a moment like they might break, but rallied under their officers and came on in a wave of human flesh. Tracers flashed through the trees and men screamed in pain and shouted encouragement to each other. The cries of "corpsman" were heard throughout the pitched battle, and with no chance for the wounded to be evacuated they lay where they were hit and bled and if they were lucky a buddy tied a touniquet or applied a compress.

Major Bud Pritchard, bleeding from the knife wound in the neck and his legs filled with holes from a fragmentation grenade, became disoriented in the dark and found himself among the NVA on the wrong side of the lines.

The fight raged for two hours and by the time dawn broke through the smoke and fog and the NVA withdrew from the banks of the Song Xau, Bud Pritchard had emptied his last magazine and lay unconscious and bleeding and surrounded by dead NVA.

Of the forty men from Second Platoon who had come to the Song Xau only ten were left alive, most of them wounded. Smoke rose from the broken trees and craters in the ground where the artillery shells had exploded and the piles of NVA dead were scattered among the Marines or floated in the eddies along the banks of the river.

PFC Billy McGarvie, black from smoke, sweat, and mud, crawled out of the foxhole and stared around him in the first light of morning. He had been shot through the left hand, and his neck and shoulder and left side of his face had taken grenade fragments. Crawling over Hillbilly's body he reached the radio and found the handset. "Mickey Mouse, Donald Duck—Mickey Mouse, Donald Duck." There was no answer and he dropped the shattered handset in the dirt and began turning over the Marine bodies and staring into the faces, looking for Bud Pritchard.

Fifty yards away another figure crawled through the blown-apart foliage and trees and stared at faces. Stopping at a body, she looked at it for a long time, touched the still warm face, then went through the pockets and collected photos and dog tags and personal items. Some of the bodies she covered with leaves and dirt, others she bypassed, and another she buried in a shallow grave, a foot and arm left poking out of the dirt. Tears stained her cheeks.

When Hai Van Phuong found Bud Pritchard he was lying with his face in the dirt and she couldn't see it. When she took the pictures from his wallet, his plastic ID card fell out and she saw Bud's photograph. She looked at it for a long time, her mind struggling; then she rolled him over and studied his face. Slowly she bent forward and touched her lips to his.

It took Hai Van Phuong two days to drag Major Bud Pritchard through the jungle to her tunnels a mile away. She pasted his wounds with root extract and wrapped them in strong-smelling leaves from the same plants from which she made the root medicine. Hai Van Phuong sat next to Bud Pritchard, and her long, tilted eyes watched his face while the candles flickered against the musty-smelling walls of the cave.

Another day passed, and Major Pritchard moaned and his eyelids opened and closed. Hai Van Phuong fed him rice soup and watched his face and her mind worked as it had when she was a child in Quang Hoa and her mother had taught her how to care for her brothers and sisters when they were hurt or sick.

The first sensation of being alive that Pritchard experienced was that of smell. The odor of mold in the tunnel and the scent of incense from the joss sticks were very real to him, and he lay on the bed of thatch and palm leaves on the earth floor and his thoughts came and went as though in a dream.

When his eyes first opened he was alone and in front of him was the earthen altar Phuong had carved out of the dirt wall. Dozens of dog tags on their chains hung from the wooden cross made from branches and reflected the candlelight back into his face.

The many photographs of men in uniform, girls back home, hot rod cars, and parents were displayed on the altar among the piles of Catholic medals, good luck charms, keys, trinkets, and other items taken from utility pockets, all dimly visible in the yellow glow six feet underground.

Full consciousness didn't come quickly and he fell in and out of awareness of his surroundings, never completely sure of anything except that he was alive.

When his eyes came open again, the altar in front of him had been replaced with a face that didn't move, made no sound, and was expressionless. From the long tangled hair he assumed that it was a female face and from the long eyes and flat nose he assumed it must be Asian, though he didn't think it important except that there was another human with him.

By now the strangeness of the surroundings became a concern to Bud Pritchard, as did the unspeaking face. He struggled for speech, but his lips seemed welded together and all he heard were grunts in his throat. The face, features hidden in the absence of full light, bent closer, and the long tangled hair fell forward and it smelled strong, like the walls of the tunnels, and it partially covered the small brown breasts.

The woman stood and he saw that she was completely naked except for a set of dog tags that hung around her neck; she looked like a prehistoric cave woman. She went to a small fire in a hole next to the altar and brought a steaming black pot to him. A broken porcelain spoon was brought to his mouth and small brown fingers pushed open his crusted lips.

The soup filled his mouth and he could feel its hotness on his tongue, and eventually his throat muscles contracted and the soup slid down and the girl poured another spoonful into his mouth.

"Where am I?" Bud Pritchard said. "Who are you?"

Hai Van Phuong said nothing and looked at him, her eyes unblinking and her mind uncomprehending the words, though faintly she recalled once hearing a voice that sounded like the one that spoke.

Through the yellow candlelight and the mask of encrusted dirt on her face, Pritchard began bit by bit to recognize the high cheeks, the round determined face, and the distant eyes (grown more distant) that seemed to see through to the back of his head. And when she returned to the fire he saw the limp and he knew that he would no longer have to search for Hai Van Phuong.

She would sit for hours staring at the altar with its icons and say nothing. She would forget to feed him and he would repeat the word *com* over and over and then she would bring him rice gruel that looked and tasted like schoolroom paste, or sometimes she would make a liquid from fruit and roots that she collected in the jungle and give it to him to drink in a bamboo tube.

Once she was gone for a whole day, and Pritchard began to despair for water and tried to locate the way out of the tunnels and managed to crawl a short distance down one of them before fainting. Upon returning, she pulled him back to the bed of thatch and palm. The word *nuoc* repeated to her several times finally brought recognition to her face, and she brought him the bamboo tube filled with water.

On the fifth day she dragged him out of the hole to a cleared area that was covered with mounds and squatted a few yards away and stared at the heaps of dirt, tears dripping from her eyes. She disappeared through the spider hole and returned with a handful of dog tags and held them out to him. When he didn't respond she looked at the name stamped into one of the rectangular pieces of metal and walked among the mounds of earth until she found the one she was looking for and laid the dog tag on it. She did this with each dog tag she had in her hand.

"Good lord," Bud whispered, "she knows the name of every man and where she buried him."

On all fours, Phuong lifted her head and quickly looked about and sniffed the air like a wild panther. Bud listened but heard nothing. The changes of expression in Phuong's face every few seconds showed the difficulty that she was having in identifying what she heard and smelled.

Out of habit she darted for the spider hole and vanished, pulling the foliage and sod cover over the opening. In a few minutes she crawled out again, cautiously, and sniffed the air and listened.

Then Pritchard heard the familiar sounds of rucksacks brushing branches, rifles on slings being transferred from one shoulder to the other, quiet cursing at the heat and thick vegetation.

He tried to call out to the Marines, but he couldn't speak above a whisper. Hai Van Phuong, eyes wide with fright, hid behind a tree and watched.

The sounds of the men became louder in the brush and then receded, and Bud's hopes faded away with the sounds. He looked down at this wounds crawling with maggots and closed his eyes and the teak and mahogany and all the rest of it swirled away into unconsciousness. He realized that he could last only a few days longer.

The blackfaced monkeys bantered in the canopy and the red-and-green parrots called to each other as they glided between the trees and Major Buddy Pritchard USMC kissed Marjorie in the back of his Ford pickup when she was only nineteen and a big yellow melon moon glistened off Lake Woodward.

Those were the days when it was only a short walk to Mrs. Jenks' corner grocery store and the cold Hires Root Beer and RC Colas tasted on a summer day like they were bottled in Heaven and it was no trouble at all (with a little luck) to come home with a string of smallmouth bass and no one paid any attention if you skinny-dipped in the creek down where the cottonwoods grew.

"He's dead."

"Look here, he's a major."

"What's a major doing out in the boonies?"

"Hey, Lieutenant!"

Bud felt someone pulling on his collar and he opened his eyes.

"He's still alive. Hey, Lieutenant! You better come over here."

To Bud Pritchard, Lieutenant, J.G., Janice Elderberry dressed in her starched whites looked like the closest thing to an angel he had ever seen. The little white Navy nurse's hat was perched on her curled short hair, and her nice mouth had a light coat of pink lipstick and she smiled prettily while she sat on a chair next to the bed and unwrapped a stick of Blackjack gum and placed it in his mouth. Billy McGarvie, covered in bandages in the bed next to Pritchard, read a Superman comic book held in his good hand.

"How you feeling?" Elderberry said.

"Better, now that I see you."

"That's the nicest thing you've ever said to me, Major; you know that?"

"I should have said more nice things to you."

"Hey, Major, you're awake," Billy McGarvie said.

Bud turned his head slowly, painfully, his neck heavily bandaged. "You made it, huh, kid?" He smiled and gave Billy a wink and the thumbs-up sign. "This time you go back to Windfall and finish school and go to work for that guy that runs the gas station." He turned back to Elderberry. "How about the rest of the guys?"

Janice Elderberry looked at her chubby hands and entwined her fingers. "Only ten survived."

"Hill?"

She shook her head.

"Stuckenburg?"

"No."

He sighed and looked back at Billy McGarvie, who had returned to reading *Superman*. "Anyway, the kid made it."

"Yeah, he sure did," Elderberry said, not knowing whether to be happy or sad. "I just hope he recovers from these wounds as well as he did from the last ones. He should never have been sent over again." She almost began to cry.

Bud felt a sense of well-being and comfort from her sensitivity and decided to let the silence ride for a while before he brought up the subject that was most on his mind. Janice Elderberry brought it up for him.

"After the patrol went past you in the brush, the girl fetched them back. They brought her in, too." She looked out the small, square window at an F-4 on the runway going into its takeoff roll. "They found her tunnel and the dog tags and stuff she had collected, and Graves Registration choppered out some men to exhume the bodies and bring them back for identification."

"Did they hurt her?"

"No—she's locked up with some shrinks and the South Vietnamese interrogators. Betty Lanterno and I cleaned her up after the doc examined her. She seems healthy enough physically, but it's going to be a long time before her mind heals."

Pritchard shook his head and looked away from Elderberry. "I wanted to help her; I wanted to make it up to her."

"Don't blame yourself." She put her hand on his shoulder. "You can still help her . . . more so than ever."

He turned back to Janice Elderberry. "Go on."

"She's not going to get the kind of treatment she needs in Vietnam. We can take her back with us and give her the care she deserves—the care you want for her."

"You said 'we.' "

"I want to help. My tour is over, Bud Pritchard; I'm going home, too . . . with you . . . if you'll let me."

"Elderberry, from now on you go everywhere I go and that's an order."

Billy McGarvie looked over the top of his comic book and smiled.